Praise for *The Marriage Portrait*

'Immersive, evocative, revisionist historical fiction, light of touch
and rich in texture'
TLS

'Nobody can manipulate and modulate time in the way Maggie
O'Farrell does. [She] is a writer who I feel is never really given
the adjectives she deserves: ingenious, inventive, humane,
wry, truthful'
The Scotsman

'Another gripping narrative with a passionate and resourceful
character at its heart'
Irish Times

'O'Farrell's writing is so vivid it melts away the time and space
between now and sixteenth century Italy . . . another
magnificently transporting page-turner'
iNews

'Finely written and vividly imagined'
Guardian

'Absorbing and delicious'
Evening Standard

'Lucrezia leaps off the page in this exquisitely detailed,
richly compelling novel. My goodness, Maggie O'Farrell
can write like nobody else'
Red Magazine

THE
MARRIAGE
PORTRAIT

Maggie O'Farrell

TINDER
PRESS

First published in Great Britain in 2022 by Tinder Press
An imprint of HEADLINE PUBLISHING GROUP

First published in paperback in 2023 by Tinder Press
An imprint of HEADLINE PUBLISHING GROUP

1

Cataloguing in Publication Data is available from the British Library

Paperback ISBN 978 1 4722 2388 3
Exclusive Paperback ISBN 978 1 0354 0964 8

Typeset in Scala 11/15 pt by Palimpsest Book Production Limited, Falkirk, Stirlingshire

Printed and bound in Great Britain by Clays Ltd, Elcograf S.p.A.

Chapter heading illustrations © Cally Conway

Headline's policy is to use papers that are natural, renewable and recyclable
products and made from wood grown in well-managed forests and other controlled
sources. The logging and manufacturing processes are expected to conform
to the environmental regulations of the country of origin.

HEADLINE PUBLISHING GROUP
An Hachette UK Company
Carmelite House
50 Victoria Embankment
London EC4Y 0DZ

www.tinderpress.co.uk
www.headline.co.uk
www.hachette.co.uk

for Mary-Anne and Victoria

Historical Note

In 1560, fifteen-year-old Lucrezia di Cosimo de' Medici left Florence to begin her married life with Alfonso II d'Este, Duke of Ferrara.

Less than a year later, she would be dead.

The official cause of her death was given as 'putrid fever', but it was rumoured that she had been murdered by her husband.

That's my last Duchess painted on the wall,
Looking as if she were alive
                    Robert Browning, 'My Last Duchess'

The ladies . . . are forced to follow the whims, fancies and dictates of their fathers, mothers, brothers and husbands, so that they spend most of their time cooped up within the narrow confines of their rooms, where they sit in apparent idleness, wishing one thing and at the same time wishing its opposite, and reflecting on various matters . . .
                    Giovanni Boccaccio, *The Decameron*

A wild and lonely place

Fortezza, near Bondeno, 1561

Lucrezia is taking her seat at the long dining table, which is polished to a watery gleam and spread with dishes, inverted cups, a woven circlet of fir. Her husband is sitting down, not in his customary place at the opposite end but next to her, close enough that she could rest her head on his shoulder, should she wish; he is unfolding his napkin and straightening a knife and moving the candle towards them both when it comes to her with a peculiar clarity, as if some coloured glass has been put in front of her eyes, or perhaps removed from them, that he intends to kill her.

She is sixteen years old, not quite a year into her marriage. They have travelled for most of the day, using what little daylight the season offers, leaving Ferrara at dawn and riding out to what he had told her was a hunting lodge, far in the north-west of the province.

But this is no hunting lodge, is what Lucrezia had wanted to say when they reached their destination: a high-walled edifice of dark stone, flanked on one side by dense forest and on the other by a twisting meander of the Po river. She would have liked to turn in her saddle and ask, why have you brought me here?

She said nothing, however, allowing her mare to follow him along the path, through dripping trees, over the arch-backed bridge and into the courtyard of the strange, fortified, star-shaped building, which seemed, even then, to strike her as peculiarly empty of people.

The horses have been led away, she has removed her sodden cloak and hat, and he has watched her do this, standing with his back to the blaze in the grate, and now he is gesturing to the country servants in the hall's outer shadows to step forward and place food on their plates, to slice the bread, to pour wine into their cups, and she is suddenly recalling the words of her sister-in-law, delivered in a hoarse whisper: You will be blamed.

Lucrezia's fingers grip the rim of her plate. The certainty that he means her to die is like a presence beside her, as if a dark-feathered bird of prey has alighted on the arm of her chair.

This is the reason for their sudden journey to such a wild and lonely place. He has brought her here, to this stone fortress, to murder her.

Astonishment yanks her up out of her body and she almost laughs; she is hovering by the vaulted ceiling, looking down at herself and him, sitting at the table, putting broth and salted bread into their mouths. She sees the way he leans towards her, resting his fingers on the bare skin of her wrist as he says something; she watches herself nodding at him, swallowing the food, speaking some words about their journey here and the interesting scenery through which they passed, as if nothing at all is amiss between them, as if this is a normal dinner, after which they will retire to bed.

In truth, she thinks, still up by the cold, sweating stone of the hall's ceiling, the ride here from court was dull, through fields stark and frozen, the sky so heavy it seemed to droop, exhausted, on the tops of bare trees. Her husband had set the pace at a trot, mile after mile of jolting up and down in the saddle, her back aching, her legs rubbed raw by wet stockings. Even inside squirrel-lined gloves, her fingers, clutching the reins, had been rigid with cold, and the horse's mane was soon cast in ice. Her husband had ridden ahead, with two guards behind. As the city had given way to countryside, Lucrezia had wanted to spur her horse, to press her heels into its flank and feel its hoofs fly over the stones and soil, to move through the flat landscape of the valley at speed, but she knew she must not, that her place was behind or next to him, if invited, never in front, so on and on they trotted.

At the table, facing the man she now suspects will kill her, she wishes she had done it, that she had urged her mare into a gallop. She wishes she had streaked by him, cackling with transgressive glee, her hair and cloak lashing out behind her, hoofs flinging mud. She wishes she had turned the reins towards the distant hills, where she could have lost herself among the rocky folds and peaks, so that he could never find her.

He is setting an elbow on either side of his plate, telling her about coming to this lodge – as he persists in calling it – when he was a child, how his father used to bring him hunting here. She is listening to a story about how he was made to release arrow after arrow towards a target on a tree until his fingers bled. She is nodding and making sympathetic murmurs at appropriate moments, but what she really wants to do is look him in the eye and say: I know what you are up to.

Would he be surprised, wrongfooted? Does he think of her as his innocent, unworldly wife, barely out of the nursery? She sees it all. She sees he has laid his scheme so carefully, so assiduously, separating her from others, ensuring that her retinue was left behind in Ferrara, that she is alone, that there are no people from the *castello* here, just him and her, two guards stationed outside, and a handful of country servants to wait on them.

How will he do it? Part of her would like to ask him this. The knife in a dark corridor? His hands about her throat? A tumble from a horse made to look like an accident? She has no doubt that all of these would fall within his repertoire. It had better be done well, would be her advice to him, because her father is not someone who will take a lenient view of his daughter's murder.

She sets down her cup; she lifts her chin; she turns her eyes on to her husband, Alfonso, Duke of Ferrara, and wonders what will happen next.

The unfortunate circumstances of Lucrezia's conception

Palazzo, Florence, 1544

I n the years to come, Eleanora would come to bitterly regret the manner in which her fifth child was conceived.

Picture Eleanora in the autumn of 1544: she is in the map room of the Florentine *palazzo*, a chart held close to her face (she is somewhat short-sighted but would never admit this to anyone). Her women stand at a distance, as near to the window as they can get; although it is September, the city is still suffocatingly hot. The well of the courtyard below seems to bake the air, wafting out more and more heat from its stone rectangle. The sky is low and motionless; no breeze stirs the silk window coverings and the flags on the *palazzo*'s ramparts hang limp and flaccid. The ladies-in-waiting fan themselves and blot their foreheads with handkerchiefs, sighing noiselessly; each of them is wondering how much longer they will be required to stand here, in this panelled room, how much more time Eleanora will desire to peruse this map, and what she can possibly find so interesting about it.

Eleanora's eyes rake over the silverpoint rendering of Tuscany: the peaks of hills, the eel-like slither of rivers, the ragged coastline climbing north. Her gaze passes over the cluster of roads that knot themselves together for the cities of Siena, Livorno and Pisa. Eleanora is a woman all too aware of her rarity and worth: she possesses not only a body able to produce a string of heirs, but also a beautiful face, with a forehead like carved ivory, eyes wide-set and deep brown, a mouth that looks well in both a smile and a pout. On top of all this, she has a quick and mercurial mind. She can look at the scratch marks on this map and can, unlike most women, translate them into fields full of grain, terraces of vines, crops, farms, convents, levy-paying tenants.

She puts down one map and, just as her women are rustling their skirts in readiness to leave for a better-ventilated room, she picks up another. She is studying the area just inland from the coast; there seem to be no marks made upon that section of the chart, other than some indistinct and irregular patches of water.

If there is one thing Eleanora cannot abide it is a lack of purpose. Under her jurisdiction, every room, every corridor, every antechamber of this *palazzo* has been renovated and put to use. Every bare plaster wall has been adorned and beautified. She will not allow her children, her servants or her women an empty minute in their days. From the moment they wake to the moment they rest their heads on their pillows, they are kept occupied by a schedule she has designed. Unless she is asleep, she will be engaged in a task: writing letters, taking lessons in languages, making plans or lists or overseeing the children's care and education.

Eleanora's head begins to teem with ideas for this marshland. They must drain it. No, they must irrigate it. They could grow crops here. They could build a city. They could instal a system of lakes for the breeding of fish. Or an aqueduct or a—

Her thoughts are interrupted by a door opening and the sound of boots on the floor: a confident, assertive stride. She does not turn but smiles to herself as she holds up the map to the light, watching how the glow of the sun illuminates the mountains and towns and fields.

A hand lands on her waist, another on her shoulder. She feels the stippled sting of a beard on her neck, the moist press of lips.

'What are you up to, my busy little bee?' her husband murmurs into her ear.

'I am wondering about this land,' she says, still holding up the map, 'near the sea, here, do you see?'

'Mmm,' he says, sliding an arm around her, burying his face in her pinned-up hair, pressing her body between his and the hard edge of the table.

'If we were to drain it, it might be possible to put it to work in some way, either by farming it or building on it and—' she breaks off because he is grappling with her skirts, hoisting them up so that his hand may roam unimpeded along her knee, up her thigh, and up, further, much further up. 'Cosimo,' she chides, in a whisper, but she needn't have worried because her women are shuffling out of the room, their dresses skimming the floor, and Cosimo's aides are leaving, all of them clustering at the exit, eager to be away.

The door closes behind them.

'The air is bad there,' she continues, displaying the map

between her pale, tapered fingers, as if nothing is happening, as if there isn't a man behind her, trying to navigate his way through layers of undergarments, 'malodorous and unhealthy, and if we were to—'

Cosimo turns her around and removes the map from her hands. 'Yes, my darling,' he says, guiding her backwards to the table, 'whatever you say, whatever you want.'

'But, Cosimo, only look—'

'Later.' He thrusts the map on to the table, then lifts her on to it, pushing at the mass of her skirts. 'Later.'

Eleanora lets out a resigned sigh, narrowing her sloping cat eyes. She can see that there is no diverting him from this. But she seizes his hand, nonetheless. 'Do you promise?' she says. 'Promise me. You'll give me leave to make use of that land?'

His hand fights hers. It is a pretence, a game, they both know. One of Cosimo's arms is twice the width of hers. He could strip this dress off her in seconds, with or without her agreement, were he an altogether different man.

'I promise,' he says, then kisses her, and she releases his hand.

She has never, she reflects as he sets to, refused him in this. She never will. There are many areas in their marriage in which she is able to hold sway, more than other wives in similar positions. As she sees it, unimpeded access to her body is a small price to pay for the numerous liberties and powers she is permitted.

She has had four children already; she intends to have more, as many as her husband will plant within her. A large ruling family is what is needed to give the province stability and longevity. Before she and Cosimo married, this dynasty was in danger of petering out, of dissolving into history. And now?

Cosimo's sovereignty and the region's power are assured. Thanks to her, there are two male heirs up in the nursery already, who will be trained to step into Cosimo's shoes, and two girls who can be married into other ruling families.

She keeps herself focused on this thought because she wants to conceive again, and because she doesn't want to dwell on the unbaptised soul she lost last year. She never speaks of this, never tells anyone, not even her confessor, that its little pearl-grey face and curled fingers still haunt her dreams, that she longs for it and wants it, even now, that its absence has pierced a hole right through her. The cure for this secret melancholy is, she tells herself, simply to have another baby as soon as she can. She needs to get pregnant again and then all will be well. Her body is strong and fruitful. The people of Tuscany, she knows, refer to her as 'La Fecundissima' and it is entirely apt: she has found birthing children not the agony and hellfire she was led to believe. She brought her own nurse, Sofia, with her when she left her father's house and this woman takes care of her offspring. She, Eleanora, is young, she is beautiful, her husband loves her and is faithful to her and would do anything to please her. She will fill that nursery up in the eaves; she will stuff it full of heirs; she will produce child after child after child. Why not? No more babies will slip away from her before time: she will not allow it.

As Cosimo labours away in the heat of the Sala delle Carte Geografiche, his aides and her women waiting listlessly in the room outside, exchanging yawns and resigned glances, Eleanora's mind shrinks away from the little lost one and towards the marshlands again, skimming over their reeds, their yellow flags, their tussocks of scrubby grass. It weaves in and out of its mists and vapours. It pictures engineers with machinery and pipes arriving, draining away all that is dank, wet and unwanted. It creates lush crops, fat livestock and villages peopled by willing, grateful subjects.

She rests her arms upon her husband's shoulders and fixes her eyes on the maps on the walls opposite as he approaches his moment of pleasure: Ancient Greece, Byzantium, the extent of the Roman Empire, constellations of the heavens, uncharted seas, islands real and imagined, mountains that disappear up into thunderstorms.

Impossible to foresee that this would prove a mistake, that she ought to have shut her eyes and brought her mind back to the room, her marital duty, her strong and handsome husband, who still desired her after all this time. How could she have known that the child born of this coupling would be unlike any of the others, all of whom were sweet in nature and agreeable in temperament? So easily forgotten, in the moment, the principle of maternal impression. Later, she will chastise herself for her distraction, her inattention. It has been drummed into her by physicians and priests alike, that the character of a child is determined by the mother's thoughts at the moment of conception.

Too late, however. Eleanora's mind, here in the map room, is unsettled, untamed, wandering at will. She is looking at maps, at landscapes, at wildernesses.

Cosimo, Grand Duke of Tuscany, finishes the act with his habitual growling gasp, clutching his wife to him in a tender grip, and she, moved but somewhat relieved (the day is hot, after all), allows him to help her down off the table. She calls for her women to accompany her back to her rooms. She would like, she tells them, a mint *tisana*, a siesta, and perhaps a clean shift.

Nine months later, when she is presented with a baby who roars and writhes and throws off its swaddling bands, a baby who will not rest or sleep or be comforted unless it is in constant motion, a baby who might accept the breast of the wet-nurse – carefully chosen by Sofia – for a few minutes but will never settle to a feed, a baby whose eyes are open, always, as if seeking distant horizons, Eleanora is filled with something close to guilt. Is it her fault, this wildness in the baby's character? Is it all down to her? She doesn't tell anyone, least of all Cosimo. The existence of this baby terrifies her, eroding as it does her conviction that she is an excellent mother, that she produces offspring healthy in mind and body. For one of her children to be so difficult, so intractable, chips away at the very quintessence of her role here in Florence.

During a visit to the nursery, where she tries for an entire morning to embrace the squalling Lucrezia, she notices how the noise affects the four older siblings, who insist on covering their ears and running off into a different room. Eleanora is seized with the fear that the behaviour of this baby will influence the others. Will they, suddenly, become unbiddable and inconsolable? She decides, on the spur of the moment, to remove Lucrezia from the nursery altogether and place her in a different part of the *palazzo*. Just for a time, she tells herself, until the child settles down. She makes enquiries, then engages the services of a different wet-nurse, one of the cooks from the kitchens. She is a broad-hipped, cheerful woman who is more than happy to take Lucrezia into her care – her own daughter, almost two years old and toddling about the flagstones, is ready to be weaned. Eleanora sends one of her ladies down every day to the kitchens to enquire how the baby fares; she does her duty by the child, of this she is certain. The only unfortunate element is that the situation goes against the opinions of Sofia, Eleanora's old nurse, who vociferously disapproves of what she refers to as Lucrezia's 'banishment' and, anyway, sees nothing wrong with the wet-nurse she herself selected. But Eleanora is strangely insistent: this child will be placed far away from the rest of the family, down in the basement kitchen, along with the servants, the maids, the noise of cooking pots and the heat of the big fires. Lucrezia's early life is spent in a laundry tub, watched over by the wet-nurse's little daughter, who pats the child's tiny tight fist, and calls for her mother whenever the baby's face creases into a wail.

When Lucrezia begins to walk, there is a near-miss with an upset pan of boiling water so she is sent back upstairs. Removed from the familiar steam and racket of the kitchens, and confronted by four children she has no memory of, she screams for two days. She screams for her basement wet-nurse, for the wooden spoons she was given to suck when her teeth hurt, for the herb bouquets silhouetted against square windows, for a hand coming down with a slice of warm bread or a rind of cheese to chew. She wants none of this room up in the eaves with bed after bed, with identical-faced children who stare at her with impassive black eyes, who whisper to each other, then suddenly get to their feet and walk away. She has a troubling recollection of an immense black pot toppling near her, and then a flood of sizzling liquid. She refuses the arms and laps of these nursery women; she won't let them dress or feed her. She wants the cook from downstairs, her milk-mother; she wants to twist a strand of her smooth hair between her finger and thumb while she dozes, curled safe in her capacious lap. She wants the kind face of her milk-sister, who sings to her and lets her draw in the fire's ashes with a stick. Sofia shakes her head, and mutters that she told Eleanora no good would come of sending the child downstairs. The only way she can get Lucrezia to eat is to leave food on the floor beside her. Like a wild animal, Sofia remarks.

When all this is reported to Eleanora, by Sofia, who makes a point of going to the chambers of her erstwhile charge and standing beside the bed, fists pressed into hips, Eleanora sighs and pushes a freshly cracked almond into her mouth. She is days away from giving birth again, her belly a mountain beneath the bedsheets; she is hoping for a boy. She took no chances this time, and arranged for her chamber to be filled with paintings of healthy young men engaged in virile, masculine pursuits – spear-throwing or jousting. She would not submit to conjugal acts anywhere in the *palazzo* but here, much to Cosimo's disappointment – he has always had a fondness for an urgent coupling in a corridor or mezzanine. But she will not make the same mistake as last time.

At four years old, Lucrezia will not play with a doll, as her sisters did, or sit at the table to eat, or join in the games of her siblings, preferring instead to spend her time on her own, running like a savage from one side of the walkway to the other or to kneel at the window, where she spends hours looking out at the city and the distant hills beyond. When she is six, she wriggles and fidgets instead of sitting nicely for a painter, so much so that Eleanora loses her temper and says there will be no portrait of her after all – she can return to the nursery. At eight or nine, she goes through a time of refusing to wear any shoes, even when Sofia smacks her for this disobedience. And at the age of fifteen, when she is about to be married, she creates an enormous fuss about the bridal dress that she, Eleanora, had commissioned herself, in a glorious combination of blue silk and gold brocade. Lucrezia bursts into her chambers, unannounced, shouting at the top of her voice about how she will not wear it, she will not, it is too big for her. Eleanora, who is in her *scrittoio*, writing to one of her favourite abbesses, tries to keep her temper and says to Lucrezia, in a firm voice, that the dress is being altered for her, as she well knows. But Lucrezia, of course, goes too far. Why, she demands, with a furious face, should she wear a dress that was made for her sister Maria, when Maria died, isn't it bad enough that she has to marry Maria's fiancé, must she really wear her dress as well? Eleanora's mind, as she sets down her stylus, raises herself from her desk and walks through the archway towards her daughter, fixes once more on Lucrezia's conception, the way her eyes had passed over the maps of ancient lands, had been focused on strange and wild seas, filled with dragons and monsters, beset by winds that might blow a ship far off course. What a mistake for her to make! How she has been haunted by it, punished for it!

At the other end of the room, Eleanora sees her daughter's angular, tear-streaked face open like a flower with hope and expectation. Here is my mother, Eleanora knows she is thinking. Perhaps she will save me, from the dress, from the marriage. Perhaps all will be well.

The first tiger in Tuscany

Palazzo, Florence, 1552

Aforeign dignitary arrived in Florence, presenting the Grand Duke with a painting of a tiger. Cosimo was very taken with the gift and it wasn't long before he expressed a desire to own one of these vicious, singular beasts. He kept a menagerie in the basement of his *palazzo*, for the diversion of visitors, and he felt that a tiger would be an excellent addition to his collection.

He gave an order to his *consigliere ducale*, Vitelli, that a tiger must be found, captured and brought to Florence. Vitelli, who had foreseen such an outcome ever since the painting arrived at court, heaved a deep and private sigh, duly making a note in his ledger. He hoped that the Grand Duke might be persuaded against the plan or even forget it, occupied as they were at that time by republican unrest in Siena.

Cosimo, however, refused to comply with Vitelli's secret hope.

'What progress on the tiger?' he asked one day, without warning, as he stood on the terrace, readying himself to leave for his daily exercise, removing his *lucco*, and strapping on his

15

weapons. Vitelli, caught off-guard, fumbled with the fastening of his ledger and managed to mumble something about difficulties with certain nautical routes from the east. Cosimo was not fooled. He fixed Vitelli with his left eye, while his errant right eye looked off to the side, at a place just beyond where Vitelli stood.

'I am disappointed to hear that,' Cosimo said, as he slid first one then two sheathed daggers into his boots, as was his habit when he was intending to step outside the *palazzo* walls. 'Greatly disappointed. As you know, the enclosure in the basement is all prepared: it has been swept clean, the bars reinforced.' He accepted a leather belt from a servant beside him, and fastened it around his waist. 'Such a pity that it lies empty. Something – or someone – will have to occupy it.'

Cosimo lifted his sword, a light and lithe one with a decorated blade that Vitelli knew he particularly liked. He swished it through the air and, for a brief moment, both of Cosimo's eyes, alight with steely amusement, landed on Vitelli.

The Grand Duke inserted the sword into the scabbard on his belt and left the terrace; Vitelli heard him descend the stairs with a flurry of purposeful strides. Behind Vitelli, the secretaries were rustling and murmuring, agog, he suspected, to have witnessed this little display – he heard, distinctly, one smothering a titter.

'Back to work,' Vitelli snapped, bringing his palms together in a loud clap. 'All of you.'

The secretaries slunk away, and Vitelli headed for his desk, where he sat down heavily, brooding for a moment, before drawing his ink and pen towards him.

The Grand Duke's peculiar fancy for a tiger was communicated to an emissary, and then an ambassador, a sea captain, a silk merchant, an adviser to a sultan, a viceroy, a spice trader, an under-secretary in a maharajah's palace, the maharajah's cousin, the maharajah himself, his wife, his son, then back to the under-secretary, and on to a band of soldiers, then the villagers in a remote part of Bengal.

Captured, netted and tied to a pole, the tiger journeyed from its place of heat and rain and foliage. It spent weeks and months at sea, below deck, in a dank and salt-crusted hold, before being delivered to the dockside in Livorno. From there, it was conveyed inland in a wooden cage lashed to a cart, pulled by six terrified mules.

When Vitelli heard that the convoy carrying the beast was nearing Florence, he sent word that they must wait outside the city walls until darkness. Do not, Vitelli instructed them, on any account bring it through the city in daylight; pull the cart into a thickly wooded place and stay there, concealed, until nightfall.

A tiger, Vitelli knew, had never before been seen in Florence. People would jostle and scream to behold such a creature in their midst; ladies would faint from the shock; young men might compete with each other to goad it as it passed them in its cage, might poke it with sticks and spears. And what if the animal became enraged and perhaps burst its bonds? It could run amok through the streets, devouring children and citizens. Better, Vitelli decided, to wait for the dim hours after midnight: no one would hear them; no one would ever find out.

Except for little Lucrezia, tucked into a bed with both her sisters in a room under the eaves of the *palazzo* roof. Lucrezia of the solemn gaze and pale, wispy hair – incongruously so, for all her siblings had the sleek, fox-dark colouring of their Spanish mamma. Lucrezia, who was slight and small for her age, and was every night shunted to the edge of the mattress by Maria, the eldest, who had sharp elbows and a predilection for lying in the centre of the bed with all her limbs stretched out. Lucrezia, who always had trouble sleeping.

She, alone, heard the tigress's cry as the cart entered the *palazzo* gates: a low, hollow call, like wind funnelled through a pipe. It severed the night with its mournful pitch – once, twice – before dying away in a hoarse rumble.

Lucrezia sat up in bed, as abruptly as if she had been stuck with a needle. What was that noise, the unfamiliar cry that had reached down into her dream and shaken her awake? She turned her head one way, she turned it the other.

She had extraordinarily sensitive hearing: she could hear what was being said, sometimes, on the floor below, or at the other end of the largest state room. The *palazzo* was a place of strange acoustics, with sound and vibrations, whispers and footsteps journeying along joists, behind the marble reliefs, up the spines of statues, through the bubbling waters of the foun- tains. Lucrezia, even aged seven, found that if she pressed the outer folds of her ear to the panelling or the frame of a door, it was possible to find out all sorts of things. The ordination of a cardinal, for example, the expected arrival of another sibling, the presence of a foreign army on the far side of the river, the sudden death of an enemy on the streets of Verona or a tigress due to arrive any day. These conversations, never meant for her, snaked into her head to take root there.

The cry again! It was not so much a roar, no, which is what Lucrezia had expected: this had a yearning, desperate rasp to it. The sound, Lucrezia thought, of a creature captured against its will, a creature whose desires have all been disregarded.

Lucrezia disentangled herself from the sheets and the folds of Maria's nightdress, and slipped from the bed. For all her clumsiness in dancing class – for which she was regularly castigated by her teacher – she was always able to glide noiselessly through the nursery, her feet finding the right tiles, never the ones that clinked or wobbled. She tiptoed past the bed where her brothers lay heaped together in a tangle of limbs, past the narrow truckle where the baby, Pietro, was held firm in the arms of his *balia*. Near the door slept two other nurses but Lucrezia stepped over them and eased back the two bolts on the door.

Slipping out, she moved along the corridor, pausing to check that Sofia, the oldest nurse, was snoring with her usual regularity, then passed a small hand along a panel in the wall. She missed the brass catch the first time, but found it the second. The panel swung inwards and Lucrezia disappeared from the corridor, through a narrow opening, no bigger than herself.

The *palazzo* was riddled with numerous hidden passages: Lucrezia sometimes pictured it, this enormous, thick-walled building, as an apple eaten through by worms. She had heard it said – by Sofia, who had no inkling that Lucrezia could understand a great deal of the Neapolitan dialect the three nurses spoke among themselves – that these passageways were there for the Duke and his family to escape, if the palace were attacked. Lucrezia had wanted to ask, attacked by whom, but had the sense not to: it was useful to understand what the nurses said to each other, over the children's heads, and this was not a skill she should divulge.

This particular passage was a shortcut to the larger courtyard, via a winding, slippery staircase of uneven steps. Lucrezia was not afraid; she was not. But she held her breath, the hem of her shift bunched in one hand, so she did not trip. Who knows how long it would be before she was found, if she were to fall and injure herself here, closeted behind the walls? How would they hear her call?

The steps curved around and around on themselves, like a coiled rope. The air was stagnant and moist, as if a living entity had been trapped there for a long time. She forced herself to keep her chin lifted, her feet moving; she had, she told herself, faced worse. And the thought of the beast spurred her on. She would see that tigress – she must.

Just as the darkness and the smell were becoming too much, a thin slice of light told her she had reached her destination. She groped for the door handle – a small, cold latch – pressed it and there she was, on the covered stairway, with slanted windows overlooking the courtyard. There were no guards or servants to be seen at this velvet-black time of night; Lucrezia checked and checked again. Then she ventured out.

From below, she could hear the nervous whinnying of the mules, the skittering of their hoofs, and then a furious rumble, like distant thunder.

Placing her hands on the marble sill, she peered over.

The courtyard was a dim vault below her, illuminated only by torches that flared from sconces on the pillars. There were the mules, six of them, lined up in harness. Around them milled a group of her father's men, dressed in their red-and-gold livery. They were circling the cart, each holding a sharpened stick, and they were calling to each other. Get back, they were saying, not so close, steady now, mind your hand there, hold the bridle, easy.

One reached up and took a torch from its sconce; he swung it at the cart, making a fiery arc through the darkness. And there came an answering hiss, the creature responding to the flames. The men laughed. The torch was swung again and Lucrezia heard once more the creature's furious fear.

And then Lucrezia, hands gripping the windowsill, saw it: a lithe, sinuous shape, moving from one side of the cage to the other. The tigress didn't so much pace as pour herself, as if her very essence was molten, simmering, like the ooze from a volcano. It was hard to distinguish the bars of the cage from the dark, repeating stripes on the creature's fur. The animal was orange, burnished gold, fire made flesh; she was power and anger, she was vicious and exquisite; she carried on her body the barred marks of a prison, as if she had been branded for exactly this, as if captivity had been her destiny all along.

The mules were struggling in their harness, tossing their heads and rolling up their lips in terror. Even though they couldn't see the tigress, so blinkered were their eyes, they could sense her, smell her; they knew she was there, and they knew they were in a confined space with her. They knew that, if not for the wooden cage, she would slay everyone and everything in this courtyard: mule and man.

All at once, the mules jerked forwards and the cart and cage were swallowed by an arch, like a mouth accepting food. Lucrezia was left staring down into an empty courtyard, the braziers still flickering and flaring, as if nothing significant had happened there.

*　*　*

The *palazzo* of Lucrezia's father was a changeable building, unstable as a weathervane. Sometimes it felt to her like the safest place in the world, a stone keep with a high garrison perimeter to enclose the Grand Duke's children like a cabinet for glass figurines; at others it felt as oppressive as a prison.

It occupied a corner of the largest piazza in Florence, its back to the river, sides soaring above the citizens like great cragged cliffs. Windows were high and narrow so that no one could ever see in. A square tower rose from its roof, with gigantic bells that tolled on the hour, giving time to the whole city. Battlements, bristling with crenellations, ran around each side of it like a brim on a hat; only rarely were the children allowed up there. Instead, they went every day with Sofia to the covered walkway to take the air. Their mamma, she would tell them, believed that children thrived with exercise, so they were encouraged to race each other there, to run from one open airy vent to the next, watching the comings and goings in the piazza far beneath their feet.

From the furthest corner of the walkway, it was possible to get a view of the statue that stood beside the *palazzo* door, a white figure who looked off to the side, as if avoiding the eye of all before him, a slingshot over his shoulder. Lucrezia might catch a glimpse of her parents, stepping around the base of the statue towards their covered carriage, her mother swathed in furs, if it was winter, or coloured silks in summer. Yellow, red, the purple of grapes were the hues of her gowns. If she saw the carriage draw up, Lucrezia leant as far over the parapet as she dared, trying to catch the sound of her parents' footsteps: the light tread of her mother, the decisive stride of her father, the plume in his hat dipping and bowing to the rhythm of his walk.

Sofia, who claimed she had been all over the *palazzo*, told them that the walls were as thick as three men laid head to toe. There was a whole room just for weapons, she said, with swords and armour lined up along the walls, and another full of books. Book after book, she told them, as she rubbed their faces with a washcloth or buttoned their smocks, filling shelves that stretched far above her head. It would, the nurse said, take a whole lifetime to read them all, maybe more. Another salon was decorated with maps of every place in the world and of all the stars in the sky. There was a vault lined with iron, with a many-bolted door, where their mamma's jewels were kept, all those that had come with her from the Spanish court and all the ones their papa had given her, although the nurse had never seen this with her own eyes: no one had, for the only hand that unlocked it was their papa's. And there was a great long room as large as a piazza, its ceiling covered with decorations. Of what? Lucrezia would ask, ducking away from the washcloth to look at the nurse, to ascertain if she was telling the truth, if she had indeed seen these frescos. Oh, angels and cherubs and great warriors and battles, the nurse said, shoving Lucrezia's head back into place, that kind of thing.

If Lucrezia had trouble sleeping – and she often did – she would think about these rooms, stacked like the blocks of the towers her little brothers liked to construct. The weapons room, the map room, the painted room, the jewels room. Her sister Isabella said she would most like to see the jewels; Maria said she would like to see the gilded cherubs on the ceiling. Francesco, who would one day be duke, said, loftily, that he had in fact seen all these rooms. Several times. Giovanni, born within a year of Isabella, rolled his eyes, which in turn made Francesco kick him in the shins.

Nobody asked which room Lucrezia would like to see, and she didn't say. But, if questioned, she would have said the Sala dei Leoni: the room of the lions. It was said that their father kept a menagerie in a specially reinforced room somewhere in the basement. He liked to display the lions, in particular, to honoured guests and sometimes to pit them against other animals, for sport: bears, boars, once a gorilla. A servant who brought up their food from the kitchens told them, in a whisper, that these lions loved the Duke so much they would permit him to enter their enclosure. In he would go, a spike with meat impaled upon it in one hand and a whip in the other. The children had never seen inside the Sala dei Leoni – although Francesco insisted he had – but if the wind blew in a certain direction, they could hear the muffled yowls of the animals. On hot days, a very specific smell would waft up to the walkway, especially at the back of the *palazzo*, which looked out over the via dei Leoni – a heavy, overpowering scent of ordure and sweat. It made Maria and Isabella complain and wrap scarves about their faces but Lucrezia hung about in the walkway above the street, hoping against hope that she might catch a glimpse of a flicking tail or a dark shaggy mane.

When Lucrezia woke on the morning after the tigress arrived, it was to a bedroom so silent she thought for a moment that her ears must be stopped with wax. Her face was pressed deeply into the pillow, and when she raised her head, she found herself stretched out in the middle of the bed, alone.

No sisters to push her to one side. And no brothers, either, in the bed across the room. No babies on the truckle.

Stunned by the peace, she took in the room: the lime-washed walls, the folded bedcoverings, the stone steps up to the window seat, the jug of water standing on a shelf.

From the open doorway, she could hear the sounds of her siblings at breakfast: the shrieks and cries of the three youngest, the clatter of spoon and plate.

Lucrezia moved her arms and legs through the cool, empty sheets, like a swimmer. For a moment, she was tempted to turn back into the pillow, to see if sleep would overcome her once more, but then she recalled an image of a rolling, loose-jointed shoulder, imprinted with black marks. A clear resolve formed in her head: she had to see that animal up close. She must. There was no other option for her. She wanted to stand before it, to see the way the black of the stripes merged with the orange of the fur. Could she sneak down to the Sala dei Leoni? There was no passage leading there, that she knew of, and someone was bound to apprehend her if she went via the walkways and corridors. How, how, how could she manage it?

Invigorated by this thought, she slid from the bed. The tiles seemed to arch their cold, gritty surfaces into the undersides of her feet. She dressed hastily, pulling her woollen *sottana* over her shift, pushing her feet into her shoes. The air in the room was frigid and still; moving across it felt, to Lucrezia, like wading through an icy lake.

At the threshold to the other room, with possible means to see the tigress flickering through her head, she paused. Along one side of the table were seated her older sisters and brothers – four children with identical red-brown hair, in neatly descending height. They were exactly a year apart in age: Maria was twelve, Francesco eleven, Isabella ten, Giovanni nine. Each followed the other like steps in a staircase. This morning, they were leaning close, their heads almost touching, as they whispered over their bread and milk.

On the other side of the table, the nurses sat with their smaller charges, the three baby boys, who were arranged in the same fashion: Garzia was three, Ferdinando almost two, and baby Pietro not yet a year.

Around Lucrezia, however, was a baffling vacancy, more than two years wide, on either side. No children occupied the years between Giovanni's birth and hers, or the gap between her and Garzia. She had once asked Sofia, the nurse, why this was. Why didn't she have a brother or a sister close in age to her? Sofia, who had been wrestling Ferdinando into a sitting position on the pot because she had decreed it was time for him to have a motion, had said exasperatedly, Maybe your poor mother needed a rest.

Lucrezia approached the table in a sideways manner, placing one foot beside the other. In her mind, she was the new tigress, pacing on powerful feet, terrifying all who saw her.

There seemed to be no place laid for her. The chair she usually occupied was currently being sat in by the wet-nurse, who had Pietro tucked up under her shawl, suckling; Lucrezia could see his feet emerging, toes clenching and unclenching as he fed.

She stood there, between the wet-nurse and Giovanni's turned-away back, for a moment, then reached forward and took a hunk of bread. She raised it to her mouth, still standing, and tore at it with her teeth. She was the tigress, devouring an enemy. She glanced around the table, almost smiling. There was a tigress among them all and they had no idea: Maria, who had her arm around Isabella's shoulders, saying something to Francesco, Garzia, who was struggling on Sofia's lap, wanting to get down and run about.

It was only when Lucrezia poured milk into a bowl and began to lap at it that she became once more visible.

'Lucrè!' Sofia yelled. 'Stop that at once! God in Heaven, what would your mother say?' She released Garzia, who immediately set off towards his wooden blocks, and came towards her. 'And what's happened to your hair? Have you been in a storm? Why is your smock on backwards? This child,' she appealed to the other nurses, as she yanked the smock over Lucrezia's head, 'will be the death of me.'

Lucrezia stood as still as the statue outside the *palazzo* gates while Sofia set about combing the knots from her hair, wiping the milk off her chin: there was no other way to be. Sofia was almost as wide as she was high, with hard palms and strong shoulders. Her smile, which came rarely, was riddled with gaps; she had barely any teeth. She had no truck with disobedience or wriggling. This was her nursery, she would remind them all the time, and things would be done her way. Isabella once muttered, it's my mother's nursery, you old cow, and Sofia's punishment for this was swift and terrible: six lashes of the switch and bed with no supper.

She didn't bear grudges, however. The next day, Lucrezia watched out of the corner of her eye as a surprisingly chastened Isabella had put her arms around Sofia's neck and kissed her cheek, whispering something into Sofia's cap. Sofia grinned, revealing the blackened gaps in her gums, and patted Isabella's arm, motioning her to the table.

Sofia pulled the brush through Lucrezia's hair, pins in her mouth, Lucrezia's ear gripped in her opposite hand. She was simultaneously telling the *balia* to stop feeding Pietro, to wind him; she was ordering Francesco not to gulp his food, to chew it properly; she was answering Maria's question about lessons this morning.

Lucrezia winced as the brush's bristles found a knot; she didn't cry out. There was no point. If you made a noise, Sofia might well remove the brush from your hair and snap it smartly against your legs. Her ear flamed hot under Sofia's grip.

She thought herself away from this situation, this moment. She pictured instead the basement in the Sala dei Leoni. The tigress would pad towards her, that rumble in her throat, but she would not bite her, no: she would regard her with a calm gaze and Lucrezia would emit an answering throaty noise and—

A sharp tug on her ear brought her back to the nursery. There was a clamour of calls and jeers around her. She had missed something – that much was clear. Her older siblings were looking at her for the first time since she had woken, laughing and pointing; Isabella was covering her mouth, bent double with mirth.

'What?' Lucrezia said, rubbing her lobe.

'You were . . .' Giovanni collapsed into giggles.

'I was what?' she said wildly, not understanding why they were all staring at her. On an impulse, she flung her arms around Sofia's familiar middle and buried her face there.

'You were growling,' she heard Maria say, with icy disapproval.

'Like a bear!' Isabella said. 'Oh, you are so funny, Lucrè.'

She heard them all leave the table and depart from the

room, still talking about Lucrè and how she thought she was a bear.

Sofia rubbed her back, between the shoulder-blades, with firm, downward strokes. Lucrezia pressed her nose into her apron and inhaled the smell that was Sofia and Sofia alone: yeast, salt, sweat, and a hint of something spicy not unlike cinnamon.

'Come,' Sofia said. 'Let go now.'

She tilted back her head to look at the nurse, arms still circling her waist. She felt the secret of the tigress move within her, like a bright ribbon weaving in and out of her ribs. Should she tell Sofia what she saw? Would she?

'Why do you have no teeth?' she asked instead.

Sofia tapped her on the head with the brush.

'Because,' she said, 'somebody had to feed your mother and her sisters and brothers, and every baby costs you a tooth. Sometimes two or three.'

Lucrezia was puzzled by this. She cast a look at the wet-nurse, who was now buttoning her smock, Pietro draped over her shoulder. Would her teeth fall out? Did it happen all at once? Babies and teeth, milk and siblings. Had she and Maria, Francesco, Isabella and Giovanni all cost the *balie* a tooth or three?

Sofia bent to hoist Garzia on to her hip and Lucrezia watched as her next-in-line brother seized Sofia around the neck, babbling sounds to her.

'But,' Lucrezia began, 'why is—?'

'Enough questions,' Sofia said. 'Lessons now. Off you go.'

Lucrezia wandered into the schoolroom, where their antiquities tutor was unrolling maps and charts, talking on and on, pointing with a cane. Francesco was staring out of the window; Maria was bent studiously over her slate, inscribing what the tutor was saying about the Trojan war; next to her, Isabella was pulling faces at Giovanni whenever the tutor turned his back. Grimaces, Lucrezia observed, which Isabella supplemented with curled, claw-like fingers, and she realised with a faint dismay that she was still being mocked for her unwitting growl.

Lucrezia slid into her place at the back of the room, a small desk behind the larger one shared by Maria and Isabella. She had been attending lessons for only a few months, since she turned seven, the age her father deemed correct for education to begin.

The antiquities tutor, a young man with a pointed beard, stood before them, a hand outstretched, his mouth moving on and on, as he spoke. After this, Lucrezia knew, the music tutor would arrive, and they would be obliged to take out their instruments, and after that, the drawing tutor would take his place, and she would be assigned the dull task of inscribing the alphabet while the others had their drawing lesson. Lucrezia had asked if she could join this lesson – it was the one that interested her most, the transferring of the world on to flat paper, conducting what a person sees through the eye, the brain, into the fingers and then the chalk – but she was told she must wait until she reached the age of ten. The days ahead, and the months and the years, seemed to jostle before her, repetitive and utterly predictable.

Lucrezia was still turning over thoughts about the feeding of babies. And Sofia's lost teeth. And the tigress. And her various longings – to see the beast, to be allowed to take part in the drawing lessons, to go once more to one of the country villas where she and her siblings were taught to ride and permitted to run about the gardens. Somehow, her mind unlatched itself from the tutor's words and drifted sideways. Lucrezia was imagining that she was an infant again, milk-fed by a fang-free tigress, a gentle creature with silken fur and caressing paws, and this baby Lucrezia spent all her days in the lion house, tucked into the warm flank of the tigress, where no one ever came and no one ever looked for her—

A crack of the cane on a map jerked her away from this vision, forcing her to focus briefly on what the antiquities tutor was saying.

'And where was it that the Greek ships were becalmed, on their way to Troy?'

Francesco was blinking, Maria twisting her lips together, as if some disparaging thought was passing through her mind; she was resting her elbow on Isabella's sleeve, and Isabella was whispering something in her ear.

Aulis, Lucrezia thought. She picked up her stylus and, on the back of the paper in front of her, drew the long line of a horizon, punctured by the masts of stationary ships; she made them tall, their sails furled, with ropes from their bows stretching to hidden anchors below the water. She then drew an altar, with people standing on its steps. And as she drew, she was recalling the lecture on perspective the art tutor had delivered to her siblings the previous week, when she was meant to be practising her letter forms. The theory was that the world had different layers and depths, like an ocean, and could be constructed from lines that converged and intersected. Lucrezia had been wanting to try this out.

'Isabella?' the tutor was saying, narrowing his eyes.

Isabella turned her head away from Maria. 'Yes?'

'The place where the Greeks were becalmed, if you please.'

Aulis, Lucrezia thought once more, as she drew. On the pathway to the altar, she added a girl in a long robe, walking towards it, and she frowned as she tried to make the lines of the path draw closer together, as required by the laws of perspective, towards what the drawing tutor had called a vanishing point.

Isabella was giving a great show of considering the matter. 'Does it perhaps begin with γ?' she asked, putting her head prettily on one side and giving him her most winning smile.

'No,' said the tutor, unmoved. 'Giovanni? Maria?'

They both shook their heads. The teacher sighed. 'Aulis,' he said. 'Remember? We went over this only last week. And how did Agamemnon, the great king, persuade the gods to give him a favourable wind?'

A pause. Isabella put a hand to her hair, tucking a stray strand behind her ear; Francesco twitched at his sleeve.

Sacrificed his daughter, Lucrezia knew. She added curtains to the altar, hanging as limply as the rigging of the ships. She would not draw Achilles, pretending to wait at the altar, she would not.

'What did Agamemnon do,' the tutor tried again, 'to get a wind so that the Greek fleet could sail on to Troy?'

Slit his daughter's throat, Lucrezia said to herself. She recalled every word of the story the tutor told them last week – it was the way her mind worked. Words pressed themselves into her memory, like a shoe sole into soft mud, which would dry and solidify, the shoe print preserved for ever. Sometimes she felt filled up, overstuffed with words, faces, names, voices, dialogues, her head throbbing with pain, and she would be set off-balance by the weight of what she carried, stumbling into tables and walls. Sofia would put her to bed, curtains drawn, and make her drink a *tisana*, and Lucrezia would sleep. When she woke her head would feel like a cupboard that had been tidied: still full but more orderly.

In the schoolroom, the teacher was asking about Agamemnon and the wind. Lucrezia laid her head on her arms and whispered a silent warning to the girl in her drawing, who was called Iphigenia, which was not a name Lucrezia had ever heard. Beware, Lucrezia mouthed to her, beware. It was unbearable that Iphigenia's father tricked her into the sacrifice by telling her she was about to be married. To Achilles, the heartless but brilliant warrior with a sea nymph for a mother. Iphigenia walked blithely to what she thought was a marriage altar but turned out to be a sacrificial altar. Agamemnon slit her throat with a knife.

Lucrezia didn't wish to think about this, didn't want the image of the unwitting girl, the glint of the knife, the eerily calm and hot sea behind, the duplicitous father, the flood and foam of blood over the altar. It would return to her, she knew, this story, in the dead of night. Iphigenia, with her slit throat, like a vibrant scarf, would shuffle up to the bed where Lucrezia lay, and she would paw at the blankets, wanting to touch Lucrezia with her cold, bloodied fingers.

Lucrezia, almost whimpering, pushed her drawing underneath a desk book and pressed her eyelids until bursts of colour shot across her vision; she could hear the tutor saying the words 'Iphigenia' and 'sacrifice' and 'daughter', and also: 'what is the matter with her? Is she ill?'

Maria was quick with her answer: 'Oh, don't pay her any mind. It is just what she does to get attention. Mamma says to ignore her when it happens and then she will stop.'

'Is that so?' the tutor's voice was uncertain, not at all as it was when he spoke of the Greeks and the Trojans, their ships and sieges. 'Should we call for the, ah, the nurse?'

Lucrezia removed her hands from her eyes. The scene before her was so bright that for a moment she could not see anything. But then she made out her siblings and the antiquities tutor, who were all looking at her.

And behind him, Lucrezia was the first to see, stepping into the room, their father.

Lucrezia's first thought, on seeing him was: Tigress, he has a tigress, hidden in the basement. Isabella immediately sat up straighter, her back like a rod. Giovanni applied himself industriously to his slate. Francesco put up a hand.

'Yes, Francesco,' the tutor said, in a neutral tone but Lucrezia could see the flush on his cheeks, the stiffness in his shoulders: he knew as well as the children that Grand Duke Cosimo I, ruler of Tuscany, was in the room.

Their father was particular and passionate about the classical world. He himself had engaged this antiquities tutor for them. They must all, she had heard him say, be educated in Greek and Roman history from the age of seven – daughters as well as sons. The Grand Duke owned, this tutor had told them, an impressive collection of ancient manuscripts, lately come from Constantinople: the tutor had been allowed to see them, even to handle some, this last part said with a shy pride.

Cosimo stepped further into the room, hands behind his

back. He strutted between the desks, looking down at what the children were writing. He laid a hand to Francesco's head, he nodded at Maria, he patted Isabella's shoulder; he passed Lucrezia's desk on slow, deliberate feet. She saw the curled-up toes of his shoes, the frilled edge of his shirt cuff. She made sure that her sketch was out of sight. He walked to the window and stood there for a moment, before saying: 'Continue, please, signore.' He smiled, revealing all his even, white teeth. 'Pretend I'm not here.'

The tutor cleared his throat, brushed a quick hand against his beard, then pointed once more at the map of Ancient Greece.

'Isabella,' he began, and Lucrezia was interested by this choice – had he deliberately chosen Cosimo's favourite for questioning? Did he know that there was no probable way that Isabella could answer? Would he give her an easy question?

'Could you tell us, please,' the tutor continued, 'how Agamemnon was drawn into the Trojan war? What was his connection to Helen of Sparta?'

Lucrezia considered Isabella's back: the conscientiously straight spine, the neat tuck of hair, the elbows held close to the body. She looked at their papa, standing by the wall, raising himself on to his toes and down again. A plan, sudden and brilliant, sprang into her head.

'Isabella?' the tutor was tapping the cane against his thigh. 'Agamemnon's connection to Helen?'

Lucrezia leant forward, as if to reach for her stylus. She cupped a casual hand around her mouth and whispered towards her sisters' backs: 'Helen was married to his brother, Menelaus.'

35

She sat back. Isabella seemed to cock her head in surprise. Maria half turned to glare at Lucrezia with a wary, disbelieving frown. Then Isabella said, in a clear voice: 'She was married to his brother . . . Meena-something.'

Lucrezia watched. The tutor smiled, visibly relieved; her father nodded as the tutor praised Isabella, saying how wonderful her answer was and that the name was pronounced 'Menelaus' and here is how you write it in Greek and would they all copy this down on their slates, please?

Lucrezia quickly took down the Greek characters and, as she finished, she leant forward again.

'Maria!' she whispered. 'Isabella! Papa has a tigress. She arrived in the night.'

Again, Maria turned towards her, then thought better of it. The tutor was walking among them, inspecting their slates, pointing out where Giovanni could perfect a letter here, a curve there. Their papa was looking towards the door again. Lucrezia held her breath. Was he leaving?

The tutor came past Isabella, said nothing, and just as he neared Lucrezia's slate, Isabella called: 'Papa!'

He turned, his hand on the door. 'Yes?'

'I have heard a rumour,' Isabella said, her fingertip pressed to her cheek.

'Is that so? And what rumour is this?'

Maria jumped in: 'That a tiger has arrived.'

Their papa stared, amazed. He was silent for a moment, and then he smiled. 'Incredible. Did you hear that, signore? My daughters know everything that goes on.' He wagged a finger at Maria and Isabella. 'You are just like your mamma, the pair of you, in every way.'

36

Isabella clasped her hands together. 'May we see it? Please, Babbo, will you let us? Will you?'

Their father laughed. 'Perhaps. I will take you all, if the signore tells me you have done well in your lessons today.'

When the lesson is over, and the children have been ushered away to their music master on the floor below, instruments tucked under their arms, the antiquities tutor will walk about the schoolroom, tidying away slates and styluses. He will be sore of foot and longing for the plate of beans and bread he will be given in the kitchens before he retires to his small cell-like room. And he will be hurrying in this, the final task of his teaching day, eager to get to his own studies. Even so, when he reaches Lucrezia's little desk, at the back of the room, he will pause, puzzled, lifting a sheet of paper between finger and thumb, examining what he sees there: not Greek lettering but a study in perspective, with all lines and principles perfectly observed. He sees, to his incredulity, Aulis: the becalmed fleet, the motionless sea, and here is Agamemnon, waiting at the duplicitous altar, and there is poor Iphigenia, making her way towards him.

He will be so taken aback that he will look up and around the room, as if he suspects some trick has been played upon him.

How can this be the work of a child so small, so quiet that he often forgets she is there? It seems so unlikely but the tutor can think of no other explanation. He tries for a feeling of outrage – that the child should have been paying attention to his lesson, instead of sketching – but the image is so compelling, so arresting, that his teacherly disapproval dissolves.

The antiquities tutor will scroll the drawing into itself, tuck it into his jacket, where it will remain for the rest of the day, its presence temporarily slipping his mind. When he undresses that night, it will fall to the floor, and he will study it again, by candlelight, once more transported to the strange and windless place of Aulis. The next day, in a back corridor, he will pass the drawing teacher – a young man with a fondness for velvet caps, from the studio of Giorgio Vasari, the court artist.

I have something I wish to show you, the antiquities tutor will say to him, producing Lucrezia's drawing out of his leather folder. What do you say to this?

The drawing tutor will stop with a smile – he has a latent fondness for this man, so scholarly and earnest, the way the lenses of his spectacles catch the light. He takes the page with a flourish and his most winning smile, shaking his cap's tassel off his brow. He is not expecting much: his thoughts are more engaged in whether or not he should invite this man to leave the *palazzo* one evening, to abandon his dusty studies, and walk out with him into narrow streets of the city. His light green eyes skim the page, considering how to frame the invitation. Then he will forget all about it. His gaze will flit from horizon to ship to altar to curtain; he will take in the walking figure's sense of motion and lightness, the waiting man's hulking threat; he will note the way the edges of the pathway are tapering, the sizes and angles of the ships, and how they are devised to give a gradation for the eye, from foreground to background.

Who did this? he will ask instead, turning it over and back. Not Maria? *Il principe* – Francesco?

The antiquities tutor will shake his head. Lucrezia, he will say.

The drawing tutor will have to think for a moment. The very little girl who sits at the back?

Yes, her. The antiquities tutor will nod gravely, then say: I thought you should know.

Then he moves off, along the corridor, books and maps held to his chest. The drawing tutor, staring after him, realises he has missed his chance, once again. He looks again at the drawing in his hand. There is something unguarded and animate about it. Something improbable. Servants and guardsmen make their way around him as he stands there, considering what to do about the drawing and the child who produced it.

The nocturnal walk to the Sala dei Leoni would be something the five children would always remember, in different ways. Francesco would recall the soldiers stationed at each gate, their weapons in their fists, saluting his father as they passed. Maria would think again and again of the water spurting up from the fountains, and how she had been surprised to see they still flowed at night, the dolphin ceaselessly swallowing and regurgitating water. Giovanni would remember most of all the way Isabella imitated the solemn expressions of the portraits they passed: the male ancestor who looked out peevishly from beneath a cornered hat, the woman who seemed very pleased with herself as she fingered a rope of pearls, the haughty man with a preposterously small dog at his heels, the pair of whey-faced children with a globe behind them. Isabella captured them all, her eyes gleaming with mockery.

Lucrezia held tight to her papa's cloak, her feet hurrying, her head turning one way then the other, taking in as much as she could. The wide stone staircases, the handrails set into the walls, the rooms leading off other rooms, the ceilings painted with stars or golden lilies, the family shields carved into the lintels, the shuffling servants, who stepped to the walls, lowering their eyes when they saw the Duke and his children, the heavy doors that her father unlatched and pushed his way through. The way the opal light of dusk fell at an oblique angle into the first courtyard, funnelled down from the sky above, but the second courtyard was darker and larger, with doorways and arches leading off it, and water spigots hidden in corners. The way it was possible to sense the Sala dei Leoni before you saw it.

How much of the *palazzo* there was to see. And how well her father knew it: how confidently he strode about it.

Cosimo stopped at a small doorway half hidden between two others, and waited as a servant sprang forward to open it. They then descended a narrow staircase, down and down. At the bottom was another door – iron-clad, reinforced with studwork. Drawing out a slender dagger from his boot, their father tapped with the hilt.

They waited. Lucrezia saw Isabella shuffle towards Maria, saw Giovanni take her hand. Francesco's face was pinched and white, looking up at their father, as if for a hint at how to behave.

The door swung open and the smell hit them: a choking stench of filth and ripe meat. The animals in there – and how many could there be? – were howling, yipping, baying, speaking in tongues that Lucrezia couldn't comprehend, telling her things she couldn't parse.

They passed a cage where two apes sat with their long arms

around each other, glistening eyes fastened on them, in their nightgowns and shawls and slippers. A silver-brown wolf lay alone in the next cage, stretched out on the stone floor, as if disguising itself as a rug; a bear slumped against a wall, all four paws manacled together, its snout lowered. Further along, there was a tank full of water, but nothing disturbed the surface: whatever was in there was keeping itself hidden tonight. At a cage near the end of the row, their father stopped. There was the staggering sight of two lions pacing, circling each other, a male and a female, and with every fourth step – Lucrezia counted them – the lion tilted back his head and let out a yowl. The lioness swung her head towards them, took them in with her lemon-brown eyes, then swivelled away.

Lucrezia glanced up at her father. Was this the lioness he loved? The one he fed off an iron spike?

Her father was looking at the animal, his eyes following her path around the cage. He clicked his tongue against the roof of his mouth. Lucrezia saw that the lioness's ears twitched at the sound but she did not stop her pacing, did not approach the bars.

'Hmm,' her father said. 'They are upset tonight.'

'Why, Papa?' Maria asked.

'They can smell the tiger. They know it is here.'

And at last, at last, their father moved on. There was an empty cage, another empty cage – and Lucrezia wondered what had happened to the animals who lived in them – and then he stopped.

It was the final cage in the row. On one side of it, Lucrezia could see, was the outer wall of the *palazzo*. They were at the very edge of the building. Beyond them now was a street, then another, and another, and then the river, cutting its ochre path through the city.

The cage had iron bars, running up, running down. The fire from the torch on the wall cast a triangular slice of light across the front of the cage but left its back recesses in darkness. A slab of meat, marbled with white fat, was lying on the floor, untouched. Other than that, there was no sign of the tigress at all.

Lucrezia looked. She looked and looked into this blackness; she strained her eyes for a glimpse of orange, a glimmer of eye, the slightest movement or sign that the creature was present. But there was nothing.

'Papa?' Isabella said, after a while. 'Is the tiger definitely in here?'

'It is,' their father said, craning his neck forward. 'Somewhere.'

There was another pause. Lucrezia pressed her hands to her chest. Please, she said inside her head, to the creature she had seen on the cart, imprisoned by a rough wooden slatted box, please show yourself. I am here. I won't be able to come again. Please come out.

'Is it sleeping?' asked Giovanni, doubtfully.

'Perhaps,' said their father.

Isabella danced up and down. 'Wake up!' she called. 'Wake up! Come on, pussycat, come on!'

Their father smiled down at her, putting a hand on her head. 'What a lazy pussycat this is,' he said at last, 'not coming to make friends with you all.'

'Babbo,' Isabella said, taking his hand, 'may we go and see the lions again? They were my favourite.'

'Yes, indeed,' their father said, delighted. 'An excellent idea.

They are much more interesting than a sleepy tiger. Come, let's go.'

He ushered his children away from the tigress's cage, back down the corridor, the servant following behind with a torch.

Not difficult at all, then, for Lucrezia to take a step or two then fall behind the servant, then stop walking altogether and allow the darkness to fold itself around her, like a cloak. Then it was perfectly possible to retrace her steps, back, back, back to the bars of the tigress's cage.

She crouched down, resting on her heels. The only light now was from the brazier on the wall. She heard the others clattering away from her, towards the lions, which were still baying and pacing. She could hear Isabella's high, questioning voice, asking about the lioness and if there might be babies soon and could she, Isabella, have one, for she would dearly love a lion cub of her own. Giovanni and Maria were saying, me too, oh, me too, can we, Papa, can we?

Lucrezia looked at the slab of darkness. It seemed to pulse and hum. She scanned it from one end to the other. She tried to think herself towards the creature it contained, tried to picture what it would have been like to be captured in a far-off place, then brought by boat to Tuscany and left here, in a stone cell.

Please, she incanted again, far more fervently than she ever did in the pews of the chapel, please.

The fat-laced meat was giving off a ferrous, acrid scent. Why hadn't the tigress eaten it? Was she not hungry? Was she too sad? Was she scared of the lions?

Lucrezia was gazing into the depthless black, searching for movement, for colour, anything, but her eyes were too weak or she must have been looking the wrong way because there was a flicker of movement next to the stone *palazzo* wall and, by the time she turned her head to see, the tigress was almost upon her.

Liquid was her motion, like honey dropping from a spoon. She emerged from the shadow of her cage as if she had the whole stretch of the jungle at her command, the filthy mud floor of Florence rolling under her paws. No pussycat, she. She simmered, she crackled, she seethed with fire, her face astonishing in its livid symmetry. Lucrezia had never seen anything so beautiful in her life. The furnace-bright back and sides, the pale underbelly. The marks on her fur, Lucrezia saw, were not stripes, no – the word was insufficient for them. They were a bold, dark lace, to adorn, to conceal; they defined her, they saved her.

Closer and closer she came, allowing the triangle of light to fall upon her. Her eyes were locked on Lucrezia. For a moment, it seemed as if she would pass her by, as the lioness had done. But the tigress paused, stopping in front of the girl. Her mind was not elsewhere, like the lioness's. She had noticed her; she was there, with Lucrezia; there was much the two of them needed to say to each other. Lucrezia knew this, the tigress knew this.

Lucrezia eased herself forward, coming to her knees. The tigress's flank was there, beside her: repeating incisions and ellipses of black in the amber. She could see the breath entering and leaving her body; she could see where the torso sloped away into her tender underside, the soft spread of her paws, the quivering in her limbs. She saw how the animal lifted her lustrous muzzle, nosing the air, sifting it for all it could tell her. Lucrezia could feel the sadness, the loneliness, emanating from her, the shock at being torn from her home, the horror of the weeks and weeks at sea. She could feel the sting of the lashes the beast had received, the bitter longing for the vaporous and humid canopy of jungle and the enticing green tunnels through its undergrowth that she alone commanded, the searing pain in her heart at the bars that now enclosed her. Was there no hope? the tigress seemed to be asking her. Will I always remain here? Will I never return home?

Lucrezia felt tears welling in her eyes. To be so alone in such a place! It wasn't fair or right. She would ask her papa to send the animal back. They could take it on to the ship, and sail to wherever they had found her, open the bars of her cage and watch her dive back into the lichenous towering trees.

Slowly, slowly, Lucrezia put out her hand. She snaked her fingers through a gap in the iron bars and stretched, spreading her fingers, reaching out of her shoulder socket, straining forward, her face pressed close to the cage.

The tigress's fur was pliant, warm, soft as down. Lucrezia eased her fingertips along the animal's back, feeling the quiver of her muscles, the flexing beads of her spine. There was no difference between the orange fur and the black, no join, as she'd thought there might be. The two colours overlapped and merged without trace.

The tigress swung her vivid, complex face around, as if to examine the person behind such a caress, as if to ascertain its meaning. To look into her eyes was to behold the visage of an incandescent, forbidden deity.

Lucrezia and the tigress regarded each other, for a stretched moment, the child's hand on the beast's back, and time stopped for Lucrezia, the turning world stilled. Her life, her name, her family and all that surrounded her receded and became void. She was aware only of her own heart, and that of the tigress, pulsing inside the ribs, drawing in scarlet blood and shooting it out again, flooding their veins. She barely breathed; she didn't blink.

Then, a sudden cry, and Maria was shrieking, Papa, Papa, look, and the world and the *palazzo* came surging back. Maria was facing her, a startling white figure printed on the darkness, arm raised, an admonishing finger pointing at Lucrezia. Feet were clattering, people were shouting, and Lucrezia was being seized from behind and dragged backwards, away from the tiger, cracking her wrist on the bars. She could hear her father calling orders; one of her siblings was screaming, and her own voice yelling, no, no, put me down.

Lucrezia was then being hurried away, down the corridor, clutched in the arms of one of her father's soldiers. Maria was somewhere nearby, saying, in her cold and instructive voice, what a stupid, stupid thing to do, she could have been killed, I told you she was too young to come, I wonder what will Mamma say when she hears. Lucrezia's wrist throbbed with the blow, her fingers felt naked and raw: they still held the sensation of warm fur, of sleek stripes.

She had no thought for her siblings or her father – she didn't know if they were with her or behind her or ahead or if they were still standing by the lions. All she knew was that she was being borne away from something she loved more than anything else in the world, that the distance between them was increasing, with every step taken. She was crying out, pleading to be let down, to be allowed back, but no one was heeding her. She kept her eyes on the cage, for as long as she could. She looked and looked over the shoulder of the man who was carrying her, strained her eyes into the dark, and saw – she was always sure of this, afterwards – the tigress gazing at her, for one final instant, then vanishing, back into her dark lair, with a whipcrack whirl of striped tail.

Venison baked in wine

Fortezza, near Bondeno, 1561

'And perhaps tomorrow,' her husband is saying, as he tips his bowl to scoop out the final dregs of soup, 'we shall go for a ride along the river. The views further west are most pleasing to the eye. I will see to it that your saddle is adjusted – I noticed today that it was listing on one side. And the hoofs of your mare will need attention, I fear, when we return, and . . .'

The sense of his words disintegrates as Lucrezia stares at him, until what comes from his mouth reaches her as a string of babble and nonsense, the squawks of a beast. Why is he saying these things? How can he sit there, serenely eating his food, talking about groomsmen and horse tack when somewhere in his mind lurks a scheme to end her life?

Once again, Lucrezia seems to hear the rasping voice of his sister Elisabetta saying into her ear: You have no idea what he is capable of.

Despite the fire that growls and pops in the large grate, despite the breath that comes from her, from her husband, from the servants in the shadows, the air in the dining hall is as frigid as iron. It has been an unusually chill winter, which yet shows no sign of ending. Even the candles, standing in ornate brass holders, seem to shiver, casting an uncertain light that doesn't reach the walls. Her husband's face comes in and out of visibility. She watches, with fixed fascination, as his expression changes with every flicker of the candle: first thoughtful, then kind, now stern, now animated, now forbidding, now handsome, then amorous and then detached. It is true: she has no idea what he is capable of, and she does not want to find out.

Again, she feels her disbelief as a bubble of mirth, just below her ribcage. If she is not careful, she will burst out laughing at the absurdity of it all, his talk, his pretence, his dissembling, his lying looks.

Her husband, who means to kill her, either by his own hand or by his order to another, takes up the end of his napkin and dabs at his cheek with its pointed corner, as if a spot of soup on one's face is a matter of importance. Her husband, who intends her death, spends a moment brushing a stray hair from his brow, then finally tucks it behind his ear. Her husband, the murderer, says, over his shoulder to the servants, that the cook should be told to add more salt. As if seasoning is important to them now. Her husband, who will kill her before long, reaches out, as if he means to fold her cold fingers into his palm. It is this that proves too much for her. She startles into life, moves her hand away, picking up her spoon and dipping it into her bowl.

And in an instant, her mirth shrivels and burns, alchemising into the purest, hottest form of fury. How dare he?

She moves her spoon from bowl to mouth, her hand trembling with the effort of not transmitting her thoughts to him. Concealment, here, is all. The broth's surface is spangled with yellow circles of oil. She fixes her eye on these instead of on him. She has a feeling that if she were to see his face, his neatly parted hair, the whiteness of his teeth, her rage would boil over and she might shout or strike him or run from the room.

She will not allow him to kill her, to extinguish her. But how can she, a small-for-her-age sixteen-year-old bride with no friends or allies present get the better of him, a soldier, a duke, a man of twenty-seven? She recalls the lessons in combat her brothers received, the hours and hours they spent practising with swords and lances and spears, with ropes to strangle, clubs to batter, daggers to slash and stab, how they learnt to parry, thrust and maim, to block a blow with one hand while delivering a counter-blow with the other, to turn and duck, to wrest themselves from the grip of another, to kill and to survive. They were taught all this, as Alfonso would have been, while she, Isabella and Maria were cloistered upstairs, learning how to replicate flowers in threads of coloured silk.

'You need a plan,' she hears – or seems to hear – her old nurse, Sofia, say, from a place near her elbow. 'To lose your temper is to lose the battle.'

A plan. A strategy. Sofia was always a woman with a plan. She would have made a wonderful *condottiero*, Lucrezia had often told her, had she been born a man.

So be it, she says to the invisible Sofia next to her. So be it.

She lets out her held breath, slowly, through her nose. Forces herself to smile at her husband, to lift her spoon, to take a sip of soup.

She had had a plan, three years previously, on the day she went to her father's office (and look how that worked out, she would like to say to Sofia, if Sofia herself was actually in the room, and wouldn't box her ears for such impertinence). She had stepped determinedly over the hallowed threshold, her hands gripped together, her head held high, her plan clear in her mind.

Several of her father's secretaries and scribes glanced up, aghast to see her there, then bowed their heads studiedly over their papers. Beyond the windows was a featureless parchment-white sky. Fragments and snippets of sound floated up from the piazza, several storeys below: her sharp ears caught a group of people singing a somewhat bawdy ditty, the spiralling cry of a tired child, a high-pitched descending laugh of a young woman.

'Papa,' she said.

Her father was standing at a lectern, reading something, his fingertip moving quickly and precisely across the page.

'Papa?'

He didn't look up. Vitelli was standing next to him, examining the document over his shoulder, and he held up a hand, blank palm facing her, to indicate that she must not interrupt.

But Lucrezia could not hold in her words. At any moment, the marriage contract might be finalised and sealed and sent back to the Ferrarese court; if she didn't speak out now, it would soon be too late.

'Babbo,' she said, employing Isabella's affectionate name for their father, trying to recall the lines she had rehearsed in her room. 'I do not wish to marry this man. I am sorry if this disappoints you but . . .'

Keeping his finger on the page, her father murmured something inaudible to Vitelli, and only then did he turn towards her.

'My dear,' he said, and moved away from his desk, towards her, his head on one side, as if considering the unprecedented sight of her, here, in his private offices. She saw at once that his wandering eye, on the right side of his face, was more than usually off-centre, which meant that he was either tired or angry. Which could it be?

'Come,' he curled his finger at her, 'come here.'

She stepped towards him, unsure if he was about to embrace or castigate her, and he regarded her approach with one eye that never left her and another that roamed around the walls, as if his attention could be in several places at once.

When she was right in front of him, he placed first one then the other hand on her shoulders, so that she was enclosed on both sides by the sweep of his cloak.

'Lucrè,' he said, dipping his head so that he was looking right into her face, inside the private space he had created, 'I understand. Marriage is a big step for a young woman. It's a daunting prospect, no? I know this, I see this. But you must not worry. Your mother will prepare you fittingly for every aspect. And I? I would only ever choose the best type of man for you. How else could I ever part with you?'

He gave her chin a gentle tweak, his eyes coming together for a fleeting moment.

'You trust your papa, don't you?' he asked.

Lucrezia nodded. 'Of course, I—'

'Have I not always taken care of you, very good care?'

'Yes, but—'

'Well, then! All this worry is for nothing. Alfonso is an excellent man. He will one day be a duke, he is cultured and—'

'He is so old!' Lucrezia burst out. 'And he—'

'He is not yet thirty. This is your idea of old? What am I, then, by this standard?' Her father removed his hands from her shoulders, mock-offended. 'An ancient old man ready for the grave?' His tone was playful, and the aides and secretaries around him gave dutiful laughs, but Lucrezia was not fooled: his gaze was serious and watchful.

'You should worry no more,' he said, drawing her arm through his, and beginning to steer her towards the door, 'because this is going to be a most successful marriage. Of that I am certain. Look at your mother and me. We had hardly met, as you know, yet we—'

Lucrezia cut across her father, blurting out the plan she had formed as she sat in her chamber that morning: 'Couldn't we marry him to my cousin instead?'

Cosimo paused, his face becoming still, as if he was only now realising the size and depth of her resistance.

'Your cousin?' Cosimo repeated, very much in the manner that he might have said, *your dog?*

'We could say that I am unwell or sickly. Or – or anything. Dianora is of marriageable age and she is beautiful. I'm sure Alfonso and his father would like her, if they saw her. Could she not be offered as—?'

'Dianora,' her father said, enunciating each syllable, 'will marry your brother Pietro.'

'Pietro?' Lucrezia was startled by this news. The lovely Dianora and the irascible boy-child Pietro? It seemed an impossible pairing. 'But what if we—?'

'It has already been decided,' Cosimo said, both eyes looking past her now, giving some indecipherable signal to a person she could not see.

'Then perhaps . . .' Lucrezia sensed her escape route narrowing, a door being slammed and locked. She tried quickly to think of an alternative plan, another idea. What would Sofia do? What would she suggest? If Dianora was really to marry Pietro, then—

'Look at your sister,' her father said, giving her hand a firm pat. 'Isabella was also nervous before her marriage, was she not? And has she not thrived?'

'I suppose,' Lucrezia said, with reluctance, thinking that Isabella had been far from nervous, and that marriage had in fact changed her life very little: she had been allowed to live in Florence while her husband returned to Rome, the couple only seeing each other several times a year. Yet she, Lucrezia, was expected to leave and go to Ferrara, a place she had never been, with a man she did not know. But Cosimo, like most adults, was working from his own version of events, so pointing this out would do little to further her cause.

'Is she not happy with the match I made for her?'

'She is, but—'

'And so will you be, Lucrè. I promise you that.' Cosimo smiled, giving a nod, as if the argument had been satisfactorily resolved. 'Alfonso's father and I have corresponded a great deal and we are both certain that this will be a celebrated marriage. In time, you will look back on this conversation and—'

'Papa,' Lucrezia said, and her voice cracked. She felt the sudden dangerous proximity of tears. 'I don't want to marry him. Please don't give me to him.'

As if the meaning and fervour of her words bore noxious fumes, everyone in the room reeled away from her. Her father spun on his heel and walked back to his lectern, Vitelli shadowing him, the hovering secretaries scurrying back behind their desks.

'This is intolerable,' she heard her father mutter, either to Vitelli or her or everyone in the room, and Lucrezia will never be sure, later, whether or not he intended her to hear what he said next. 'There has always been something in her that makes me wonder if she is unsuited to marriage – it will be a miracle if they don't regret the union, and return her to us within a month.'

Alfonso is keen for her to eat a good dinner but the thought of her impending death has stolen her appetite. He persists, however, encouraging her to try the venison baked in wine, to take one more mouthful, then another. She is, he tells her, looking thin – he wants her to regain her strength after her recent illness. Venison is good for the blood, he says: a person needs meat juices circulating through them. She eats a mouthful or two but most of her portion she cuts into small pieces and drops into her napkin. He tears off a hunk of bread and, carefully removing the crust, mops up the sauce and holds it, dripping, to her mouth. She doesn't like to say that the fluid oozing out of the slab of venison, with its transverse fibres of muscle and fat, the way it stands in puddles of red, which could be either wine or blood, makes her stomach heave.

She opens her mouth, takes the sodden bread from his hands, and forces the muscles of her throat to swallow it down.

He tells her about a hunting trip here with his father, when he was young – 'perhaps eight or nine' – and he came across a wild boar in a clearing. He had raised his bow but had been unable to fire an arrow.

'It was a female,' he says, 'and she had three young ones with her. They looked quite different from her, small and pale brown, with stripes running down their backs. I knew I should do it, that I should let fly the arrow, that my father would be angry if he found out I'd missed the chance, but I could not. So I just watched them, from horseback, until they disappeared into the undergrowth.'

'And was your father angry?'

The lower part of Alfonso's face is caught by a wavering circle of light. His lips are parted in a smile or a grimace – impossible to say which.

'He got his steward to beat me. I couldn't sit down for three days. He told me it was so I should always remember that I must never let sentiment get in the way of necessary action.'

She considers this advice, dispensed by a deceased father: sentiment and necessary action. Could the two, she wants to ask, not coexist? Has necessary action ever been dictated by emotion? Could the heart not have a say? As she lifts her cup to take a sip of wine, she pictures him as a small boy, in a sun-shot clearing, watching transfixed as a boar truffles for food, trailed by three offspring, their tiny hoofs treading down the soil. Then she sees him being beaten while his father watches.

'My father,' Lucrezia hears herself say, 'keeps animals –

exotic creatures – at the *palazzo*. He has a menagerie in the basement.'

'Ah,' Alfonso says. 'I have heard of this. Did you ever see them fight?'

'No. He never . . . That was only for visitors. And perhaps my brothers, I don't know. He let us visit, my older siblings and me, when I was a little girl. I was very pleased to be included, that he considered me old enough – all my younger brothers were left behind in the nursery. There was a tigress, you see, and I—'

Lucrezia breaks off; she may already have said too much. And why is she saying these things? She never talks about the tigress; she never has and never will.

Alfonso, leaning forward into the light, is regarding her with interest, his eyes moving about her face in that way he has, gathering information and insights. What might this mean? he is thinking. She is sure of it. This story is about a tiger, yes, but what is she really telling me? And why the hesitation? What is she hiding?

She could tell him everything, she knows. From the fiery feel of the fur to the crack of the iron bar on her wrist as she was dragged away. She could describe for him the foetid air of the menagerie, the shackled ankles of the bear. She could tell him that a few weeks after their visit to the Sala dei Leoni she plucked up the courage to approach her father during a music lesson, which he sometimes attended, if he could spare the time, and ask him if she could see the animal again, and her father had ripped open her heart, with words like blades.

Unfortunately, he had said, with apparent unconcern, the tiger has been killed.

Killed? Lucrezia echoed, as if she couldn't make sense of the word, as if it was from a language she hadn't yet encountered. How could such a creature die, be extinguished, when it was the distillation of life itself? It was impossible.

The lion and lioness, her father explained, had set upon the tiger together. A careless servant left the interconnecting doors of their cages open. The beast fought bravely, he added, turning over the page of music he was looking at, injuring both lions rather badly. The tiger battled for life, but in the end the two lions were too much and they overpowered her. The servants were unable to separate them, he said, with a shrug of annoyance. And, what's more, the pelt was ruined, so it couldn't even be taken from the carcass, which had greatly disappointed Lucrezia's mother.

She could confide in Alfonso that she was taken ill that afternoon. The physician was called; he bled her, he laid a poultice on her chest, he administered a sedative, and a tincture of valerian. He diagnosed a fever of the nerves and put her in quarantine on a lower floor. It was difficult to know, he regretted to say, whether or not Lucrezia would survive.

She spent several weeks alone in the lower chamber, seeing only the *palazzo* physician and the servant who was charged with giving her soup and changing her linens. She began to rally only when her mother came to visit her. Lucrezia swam up from a fitful sleep to find Eleanora at her bedside, the lower part of her face behind a scarf, to prevent inhalation of the sickness. She gazed up, stunned, at her mother, who was unwrapping tiny parcels tied with paper and string, inside which were numerous glass *animaletti*, in different colours. Eleanora was placing them around the bedsheets – a blue fox, a yellow bear, a fish with a golden fantail – saying that she herself had ordered them especially for Lucrezia, from a city famous for glass. And also that the art tutor had seen a drawing Lucrezia had made, and he had shown it to his master, the court artist, Signor Vasari. He, in turn, had brought it to Eleanora's attention. It was Signor Vasari's opinion, she said, that Lucrezia should be allowed to join in the drawing lessons. Eleanora's eyes, above the mask, seemed to gleam with a desperate hope. Would you like that, Lucrè? she asked, dancing the little glass bear up and down in front of Lucrezia's face. Lucrezia could not think what drawing her mother was talking about, could not understand what was being said to her. But she said, Yes, Mamma, thank you, because she knew that this was the reply to make her mother happy. Then, Eleanora said, with a catch in her voice, You must get well, yes? So you can begin your art tuition?

When Lucrezia returned to the nursery and schoolroom, she was thinner and quieter than ever before. She spent hours arranging and rearranging her *animaletti* on the nursery windowsills. She was allowed to take part in the drawing lessons; after several weeks, the art tutor began to stay behind after his lesson to tutor her, and only her. He didn't so much teach as sit next to her while they drew together, and occasionally he said, Like this, do you see that, is that what a horse or a butterfly looks like to you, think again, look again, really look, and now does it perhaps seem like this or this?

She never saw the Sala dei Leoni again.

She could tell Alfonso all this, thereby giving him keys to certain gates and alleyways inside her. So she will not. She will not permit him access. She will not say that without the art tuition, which continued until her marriage, she doesn't think she would have recovered or survived, but would instead have sunk beneath some hidden surface. She will keep these words safely inside her, where no one may look at or pore over them.

So when Alfonso asks what happened to the tigress, she gives him a bland smile and says: 'I'm afraid I've no idea. My father may have sold her. My mother hates the menagerie – she complains about the smell and the noise, and my father is always eager to make her happy.'

He looks at her for a moment longer, then reaches out and takes her hand, lacing his fingers between hers.

'You are cold, my darling,' he says. 'Have some more of the venison. It will warm you.'

Seven galleys laden with gold

Palazzo, Florence, 1550s

When she was young, Lucrezia had a curious habit of asking her parents, whenever she could, to tell her the story of their initial meeting. She would beg Eleanora, then Cosimo, then Eleanora again, until they became exasperated by the demand. In truth, Eleanora and Cosimo liked to relate it, and they were pleased that their troublesome fifth child appeared attached to the narrative: it was romantic, it showed the feminine sensibility so often lacking in her. But Lucrezia's reasons had nothing to do with sentiment or romanticism. Her desire to hear about them first catching a glimpse of the other was a groping towards an understanding of the mysterious and glamorous people from whom she had sprung, and with whom she felt so little in common. She would listen to one version from Cosimo, then compare it to another she was told a few days later by Eleanora, then demand a further version from Cosimo, so she could see how they all measured up. It was a way for her to puzzle out what marriage meant, what this contract between a man and a woman entailed.

In bed, at night, lying awake, or kneeling on the floor during Mass, she would consider the pieces and fragments of the story she had heard, like a gambler sifting through game counters, weighing them up, trying to put them into order. As her little brothers snored or sighed in their sleep, or her family murmured responses in Latin to the priest, she would be picturing her father, a visitor to Naples, aged fifteen and a mere page, at the house of the Holy Roman Emperor's Spanish viceroy, glancing through a thin curtain and seeing the youngest daughter: Eleanora, just thirteen years old. Lucrezia, in her mind, gave the room columns, and heavy drapes on either side of a carved fireplace. The young Eleanora's hair was perhaps in a shining plait down her back and Lucrezia imagined her chin would have been raised a notch or two higher than was strictly seemly, eyes wandering not dreamily but restlessly about the ceiling. Lucrezia knew each of the story's elements so well they were like familiar, over-handled gems, their corners softened, their gleam dimmed.

She knew how curious and alluring Eleanora would have appeared to her father: the foreign style of her dress, the decorated braiding of her hair. How her father returned to Florence and for two years held the image of this young Spanish girl in his heart, and when chosen to be the Grand Duke of Tuscany, and head of the dynasty, he asked for this girl to be his wife. No, he would not take the politically advantageous hand of a Dutch princess or the daughter of neighbouring rulers: he wanted the girl he had seen in

Naples. The Spanish viceroy considered his plea, then offered his elder daughter but, no, Cosimo would not have her: he would marry for love and the only woman he wanted was Eleanora. Eventually the viceroy agreed and they were married by proxy; Eleanora began to learn Tuscan so that she could write to her husband rather than using a translator to transcribe their letters.

Four years after Cosimo had first seen her, Eleanora set sail from Naples, accompanied by five maids, her old nurse, Sofia, and seven galleys laden with her dowry of gold, plate, silks, brocades, beads and oils. Lucrezia knew – because her papa liked to tell them – that he had waited impatiently for news of Eleanora, staying awake to hear if any messenger came in the night, praying that the winds would be fair. As soon as he received word that they had landed at Livorno, he made preparations to leave Florence and set off for the coast, to meet his bride. The court advisers frowned at such impetuous behaviour: it was unthinkable, unbecoming for a man to travel towards a woman. It would give the wrong impression to her of the balance of power in their marriage: Cosimo should stay put, in his *palazzo*, waiting for her to come to him. But Cosimo did not listen. He took the road to Livorno and met Eleanora halfway, to bear her, like a prize, back to Florence. When they arrived, the people of the city lined the streets to be the first to see this new, exotic grand duchess.

Lucrezia met her future husband only once before their wedding, and he was, at the time, betrothed to her sister Maria.

They passed by her on the highest battlement surrounding the bell-tower, Maria and her fiancé, his head inclined towards Maria's nervous chatter. Lucrezia was perhaps ten at the time, with the flat and featureless body of a child, and she stood there, holding her pet mouse cupped in her palm. The fiancé's eyes had left Maria – her flushed cheeks and trembling chin – and travelled over Lucrezia's face, to the mouse, then back to her face, and his lips curved up in a wry smile. Maria's hand had been hooked into the green velvet of his sleeve, with her opposite hand pressed on top of it, as if she was afraid he might attempt an escape. Lucrezia had flattened herself against the rough stone of the wall as they approached, nestling the mouse close to her chest. The fiancé, who would one day be a duke and came from a very old family – one that could be traced back to the time of the Roman Empire, she had heard her father say, more than once – paused, his boots slowing down, and he said, who is this child?

Maria's gaze swung towards Lucrezia, then away. One of my sisters, she said, and they sidestepped her, moving on, past the columns, to the opposite side of the tower where, as Maria was telling him, they might see a view of the cupola.

As he walked away, the fiancé, whose ancestors had defended the Emperor, brushed his thumb along Lucrezia's cheek, and then, very quickly, so quickly that afterwards she was never sure if it had actually happened, he twitched his nose at her and pulled – she was sure of it – a face like a mouse. One sniffing at something it liked, cheese perhaps or a tasty breadcrumb.

Lucrezia laughed, up there on the tower, at the accuracy of this impression, at the unexpectedness of a revered man making such a face. How did he know so well the way mice

64

could look? And for him to have done that, without Maria seeing, just for her, Lucrezia. Delighted, she watched her sister and her husband-to-be walk away from her.

The end of the meal

Fortezza, near Bondeno, 1561

'**Y**ou look cold, my love.'

Lucrezia shakes her head and shivers, all at the same time. Alfonso is looking at her intently, leaning in close, his hair falling over his brow, his expression solicitous.

Then he stands, pushing back his chair, takes her hand and leads her towards the fire. Beneath her skirts, beneath her damp stockings, she is aware of a tightening in the muscles of her legs, urging her to run, to sprint away.

She moves to sit in the smaller fireside chair, but he draws her towards him, on to his lap, putting his arms about her. It is a strange moment as she allows herself to be settled there. Feeling his grip tighten, she finds herself wondering if this is indeed affection or if he means to finish her right here.

Lucrezia is finding it hard to meet his eye, to behold him at this proximity, but she forces her gaze towards him and sees him looking back at her, smiling gently. His face, she knows, is handsome. People comment on this all the time. He has a well-formed physique with broad shoulders and strong limbs. Placed on his lap, however, and in this shuddering light, she cannot tell, cannot say whether his visage is pleasing or threatening. She can see only parts of him: now his brow, now his cheek, the whorl of his ear.

Is it possible that she has made a mistake, that she has misjudged the situation here at the *fortezza*? Perhaps he is as good as his word; maybe he has brought her here for a rest, for a change of air. Is it just her imagination – which all her life she has been told is too active, too excessive – or a trick of the mind that has persuaded her he intends to harm her?

His arms are about her waist; his legs support her; she rests her fingers on the back of his collar. In the amber-coloured firelight, out of the corner of her eye she is almost convinced that he is, once again, wearing slashed green velvet sleeves, even when she knows that he is dressed in a travelling suit of worsted wool.

On an impulse, she leans forward and kisses his cheek. His skin is prickly with a day's growth of beard, and his face, when she moves upright again, is pleased and quizzical.

'What was that for?'

'To . . .' she improvises '. . . say thank you.'

'For what?'

'For . . . bringing me here.' She sifts her mind, rapidly, for any words that might persuade him to spare her, if that is indeed his plan. 'For taking care of me. For . . .'

His arms press closer; she hears the struts of her bodice creak under the strain.

'You don't need to thank me,' he says. 'But you can give me another kiss.'

He turns his head, away from the light, and indicates his other cheek. After a moment, she dips her head and kisses it. Then he turns towards her and raises his mouth.

She makes herself smile. She makes herself move towards him. His features, the closer she gets, merge together, and she lowers her eyelids. He cannot mean her harm, because he wants her to kiss him, and here are his lips, beneath hers now, and there is pressure, his mouth covering hers, his large hand closing around the back of her head, and no one would do that if they meant to, if they intended to, if they were planning to— No, it is impossible, she must be mistaken, he must love her after all, he must treasure and respect her, because no one would kiss someone like this, with passion and heat and mouth and the slash of a tongue-tip, would they, no one would think of killing someone at the same time as kissing them as if they meant to pour their very soul into them?

She must have been wrong. She is overwrought from the journey, from her recent illness. She has let her imagination get away from her. Yet again she has let it lead her astray. Her handsome and sophisticated husband means her no harm. He loves her. He must do. He is kissing her at such length. How lucky she is, to be married to someone so devoted.

The kiss goes on. And on. She allows it. She laces her hands together around his neck and lets her thoughts wander. There is something incompatible about the temperatures in the room. One side of her is too hot, her left cheek and arm scorching in the fire's heat. The other, facing the room, is too cold, the freezing miasma of the *fortezza* coating her.

His hands are brushing the fabric of her sleeves. Then, all at once, he pulls away.

'Come,' he says. 'I will show you to your chamber.'

Lucrezia raises herself from his lap and decides to broach the subject that has been worrying her since they left court this morning.

'I wonder,' she says, in the lightest tone she can manage, as he lifts a candle from the table and takes her hand in his, as if the matter is of no consequence at all, 'when my maid-servants will arrive. It is getting so late and . . .'

He doesn't look at her when he says: 'I expect it will be tomorrow or the day after.'

'But I thought they were coming directly after us, because you said—'

'Can you not survive without your women?' He seems amused. 'Even for one night?'

He moves towards the door and opens it, standing to one side to let her pass through.

'I suppose I could,' she says, stepping out into the corridor. He means me no harm, she says to herself. He loves me, he does – he says he does.

'They will come as soon as they can.' Alfonso takes her elbow, moves off down the corridor, the circle of candlelight tremulous around him; she has to lengthen her stride to keep up. 'The roads would not be safe for travel after dark. You wouldn't want your women to run into danger, would you?'

He reaches out and touches her chin, pinching it between thumb and finger, angling her face to the light. He tells her she looks beautiful. The country air is agreeing with her already.

'I miss your hair,' he says, letting her shortened plait run through his palm, 'but it is still lovely.'

She nods, says, 'Thank you.'

He leads her up a spiral staircase slippery with moisture and moss. She must cling to his hand so her shoes don't skid, so she doesn't stumble on the hem of her gown. It is only by the candle's weak yellow penumbra that she can see where she is, the walls and corridors of this place. They go up a flight of stairs, along a corridor, and up a narrower set of steps. She finds she is trying to remember the way, to create a map of this building in her head, just in case: left out of the hall, then up the stairs, then right along a low corridor, then through an archway and—

'Here,' he says, stopping just ahead of her and pushing open a heavy wooden door. 'This is where you shall sleep. I ordered a fire to be lit, so it will be warm and aired. After you, my darling.'

Everything changes

Palazzo, Florence, 1557

By the time the four eldest children of the ruling family were approaching the end of their childhood, their futures were already mapped out for them. Their parents and emissaries and secretaries and advisers had been working on these plans since the children's births.

Maria would marry the son of the Duke of Ferrara. Isabella was betrothed to Paolo Giordano Orsini of Rome. Francesco would one day be Grand Duke of Florence. Giovanni would excel as a cardinal.

One by one, Lucrezia's elder siblings left the nursery. If she had felt lonely before, she was unprepared for how it would be when her older siblings grew up. To mark their betrothals, Isabella and Maria were given their own chambers. Francesco and Giovanni, on their thirteenth birthdays, also took rooms on the second floor, and Francesco was expected to join his father every day in his offices, to learn about matters of state.

Lucrezia slept alone then, on a narrow truckle, while her younger brothers took the larger bed. She sat at a desk on the other side of the schoolroom from Pietro, Ferdinando and Garzia, who were just learning their numbers and letters. She stayed up in the evenings, listening to Sofia and the other nurses converse in their native tongue: malleable vowels with interesting stresses, occasional words that were half familiar to Lucrezia's Florentine ear. It was well known in the *palazzo* that Sofia would permit only young women from her Neapolitan home village to work alongside her in the nursery. Lucrezia sometimes wondered if the reason for this was really what Sofia claimed – that these girls made the best nursemaids – or whether it was because the arrangement enabled her to talk with her helpers in their own secret dialect, believing that no one else understood.

Glimpses of Lucrezia's four elder brothers and sisters were brief: the sound of their footsteps as they moved along corridors, a flash of fabric as they descended a staircase, Isabella's laugh at a gathering in the salon, Francesco's dry cough coming through the walls of the state room, where he was attending their father. They never came up to the nursery. Lucrezia, sidling along passageways, caught snippets of information: that Maria's wedding would be lavish, with the church of Santa Maria Novella bedecked in myrtle branches; later in the evening, a hundred Florentine ladies would dance the length of the great hall, and there would be masques, and acrobats from the Orient. Nothing, however, Lucrezia heard, as she loitered behind the panels of her mother's chambers, would surpass in opulence the dress Maria would wear. It would be spun from pure gold, overlaid with silk from her mother's insectarium. Eleanora would herself oversee the whole process. Maria would glow as she walked up the aisle of the church, the gold chosen to enhance her creamy complexion and the blue to bring out the chestnut glints in her hair: a gown such as this would never have been seen before.

The day that everything changed was damp and thunderous. It had rained all night and all morning, the *palazzo* roof giving off a staccato thrum. The piazza, when Lucrezia gazed down at it from the nursery windows, was slick with water, flagstones gleaming and reptilian, fallen leaves choking the gutters. The Arno, she knew, would be swollen and silt-saturated. The usually healthy and robust Maria had caught a contagion of the lungs, Sofia had told them a few days before, and had been put to bed. The air is bad today, she said, waving a hand before her, as if her palm and fingers had the power to clear terrible miasmas from the room.

Lucrezia was in the schoolroom, copying a map of Mesopotamia, filling the wide oceanic spaces with cresting waves. She was sketching a sea monster, giving it sinuous coils that rose out of the water, and she was imagining how much more of it there might be below the surface when she heard the noise. A long keening howl that made her lift her head. At first, she thought it was one of the dogs, perhaps injured or beaten, but it tapered off with a human cry, a repeated word: No-no-no-no.

Lucrezia half rose, the stylus slipping from her fingers. Her mother? Isabella? It came from the floor below, she could tell, rising through the walls and ceilings.

There it was again. No-no-no. Then a screaming sob.

Lucrezia ran across the room, through the door and leant into the stairwell. 'Mamma?' she called.

There was silence from below. Then a door slammed. The sound of feet coming quickly along a corridor, the sweep of a robe or a gown hem.

'Isabella?' Lucrezia tried. 'Is that you?'

There was a low murmur, then a door opened, and the noise of sobbing drifted up towards her, like smoke, over which could be heard the rumble of prayer: the *palazzo* priest, Lucrezia realised, intoning in Latin.

'Mamma?' Lucrezia tried to call again but all that came out was a croak. She was seized with the feeling that something dreadful had happened: this certainty clamped its jaws around her. From somewhere below came the thunder of several people descending the stairs at speed. Someone was crying, where is His Excellency? Have you seen him? Fetch him here now.

Sofia found Lucrezia, a little later, clinging to the stair-rail. She had to prise her fingers off the carved stone and pull her back to the nursery. Lucrezia's younger siblings had been made to kneel before the wooden statue of the Madonna and, as was her custom, Sofia had opened all the windows, to let Maria's soul fly to Heaven.

The rug pressed its fibres into Lucrezia's knees. She placed her palms together; she said the words of the prayer; she avoided the painted eye of the wooden Madonna but instead looked at the windows, flung wide, and the city beyond. The sky was an uneasy grey, swollen with more rain. It made Lucrezia shudder – she did not want Maria to fly from this place, alone, from these windows, up towards that forbidding sky. This was where she belonged. Lucrezia wanted to turn her head and find Maria there, walking into the room, her chin firm, her arms folded, talking about the fabric of her wedding dress, the arrangements for the dancing. How was it possible for someone to be there one day and gone the next?

Lucrezia felt Sofia tug on her sleeve, which meant, she knew, that she was expected to face the Madonna, whose expression was mournful and universally forgiving, her feet ringed by quivering candle flames. But Lucrezia was unable to remove her gaze from the windows and their framed oblongs of sky, their twisting skeins of birds.

She could see nothing that might have been Maria's departing soul. No breeze, no motion, no flicker of light. Only the rain, which continued to fall, thousands and thousands of silver needles, dropping from above, flecking the nursery sills and the floor and the greenish panes and the streets and the houses all across the city.

A month or so after Maria's burial, an ear pressed to the splintery wood of a passageway that ran behind the Grand Duke's private rooms might have heard the following sounds: the muffled tap of boots, pacing meditatively from one side of the chamber to the other, the scratch of a quill on paper, a smothered throat-clearing, the breathing of someone just on the other side of the panelling. And then the voice of Vitelli, adviser to the Grand Duke Cosimo: 'It is highly regrettable,' he said, and then after a moment continued: 'But nothing, of course, compared with the tragic loss of Lady Maria.'

There was a pause and a noise of assent: Cosimo.

'The letter from Ferrara,' Vitelli said, 'is everything it should be.'

A crackle of paper, as if the letter itself was being perused.

'You will see,' Vitelli said, closer to the panelling now, as if he had moved towards Cosimo to read over his shoulder, 'that the young man, and his father, the Duke, are devastated by the loss but they are also very gracious in expressing their sorrow on behalf of you and the Lady Maria's mother.'

'Yes, yes,' Cosimo said, with a hint of impatience.

If the person to whom the listening ear belonged were to shift to the left, they might find a sliver of light betraying a chink in the panelling. And if the eye were pressed as close as possible to the gap, the person could make out the glow of candelabra, the shapes of chairs, a standing figure, presumably Vitelli, and a seated person attired in something lustrous and brown. The Grand Duke Cosimo, in his sable robe, which he wore on cold days in his bedchamber.

'A second letter,' Vitelli said, after a moment, for he knew when to stay silent and when to speak, 'has reached me, from one of Ferrara's retinue.'

Cosimo leant heavily back in his chair. 'And?'

'It is implied that the Duke is as sorry as you to miss the chance of a union between your children. It further mentions, delicately so I might add, that the old Duke's health is not good and that it can be only a matter of time before the son, Alfonso, succeeds him. Therefore, I need hardly tell you, it is pressing that we respond quickly. There are many keen to fill this vacancy so—'

'Yes, but what can be done? It isn't as if—'

'It has been hinted,' Vitelli said, 'that he might be open to marriage between his son and another of your daughters.'

'But . . .' Cosimo scratched at his beard '. . . Lady Isabella

76

is already betrothed and I cannot easily undo such a match so how does he anticipate . . .?'

Vitelli cleared his throat respectfully. 'I believe, Your Grace, that they may be referring to the Lady Lucrezia.'

The eavesdropper in the passage might then have drawn back from the sliver of light. The shock was as great as if the people in the room had turned and seen through the solid wood of the wall, seen everything, seen her standing behind them, eye to the crack.

'Lucrezia?' Cosimo was repeating. 'But she is just a child, a . . .'

Vitelli coughed again. 'She will be thirteen soon.'

'Thirteen? No, she is . . . ten, perhaps? She is still in the nursery, she still plays with a doll. How can Ferrara be thinking of—?'

Some movement from Vitelli made him stop.

'She is young, yes, and small in stature, but she will be thirteen before long, my lord. It would be a very advantageous match, as you yourself have said, many times. Only think: this is another chance to formalise a union between our region and that of Ferrara. The son will soon become duke. Yes, there is the trouble with his mother and her religious tendencies, but that situation may be managed, if the son is as able as my informant claims. And if we pass up this opportunity, there will be many others who rush to seize it. And it cannot be long until Lucrezia . . .' Vitelli allows a fastidious pause '. . . reaches womanhood. If she has not already. I can make enquiries. So it may be a matter your lordship would like to consider.'

From elsewhere in the building, another, rougher, voice

might be heard to call, in exasperated tones: 'Lucrezia! Lucrezia! Where has the girl got to?'

The listener backed away from the passage wall and ran up to the next floor, on swift and panicked feet.

Sofia was doling out soup when Lucrezia came streaking into the nursery, as if pursued by a pack of wolves, her hair disarrayed, the door banging shut behind her.

'You,' Sofia said, brandishing the ladle. 'Where on earth have you been? I was calling and calling. Sit down this instant.'

Lucrezia slid into her chair at the table and took up her spoon. Sofia continued to castigate her but the sound rippled over Lucrezia's head. She didn't eat, but let her spoon sweep from one side of the bowl to the other, like an oar pushing a galley ship through the sea. Eventually, Garzia took the soup from her and ate it himself.

She thought of the conversation she had just overheard, between Vitelli and her father. She thought of the son of the Duke of Ferrara, the shine of his boots, the way he had stepped past her at the top of the tower, the brush of his thumb against her cheek. She thought of Maria, and how the doctors came and went from her chamber for two nights, the shuffle of their feet along the passages, and then all that was left of her eldest sister was nailed into a long wooden box. Maria was gone from among them; they had lost the head of the creature that was the *palazzo* children. Lucrezia had heard that their father had ordered Maria's portrait to be taken from the mezzanine and hung in his private rooms. She thought of Maria's impassive, pretty eyes scrutinising the chamber for evermore. Did their father look upon it daily? Did he memorise the contours of his lost daughter's face? Did he stand before it when he received the letter from Maria's fiancé's father, the one that asked if Alfonso might marry a different daughter?

What might Maria have said?

The thought that she, Lucrezia, might now be promised to this man, this son of Ferrara, was so shocking, so unexpected, she didn't know what to do. She didn't know how to approach the idea. That she might be expected to take the place of her dead sister struck her with a terrible, immobilising unease. Her mind began to occupy itself with all the differences between her and Maria: Lucrezia was smaller; she was not nearly so accomplished in music and dancing; she never could think of what to say to visitors and courtiers; she tended to day-dream and drift off, instead of paying attention to the conversation in a room; she wasn't nearly so pretty; she had no skill with dress or ornament.

She rested her elbows on the nursery table, in the rooms she had lived in all her life, but her very body felt unfamiliar to her, as if it wasn't hers, as if these arms and legs and head belonged to another, as if she could no longer tell it how to sit in a chair, to raise a spoon to the lips, to breathe in and out. Dread began to cover her, like moss on a stone. There was a sense that something or someone had crept up unseen and now stood at her back. She sat there in front of her empty plate, with a growing horror of what was behind her. It was dark, this thing, and gelatinous, with an uncertain, shifting outline; it had no eyes but a wet, open mouth that emitted a damp, gaseous breath. It was, she knew, without looking around, her death. If this marriage went ahead, she would die, she suddenly saw, perhaps now, perhaps later, but soon. She would never get away from this spectre, this ghost of her own demise.

Lucrezia pressed herself into the edge of the table. The lights in the room seemed to blaze brighter, unbearably so, then die down. There was a cramped, airless feeling in her chest: the thing had her by the throat, it had already clamped cold fingers over her mouth.

Without warning, she slithered down between chair and table, groping her way under the cloth. It was the only way: she could not run from the table for the thing would stretch out an arm and seize her. No, she must evade it like this, diving from sight, then scrambling out between the chair legs and people's feet on the other side.

Lucrezia resurfaced in the room. All around her were the cries of the nurses, Sofia admonishing her, saying, what in the name of all that is holy are you doing now? They could not see it, Lucrezia realised, the horrible thing, they could not see it or sense it as she could. She darted forward but someone caught her arm. Was it the spectre? Had her end come so soon? Would she now be nailed into a wooden box and placed in the family tomb, to lie next to poor Maria?

She yanked her arm away and made a dash for it, across the carpet, towards the door, but she could still get no breath into her body and her head was full of heat. The fireplace, the tapestries, the coffer, the door out seemed to float before her in a pool of fiery light. And then it all stopped, as if a curtain had been drawn across it, and Lucrezia fell to the floor.

When she returned, it was as if she had been deeply asleep for many hours. But then she saw that she was lying on the nursery floor and Sofia was standing above her, frowning, and the other nurses and her brothers were crowded around saying, is she dead, will she wake up, should we ask Papa to call the physician?

On seeing Lucrezia's eyes open, Sofia snapped her fingers and hustled them all away. 'Out,' she ordered. 'All of you. Now.'

The nurses and the brothers milled reluctantly towards the door, and Sofia returned with a cushion in her hands. She lifted Lucrezia's head, gently, ever so gently, and placed the cushion behind it. 'Always the same with you,' she was murmuring. 'Never know what's going to happen next.'

She fetched some water from the table and held it to Lucrezia's lips, lowering herself stiffly to the carpet, where she sat with her skirts puffed up around her, a pigeon on a nest. She loosened the ties of Lucrezia's smock, and smoothed the hair away from her brow.

'So,' Sofia said, 'tell me. What is all this about?'

Lucrezia shook her head and looked away, knowing all the while that Sofia would get it out of her.

Sure enough, when she looked back at the nurse, Sofia was regarding her with narrow eyes.

'Stomach ache?' she demanded. 'Your head hurts? You ate no lunch, I saw. What is it?'

Lucrezia squeezed shut her eyes so that the tears wouldn't fall but she felt them leaking out between her lashes. The story seemed so enormous, so unwieldy, that she didn't know where to start: at the letter, at Maria's death, at the man at the top of the tower?

'Come,' said Sofia, taking Lucrezia's hand in hers, with unaccustomed kindness, 'you can tell old Sofia.'

'They . . .' Lucrezia tried, curling her fingers into Sofia's roughened palm '. . . I mean, my father . . . or perhaps Vitelli . . . I don't know . . . they want . . .'

Sofia was looking at her very closely. 'They want what?'

Lucrezia took in a gulp of air. She felt the proximity of the grey monster again but she knew it wouldn't dare to come close if Sofia was there. 'They want . . . the son of the Duke, the one Maria would have . . . that is, they . . . my father and Vitelli think the Duke's father will . . .'

Sofia was listening, leaning in, as if every syllable Lucrezia spoke was a fragile airborne filament of gold, to be caught, not permitted to float away.

They were both silent for a moment. Sofia stared at her, brows drawn down. Then she said: 'You?'

And, relieved that quick-witted Sofia had understood, that she didn't need to speak the words, Lucrezia nodded.

'They want you to marry the Duke's son? You heard them say this?'

Sofia seemed to consider the idea, lifting her head and working her mouth, as if she was tasting something for the first time. When she looked back, her face was enraged. For a moment, she lapsed into dialect, muttering a string of words that had the Madonna and the devil and something else in them.

'You are twelve years old,' she said, almost to herself. 'And the heir to Ferrara is a man of twenty-four.'

She was silent for a moment or two. Then she tapped Lucrezia's knuckles. 'I suppose I should ask you how you found out about this,' she said, 'but I won't.'

Sofia let go of Lucrezia's hand, struggling upright, her breath coming in short gasps. She walked to the window, with her uneven, limping gait, one hand held to her lower back, and looked out at the piazza. Then she paced to the fireplace, where she seized the poker and plunged it into the blaze, the logs spitting and protesting at the disturbance, sending a constellation of sparks flying up the blackened, soot-furred chimney.

'We may,' she said, seemingly addressing the logs, 'need to be clever about this, you and me. Like a pair of foxes. Do you understand what I'm saying?'

Lucrezia said she did but had no real inkling of what Sofia meant. She turned on to her side and began to raise herself on her elbows. Sofia came over to her and gripped her under the arm, raising her to her feet. Then she pressed a palm to each side of Lucrezia's face. 'Vitelli will come up here soon,' she whispered. 'He will want an interview with you and me.'

'He will?'

Sofia pressed harder on Lucrezia's face. It was a peculiar embrace – uncomfortable yet kind, urgent yet fond. 'Whatever I say, whatever answer I give him, you follow my lead. Do you hear me?'

Lucrezia nodded, baffled.

'He will ask questions and I will answer, not you. Whatever I say, just nod your head. And don't tell anyone about this. Promise?'

'Yes.'

'Not your mamma, not Isabella, not anyone.'

'I promise.'

'We won't be able to stop this marriage but, with God's help, we can delay it, just a little. Until you are grown. A year or two's grace. Yes?'

For a moment, and just for a moment, Sofia caught Lucrezia to her chest, hard. Lucrezia's nose and cheek were crushed to her apron. Then she released her and moved quickly towards the table, saying something about the mess and the dishes and why doesn't anyone ever lend a hand to help her, what do they take her for, some kind of workhorse?

Sofia was, of course, right.

Vitelli appeared the very next day, late in the evening, announced by two sharp raps at the nursery door.

The younger boys had been put to bed; the two other nurses had been told to darn the children's winter stockings; at the request of the art tutor, Lucrezia was making a study in oils of a dead starling she had found on the mezzanine, turning it one way, then turning it over, trying to capture the fleeting iridescence of its wing feathers. Sofia was counting linens in and out of a chest.

When the knock came at the door, Sofia's head jerked up. She looked at the door, she looked at Lucrezia. Then she did a strange thing: she carried on counting linens. Lucrezia saw the two younger nurses exchange puzzled glances but they knew better than to answer. This was Sofia's dominion and no one would open that door but her.

The knock came again, this time sharper and louder.

'Seven,' said Sofia, unperturbed, to her stack of linens, 'eight, nine.' She sighed with satisfaction, putting the last folded square on its pile with a pat. 'And ten.'

Lucrezia and the other nurses watched as Sofia opened the coffer lid and placed the stack of linens in its depths, carefully, without a hint of hurry.

Again, the door resounded with a deep, insistent knock.

'Just a moment,' Sofia called. 'I'm coming.'

She took a cloth to the top of the coffer, wiping away imaginary dust. She edged across the room, crooning a song to herself, taking a moment to straighten a bowl on the table, and another to tuck a stool underneath it. She whisked her duster over the door handle, then straightened her cap in the mirror above the fireplace.

When she at last opened the door, she looked the caller up and down.

'Signor Vitelli?' she exclaimed. 'What a surprise. Will you step inside?'

Vitelli strode into the room, coming to a stop in the middle of the rug. He was holding a leather-bound desk book to his chest and was wearing a long cloak trimmed with rabbit fur, which swirled about his legs.

'You,' he pointed at the nurses, whose needles were poised above their darning, 'and you. Leave.'

The two nurses turned frightened eyes to Sofia, who was standing by the door, her duster still in her hand.

Sofia waited, regarding Vitelli as if examining his attire for spots of dirt, then nodded to them. They gathered up their work and their threads and scuttled to the chamber, shutting the door behind them.

'What can I do for you, signore?' Sofia said, squinting up at him. 'Will you take a drink? Lucrezia and I were just about to—'

'No,' Vitelli cut across her, opening his book and peering down at something written there. 'I shall not stay long. There is a matter on which I wish to consult you.' He cleared his throat, a two-note sound. 'A rather delicate matter.'

Lucrezia shifted in her chair. She passed her paintbrush from one hand to the other, teasing its damp bristles into a narrow point. She had made this brush from a patch of fur she had snipped – guiltily, furtively – from one of the *palazzo* cats; she'd come across it, stretched out and napping beside a fire. The cat hadn't even woken up and, Lucrezia saw only the other day, its fur had completely grown back.

She was just moving the brush's wetted tip back and forth in the dab of blue paint – she had only the tiniest amount of this colour, so had to be careful about how she used it – when Vitelli spoke again.

'We have received assurance that Alfonso, heir to the Duke of Ferrara, Modena and Reggio, would be willing to enter into a state of matrimony with the Lady Lucrezia.'

Lucrezia held herself very still, her brush – loaded with the rare and costly ultramarine – poised. She could not breathe, could not raise her gaze, for she was convinced that Vitelli and his pale eyes would be able to bore through her skin and see that she already knew this, would discern her habit of loitering in passageways, ear pressed to walls and panels.

She needed to have no such fears for Sofia, it seemed.

'The son of the Duke of Ferrara?' Sofia was repeating, in shocked tones. 'Him that was promised to Lady Maria, God rest her soul?' Sofia crossed herself, piously.

Again, Vitelli cleared his throat. 'Yes, the very same.' He skimmed over these words, efficiently, impatiently. 'They are naturally distressed by the loss of Lady Maria but the fact remains that the Duke is in want of a wife for his son. Alfonso remembers meeting Lady Lucrezia and took away with him a favourable impression. He has indicated that he wishes to be espoused to her. It is,' Vitelli snapped shut his book and began to fasten the long leather tie, 'entirely fitting to propose marriage to a sister of the deceased. It shows great affection and respect for this house. Not to mention,' he added quickly, 'the great esteem in which he holds the Lady Lucrezia.'

Hunched over the table, Lucrezia lowered her brush, fraction by fraction, to add a streak of ultramarine along the starling's wing. The colour appeared to vibrate and push against the dark gloss of the feathers; Lucrezia could almost hear this, a warring between two dissonant notes.

'What an honour for her,' Sofia murmured, stretching the duster between her hands as if she might tear it, and Lucrezia believed that Vitelli would never be able to tell that Sofia meant the exact opposite of what she was saying.

'Indeed,' Vitelli remarked, inclining his head, then he pulled an odd face, his eyes creased, his lips retreating from his teeth. It took Lucrezia a moment to realise that Vitelli was attempting a smile.

'Perhaps,' Sofia said, shifting her feet on the rug, 'the Duke and his son do not realise that Lucrezia is still very young.'

'She will be thirteen on her next birthday and—'

'She is barely twelve,' Sofia cut in, 'and the Duke's heir is, I believe—'

'The Lady Maria, God have mercy upon her, was certainly a more appropriate age, but Alfonso is undoubtedly looking ahead to the day when he will be Duke of Ferrara, and wishing to take a wife is, of course, a great part of that. This would be an advantageous match for both.'

'She is a child, signore.'

'Many women are married at—'

Sofia lifted her chin. 'She is still a child,' she repeated, and her quiet, emphatic tone made Lucrezia glance up. She saw Sofia's fingers, behind her back, crossed over each other. The superstitious nurse, who would never lay a hat on a bed, never pass another person on the stairs.

Vitelli narrowed his eyes. He swallowed, the protrusion in his white neck bobbing up and down. 'Am I to understand, signora, that she is yet to . . .?' Vitelli trailed away, expectantly.

The nurse allowed for a pause. She tilted her head, with an air of puzzlement. 'Yet to?' she prompted.

Vitelli shifted his gaze to the floor, the window, the ceiling. 'That she has not . . . that is to say . . . ah . . . she hasn't . . .?'

Again, Sofia permitted a silence, one that widened and expanded between her and the senior adviser. Lucrezia peered at them both from under her lashes. She had no inkling of what they were speaking. All she knew was that Vitelli was deflating, emptying, like a cloud that had been filled with rain and was now breaking apart into harmless wisps.

Vitelli was trying again: 'She has not . . .' he faltered, a boat adrift on a current, but Sofia refused to catch the rope he was desperately tossing towards her.

'Not what?' she said innocently.

Vitelli set his jaw, still not meeting her eye. 'Signora, has Lucrezia begun her . . .' he broke off but, shutting his eyes briefly, he summoned courage '. . . monthly bleedings?'

'No,' Sofia said.

Lucrezia looked down, not at her painting but at the starling laid alongside her brushes and oil vial. The bird, the picture. She looked nowhere else. She looked at the delicate, scaled feet, which would never again cling to the twig of a tree or the stone lintel of a window; she looked at the folded, layered wings, which would not be outstretched, catching the upwards motion of a breeze, would not carry the bird over roofs and streets. She looked at her painting, saw where it had failed to capture the exact line of the beak, the lustrous green of the soft throat.

Sofia's 'no' tolled through her head. No, she had said, definite and sure. She had looked at Vitelli and said: No.

Lucrezia touched her fingertip to the starling's tail. She had found it early that morning, on the mezzanine. It had flown in through an open window and then been unable to find its way out again. She wondered if it had spent all night fluttering back and forth, in ever-rising panic, butting its beak again and again against the glass, wings a desperate whir. She stroked the plush throat with a curled finger. Had its heart emptied gradually of hope? Had it looked through the glass and seen where its companions were wheeling and massing in a large, oscillating cloud above the *palazzo*? Had it watched as they all flew away, leaving it there, trapped in the building? She could not bear it, could not find capacity within herself for the sudden sympathy she felt for this bird.

No, Sofia had said. And she, Lucrezia, must do her part. She must keep her head lowered, like this, keep looking at the starling, at the imperfect picture she has made of it. She must never let on to Vitelli that Sofia had crossed her fingers, behind her back, that Sofia had shown Lucrezia what to do when the bleedings come: fold and fold a cloth to pad herself; take a stone that has been smoothed by the river and heat it in the fire, just enough, then wrap it in linen and lay it on your stomach. To draw the blood down, to ease its passage,

Sofia had said, as Lucrezia lay on the bed, stupefied by the cramping ache. Twice, this had happened to Lucrezia. And Sofia said, It will come every month, just like the fullness of the moon. It comes to all women. Even Mamma? Lucrezia asked, incredulous, unable to believe that her serene, bejewelled mother could ever be laid low by something like this. Sofia had nodded. Even Mamma, she said.

And now, in the hot room, with Vitelli looking so furious and thwarted, and Sofia so small yet obdurate before him, Lucrezia would have liked to ask: what has this to do with the Duke's heir, with marriage, with her age, with anything? But she could not. She must pick up her paintbrush and rinse the traces of ultramarine from its cat-fur bristles, and she must survey her painting with a face of absolute stillness, as still as the starling on the table before her. She must not give anything away – the bleeding, the cloths, the hot stones, Sofia.

'I see,' Vitelli said. His tone is clipped, disappointed. 'Well, she has always been small for her age, I suppose. Undergrown.'

Sofia shrugged. The fingers behind her back relaxed, untangled.

'We can proceed with the betrothal negotiations but we shall tell the Ferrara court that the marriage will have to wait until such time that the Lady Lucrezia begins her . . .' Vitelli waved a hand through the air. He was not about to repeat the words for the subject under discussion, unless strictly necessary. 'You will inform me, signora, please, when this commences?'

'Certainly,' said Sofia. She moved sideways slightly, then back, as if to make her skirts swish one way, then the other. It was an act that carried a vague yet indiscernible hint of triumph, the sense of a point won.

Vitelli must have felt this, too, because he frowned and turned stern. 'In person, if you please.'

'Of course, signore.' Sofia smiled, showing all the dark vacancies in her mouth. 'I shall come to you myself, as soon as I know anything. And we shall look forward to the wedding day, with much excitement.'

Vitelli held her gaze, as if ascertaining whether or not she was in earnest, then moved away. He was about to stride out of the door, when he seemed to think better of it, and walked towards the table where Lucrezia was sitting.

She watched as he advanced, getting closer and closer and taller and taller, until her neck was craned backwards. Her mouth felt suddenly dry, her heart thumping in her chest. What if he were to put the same question to her? How could she lie to him? What if he asked her if Sofia told the truth? What could she say? And what would he do to Sofia, if he knew?

Vitelli was so close to her now she could see the individual hairs in the fur of his cloak trim: flecked, they were, with lighter, almost golden, tips and darker roots. She wondered how many rabbits had had to die to make this cloak for him. Seven, eight, nine? Were they old rabbits, ready to die, or young ones with soft, unlived-in fur?

Vitelli was leaning over her. For a strange moment, she thought he might envelop her, throw the cloak around her and carry her off, away from the safe walls of the nursery, away from Sofia, and down to the depths of the *palazzo* where the son of the Duke of Ferrara would be waiting, slowly removing his slashed sleeves, and his face would not be that of a mouse, it would be grim and carnivorous and he would want to know why she had done nothing to save her sister, why Maria had died, how she could think she might ever take her place as his wife, how dare she?

But Vitelli was putting his hand to her painting. He was lifting the small square of *tavola* by its corner and holding it to his face.

'Whose work is this?' he asked.

Lucrezia, unable to speak, turned her finger upon herself and pointed at her chest.

Vitelli didn't see. He was taking out his eyeglasses and positioning them on the bridge of his nose so that he could examine the painting at close quarters. His face, beholding the tiny rendering of the starling – he ignored the corpse she was copying – was a mixture of surprise and disbelief.

'Who did this?' he asked again.

'I did,' Lucrezia said, in a croaking voice. Please, she was thinking, please. Don't ask about the blood. Don't look at me. She would guess that a man like Vitelli could see the truth written on someone's skin.

But perhaps not. He was staring at her now with an expression of puzzlement.

'You?' Vitelli said. 'No. I think not. Was it your tutor? He did this and you finished it, yes?'

Lucrezia, confused, nodded. Then she shook her head.

'It is Lucrezia's,' Sofia said, stepping towards them and putting a hand on her shoulder. 'She likes to make these tiny little paintings on bits of wood. She does them all the time. There are boxes and boxes of them in the cupboard.'

Vitelli looked at Lucrezia for a long moment. His eyes travelled from her hair, divided down the centre, to her temples, to her eyes, cheeks, neck, arms, hands. Lucrezia quailed, trembling. She felt like a floor being swept by a brush, again and again.

Vitelli continued to look from the bird to her, and back again.

'Hmm,' he said, eventually, weighing the *tavola* in his hand. The starling's wings were tucked, feet drawn up, head drooping in defeat, in acceptance of its death. Lucrezia had put a border of ivy and mistletoe around it. 'May I keep this?'

It was not a question. He was already turning away, placing her miniature painting inside his leather book and tying the straps, so that the bird could never fly away again, even if it had lived.

This journey's true design

Without warning, Lucrezia receives a signal, a glimmer of this journey's true design.

Alfonso has shifted himself off her and fallen into a shallow slumber, one hand still buried in her shift. The candle has been snuffed out and the room is thick with a dark that feels almost animate – a breathing presence, with heavy, furred flanks.

But, all of a sudden, in this unfamiliar room, something descends upon her. It has the quality of a vision but it is frailer than that, and brighter in its urgency, arriving unbidden in her head.

What has come to her is a painting, entire and robust in its untested perfection. A painting on an elongated rectangle of *tavola* – she will cut herself the exact size she needs, at the precise angle she favours – at the centre of which will be a castle. No, a white mule. No, a stone marten, with streaks on its face. Or a centaur? Or all of them. Not one painting, then, but a series, all miniature, all ornate, the confines of the

94

wooden boards filled with details and clues and decorations. She will cut the board now – no, it will have to be tomorrow, for she shouldn't wake Alfonso with the sawing. But did she pack the right tools? The small handsaw, the planing knife? She thinks she did not.

The disappointment is keen. It leaves sharp icicles in her chest. To have this idea but no means to act upon it: the thwarted frustration of it. No matter. She will sketch the ideas tomorrow. Or perhaps now, this minute. She will ease herself from the bed and strike the tinder, relight the candle and take up the roll of vellum she knows is in the travelling box.

All is not lost. She knows this. She slips her feet out of the bed and, wrapping herself in the furs discarded by her husband, she moves towards the candle.

Everything is working out, and life is continuing after all. Alfonso is not the murderer or monster she perceived him to be at dinner – what temporary madness was that, what devils whispered all that in her ear? She has been told, over and over again, by her mother, by Sofia, that she is far too fanciful, far too susceptible to strange imaginings and fears, and that she should show more sense. Perhaps they are right. She will recover here, and so will this marriage. He has brought her to this place for the simple reason that he has loved it since childhood and wants to share it with her. She will spend the days with him, so that he feels attended to, taken notice of, and she will work at night. All, she thinks, as the candle catches at first try, will be well, and she sits, placing her hands, palm down, on the surface of the desk, and she smiles.

Something read in the pages of a book

Palazzo, Florence, 1557

Sofia managed to keep Lucrezia's secret, and delay the wedding, for almost a year. Any soiled clothes or bedding, she scrubbed in a bowl and dried in a cupboard. She tossed anything irreparably stained on to the fire with a quick flick of her wrist, and together they watched the flames devour the evidence. If the other nurses knew, they never said anything: they were both fierce in their loyalty to Sofia.

Betrothal and dowry negotiations between the two families continued, at a distance. Lucrezia learnt, from listening to a conversation between Vitelli and a clerk, that her father desired the terms of her potential marriage to match those of Maria, but the House of Ferrara was asking for an increase in the settlement, due to the delay. Loitering in an antechamber near the offices, while waiting for an audience with her mother, she heard Vitelli recommend that perhaps a certain amount of *scudi* be held in reserve, until such time as a male heir was produced, and then that portion of the dowry could be considered paid. Lucrezia saw her father nod, reach for the latest letter from Ferrara and hold it close to his face.

Winter began its slow tilt towards spring, the snows melted, a new *nano* arrived at the *palazzo* and was named, like all the others, Morgante, and word was that Eleanora was much diverted by his antics. The citizens in the streets below laid by their woollen caps and shawls, and the children, leaning over the *palazzo* parapet, were pleased to see the flower-seller return to the western corner of the piazza, her basket filled with thickly fleeced lilac blooms. Their father resumed his daily swim in the Arno; it was reported that another attempt had been made on his life but he and his Swiss Guard had seen off the assassins. He was called away to attend an uprising in Arezzo. Eleanora held a party, the first since Maria's death, at which acrobats put on a display, and musicians played while guests danced. The food was said to have surpassed anything Eleanora had served before. Lucrezia studied accounts of Greek military tactics, painted a scene from Homer and walked whenever she was allowed to around the battlements of the tower, watching great nets of starlings spill themselves one way then the other above her head. Her brothers were taught the rules of *calcio* in the courtyard below; Garzia received an injury to his arm when Ferdinando tackled him too hard; Pietro took to biting his brothers, if provoked, and the doctor was summoned to bleed him twice a week in an attempt to rebalance his humours. One of the guard's dogs gave birth to puppies. The silkworms in Eleanora's insectarium continued to ingest mulberry foliage; their gossamer trails, stretching from leaf to leaf, sparked into visibility in the morning light.

Her imminent betrothal, her marriage, the man designated to be her husband, the life in Ferrara that awaited her seemed to Lucrezia, during this time, so distant and abstract that it resembled something read in the pages of a book or heard in the lines of a song. She was to be betrothed: it remained a fact that she knew, had learnt by heart, like Latin poetry drummed into her by the tutor. The meaning of it, its significance, failed to touch her. Life at the *palazzo* went on as before. Isabella still dressed in her finery to walk from courtyard to salon, trailing peals of laughter behind her, like bright scarves; Pietro still had tantrums when he roared until red in the face, drumming his fists on the carpet; Sofia still ladled out their midday soup in the same bowls, at the same table; the sun still poured in on the far side of the schoolroom in the morning, then swung round to the bedroom windows by the evening. Maria's chamber door remained shut. It seemed to Lucrezia some days that nothing would ever change, that she would spend her whole life in these rooms, with her brothers, dressed in stockings and smocks.

Shortly after her thirteenth birthday, Lucrezia rose from her bed and was crossing the room to peer out of the window, to see what weather was filling the sky, when she was startled by a cry. She turned to see her mother standing in the doorway, flanked by two of her women, and her face was lit, beaming.

'Look, look at Lucrè!' her mother was saying, clapping her hands. 'Oh, what a momentous day!'

Lucrezia smiled uncertainly at Eleanora. Whatever could she have done to merit such praise, such attention?

Everyone in the room turned to her; the three nurses stopped dressing the boys. Their hands fell to their sides. Eleanora was pointing and Lucrezia looked down at herself. What about her had changed so much as to produce this reaction in her mother? She saw only the pale length of her *camiciotto*, her bare feet, the floorboards beneath.

'Look,' her mother exhorted again. Then she strode across the room and, taking Lucrezia by the upper arm, turned her so that she was facing the wall.

Behind her there was a chorus of cries: 'Ooh,' cooed one of the ladies; 'Ah,' sighed the other. 'Congratulations.'

'Do you see?' Eleanora demanded, delighted, but she wasn't talking to Lucrezia.

Lucrezia twisted one way, then the other, baffled, trying to see what they could see. What was it about her back that was so remarkable today?

Then she saw it. A patch on her shift, halfway down, dark red and the shape of a landform, a distant and unmapped island surrounded by a vast white sea. She realised there was a familiar heavy feeling in her abdomen, as if a fist was clenching and unclenching

Eleanora was talking about how someone must go down, now, to His Excellency; they will send word this very day to Ferrara and arrangements can be made for the wedding, for the Ferrarese to come to Florence. How terribly exciting it all was.

Lucrezia's face felt hot, as if she was standing close to naked flames, but her hands and feet were stiff with cold. Her mother's words fell about her, like ash descending from the sky. She gripped the folds of her shift and stared at the floorboards.

Her mother was back among her ladies. They were still talking about arrangements, about a seamstress for the alterations, about getting sight of the dress today. Lucrezia lifted her gaze and met that of Sofia, across the room. The old nurse was standing by the coffer, with Pietro on one side and Garzia on the other. The three of them stared back at her, her brothers confused by all the fuss. Sofia's face was expressionless, unreadable. She seemed to clutch the boys' hands ever tighter, and her lips moved, ever so slightly, as if in apology or perhaps in prayer.

Eleanora's ladies sent word to Vitelli, who selected the correct way to delicately communicate the news to Lucrezia's father. Eleanora and Cosimo met in her apartment and clasped each other in joy. Cosimo authorised a letter to be written to the Ferrarese court, informing them of the welcome arrival of Lucrezia's womanhood. The following week, a stamped and signed contract, with the wax seal of the Duke of Ferrara, was brought by messenger, carried overland via Bologna, and delivered to the desk of Cosimo. It was accompanied by a letter from the Duke himself: he looked forward with joy and anticipation to sanctification of the union between his son and the Lady Lucrezia; he sent his sincere felicitations to the Grand Duke of Tuscany and his family; he was including them in his prayers. He only regretted that his son, Alfonso, was shortly to go to France, to fight for the King. If the Grand Duke was in accord, the wedding could take place upon Alfonso's return. He would, in the intervening time, look forward every moment to this happy occasion.

Cosimo read this letter through, leaning back in his chair. He let it drop to the desk and picked up the marriage contract. This he read four or five times, rubbing his thumb back and forth on the bearded underside of his chin. Then he took a quill from the array held out to him on a tray by a bowing clerk and put a line through several of Ferrara's clauses. He wrote adjustments to certain sums and struck out a demand about inheritance of lands to the north. He then wrote a brief note explaining his amendments and asking for Ferrara's agreement; he referred the Duke back to his earlier letter last spring, which requested these points be removed from the contract. He stated that the wedding could indeed take place on Alfonso's return from fighting in France – which might, he commented to Vitelli, who stood behind him, be a year or more from now.

Cosimo signed his name and, pushing a stick of sealing wax to a flame, allowed the wax to bleed on to the document, then pressed his signet ring to the scalding circle of red, thereby sanctioning the marriage between his fifth child and the representative of an ancient imperial family.

Not long after this, an emissary arrived from Ferrara, bearing missives for the Lady Lucrezia in the region of Florence.

They were borne from the *palazzo* gates, to the offices of Cosimo, where the contents underwent an initial inspection, to Eleanora's salon, where first the Grand Duchess and then all her ladies examined them, and then to the chamber that was now Lucrezia's, a high-ceilinged square room tucked behind the chapel.

Seated at a table by the fireplace, Lucrezia took the papers from the servant and put them on to her desk, where she regarded them with narrow eyes. She was at this time still maintaining to everyone that she did not want to marry the Duke's son, she would not be a substitute for her sister, but she was nevertheless aware that the machinery of the betrothal had been grinding inexorably on. Her parents and their entire staff seemed to have tacitly agreed to ignore her protests, continuing with plans for the wedding, discussing recipes for the various feasts, debating whether the great hall should be given new wall hangings, if they should serve only Tuscan wines at the dinners, which musicians should be allowed to play from the gallery and which from the floor, engaging seamstresses to make wedding clothes for the whole family. And now this: a letter from the son and heir himself.

She slid a fingernail beneath the seal to lift it, noticing, with only a minor pulse of surprise, that it had already been broken. Of course. Her parents would both have read it before it was brought to her. The letter was folded into quarters, like a book, and when Lucrezia smoothed it flat against the table surface, she saw that a confident looping script covered the whole sheet. It opened with the words *My dear Lucrezia.*

A sudden heat broke out on her face. It was hard to identify what was more startling – the possessive 'my' or the disturbing tenderness of 'dear', or indeed the sight of her own name in his writing. No one had ever addressed her like that. She was somebody's 'dear', somebody's Lucrezia: the three words seemed to snake themselves around her, and she saw herself, just for a moment, encircled by a pair of arms, her body held inside an embrace.

Her eyes read it again – *My dear Lucrezia* – then passed on to the words that followed: *May I address you thus? It is what you are and will be to me.*

The paper was trembling in her fingers so she laid it flat upon her lap, where the fabric of her skirt gave it a steady resting place, but she was still unable to prevent her gaze from skittering over the page, darting from one random word to another. *Cherish,* her eyes told her, *fervently, anticipation, fruitful, fight for the King, pray, true.*

Still gripping the edges of the letter, she forced herself to follow the lines, one after another. He was, the writing went on to say, filled with great joy that their marriage would soon take place. What a happy day that would be. He and his family and, indeed, the entire court were greatly anticipating this event. He was sad, however, to be leaving that very week for France: he had promised to fight for King Henri. He would think of her, his Lucrezia, every day while he was in that far land. He asked her to pray for him, her future husband, and for his safe return. Might she spare the time to write some lines to him? Please would she tell him about her days and pastimes? He would cherish her letters and fervently hoped that their marriage would be fruitful and happy. He remained her loving and true fiancé, Alfonso.

Her immediate desire was to write to him saying that she regretted she could not marry him and that she hoped he understood. She knew, though, that there was no hope of such a message getting through to him. Her father, his secretaries and assistants would intercept it, and her mother would punish her for writing it.

She would have to send some form of reply, however. That was the correct course of action. A man wrote to a woman – she would not use the term 'fiancée', she could not attach that word to herself – and the woman wrote back. But what could Lucrezia say in these letters? That she walked about the mezzanine? That she spent hours staring out at the piazza? That she practised her lute and worked on a Greek translation, then searched for something to paint? What could she possibly write that might catch the interest of a man like the future Duke of Ferrara?

At the sound of a cough, Lucrezia looked up. The servant who brought the letter was still standing by the door. She had forgotten she was there.

'Yes?' Lucrezia said, trying to comport herself like a woman who was used to receiving letters from the man to whom she was betrothed (fervently, fruitfully, happily).

'If you please,' the servant whispered, 'Her Ladyship your mother said to tell you that the emissary is waiting on your reply.'

'Oh,' Lucrezia said. Waiting? Was she meant to write a reply this minute? She had no idea such a thing would be required of her so quickly. What to say? How to find the words?

She turned to her desk. It was covered with sextants, an astrological map, a telescope pushed inside itself, several reed pens that she had been cutting, a penknife, a bowl encrusted with a mixture of linseed oil and smears of powdered verdigris. She pushed these items to the left, then the right, searching for something – anything – she might write on or with, a clean sheet of paper. She couldn't write to a man about to leave for war on a parchment stained with paint mixes or punctured by compasses. Her mother would need to see this letter, and if Lucrezia didn't present something well worded and perfect and—

The servant was stepping into her sightline, placing two items on the very edge of the table. Lucrezia wanted to say, don't put anything else there, can't you see I'm trying to clear space, but the servant was speaking again: 'The emissary brought these, if you please. For you, Your Ladyship.'

Lucrezia looked up from her search, and regarded the parcels: one was small, covered in cloth and bound tightly with twine; the other was flat and packed with linen. She reached out a hand to the smaller parcel, about to pick apart the knot and slide off the wrappings, when she found herself examining the dimensions of the other. Long and rectangular, with sharp corners. Her hand wavered, moved away from the smaller parcel towards the larger. She hooked a finger into the cord tied around it and drew it across the desk.

She could guess what this one would be: a portrait of Alfonso. She would be able to look at his face, to see into his eyes.

Where was her penknife? Where was it? She opened her desk box, riffled through quills and ink pots. She turned to the serving girl. 'Have you a knife?' she asked. 'Or scissors?'

The girl stared at her, then shook her head.

Lucrezia turned back to her desk and, seizing a pair of compasses, she picked at the knot with its spiked end. The third time she yanked, she felt a sliding, a give. She tossed aside the instrument and disentangled the knot, stripped away the twine, the coverings. She ripped away cover after cover, layers of straw and linen padding, and then she was rewarded with the back of a wooden board. Yes, she had been right: it would be a betrothal portrait. Let's see you, then, was what she was thinking as she turned it over.

But she was entirely mistaken. What he had sent in this parcel utterly confounded her. Instead of the face she was expecting, half remembered from a moment at the top of the tower, there was something else. There, on the *tavola*, bead-bright eyes turned inquisitively towards her, a tail curled about its feet, one front paw raised, was a creature. She had never seen anything like it before. It was the colour of wood, with a sleek pelt and clawed feet. Its muzzle was narrow, with a pinkish-brown nose, a milk-white underside, and delicate sprays of whiskers.

It was like an otter, or a mink, or a tiny bear: it was all yet none of these. She let out a small, involuntary noise of surprise. It was shocking that such a man would send a gift so improbable, so unconventional. Betrothal gifts were only ever portraits or jewels, she knew. And yet her husband-to-be had sent this. She was filled, instantly, from her feet to her head, with absolute and uncomplicated love for the animal in the painting. She gripped her hands together under her chin, unable to withstand the joy of it.

The serving girl, who had, unnoticed by Lucrezia, stepped forward to pick up the discarded linen and string, handed her a piece of folded paper that had fallen from the padding.

Lucrezia took it, distractedly, and unfolded it.

Another letter, shorter this time:

My dearest,

I am sending this to you as I recall that you have a certain affinity with beasts, and I am told that you are fond of painting.

This is a work I have always loved – it has hung in my rooms since I was a boy, and now I would like you to have it. It is a portrait of a stone marten, or la faina, *as it is called here, an attractive yet shy animal which makes its home in the forests of Ferrara. We will see many of its kind when we ride out together.*

They are wild, of course, but perhaps you will accept this one, tamed for you here in oils? I hope you will remember me and our betrothal when you look upon it.

Ever your loving,

Alfonso

Lucrezia placed the letter on the table. She stretched out and ran a tentative finger along the creature's painted spine, feeling the contours and ripples of the oil and pigments – a series of secret messages from whoever had created it. A kit from the forest, in the place of a dull portrait of a husband-to-be. What would her mother say? And her father? They would greatly disapprove. Lucrezia put a hand over her mouth to stop her laughter.

'*La faina*,' she whispered, tasting the word, the two incarnations of the *a* vowel, the friction of the *f*. It was her first word of Ferrarese. The stone marten – woodland sprite, tree-dweller, forest spirit – gazed back at her with impish eyes.

Lucrezia touched the darker furze of the tail, the pearled spikes of the claws. She was taken aback to feel the thickness of the paint, its luxuriant, textured layers, how the oils stood proud of the *tavola*. It was at once touching and unnerving that someone had known or divined that this was the way to her heart. How had he intuited so much about her from one very brief meeting, years ago?

With a sudden bang, the door was pushed unceremoniously open, and Isabella swept into the room. Dangling from her wrist was a golden cage containing her canary, a dainty creature that, if left in a sunbeam, would raise its head and pour forth bright surges of notes from its sharp little beak. Isabella liked to walk about the *palazzo* with it, so that the bird got fresh air.

'I hear,' she said, setting down the cage, 'that presents have arrived from Ferrara. Let's see.'

Lucrezia lifted the painting from the desk, her eyes radiant. 'Look,' she said, 'you'll never guess—'

'Is it a portrait? Show me.' Isabella said, advancing across the chamber on noisily heeled shoes. Peering over Lucrezia's shoulder, she let out a small shriek. 'My God,' she said, recoiling, 'what is that?'

'It's a *faina*, from the trees of—'

'It looks like a rat. Is that all he sent?' Isabella's face was disgusted. 'The man must be out of his mind. Does Papa know he's given you an old painting of a rat? It's an outrage, an insult to our family, and to you, a complete—'

'There was something else,' Lucrezia said dreamily, looking at how the artist had contrasted the stiffness of the marten's whiskers with the lush softness of its belly. 'I think.'

'Where?' Isabella demanded.

Lucrezia gestured vaguely. 'Somewhere.'

The servant stepped forward and, retrieving the small box from under some papers, handed it to Isabella.

'Hmm.' Isabella turned it over in her hands; she brought it up to her ear and gave it a shake. There was an answering metallic rattle. 'This is more promising.'

Without so much as a glance in Lucrezia's direction, Isabella stripped off the string and cloth, discarding them to the floor, to reveal a leather-covered box.

'Aha,' she said, and flipped open the lid.

Lucrezia was still examining the marten, puzzling over the

marked thickness of the paint, so she missed the discovery her sister made. All she knew was that, behind her, Isabella gasped and said: 'Lucrè, look.'

'Yes?' Lucrezia murmured, without turning round.

'Look!' Isabella insisted, slapping Lucrezia on the shoulder. 'Forget that horrible rat for a moment, would you, and—'

'That hurt,' Lucrezia said, rubbing the spot, 'and you mustn't—'

'I'm going to box your ears, you little flea,' Isabella shrieked, 'unless you look, right now. You're driving me to distraction.'

Lucrezia sighed and tore herself from the painting. 'What is it?' she said, turning in her chair.

Despite everything, Lucrezia caught her breath at what she saw. Her sister was holding up a jewel of startling crimson. An enormous ruby set in gold, surrounded by pearls, and strung on a slippery, linked collar, encrusted with more rubies, to be worn about the neck, Lucrezia supposed. The colour of the larger stone was pure and searing, like a frozen drop of wine. It drew the eye to itself, unerringly; it was the brightest element in the room.

'Now this,' Isabella was saying, 'is what I call a betrothal gift.'

Lucrezia didn't say anything. She stared at the pendant, the way the light seemed to gather around it, the way it made everything else seem pallid and unobtrusive. How heavy it would feel, around the throat. How it would tug and weigh upon the skin there.

'So unfair,' Isabella was muttering, holding the pendant up to her own neck and gazing petulantly into the glass above the mantel, turning one way, then the other. 'Paolo never sent me anything half as fine. Suits my colouring best as well. It's wasted on you.'

'Why?' Lucrezia said.

'Why what?'

'Why is it wasted on me?'

'Well,' Isabella, still looking at her reflection, said, 'you don't care for such things, do you?'

Lucrezia glanced back at the rendering of the animal, the gleaming gilded frame. 'I suppose not,' she mumbled.

'I want it,' Isabella declared, holding the pendant out at arm's length. 'I can have it, can't I? You will give it to me.'

Lucrezia looked at her sister, at the combative, acquisitive glint in her eye, the determined set of her mouth. She allowed there to be a slight pause. 'You want me to write back to him and say, thank you for the gift, which my sister has decided must be hers?'

Isabella held her gaze for a moment longer, calculating the various outcomes of this situation, then let out a cross sigh.

'Papa wouldn't allow it,' she said, more to herself than Lucrezia. 'So unfair,' she said again, and let the pendant and its collar coil back into the box. She was about to snap the lid shut, when she paused. 'He's written something here, inside the lid.'

'Has he?'

'Yes. Shall I read it to you?' Without waiting for a reply, Isabella put on a deep, masculine voice and intoned: '*This belonged to my grandmother, who had the same name as you: from one Lucrezia to another.*' She snapped shut the box with one hand and tossed it into Lucrezia's lap. 'There,' she said, waspishly. 'All yours. Good luck with him. The pompous ass.'

Isabella turned and marched across the room; when she reached the bed, she threw herself on to it, face down.

Lucrezia placed the box on the table next to her. She lifted the lid and examined the pendant. Its splendour and unsettling beauty were dimmed slightly by its leather surround. It felt manageable, approachable. Someone had decided it would be set in pearls, which surrounded it like a mouth of tiny teeth: had it been the artisan or the grandmother? She wondered what this other Lucrezia had been like. She knew from her father that Alfonso's grandmother had been a famous beauty, and had been painted by many artists. Might this pendant have appeared in one of those portraits? She could ask Alfonso, she supposed, in her letter. Lucrezia reached for a quill and her penknife, and began to whittle herself a sharp point.

Behind her, she was aware of Isabella, lying on her bed, muttering to herself: 'The Duke of Pomposity. From one Lucrezia to another. What an ass. Duke of Far-away-i-a. Who sends a rat and a jewel? Ass.'

Lucrezia said nothing, just pulled a piece of parchment towards her. It was the only way to deal with Isabella's fits of temper: ignore them, let them run their course. Securing the page with one hand, she held her pen poised. How to begin? Dearest Alfonso? Your Excellency? *L'Altura?* My dear?

Lucrezia bit her lip, aware of the ink drying on her quill, of the empty page, of the emissary waiting for this reply, of Isabella on the bed, now singing a breathy song about husbands with tight purse strings and small—

Lucrezia shut her ears and mind to everything around her. She propped the painting of the stone marten in front of her, leaning it against a vase. She gazed at it, gazed and gazed. She had the strange and unaccustomed sensation of having been observed and, perhaps, understood. How odd it was that the person who seemed to comprehend her, to see into her very soul, should be a man who had glimpsed her only once.

She thought for a moment of her father spying her mother, through a diaphanous hanging, in Naples, and how he had resolved there and then to take that girl as his wife. Could it be possible that this duke's son had held her image in his heart, a child on a battlement, holding a mouse? And when Maria, his first betrothed, had died, might his affections have turned towards Lucrezia?

In a day or two, Lucrezia would tuck the oil painting of the stone marten under her arm and, accompanied reluctantly by one of her mother's ladies, go in search of her art tutor, who was often at work somewhere in the *palazzo*. She would find him eventually, up a ladder in a corridor, with Signor Vasari himself, making an initial sketch on the ceiling for a fresco of the goddess Juno in a peacock-drawn carriage. Lucrezia would place the painting on the table next to their chalks and watch as their eyes seemed to fasten upon it, like cats with prey. The tutor descended his ladder, reached for it and held it carefully in both hands, keeping his fingers clear of the painting's surface, while Vasari came to look over his shoulder. This, the tutor would tell her, is the work of a skilled master. Do you see the gradation of colour here, the careful brushmarks there, how the animal appears to be in motion? Vasari would nod and say, exceptional, in his grave voice. She would ask them what she had come to find out: why the paint was so thick, why the artist had applied so much of it. Vasari and the tutor would consider this for a moment, still taking in the stone marten, its animated face, its raised paw, and Vasari would take the painting from the tutor, tilting it so that he could look at it from its side. Then he would describe for her the practice of underpaintings. An artist might paint a scene or a portrait, then cover it with an entirely different painting. It happened all the time, if an artist was unsatisfied with the first attempt or was short of money to buy materials or if he wished to conceal the work he had produced, for whatever reason, or desired merely to give the finished work a sense of light and shade. A *tavola* or a canvas, Vasari explained, might have three or four different paintings on it, all existing in secret layers. As with this one. I want to try, she would say to the young tutor. Please show me how. The tutor would glance at his master, and Vasari would sigh, then wave them away. The tutor would wipe his hands with a rag. Come, he would say, let's begin.

In her chamber, with Isabella still lying on the bed, and her canary regarding Lucrezia from its cage with a single glistening eye, Lucrezia straightened her page, readied her quill, and inscribed the letters of his name, for the first time: *Dear Alfonso.*

Somewhere in the darkness

Fortezza, near Bondeno, 1561

When she wakes, later, it is with a swooping sensation, as if she is moving up a slope at speed or passing from one realm to another.

She lifts her head from the pillow and peers into a thick, oppressive dark. Where is she and what place is this? She looks for the geometric *castello* windows, to her right, but there is nothing. She turns her head to see the high opaque panes of the *palazzo* but, again, nothing. She wonders, Where is the painting of *la faina*, why is it not on the mantel?

Then she sees a single bed curtain, pulled back, as if someone has left in haste, and beyond it, the angled slant of a wall, cast in midnight gloom, and she remembers: the *fortezza*. She is at the *fortezza*.

But where is Alfonso? Nowhere to be seen. He has gone. The bed is empty. Over to the left will be the table, spread with sketches for the painting she conceived last night, and then to the other side—

She is beset, with a horrible swiftness, by the knowledge that she is about to be sick.

She lurches upright, scrabbling for the edge of the bed. If she can just get clear of the curtains, of the mattress—

'Emilia?' she calls, and her voice is unfamiliar to her, rasping and indistinct, seeming to come from a long way off. 'Clelia?'

Then she remembers that they are not with her, that they were left behind in Ferrara.

Her head pulses with pain, as if her jaw is hinged too tightly to her skull. The muscles in her neck have snarled themselves into bright, fierce knots that press at the passages of blood through her head. She can feel the bone sockets of her eyes, the roots of her back teeth, the cavities of her nose – they seem to be inscribed on the darkness in glaring ink; they seem to sing with a high-pitched agony.

She gropes for the curtain and yanks it back, falling from the bed to the floor. She retches, her stomach convulsing, pushing bitter acid into her mouth; she retches again, and this time a flood of liquid pours from her, burning and foul. It is like lava from a volcano, forcing its way out of the ground, bubbling up and erupting forth.

Her mind is sheer and startled. Whatever is in her will come out. She crouches on all fours, like an animal, coughing and vomiting until her stomach is hollow, until she is spitting blood and bile from a sore, scalded mouth.

She calls out again, but the thickness of the walls mocks her, throwing back a voice so feeble and irrelevant that she is silenced. She eases off her sodden shift and, not knowing what else to do, steps back into the bed. Never before, it distantly occurs to her, has she been so alone: there has always been someone to call, someone to summon, all her life.

Moments later, she starts to shake. It begins at her feet, a tremble that seizes her ankles then her legs, causing the blankets to be disturbed, releasing pockets of warm air, making her whimper and curl into herself. Then it is as if the malady has taken her by the scruff of her neck. It is angry with her – this much is clear. It is furious. She has done something terrible and unforgivable to it, something that has riled it to a towering temper. It rattles her back and forth in its grasp, it shakes her teeth in their gums, it makes her arms and legs flail and thrash. The bedclothes are tossed to the floor, her hands are knotted into themselves, wrists turned back, the muscles in her legs convulse and solidify. She is unrecognisable to herself; she is a creature entirely at the mercy of a stronger power, a flea on the back of a rabid beast, a plucked quince in a pot of bubbling water.

There is nothing she can do. She is powerless, entirely at the mercy of a heartless force. She is thrown one way, then the other; her head is pressed down into the pillows, snapped forward, then back. Her arms are pulled rigid, her fingers retract into claws. It is difficult to get breath past her frozen throat, down into her petrified lungs.

She might die. This fact presents itself to her, like a gull flying out of a storm, and she examines it, dully, through the churning mists of the sickness. She might. She recognises this; she accepts it. She has reached a place where all she craves is an end to the torment, the bodily suffering. Any end at all.

The Duchess Lucrezia on her wedding day

Palazzo, Florence, 1560

The chamber is filled with people and the wedding gown waits for her on the bed.

Lilies stand tall in a vase on the mantel, their stems offering up blooms as if for scrutiny. The air moving in and out of her is heavy with their scent. When she'd woken, just after dawn, the buds had been closed but now, the full complexity of their petals and stamens is open for all to see. The sweet, cloying smell of them fills her chest, leaves it, fills it again. A rust-red shadow of pollen encircles the base of the vase.

Behind them, servants come and servants go, their shoes rushing one way and the other. Someone knocks at the door, delivering a wooden box; another person opens the box and takes out jewels from inside it, one by one. Someone else lifts Lucrezia's arm and places bracelets on it, pushes earrings through her lobes, fastens her betrothal ruby about her neck. Lucrezia is the only motionless being. She sits at the centre of this activity, a reed caught in the eddy of a stream.

Three maids are stationed around her, each unknotting a section of her hair, tugging and pulling at the scalp with combs. One of them, a girl of about Lucrezia's age, with a puckered scar curving from the corner of her mouth to her neck, has a particularly gentle touch, disentangling the knots with careful fingers, instead of yanking the comb through them, and Lucrezia would like to tell her how grateful she is for this.

Lucrezia has been occupying herself, as she sits here, with planning how she would paint the lilies, how she could capture the flecked pink stains of their interiors, the swan-white of the outer petals, the stamens sticky with nectar, their simultaneous strength and fragility. Her leg, beneath her *camiciotto*, is bouncing up and down, up and down. She cannot stop it: sitting still for so long is intolerable for her. She wants to leap up, to bat these women away from her, to yank her hair out of their grasp and move about the room, pulling off the clinking bracelets, rolling her shoulders in their sockets, stretching her neck from one side to the other. Most of all, she would like to clear everyone from the room with a loud cry, so that she might have a moment to gather her thoughts.

But there will be no sketching today. The wedding gown is waiting and the lilies will be bound and placed in her hands, and she will carry them before her, like a shield or a lance, all the way to the altar.

A long triangle of light, an exact yellow replica of the window behind it, makes a sudden appearance at her feet, spreading itself out across the floor, as if reaching for her ankle. Lucrezia observes how it bends around objects in its path, drapes itself over a pair of shoes, a dropped cloth, a discarded shift.

Near the bed, two servants are arguing in impassioned

whispers. Something about the dress, and the order in which it must be donned. Lucrezia sees one of them pick up a sleeve and say, this, in a peremptory tone, and the other shakes her head, bringing her hand down emphatically on the bodice. The first servant clutches her forehead dramatically, and says if they weren't taking so long with the hair she would already be dressed. They are anxious because Eleanora has instructed them, in commanding tones, to make Lucrezia look like a duchess because this, she said, with a rare smile on her face, is what she will be. The old Duke, the father, has died and Alfonso is now the Duke of Ferrara; Lucrezia has heard rumours that this is why he has returned from France, to assume control of his court, and not, as Eleanora says, to claim Lucrezia as his bride. Either way, she will become a duchess today, from the moment she is married. She sometimes says this word to herself – *duchessa, duchessa* – over and over, when she is alone, rendering the word into a slurry of sound. Its three syllables seem to battle against each other, the peremptory *du*, the harsh *che* and the final susurrating *ssa*. How strange that it will soon be forever part of her name.

Lucrezia knows there was a series of masques at the *palazzo* last night, in honour of the new Duke, with the players dressed in embroidered velvet. There were twelve Indians and twelve Greeks, accompanied by heavenly music. The Florentine ladies danced and course after course of delicacies were served on the salon's long tables. This may also be why the servants are tired and tetchy: they will have been up most of the night. Across the city, there have been feasts, with pigs roasted above fires, and citizens carousing through the night. Her father arranged for a game of *calcio* to be played in front of Santa

Croce, which was attended by thousands, and a young man from the eastern quarter has been grievously injured while defending his team's goal. Her father has dispatched a purse of *scudi* to his family, in honour of his bravery and grit.

She knows all this not because she was there but because she has overheard the servants talking of it all – the masques, the candles, the pig-roasts, the *calcio*, the *scudi*. She longed to see it, to stand in the rooms, or perhaps even the gallery above, and watch the dancing, to see all those faces. She begged and begged her father and mother, but they refused. She had stamped her foot and cried, why can't I, why? But her parents turned away, shaking their heads, saying that she, Lucrezia, must remain here, in her chamber. It is not right for young brides to be seen before the wedding.

The mirror gives back to her a face with cheeks high in colour, eyes glittering, hair held away in looping ropes by the six hands of servants, who are combing and plaiting it, and this gives her an unearthly look, as if she is floating up and into the sky.

The wedding gown waits; she can sense it behind her, biding its time, its empty shape poised to encase her body.

There comes into the air around them the sound of the bell in the campanile. It strikes five, it strikes six, then seven. Behind it, by just a fraction, come Florence's other bells, as if the city is an echo chamber, calling and responding to itself. As the final tolls still shiver against the walls of the room, the maids begin to panic. They dart from door to window, from coffer to bed, calling to each other to hurry, quick, hurry. The woman still holding the dress sleeve begins to castigate the ones still plaiting her hair, saying, why aren't you finished yet, you're so slow, you're going to get us all into trouble. The older maid, who is beginning to coil the long plaits around and around and pin them to Lucrezia's scalp, tells the woman to shut her mouth or she'll shut it for her.

Lucrezia's hair has never been cut, not since the day she was born: if unbound, it reaches to her ankles, a burnished copper river that falls from her head to the ground. She can wear it around herself like a shroud. It can conceal much: her whole self, if loose, or flowers, seeds, even small pets, if piled up. Brushed, it comes to life, transforming and separating into sinuous tendrils, the edges of which crackle and rise into the air, like severed spider weave. If dressed, like this, by the hands of expert servants, it can be pinned and woven into a crown or a halo.

The plaits are arranged, criss-crossing her head, looping over her ears and the jewels there, up the curve of her neck, and secured at the crown of her head. The veil is brought down around her while they affix the golden diadem, brought by Vitelli himself, from the iron-lined strongroom.

The maids are still squabbling among themselves. One makes a slightly bawdy remark about husbands, another titters, and the older one tells them sharply to hush. The diadem suddenly feels too tight around Lucrezia's head: she can feel it pressing upon her skull, along with a hundred bristling brass pins, keeping her hair in place. She curls up her toes inside her slippers and repeats to herself Sofia's advice on the matter of her wedding night: let the man do what he will, don't fight or struggle, breathe deeply, and it will soon be over. But it is not, she had wanted to say to Sofia, in my nature to acquiesce, to submit.

Then the veil is lifted back and she sees that the maidservant with the gentle hands and the scarred face is motioning to Lucrezia to stand up.

Lucrezia turns and faces the dress.

Here it comes now, cradled in the arms of the two servants. It travels, like a full sail, to where she stands, made ready in her shift and veil. Its fabric ripples like running water; the silk carries in itself myriad blues, from the light cerulean of a clear sky to a dark, inscrutable ink. The gold organza divides the blue down the centre, a glinting, shining road.

It opens, the dress, in the many deft hands of the maids, unfolding like a map, and it hovers – flat and unreadable – for a moment. Then they pass it in front of her and it is wrapped around her. The bodice is laced, one maid pulling on the ties, the other holding the fabric together; the sleeves, stiff and voluminous, are eased on to her arms and the scarred girl stands at her shoulder, fastening them with quick movements. Lucrezia finds herself wondering about this girl who treats her with such kindness. She is perhaps not much older than Lucrezia; she has light hair, not dissimilar to Lucrezia's in colour, curling out from under her cap. Patches of sweat mark her gown under the arms and along the collar. The crescent-shaped scar curves from the corner of her mouth to her neck and this throws her beauty into relief, making it somehow more apparent.

Lucrezia can feel the bodice drawing together at her waist in the small of her back. She feels the colour rise to her cheeks and neck, and a dangerous pricking at her eyelids. The girl lacing the sleeves, who is in front of her now, tying the threads under her armpits, glances quickly at her, then away, and is it Lucrezia's imagination but does the girl look at her, once more, with pity and sympathy? How can such a girl, maimed like this and living as a servant, feel sorry for her?

And then it is done. The dress is on her. It reaches her ankles, it covers her wrists, it stands up on all sides of her, a fortress of silk. Above it is her piled hair, the ruby collar, below it her feet, now in satin shoes.

In the mirror, she sees a girl surrounded by a sea of blue and gold, like an archangel fallen to earth.

And, with the servants ushering her forward, placing the bound lilies in her hands, she steps towards the door.

The gown rustles and slides around her, speaking a glossolalia all of its own, the silk moving against the rougher nap of the underskirts, the bone supports of the bodice straining and squealing against their coverings, the cuffs scuffing and chafing the skin of her wrists, the stiffened collar hooking and nibbling at her nape, the hip supports creaking like the rigging of a ship. It is a symphony, an orchestra of fabrics, and Lucrezia would like to cover her ears, to stop them with her palms, but she cannot. She must continue like this to the door; she must walk through it, out into the corridor, where there are people – her father's officials, her mother's retinue – waiting for her. She must leave behind this chamber and this *palazzo* and it may be that she will never sleep here again.

She is ushered along, through room after room, passing under marble portals, through archways. Doors are opened for her, faces peer out at her.

She averts her eyes as they approach what used to be Maria's chamber, but not before she sees, unbelievably, that the door is ajar. A sliver of light reaches out from it, into the corridor.

Lucrezia grips the lily stems. Can someone be staying in there? Has Maria's room been given to someone?

The idea that it will be the Duke of Ferrara rears into her mind. It will be him, of course it will. Where else would they put him, when the *palazzo* is stuffed with guests and visitors, servants and courtiers? What other room would befit his status?

Maria's room: her bed, the heavy red drapes, the coffer with golden lacquer, the high window with a table beneath it. There used to be a quartz vase there, with patterns cut into the rim. Maria liked it to be filled with anemones in spring, then bougainvillaea in summer. Will it still be there, filled with delicate purple-pink blossoms, as it would be if she were alive?

If she were alive, it would be her, now, coming out of that door and walking towards the staircase, trailed by maids, flanked by courtiers, and here is Vitelli, at the bottom, looking up at her, then glancing towards the courtyard, giving a signal to whoever is waiting there. Here she comes now, he is telling someone just out of sight.

It should have been her, Maria, is what everyone around her is thinking. Lucrezia is sure of this. It should have been Maria in this dress, with these lilies. Not this one, who is smaller, younger, not nearly so pretty and altogether less agreeable.

At the top of the stairs, she is seized with an urge to double back and push at that door, just in case there has been a mistake and Maria is in there, sitting at her table, writing letters, her vase of flowers before her, light from the window falling on to her shining head of hair, and she will turn, displeased at the interruption, and see Lucrezia there, and she will say, what on earth are you doing? Why are you wearing my dress? Remove it this instant.

Lucrezia takes a step down, then another and another, the thin soles of her slippers meeting each tread. The girl with the scarred face is just to her right; she is holding Lucrezia's wrist, steadying her on the stairs. Does she think Lucrezia will fall?

Vitelli is at her side, gripping her arm; the two of them move through the velvet dark of the gatehouse. It feels oddly intimate, enveloped as they are, together. Lucrezia finds she wants to lean towards him and say – what? Let me go. Let me run. Release my arm so that I may—

The gates creak open and a waterfall of noise crashes down on her. She doesn't know it but she has departed from the only quiet of the day: the rest will be motion and jostling and talk and commands and obligations. Here she stands, on the threshold of the *palazzo* where she was born, and now she is stepping forward, outside its tall, tall walls. She has to close her eyes against the glare. A huge sound rolls around her, like a wave. It is enough to knock her off her feet so she is glad, in a way, that Vitelli still has her by the arm. When she opens her eyes, she sees that the piazza is crammed. The people of Florence are waving scarves and flags in the air, shouting, all their faces turned her way. So many faces! It is quite astounding. All so different: some old, some with wide eyes, some narrow, mouths with white teeth, mouths with none, hair that curls and hair shorn close to the head. There are babies held in arms, there are children straining their necks to see. How many iterations of the human face exist, how many ways in which mouth, nose and eyes can be arranged! It astounds Lucrezia. She would like to stop and look at them all, one by one, to speak to them, ask what is their name and what are they doing here. A woman near her, held back by a guard, is saying something, over and over, stretching out an imploring hand. Lucrezia looks at her. She could reach out and touch this woman, this person in a grimy smock with hair unravelled down her back. She realises, with a small shock, that the woman is calling her name – Lucrezia, Lucrezia – and how can this person know her name, and what is it to her, what is she to her?

Here is the carriage, suddenly, not the covered one her parents usually use but the other, with an open top, its door held for her by a guard. She puts her toe on the footrest and Vitelli and the guard hoist her, her flowers and her dress up and into the carriage, and close the door with a snap.

The carriage is high, and precarious-seeming; the glare and noise of the piazza feel close but not overwhelming, and Lucrezia is trying to find a comfortable seated position inside the cage of her dress, so it takes her a moment to realise that she is sitting opposite her parents.

Eleanora sits in a nimbus of cross-hatched fabric, one hand supporting her chin, the other hooked through Cosimo's arm. She considers her daughter with thick-lashed eyes.

'Yes,' she murmurs, as if they are continuing a conversation from earlier, 'the colour does suit. It complements your eyes, your hair. I thought as much, although some of my ladies warned it might emphasise your pallor, but I was right, after all.' She continues to examine the dress, from the bodice, all the way down to the hem and back again, leaning forward to scrutinise the sleeves.

Then Eleanora puts her head on one side. 'Don't you have a kiss for your mamma, on a day such as this?'

'Yes,' Lucrezia says. 'Sorry, Mamma.' She gets cautiously to her feet, clutching the lilies. She struggles for a moment to find her balance – the dress is so enormous, so burdensome – and leans forward carefully to plant a kiss on her mother's face.

The cheek is cool and soft, the texture of an overripe apricot, with that same slackness and deliquescent give. Her mother's scent is always the same: hair pomade, violet oil, cloves.

At the sight of this kiss between mother and daughter, the crowd gives up a great cheer, which bounces over them and back. It is as if someone is tossing a bright golden ball from one side of the carriage to the other.

The horses, at the touch of the whip, jolt forward and Lucrezia is shunted back to the opposite seat.

'Do you see,' Eleanora says, 'these people, Lucrezia? How they love us.'

Lucrezia looks at her mother, who holds a handkerchief aloft; its lace edges flutter prettily in the warm air; Eleanora smiles out of the carriage. Cosimo sits with a straight spine, his head high; he doesn't smile but every now and again inclines his chin in a regal nod. Lucrezia sees a metallic glint at the neck of his *camicia* and realises that even today he is wearing chainmail beneath his clothes: she has heard he never leaves the *palazzo* without it, so sure is he that an attempt will be made on his life. She turns her head one way, then the other, fearing an assassin might burst from the crowd. But the faces of the Florentines lining the street are blurred by motion, daubs of paint dissolving in water.

'They do, Mamma,' Lucrezia says.

The carriage swings left then right, the horses straining against their harnesses, and Lucrezia is thrown one way, then the other. She holds up the lilies so their petals won't bruise. Her parents, she sees, are buttressed against each other and barely move. They continue to gaze out into the crowds, Eleanora waving with a vague smile.

'Mamma?' Lucrezia says, leaning forward and clutching at her mother's hand, pulling it towards her, as if closing this gap might rescind and rewrite all that has happened between them since Lucrezia's birth. It seems suddenly clear to Lucrezia, as their carriage moves through the city, on their way to her wedding, that the bond between her and her mother is fraught and frayed, with knots and kinks she will never understand, and always has been thus. Why, she wants to say to Eleanora, as they sit opposite each other, why must it be like this with us? Do you not remember the *animaletti*? How I loved them, how surprised I was by you bringing them to me. How inconsolable I was when my brothers knocked them off the windowsill. Do you remember when you arranged for me to have art tuition?

'Mamma?' she whispers again, gripping her mother's fingers, wanting more than anything to smooth the invisible rope that tethers them so uncomfortably to each other, to make it right somehow.

The noise of the wheels, the crowds, the air rushing past, whisk away the word. Lucrezia can see that they are nearing Santa Maria Novella; there isn't much time. These are the last moments of her girlhood – with every passing second, her time with her family is ebbing away. Very soon, she will be married. The feasting, the dancing and the gaming have already taken place – the celebrations have been going on for days – and by the end of the day, she will be gone.

Lucrezia places her other hand on her mother's knee. Her fingertips tap the cloth, as if seeking entry.

Eleanora looks down, surprised, then up at Lucrezia. Her perfect arched brows lift, and her mother looks at her, properly and for the first time that day, and something flickers across Eleanora's face, softening her features, as if her youngest daughter's voice is piercing some central part of her, activating a flow of sympathy within her.

'Yes?' Eleanora says.

'Mamma, I . . .' Lucrezia tries to find the words, tries to locate what she wants to say. She cannot talk about the complex, snarled thread between them, not now, with the cathedral around the corner, cannot say that she is scared, that her fear of marriage and what lies ahead is so consuming that it fills the vacant space beside her in the carriage, travels along with them, its clawed feet hooked into the seat. There is no time to say all this, the moment to speak it has passed, so instead she returns to a topic that has always been safe between them, and says: 'When you . . . when you . . . first saw Papa, on the road from Livorno . . . did you . . . how did you . . .'

Eleanora looks at her youngest daughter, perplexed. Lucrezia gazes back, willing her to understand what she herself cannot say.

'How did I what?' Eleanora says.

'Was it . . . did you feel love for him then . . . straight away . . . or was it later?'

Eleanora considers this, then gives a minuscule shrug. 'I saw him first at the viceroy's house in Naples so—'

'I thought only Papa saw you.' Lucrezia is shocked by this

new version of a story she thought she knew backwards. 'You were facing away from him, looking up at the ceiling.'

Her parents glance at each other and a private thread is being spun between them, as if one of Eleanora's silkworms is at work in the air. Lucrezia's father blinks, taking his wife's pale fingers.

'No,' Eleanora's jewels tinkle as she shakes her head, 'I saw him but I pretended not to. I knew he was there. I knew he admired me. I knew, in that moment, how things would be.'

Her father holds his wife's gaze and wets his lips, which always look so red inside the hair of his beard. Lucrezia averts her eyes. The church of Santa Maria Novella is behind her now, she knows, its great height looming up from the streets. Her mother is turning her head, asking if the other carriage is coming with the boys, and Lucrezia feels once more, like a heavy sack strapped to her back that she must forever carry, the knowledge that her mother loves the boys best, that nothing can replace them in her eyes, that Isabella is her father's favourite and can do no wrong, that there has never been enough love left over for her, that she will always be the afterthought, tolerated at best, and she wants to say, why is it them you love, why not me, can you not see how cold Francesco is and how cruel Pietro is turning out to be, why am I being made to marry this man who will take me away to Ferrara, when Isabella is allowed to stay here, why am I the one who will be sent away?

The carriage pulls to a stop. Lucrezia swallows down these words like a bitter medicine. It is too late for such subjects: the time for them has elapsed and they don't matter any more. Her new life is about to begin. She, Lucrezia, will be born anew, no longer the fifth daughter of Florence, small for her age and overlooked: she will be the Duchess of Ferrara.

She lifts her eyes to the stone cliff-face of the church; she sees where its campanile has stitched itself to the summer sky, the brown brick meeting blue, and she gets unsteadily to her feet.

The interior of the church is a relief: the noise of the city falls from her as she steps through the doors.

Her father and mother pause at the font, dipping their hands into the water; Lucrezia is about to do the same, but then, turning, she stops. The building ahead of her is astonishing: she has never seen anything like it. A long stretch of red-tiled floor sweeps away from her, with pale repeating arches on either side. Light enters at an oblique angle from invisible lofty windows, high above their heads, warming the apex of the arches, alchemising the white plaster to lozenges of gold. Candles gutter and flare, piercing the dusk, each at the centre of their own glowing corona. The lines of the roof, the lines of the aisle lead the eye irrevocably all the way to an altar surrounded by painted saints with golden halos, and windows of many-coloured glass.

Lucrezia steps forward, awed; she casts her eyes up, to one side, to the other, wanting to memorise it, so that she may be able to replicate it later. She will need paper, chalk, the colours of white, red, the azure blue of the windows, the vivid yellow, the gilt of the halos – and she feels a pulse of something like excitement or panic. How soon can she do this? How can she remember it all? And is it not incredible that a building of plain stone can conceal such a heart as this, a kernel of glory, fire and gold?

They are proceeding up the aisle. The air is laced with incense and smoke; she can see it coiling and turning in the narrow spears of sunbeams; somewhere there is low singing in Latin. Beneath her feet, Lucrezia sees a face cast in white marble, eyes shut, partially worn away, its body half submerged in the floor, like a person floating down a stream on their back. A strange place for a tomb, she thinks, the floor of a church, where all may scuff their feet against you, tread on your eternal rest.

They are reaching the altar, where a group of people are standing, one of them a priest in a white-and-gold robe so long it appears he has no feet, that he moves on wheels, or floats just above the floor.

Lucrezia is smiling at this thought for nothing can touch her in a place as beautiful as this, as heavenly, no bad thing could possibly take place here; she is filled to her outer edges with the soaring space, the insubstantial celestial rafters of light that mimic the prosaic wooden ones above. She is aware of her father stepping away from her, for a moment, she believes, and then she feels a sudden touch – respectful but sure.

A hand is taking hers. It is large, with long fingers and a warm palm. She can glimpse part of its wrist, in the gap between veil and dress; the rest is swallowed by fabric. Black hairs are growing in a single direction, away from the cuff, like a crop blown by a prevailing wind; it belongs to a tall person who is standing next to her. This hand covers the whole of hers.

Lucrezia hears herself gasp – a small inhalation inside the private space of her veil. Her hand appears to be gone, subsumed, her sleeve ending in the strong, proprietorial clasp of a stranger.

And so this is Alfonso. He is here, next to her, waiting for the ceremony to begin. How stupid of her not to realise. It is him, Alfonso, Duke of Ferrara, the man who will stow her and her bags and her dowry and return with her to his castle. He is here and he is real.

A sword is raised and held over their heads and Alfonso is presenting her with a gold *cintura*, heavy with rubies and pearls, which he fastens around her waist. Then he straightens and places first one ring, then another, then another, on her hand. The third, bearing the impression of his crest, an eagle with outstretched wings, is slightly too large. She has to curl her fingers to keep it in place, and she feels its unfamiliar press on her flesh as she watches her father ceremoniously hand Alfonso a silver dish and *boccale*. The men bow gravely to each other.

Alfonso passes the goods to a man who stands just behind him, and he turns to Lucrezia, takes the hem of her veil and lifts it, up, up, over her head, and suddenly she can see, she can breathe. There is nothing between her and the world, nothing screening her vision, nothing to stop her eyes moving freely about the church, drinking it in, nothing between her skin and the incense-heavy air, and nothing between her and the man in front of her.

The priest has indicated that the Mass will begin and Alfonso adjusts his body so that he is facing the altar. It takes Lucrezia a moment to follow suit.

There are many words in Latin, flowing over their heads or perhaps floating up to the ceiling. Lucrezia is finding that she cannot concentrate, cannot interpret what the priest is saying. Every now and again she catches a word and she can make it mean something – the Father, the soul, a union – but she cannot stitch it into a sentence or even a clause. She knows she should be absorbing the solemnity and significance of the ceremony but all she can do is examine as much of Alfonso as she can see: his shoes, their polished brown sides, the places where it is possible to see the outline of his feet through the leather, the curve of his long calves through his hose, the way the cuffs of his shirt are fastened with a fine twist of silver. His hair is dark, longer than that of other men she has met; it falls across his brow. And he is tall, just as she remembered, with the broad body of a soldier. Her head barely reaches his shoulder, her feet take up less than half the space of his.

She is aware of his in-breath and out-breath, the rasp of cloth as he moves to take the cup and then to pass it to her.

The priest removes the lilies from her, joins their hands together and motions them to face each other. He is saying more words now and Lucrezia can grasp 'husband' and 'wife' and 'life' and she knows then that it is done, she is married, that it can never be undone. She is no longer the person she has always been but someone else she doesn't yet know, with a different name, a different home. She now belongs to this man standing before her, and when she raises her eyes she is expecting him to look solemn and grave.

Instead, on the face of Duke Alfonso, Lucrezia is taken aback to see, there is something else. Alfonso has been as little affected by the seriousness of the religious ceremony as she has. When her eyes meet his, it is clear that he has been waiting for her gaze; his mouth turns up a little at the corners.

He slides his eyes towards the priest – still reciting words pertaining to God and duty – then flicks them back to hers, with a slight raise of one eyebrow.

It is an expression of amusement, one that casts a cloak of collusion around her and him, together. It says, this priest is really quite dull, isn't he? And: when will this be over?

Lucrezia couldn't have been more surprised than if Alfonso had performed a dance up there on the altar. She feels her own mouth beginning to curve into a smile.

A pressure is applied to her hand, joined to his, and she realises he is squeezing her fingers. She glances at him again and sees that he is twitching his nose, just a tiny amount. It is the same face he pulled all those years ago, on the battlements of the tower, the mouse face. She wants to say to him: you remember that? You remember seeing me there, with my pet mouse? And also: do you regret that it is not Maria here today, in this dress, with her hands in yours? Do you really not mind that it is me and not her?

But there would be no sense in saying any of these things to him. They are now turning to face the back of the church and they are moving down the aisle, through the yellow arches of light, over the red diamond tiles and the marble tombs; they are passing out through the enormous doors and Alfonso is linking her arm through his, and she can feel the crackle of embroidery, and also something else – the shift and spring of muscle and sinew beneath his clothes.

When they come out on to the steps of the church, he waves at the gathered crowds and Lucrezia does the same. Her veil is thrown back, the sun on her face, and the crowds are shouting and cheering, holding up small flags and handkerchiefs, under the stern gaze of her father's guards. Alfonso is nodding at the people of Florence, his black hair gleaming in the light, and he turns and speaks his first words as her husband: 'Do you still have the painting of the stone marten?'

'*La faina?*' she says. 'Of course! She is one of my most treasured possessions. I keep her beside my table and she is the first thing I see every day.'

He looks at her, his head on one side, a quizzical smile playing around his lips.

'Her?' he says.

Lucrezia nods. 'She looks like a her to me.'

'And do you think she will be happy to leave Florence and go to Ferrara?'

Lucrezia looks up at this man, her husband, who broke with tradition and selected this painting for her as a bridal gift, just over two years ago, who had noticed and remembered her love for animals – that pink-nosed mouse held in her palm – who had sent it to her, the first painting she ever owned.

'Yes,' Lucrezia says. 'I think she will.'

And there, on the steps of Santa Maria Novella, Alfonso presses his hand to hers, as the sun beats down on them both, on the crowds, on the intersecting stones of the piazza, the battlements of the *palazzo*, the streets and gutters and archways, on the red roofs all over the city, and the hills and trees and fields of the surrounding land.

Scorched earth

Fortezza, near Bondeno, 1561

Someone is at her bedside, talking in soothing phrases. A hand touches her brow; hair is cleared from her face, a cup is held to her lips and water invades her mouth. She swallows and feels it cut a cool trail through her.

'Not too much,' the person is saying, 'just a little.'

For a moment, Lucrezia believes that it is Sofia, come to take care of her, come to save her, once more. Word of her malady must have reached Florence and Sofia will have mounted a horse and ridden through the night, over the mountains, her steed plunging through snowdrifts and ice floes, Sofia an avenging maenad, swollen joints forgotten, suddenly able to ride. She will tell Alfonso that Lucrezia is not to stay here, she will stand up to him, in that way she has, and together they will leave and go back to Florence – no, somewhere else. Urbino, perhaps, or Rome. Sofia and Lucrezia will go, together, and take up residence somewhere far away, in another region or another land.

But it cannot be Sofia. Lucrezia knows this. She cracks open her eyes and, despite the pain the light brings to her head, peers up through her lashes.

It is only her maid Emilia who is sponging her forehead, straightening the bedclothes around her, saying, 'Oh, madam, you poor thing. Was it something you ate? You must drink a little water, only a sip at a time. Your stomach will not want any more than that.'

Emilia puts down the cup, rises, and starts dropping soiled linens into a bucket. Lucrezia watches her with dull, amazed eyes.

'I am so sorry I wasn't here last night,' Emilia is saying. 'The horses left and I thought we would be following straight after but then we were told the weather was bad and the roads weren't safe and we were to stay behind. I was so worried about you, all alone, with no one to help you. I tried to get the groom to let me go but he said he had orders from Signor Baldassare and—'

'Baldassare?' Lucrezia repeats, through a mouth that feels as dry and cracked as scorched earth.

'Yes, madam. He ordered the servants to remain in Ferrara when he left so that—'

'He left?'

'Yes, at first light.'

'Where was he going?'

'Well, here, of course. His Grace, the Duke, never goes far without him so—'

'Baldassare is here?'

'Yes.'

'In this *fortezza*?'

'I think so.'

'He has already arrived?'

'I would expect so. He rode out early this morning, with a—'

'Who else was with him?'

Emilia is scrubbing at the floor with rags she has taken from under the bed. 'Ah, now let me see, there was—'

'Who?' Lucrezia says, more sharply than she intended. 'Think, Emilia.'

'Very few people, I believe, madam. There was Signor Baldassare, and some of the Duke's men, three guards, one of the grooms. The cook sent a ham and—'

'And you came with them?'

'No, I told you . . .' Emilia pauses to wring out her rag. 'They wouldn't let me join them, so when, later on, I heard that there was another party of people leaving for—'

'Who knows you are here, Emilia?'

'Well, I suppose . . .'

Emilia's story rattles on, with words and names and reversals and qualifications, so many of them that Lucrezia cannot grasp. She tries to follow but it feels as though she is filled with sand – soft, dry sand that collects in one corner and, if she tilts her head, slides to fill the other.

'. . . so I just slipped out,' Emilia is saying, cheerfully scrubbing the floor, 'because I didn't think anyone at the court would miss me and I knew that you would need me so I thought the best thing was not to ask permission. If you don't ask then you can't be—'

'Did you tell anyone you were coming?' Lucrezia demands, cutting across this deluge of words.

'I just told you – no.'

'Did anyone see you leave?'

'Don't think so.' Emilia purses her lips. 'Why do you ask, madam? Are you—'

'Think carefully,' she urges the maid. 'Clelia? Nunciata's women?'

Emilia shakes her head, frowning. 'No. I don't think so. I just packed a bundle and slipped away while—'

'The grooms? Any of them?'

'Impossible,' Emilia scoffs. 'They broke into the wine last night, I heard, and they were all—'

'What about the horse you rode? Did anyone know you'd taken it?'

'But I've already told you, madam,' Emilia says, getting to her feet, 'I didn't come on a *castello* horse. They had a spare so I—'

'So no one knows you are here?'

'No.'

'Baldassare doesn't know? Or His Grace, the Duke?'

'No,' Emilia says, with a baffled pout, releasing the window catch and tossing the foul water out – Lucrezia hears it, a moment later, land with a spatter on the *fortezza*'s lower walls. 'Why do you ask so many questions? You look so pale. Are you feeling sick again? Do you want—'

'There isn't time to explain now,' Lucrezia says, shutting her eyes. She is trying to gather her thoughts – Alfonso, the *fortezza*, the dinner last night, Baldassare leaving at dawn, the telling of Emilia not to come, forbidding her to follow Lucrezia. What does it all signify for her? What can she do? 'I need . . .' She gropes about for something in the bedclothes – the sketches she did last night, her wrap, anything to give her a sense of anchorage in this strange morning, which seems so unmoored, so startling. 'I need . . .' What does she need? Lucrezia tries to raise herself from the pillow. 'I must . . .'

Emilia is putting a hand on Lucrezia's shoulder. 'You must stay there, lying down. You need to rest. I will go to the Duke and tell him you are unwell and he will send for—'

'No!' Lucrezia grasps Emilia's hand. 'Don't go downstairs. Don't leave this room, do you understand? Neither of us will leave. Don't tell anyone you are here. I have to think, I have to—'

'Madam, you need a doctor. I will ask—'

'Emilia,' Lucrezia whispers, pulling the maid close. 'Emilia. Listen.' She wonders for a moment what she has to disclose, how to make Emilia understand, but then she finds she is speaking the words before she has even decided what to say: 'He means to kill me.'

If Emilia is startled by this utterance, it is no more so than Lucrezia herself. The sentence seems to slide from her mouth and gather like smoke in the air between them. It is the truth, Lucrezia realises in that moment. She knew it last night, at dinner, but somehow she persuaded herself – or perhaps clever Alfonso convinced her – that she was mistaken. But this is what she is facing. Death has come for her. It is knocking at her door; it is sliding its fingers through the keyhole; it is searching for a way past the lock.

Emilia has her head on one side, gazing down at her. She has heard the words; she is considering them, but instead of gasping and starting to wail, she pats Lucrezia's fingers.

'Your Highness,' she says, 'fever can fill a head with all—'

'Please listen to me,' Lucrezia gets out from her raw throat. 'Please. You have to believe me. He will kill me. You understand? That is why he brought me here, without you, without anyone. No witnesses. You see?'

'Madam,' Emilia glances nervously towards the door, shifting from foot to foot, 'remember, you have not been yourself for a while now, and perhaps—'

'He poisoned me,' Lucrezia says, gripping Emilia's hand as tightly as she can. 'Last night. I know it. The venison or the soup or the wine – I don't know. But he did. You have to believe me.'

In the white winter light of the room, Emilia's face undergoes a change. She looks at her mistress, she looks at the recently scrubbed floor, she looks at the sketches on the table, she looks out of the window at the fringes of the river. When she turns back to Lucrezia, her expression is tempered with a frown.

'I cannot believe it,' she says. 'The Duke is a man of honour, and he loves you. He would never do such a thing. Not to you. Not to his wife.' As Emilia speaks, as she debates the subject with herself, Lucrezia can see the idea spreading its roots, slowly and stealthily, into her thinking. She can see Emilia begin to believe her, little by little.

'But he loves you,' Emilia says again, in a whisper this time. 'He does. Anyone can see that.'

Lucrezia says nothing but keeps her eyes on the maid's face.

'How could he ever . . .' Emilia exclaims '. . . how is it possible . . . What kind of a man would do that?'

Emilia sinks to the bed. She grips Lucrezia's limp hand. 'Oh, madam,' she says. 'Whatever shall we do?'

Lucrezia loves her for that 'we'. She revels in the sound of it. That single syllable is a balm to her disordered mind, to her aching and empty body.

'I don't know,' Lucrezia says. She rubs her forehead, as if trying to erase the pain there. 'I cannot say.'

Man Asleep, Ruler at Rest

Palazzo, Florence, & Delizia, Voghiera, 1560

I t is the very end of her wedding day and she is sitting in darkness so profound she cannot see her hands in front of her face. It is the middle of the night, deep in the sunless hours, and the covered carriage waits just inside the bolted gates of the *palazzo*, under the arch. Outside, she can hear servants talking to each other, discussing how to secure this box here, to move that bag there, to add more straps to the luggage, to ensure that the horse is properly harnessed.

In her lap there is a rosary, a nosegay, and a woollen shawl with a slippery fringe. The seat beneath her is padded with a velvet cushion, studded with gold buttons, but she is only too aware of the unforgiving wooden slats of her father's carriage beneath her.

Perhaps dawn is about to break: the starlings outside in the piazza are beginning their percussive chatter. It is possible to hear them through the darkness and the heavy wooden *palazzo* gates. She had thought that she and Alfonso would leave straight away, after the wedding Mass, that she would move seamlessly from the church into her new life. But no. No one had thought to inform her that after the Mass came an interminable wedding feast: long tables heaped with roasted meats and herbed breads, Lucrezia only managing to swallow a few morsels, and then the men left to watch the chariot race put on by Lucrezia's father, and then, just as it seemed the feast might end, that she might be permitted to rise from her place at the table, the men returned, flushed and excited, and then musicians were entering and they began to play, while a tumbling troupe came leaping into the salon, and the *nano* Morgante got into a fight with one of the acrobats, and then came some dancing, and Alfonso partnered her, then Eleanora, then Isabella, and then he asked her again, and Lucrezia was by this time so exhausted that even to stand made her feel dizzy but she knew that her parents were watching, and members of the Ferrarese court, so she had to smile and put her hand into his, and to compel her feet to perform the steps, her head to stand upright on the stem of the neck, her face to appear agreeable; she was required to make her movements as graceful as possible – but not too much – when really all she wanted to do was to go to her chamber, strip off the heavy gold *cintura* and the cage of a wedding dress, and fall asleep.

Lucrezia grips the crucifix at the end of the rosary, its corners digging into her palms, and winds the shawl about her hands. The air here in this carriage, under the archway, is dank and cool.

She has not been able to bid farewell to Sofia: there has not been a moment for her to slip away to the nursery. She does not know how this is possible. She cannot leave without laying eyes on Sofia, without saying goodbye: it cannot be.

There was a gap of time in her chamber, when she'd thought of requesting for Sofia to be brought to her, but first there was the bewildering experience of her father saying goodbye, and leaving the room, as if he might see her again tomorrow, and then her mother directing the servants in the correct way to remove and store the wedding dress: Like this, no, not like that, careful, don't, you'll tear it, lift it over her head, over, I said, are you listening to me? And then Lucrezia was out of the blue-and-gold dress and the relief was like a burst of sunshine after rain. Her ribcage moving in and out, unimpeded, her arms so light-feeling. Isabella was there for a while, yawning, a sweetmeat in her hand, saying something to their mother about one of the ladies at the dance, how her shoes were so ugly, and do you think her husband knows? Then Isabella said, Good luck, Lucrè, and left, still yawning. And instead of being permitted to go to bed, like Isabella, Lucrezia was being laced into another dress, one she likes, in a light lavender-grey, and her mother was giving her instructions: always listen to Alfonso when he talks, always conduct herself with piety and obedience, be careful of consorting with unsuitable people, especially all the artists and composers and sculptors and poets, for it is said that the Ferrara court is full of people of that ilk; she must take care not to form any unseemly attachments; she must be careful with her appearance, always attire herself in a manner appropriate to her station, to eat enough but not too much, to keep up her music, be courteous and respectful to Alfonso's mother and sisters, always smile and stand when Alfonso enters a room.

Yes, Mamma, Lucrezia had said. Yes, Mamma, yes.

And her mother kissed her, and they were bidding each other goodbye, and she was being escorted down the stairs and all she could think was that she hadn't yet taken her leave of Sofia, that she couldn't drive away without seeing the old nurse: what would Sofia think if Lucrezia left for Ferrara without bidding her farewell? Would she think that she didn't matter to Lucrezia any more, that she had forgotten her, that she had shed her as a dog discards a picked-clean bone?

Lucrezia said to the courtiers helping her down the stairs: I need to go back, I need to go to the nursery. But the courtiers shook their heads or pretended not to hear her. I need to see Sofia, Lucrezia said, in what she thought was a clear voice. But here was the end of the staircase and here was the first courtyard with the dolphin spouting water and here was the second, with the door to the carriage, wide open, ready to receive her.

There was no option. She saw this. She would not be allowed to turn back, to climb to the nursery, not even for a moment.

She put her foot on the carriage step, pulling her skirts out of the way, turning her head, as if to seek an opportunity or an excuse to run upstairs, and some figures appeared in the courtyard, and it wasn't her old nurse, it was the groomsmen, who started forward and, saying that she mustn't be exposed to the night air, secured the doors behind her, locking her inside.

Lucrezia leans forward and tries the handle; perhaps she will ask for leave to go back up the stairs – she could say she has forgotten something or left a bag behind – but without warning, the door is pulled open from the other side, and Lucrezia is yanked off the seat, on to the floor.

'Ah,' a voice exclaims, 'the Duchess has fainted.'

A plinth of yellow light has fallen across the carriage floor, with the dark outline of a figure at its centre.

'No, no,' she says, struggling upright, her face hot with embarrassment, 'I am well, I—'

'Bring a lantern, quickly.'

His tone, Lucrezia thinks, as a hand closes about her upper arm and another on her shoulder, is measured and authoritative. It is a voice that assumes – knows – it will be instantly obeyed. Her father, in the same situation, she suddenly sees, would have been shouting, his words pitched to fury. But Alfonso is unruffled, controlled.

She hears the rapid shuffling of servants doing his bidding: a lantern is brought, people crowd the doorway, she is lifted upright and shunted back against the cushions.

Alfonso, her husband of ten or eleven hours, kneels before her. He puts a palm to her forehead, he holds her wrist, as if to feel for a pulse; he will not let anyone else touch her, she sees. He holds them off with just his presence, his ducal demeanour. And all the while he speaks in his low voice: not so close, give her space, she is looking better already.

'I am quite well,' she tries to say, 'I assure you. I was just trying the door handle when you—'

'Take this,' she hears Alfonso say, to an unseen servant, and he passes a bag out of the carriage. 'Prepare, please, to depart immediately.'

The 'please' intrigues her. Never has she heard this word fall from the lips of her father or her mother when speaking to their staff.

Alfonso is leaning close to her now, raising the lantern, and out of the darkness emerges his neck, the shirt open at the collar, then his throat and chin, then his lips, his nose, his cheeks, his large dark eyes, then the fall of his hair over his brow.

They stare at each other: Lucrezia at Alfonso, Alfonso at Lucrezia.

It is the first time they have ever been alone together.

'Are you well enough to travel?' he says softly.

'Yes, of course.'

'Can I fetch you anything? What do you need?'

'Nothing. I promise.'

'Here is some food for the journey. I noticed you ate very little at supper.'

He lays a knotted cloth in her lap and, startled, she puts her hands around it. She can feel the mound of a loaf, the hard sides of the cheese they make in the kitchens, and the soft orb of a fruit – apricot, perhaps.

'Thank you,' she says.

He takes her fingers in his and raises them to his lips. She observes this, as if the hand belongs to someone else. His mouth brushes her skin; she feels the press of it, the sharp sting of his emerging stubble, the heat of an exhalation.

'So,' he tilts his head, 'if there is nothing you need, we shall begin our journey, yes?'

And without waiting for a response, he leans forward, out of the carriage, and hands the lantern to someone just outside. She hears him murmur his orders: make everything ready, check that all the luggage is secure, ask them to open up the gates.

He pulls the door closed and sits beside her. Lucrezia tries to steady her breaths: in, out, in, out. The gates of the *palazzo*

149

are opening. It is nearly dawn. She is leaving. Outside, she can hear the groomsmen gathering up the reins, snapping a whip in the air. Alfonso is telling her that they will take the carriage through the city and beyond, after which they will switch to horseback because the road over the mountains is too rocky for anything else, and she does not say that her father has already told her this, but she listens, to his voice, to his words, to his talk of the mountainous ascent and the wild beauty of the Apennine peaks, and then the flat plain of the Po valley, where their journey will end.

The gates rattle as they open, and Lucrezia wants to push at the carriage door, one last time, to say goodbye to the courtyard, to the white figure of David, the battlements around the campanile, as they pass by, but she dares not. The coachman whistles now and she braces herself for the forward jolt of the wheels.

But instead there is a call from outside, a shout: 'Stop! Wait! Stop!'

Alfonso turns his head. Although it is dark, Lucrezia knows he is frowning. This was not part of his orders.

'Wait!' the voice calls, ending on a wail. The next moment, the carriage door is wrenched open, and Lucrezia is startled to see Sofia, a shawl over her nightgown, her hair in a twist over her shoulder. Her face is flushed and stricken, her eyes wet. She gropes a hand towards her and Lucrezia seizes it. Then the nurse is in the carriage with them, enveloping her in an embrace that is desperate and strong.

'Goodbye, little Lucrè, goodbye,' the nurse is saying. 'May he be good and kind to you, for you deserve nothing less. Never forget that.' She fumbles under her shawl and then

Lucrezia feels something pressed into her hand; it is hard and flat; Sofia curls her fingers over it. 'You left this,' she says, 'upstairs in the nursery. I thought—'

'It's for you,' Lucrezia is able to say, pushing the tiny painting back into her hand. 'I made it for you, to keep.'

Sofia nods her thanks, her cheek pressed to Lucrezia's, as if she is hoping to draw into herself some part of the girl's essence.

'Live a long life,' Sofia whispers fiercely, into Lucrezia's hair, 'be happy.'

Then she pulls away and gives Alfonso a stern, searching look. For a moment it seems that she will speak, she will say something to him. But she doesn't. It is enough, for her, to cast her eye on him, to examine him as a scholar will a manuscript.

She leaves.

It is only after the carriage door closes, and the coachman snaps his whip, and the horses startle in their harnesses, stepping forward, and they pass under the archway and into the deserted piazza, Alfonso saying, who on earth was that person, that Lucrezia realises something. For the first time ever, Sofia had spoken to her in Neapolitan dialect, which meant that Sofia had always known that Lucrezia could understand it.

'What was it she tried to give you?' Alfonso is asking, as they weave their way through the city, her father's battalion riding alongside them, the sounds of hundreds of horses' hoofs clattering against the streets.

She tightens her fingers around the rosary, once more, and thinks of the small painting she has been working on for

weeks: a nurse standing in the middle of a rug, looking defi-
antly up at a tall adviser; rabbits, many of them, gambol
delightedly around her feet, their silver-brown coats glinting
in the light. If looked at very closely, it could be seen that the
nurse has her fingers crossed. Lucrezia made it specially for
Sofia, the keeper of all her secrets.

'Nothing,' she says.

The carriage trundles through a deserted Florence. Lucrezia
presses an eye to the gap around the door and, flickering past
in the weak light, sees houses, windows, shutters, small
squares, water troughs, bridges, the wooden door of a church,
a dog asleep on a doorstep, a guttering lantern on a balcony.
Her father's city, still in a state of slumber.

The walls cast deep shadow on the streets around them;
the horses pass through the narrow gates like a knife through
bread: the only sense Lucrezia has of this is a momentary
darkening of the carriage as they travel beneath the walls, and
then they are out the other side, and she is clasping her hands
together, the wedding rings unfamiliar hard circles.

She is thinking about the man next to her, his head leaning
back on the cushions, and about the parcel of food he brought
her, and also about the portrait of a stone marten and the
dancing and music from earlier. Her mind is restive, flittering
from images of blue silk to lilies bound by string to a bristling
fistful of hairpins to a brush moving to and fro across a piece
of paper to a lantern on a balcony to a flat river cutting through
a green and fertile plain.

When she wakes, much later, she finds she is lying on the
seat, alone, with buttons pressing uncomfortably into her

cheek. A blinding sunbeam is illuminating the carriage, entering through the open door. They have stopped; outside is the murmur of conversation, bird calls, and the sound of horses cropping grass.

'Alfonso?' she says timidly, then wonders if she is permitted to address him thus. Perhaps he would prefer her to use his title. 'Your Grace?' she tries, a little louder.

Someone outside the carriage makes a noise of surprise; she hears feet crunching over stones and then a person appears. It is a guard, dressed not in the red livery of her father's soldiers but a green-and-silver tunic; he bows his head to her, saying something in an unfamiliar tongue, holding out his hand. It is clear that she is meant to descend from the carriage.

So she does. She takes the hand of this guard who is speaking to her confidently and fluently in Ferrarese dialect – for what else can it be? – and she steps down to the ground.

They have stopped at a point where the road vanishes under a clear, pleated brook. The carriage horses have lowered their heads into it, their harnesses clanking as they drink. Ahead are mountains, layered peaks and slopes violet against the sky, the road disappearing and reappearing over their rumps. The heat of the day is rising around them. Her shadow at her feet is foreshortened, a folded-up version of her. Moisture is rising from the damp stones at the river's edge; a bird with a blue stripe on its wing skims along the surface of the water, turning a tight circle, then retracing its route.

The carriage is surrounded by guardsmen and servants all dressed the same, in silver and green. They are talking eagerly, bowing to her, their faces animated, delighted even. Some seem to be holding boxes and packs belonging to her. She smiles at them, inclining her head, and they gesture to her, beckoning.

'Alfonso?' she asks, keeping her fingers hooked into the door of the carriage belonging to her father. 'The Duke?'

The servants nod enthusiastically, still gesturing.

'His Grace?' she says. 'Ferrara?'

Yes, yes, they seem to say. Ferrara, yes. And, beckoning, this way, come this way.

There is no sign of Alfonso anywhere. Lucrezia looks to her left, then her right, then turns in a circle. A guard is coming towards her, leading a horse the colour of fresh cream. Saddlebags adorn each side of it. This must be the biddable mare, sent from Ferrara to carry her; her father's soldiers have disappeared, and the carriage is preparing to return to Florence, without her.

Lucrezia swallows. She isn't sure how to behave. Nothing in her mother's advice, Sofia's stories, her schooling has prepared her for this, being abandoned at the side of a road, with people speaking a language she cannot understand. Where is Alfonso? How can he have gone?

The pale horse is tall, its flanks high above ground. How will she ever get up there?

The urge to climb into the carriage and be conveyed back to Florence courses through her. But Lucrezia takes a step away from it. She looks at the familiar packs on the ground, at the twisting surface of the water, at the glint of the eager faces of these men, at their ornate green uniforms, at the bridle of the horse, which is decorated with gryphons and eagles.

'Ferrara?' she says again, and the word is like magic. It is the only word both she and they mutually understand.

'Ferrara!' they cry back to her. Ferrara! And, animated, they nod and beckon.

One springs forward, saying something, exhorting her in some way. He claps his hands and calls the word again, and around the side of the carriage comes a woman. For a moment, Lucrezia cannot tell who it is – a relative of Alfonso, a sister, come to accompany her across the mountains? But there is something familiar about her gait, that brown dress, the apron. It is, Lucrezia is staggered to see, the maid from the *palazzo*, the one with the scarred face.

'It's you,' Lucrezia says. It seems unaccountable to see her here, in this lonely spot in the lee of the Apennines.

'Your Highness,' the girl murmurs, dropping a curtsey.

'What are you doing here?'

'I am to travel to Ferrara, my lady.'

'You are?'

'With you,' the girl adds deferentially, her eyes cast down.

'Who said this?'

'Your father, if you please.'

Lucrezia turns away from her, and finds the Ferrarese servants and the horse all staring at her, so she turns back.

'What is your name?' Lucrezia asks.

'My mother called me Emilia, my lady.'

'Emilia,' Lucrezia repeats, and only then does she realise the joy of speaking Tuscan, the flow of the familiar words between them, 'do you know where the Duke is?'

Emilia shifts uneasily from foot to foot, then thrusts out a hand, pointing towards the mountains.

'He has . . .' Lucrezia struggles to find a reason why he might have deserted her like this '. . . gone ahead?'

'He left, my lady. In a great hurry. I think to go to court.'

'Do you know why?'

The maid hesitates. 'There was a letter,' she whispers, and Lucrezia steps forward, even though it is evident no one around them understands what they are saying. 'A messenger came galloping from over the hills with it, all in a panic. The Duke read it and he . . .'

'He?'

'With respect, my lady . . . he became. . .' Emilia pauses, searching for the right word '. . . angry.'

'Something in the letter made him angry?'

'Yes. He threw his gloves to the ground and I heard him . . .' again, Emilia falters '. . . at least, I think I heard him curse his . . .'

'His what?'

'His mother, my lady,' the maid murmurs apologetically.

Lucrezia stares at Emilia for a moment, then bows her head. She needs to think, she needs to assess, and whatever deductions pass through her must be concealed from servants, who will always talk and gossip among themselves. Her mind is muddied by exhaustion but still she is hotly aware that to be left at the side of a road by your husband of several hours is a terrible slight, and that many, many pairs of eyes are upon her at this very moment, watching to see how she will react. So Lucrezia looks down. She sees her travelling gown, her feet, shod in thin leather slippers, standing on a stony path, her hands clasped tightly together. She thinks: His mother, my feet, my slippers, a messenger, a curse. She thinks: Biddable mare, throwing his gloves to the ground, how tired I am, his mother. She shakes her head and presses her fingers to her brow, trying to master her thoughts. Alfonso's mother, she knows, has been the cause of much trouble in the Ferrarese court because . . . What was it Lucrezia's father told her? That she was born a Protestant, in France, but renounced her faith to marry the old Duke. Lucrezia is relieved to remember this. But then? There was something else, another chapter to the story. She strains to recall what her father said (she had been only half listening at the time, instead craning her neck to peer at the rarely seen curios and treasures that lined the shelves of her father's inner sanctum). Then it comes to her: a discovery that, years ago, the mother had been secretly attending Protestant Mass and consorting with Protestant sympathisers and – she remembers the shock of this – the old Duke had taken the children from her and imprisoned her somewhere in their *castello*. Lucrezia's father had wagged his finger at her and said to her jestingly, so be on your guard, Lucrè. And they had laughed together, she and her father, and the attendants standing behind him. Later, however, this story had caused Lucrezia some disquiet, giving rise as it did to more questions than answers. How could a man imprison his own wife? Did the young Alfonso and his siblings not suffer at being taken away from their mother? The old Duchess, her father had assured her, was now freed from her imprisonment, after promising Alfonso not to revert to Protestantism again, but that such a thing happened to a duchess, Lucrezia's predecessor, is confusing. How should Lucrezia greet such a woman? Should she affect to have no knowledge of the old Duchess's religious rebellion or her incarceration? And, most pressingly, what can have been written in that letter to make Alfonso ride off, leaving her here?

'His Grace,' Emilia, still at her side, is venturing to speak, 'said not to wake you. That he wanted you to sleep. He told me to tell you that he will deal with the matter at court and then he will meet you at the villa.'

'The villa?'

Emilia bites her lip, scanning Lucrezia's face with an imploring expression. 'Yes, madam.'

'But we are going to the *castello*, we are going to Ferrara,' Lucrezia says, her voice rising. Her father had told her that this was what would happen, so it must be true. 'I will have the formal *entrata* to the city, and be met there by his mother and his sisters for the *menare a casa*,' she persists, 'because . . .'

The girl is shaking her head. 'I'm sorry, Your Highness, I am so sorry. His Grace, the Duke, has decided that we are instead to travel to a *delizia*, his villa in the country.' She points to the cream-flanked horse. 'His Grace selected this horse for you. Also,' she says, holding up something, 'I am carrying your painting.'

The oblong parcel, which Lucrezia had tied up, wrapping the stone marten in layers and layers of cloth, is gripped in the maid's fist.

Afterwards, the journey over the mountains will assume the quality of a dream – something fleeting, evanescent, an experience outside life.

Images and impressions will intrude upon her over the coming weeks, like unwanted visitors to a room. She will be writing correspondence or listening to a courtier when her mind will be filled with the memory of a saddle, the way its leather squeaked as it moved, the neck of the horse, the lulling rhythm of hoofs on the mountainous path, how there was an indent she would grip whenever the horse missed its footing. She might be at the table, faced with a plate of roast swine on a bed of artichokes, and across her mind will flit the image of a torn crust of bread, eaten while sheltering behind a rock on a blustery mountain pass, while the guards milled about, blowing warmth into their cupped hands. She might be lying in bed, watching as Emilia glides about the room, shaking out and folding clothes, and Lucrezia will remember how, after several hours of riding uphill, she had asked for Emilia to be placed behind her on the horse, and they rode like that the rest of the way, the two of them, mistress and servant, Emilia's hands resting on her waist, and how Lucrezia could feel the girl's fear in the tremble of her fingers. Lucrezia had not known it was possible to fall asleep – or, at least, a halfway version of it – on horseback. That you could be riding along, a leading rein stretching from your horse's bridle to the hand of a groomsman, mounted beside you, and your head could tilt forward, slowly, so slowly, and you would believe you were just resting your eyes for a moment, but then you would jerk it upright again and see that the sun had slipped down behind the rocks and the trees had clothed themselves in darkness and the night sky was a black bowl upturned over your head.

They travel up and over the Apennines in daylight, Lucrezia clinging to the pommel on the saddle, Emilia clinging to her, the oil painting of the stone marten strapped to a saddlebag. Lucrezia has painted mountains, many times, but only in miniature, shrunk down, as backdrop to a scene, as a means of giving perspective to a composition. She has never seen them up close, never ridden across one, never realised that what might appear green or grey from a distance proves, up close, to be a collision of colours and textures: thick black-brown mud, rich green conifers, trees whose leaves shudder and twist in the wind, revealing silver undersides, grey rock, the dank rust of a pool where the horses dip their heads.

Behind her, Emilia's teeth chatter, either from fear or from the cold, and she intermittently whispers a prayer under her breath.

'Do not be afraid,' Lucrezia says to her, over and over.

'Yes, madam,' she replies.

But as they descend on the other side, and darkness begins to fall once more, and Florence feels very far away, and up ahead is a villa where a husband may or may not be waiting, and neither she nor Emilia can make themselves understood to these men who are leading them into the night, it is Lucrezia whose courage begins to fail her. Where is Alfonso? What kind of a man leaves his new bride alone like this?

They rest the horses; Lucrezia is given cheese and dry flat bread, studded with olives. When the servants gesture to her to remount, she feels fear engulf her with a slow creep.

'Ferrara,' she says again, hauling herself to her feet, and the servants nod and smile. 'His Grace? The Duke?'

The servants let forth a slew of words. Lucrezia can discern the word 'Ferrara' and '*delizia*' and 'Duke' and something that could be 'garden' or 'game'.

She reaches for Emilia's hand; the maid's answering touch is steady. The two girls stand there, hands linked, facing the servants, Lucrezia sees how similar they are in height and colouring, how with the same clothes or mantle, they might, from the back, be taken for the other. She finds no comfort in this realisation; instead it feels like another strange and unaccountable trick being played on her.

'What do you think?' Lucrezia murmurs.

'We cannot stay here,' Emilia says. 'It is getting dark.'

'If only I could be sure that they really mean to take us to the Duke, if only there was some way to—'

'Ferrara?' Emilia asks again, in a loud voice.

Yes, yes, the servants cry, echoing the word back to them, pointing to the mare, whose mane glows like marble through the dark. Lucrezia steps forward, towards the horse, keeping a tight grip on Emilia's fingers.

'Come,' Lucrezia says, trying to take command of the situation, trying to behave as the duchess she now is. 'We will go. We have no choice.'

She puts a toe into the stirrup and many hands rush to assist her but she hoists herself up on to the mare's saddle, then holds out her arm to help Emilia. The girl is whimpering with unhappiness but Lucrezia turns the horse's head, taps her heels against its flanks and takes once again to the path.

Night gathers itself around them, the darkness intensifying, as if black paint is being swirled into the air. They travel along a wide road, on either side of which are rows and rows of fruit trees – Lucrezia could, for a while, make out branches heavy with the round curves of peaches and perhaps the tear shapes of lemons. But now it is too dark to see anything at all. The servants at the back of the procession call to those at the front, and the call is returned, their voices arrowing past Lucrezia. She can feel the damp breath of Emilia on her neck, the clutch of the girl about her waist, and these are a small comfort. She hopes against hope that soon, from out of the darkness, some form of archway, perhaps in stone, will appear and it will be lit with flaring torches, and beyond it will be an open doorway, burnished and bathed in candlelight. There will be a bed, a chamber, a meal, warm clothes.

Instead, though, they turn into another, narrower, road, and there are no more fruit trees, just fields where low-growing crops rustle and whisper to them as they pass, or the numerous moist eyes of fenced cattle regard them; occasionally, the black shape of a roof appears in the distance and Lucrezia's heart gives a hard knock, but they pass it, and she can see by its size that it is no place for a duke with an ancient name.

All at once, they turn off down a track, lined on each side by cypresses, and Lucrezia thinks that whatever will happen will happen now: she and Emilia will be carried off, ravished, stolen. She has stopped wondering where Alfonso is, whether she will ever see him again. But she will be—

Then she sees up ahead an archway, with doors thrown open, and people are approaching with torches, calling to the servants on horseback.

Lucrezia is helped down by unseen hands and led across a square courtyard and, in language she doesn't understand, is ushered by two men in country clothes up a staircase and in through the door of a room. The men light a candle, which was waiting on a low table, and leave, with many incomprehensible words and smiles.

Still clutching each other's hands, Lucrezia and Emilia advance into the room, Emilia holding the candle. The chamber before them is a dark cavern, in any corner of which may be waiting a monster as yet unknown to them. The trembling circle of waxy light pushes at the blackness. Lucrezia feels, within her, the rise of what she thinks of as her spirit – the unfettered part of herself to which no one, not even she, has access. It lives somewhere deep inside her, under the layers of costly *palazzo* clothes, mostly hibernating, as if under a covering of leaves, until called into action. Then it might uncurl, crawl out into the light, blinking, bristling, furling its filthy fists and opening its jagged red mouth. In this black and unfamiliar room, Lucrezia feels it, senses it stirring, raising its head, and starting to howl.

She lifts her chin, seizes the candle from Emilia and thrusts it out at arm's length. She is not afraid, no, she is not. A beast – muscled and brave – lives within her. She tells herself this over the cantering of her heart. Let the ghouls that hover in the corners of the room see what they are dealing with: she is the fifth child of the ruler of Tuscany; she has touched the fur of a tigress; she has scaled a mountain range to be here. Take that, darkness.

She edges forward into the chamber. She sees walls of the palest distemper, veering off into shadows. She looks up and there is the lofty curve of the ceiling and it is alive with writhing frescos. Above her head, a man with a rippling beard and a bright staff drives a chariot through pearly storm clouds; next to him, dryads in scant robes disport themselves in a waterfall; in the corner, Lucrezia sees a goddess casting a prismatic streak of rainbow with a languid turn of her wrist, her golden curls blowing about her shoulders.

Lucrezia feels a tug on her hand and, with effort, she tears away her gaze. Emilia is pointing at something to their right.

A square structure is looming out of the darkness. Lucrezia

stares at it. It is higher than her, with a long flat base and a lid above. For a moment, in her fear and exhaustion, she cannot tell what it is. A box, her disturbed mind hisses to her, a cage.

She raises the candle, the rim of its light circle trembling, and when she sees what it is, she lets out a short, high laugh.

It is a bed. Of course. What else would be in a bedchamber? It is a bed, nothing more, with swollen goose-feather pillows, a coverlet of padded rose silk and thick bed curtains, held back by twisted gold ropes.

The sight of something so ordinary, and so welcome, is such a relief, that both girls laugh and, spontaneously, grip each other in an embrace.

'I thought it was—' Lucrezia says, unable to get out the words.

'I know,' Emilia cuts in.

'A cage!'

They laugh. Then Emilia, almost as if she has remembered her role, steps behind her mistress and begins to unlace the travelling dress. Lucrezia realises that there is no more welcome sight at this moment than a bed: it is what she needs more than anything else. She puts down the candle on the bedside table, then holds out her arms for Emilia to remove the sleeves. The maid folds back the bedclothes, then walks to the door, where she turns the big iron key; both girls hear the clunk of the lock.

They are safe: Lucrezia permits these words to ripple through her mind.

She exhales a long breath that feels as though it has been held since Florence. She allows herself to sink down to the bed. She is so tired that it feels like too much of an effort to lift her feet under the sheets. But she does. The pillow cradles the back of her head; she hears the narrow shafts of the feathers crack and resettle under its weight.

Emilia moves about the dim room, lifting discarded clothing and placing it on a chair. Lucrezia closes her eyes and sees, behind the lids, the drape of a horse's mane, the sight of trees flashing by, a windy mountain pass, so she opens them again.

Emilia, she sees, is lying on the floor, not far from the foot of the bed, arranging her cloak so that it covers her, cushioning her head from the bare boards with her shoes.

'Emilia,' Lucrezia says.

The maid lifts her head. 'Yes, Your Highness?'

'You can't sleep there.'

'No, it is fine, I am—'

'Sleep here,' Lucrezia pats the space next to her.

'No, madam, it would not be right. I assure you that I am—'

'Emilia, please. It is . . . this room is so big and I . . . I won't sleep anyway. Please. I want you to. I'm scared to be alone.'

Emilia raises herself up and tiptoes across to her. Lucrezia feels the mattress sag as Emilia climbs into bed.

Lucrezia blows out the candle.

'Good night,' she whispers to Emilia's back.

It is the dead of night. Outside, she can hear the strange rustles and hoots of forest creatures, the occasional shriek. Lucrezia pictures some small mammal being caught by a predator. Next to her, she hears the breathing of the maid, slowing, deepening. But she, Lucrezia, will not sleep. She cannot: it is impossible.

And yet she does. Quite without warning, Lucrezia drops, like someone falling from a high wall, into a deep and profound unconsciousness. The forest, at night, seems to come right up to the walls of the villa and press itself close, encircling the inhabitants in its green, quickening world; it wreathes into their dreams the snap of branches, the creep of lichen, frail light-seeking shoots, with web-veined foliage. Its sharp, loamy air penetrates their slumbering lungs.

Lucrezia sleeps as a deer emerges from the tangle of the forest, picks its way on soft hoofs across the driveway of the villa, lifting its head at the sound of a fruit dropping from a nearby tree. She sleeps as wild boar bludgeon their bristly, squat bodies, heavy as travelling boxes, through the thorned underbrush, snouts held to the ground. She sleeps as the dawn birds unfold their wings, as a porcupine snuffles along a pine-needled path known only to itself, as the servants wake, pile kindling into the stoves and strike flints and lift pots and scatter yeast into flour. She sleeps as the farmers pull on their clothes, clap on their hats and take to their fields. She sleeps as the pot boys are sent out to draw water from the well, as the first fragile light is seen in the valley, as its first heat is felt.

She sleeps off the long preparation for her wedding, the hair combing, the dress on the bed. She sleeps off the Mass, the feast, the dancing, the acrobats. She sleeps off the farewells with her parents, her indifferent sister, with Sofia. She sleeps off two wakeful nights. She sleeps off many months of disquiet about her marriage. She sleeps off the carriage ride with Alfonso through Florence at dawn, the discovery of his vanishing, the ascent of the Apennines, the journey at dusk down the other side to the valley. She sleeps and sleeps and sleeps and, as with all good sleeps, everything bad is sloughed off her.

The villa prepares breakfast; it consumes it. Floors are scrubbed, windows are thrown open, tables are dusted, dogs are let outside, bread is baked, then eaten, then baked again, loggias are swept, door handles are polished. The midday meal is cooked; it is eaten; it is cleared away. Dishes are washed, dried, then put back into the cupboard. The dogs take to the shade, to doze with lowered muzzles; the farmers seek shelter from the hottest part of the day, under the trees, in the cool of their houses. Servants sit in a chair, if they can find one; the cook puts her feet up on a barrel.

When Lucrezia wakes, she finds herself in a room filled with light the colour of honey. Everything seems burnished, tinted with its warm, dappled glow: the bed curtains, their gold ties, a coffer near the door, a table with a bowl of yellow roses on it, two chairs on either side of a fireplace, the carved dryads who dance and chase each other along the lintel. Lucrezia lies there, taking it all in.

It is as if she has travelled during the dawn, as if she has left the room where she fell asleep – that black and perilous cavern – and been transported, by witchcraft, to this place of sun and heat and beauty. Emilia is nowhere to be seen; that side of the bed is smooth, the pillow plumped, as if no one had ever been there. Above her head are celestial creatures with trumpets and lyres, flying across the plaster of the ceiling, wings outstretched to catch the heavenly zephyrs. Neptune, with a long, damp beard and a weed-draped trident, stands guard over the doorway, his hips tailing away into foamy sea. Only the sight of the yellow-haired Iris, still spilling a rainbow from her palm, convinces Lucrezia that this is the same room, that she hasn't been spirited away by night.

She sits up, raises one arm above her head, and then the other. She has no idea what the hour is or how long she has slept: cicadas are pulsing outside the window, her stomach feels hollow and empty. Heat seems to be filtering through the gaps in the shutters, but it cannot be past midday. Can it? She never sleeps this late.

She is about to push back the sheets and stand up, when there comes a knock at the door, and because she is sure it is morning, and this must therefore be a servant, most likely Emilia, with breakfast and clothes, she says: 'Come in.'

The door is flung open and, with confident strides and the tap of heeled boots, a man enters the room. Lucrezia is so taken aback that he is halfway across the floor before his name pushes its way into her mind. The Duke of Ferrara. Alfonso. It is he, entering her chamber, looking suddenly so different, with his hair tied back and in shirt sleeves, which fill and empty as he moves towards her.

'Y-your Grace,' she stammers, sitting straight and casting about for a wrap or a mantle, anything with which she might cover herself. She has never, in all her life, been seen in her nightshirt by anyone other than her mother or her sisters. 'You're here. I didn't know . . . I was . . . I . . . Let me just . . .'

He arrives at the bed and, without the slightest hesitation, sits down upon it, as if it belongs to him. Which, Lucrezia is able to reflect, it does. The mattress shudders and tilts as it accepts his weight.

'Your Grace?' he exclaims. 'Are we to address each other thus?'

'I . . .' Lucrezia's fingers find the neck ribbons of her nightdress and draw them together '. . . that is, I was always taught to—'

'Never mind what you've been taught,' he says. 'My given name is Alfonso, as you know, which is what my family and my friends call me – those who love me. Among whom I hope I may now number you.'

There is a pause. He raises his eyebrows with an expectant air. She is having trouble following the circling pathways of his sentences. Did he ask her a question? She can't recall, and is it her imagination or is he edging closer to her, along the side of the bed?

'May I?'

'May you what?' Her confusion is making her stupid, when all she really wants to know is what happened at court and why he abandoned her like that. He had been talking about names, hadn't he? But what is he asking of her?

'May I number you among those who love me?'

Lucrezia stares at him. She sees a stranger with an unlaced shirt, sitting close to her on a bed, in a deserted room. She sees muscles stretched beneath the skin of a chest that is damp and beaded with perspiration, a pair of hands with broad knuckles and long fingers, elegant yet strong, the nails clipped to clean half-moons. He doesn't look like someone who has just been faced with an emergency at his court. There is a distinct smell coming off him – sweat and heat and the outdoors and something vegetal and fresh, like leaves or bark or sap. It is an overwhelming odour, both pleasant and unpleasant. She would like to draw nearer to sniff it out;

she would like to draw back, to pull up the sheets to cover her face, to dive down into that cocoon of linen and never come out.

He has asked her a question, again, for the second time. And she must answer: her mother's lessons in manners and etiquette surge through her mind. Answer any query put to you promptly, with a pleasant expression on the face, with a light voice, with an affirmative response, if required.

'Yes,' she replies, 'naturally.' She almost adds 'Your Grace' but manages to stop herself.

He gives her a smile and there is something playful, something irreverent in it; his eyes glint with suppressed glee. She has the distinct feeling that the whole conversation has been a diversion for him, or perhaps some kind of test.

He nods, once, and says: 'Good.'

And then he moves closer again, so close that she can feel his leg against her hip, beneath the bedsheets. And the thought that Lucrezia has been holding at bay ever since he entered the room now opens its startling petals in her head.

He means to take her, here and now. He means to perform upon her the act she has been dreading, with all her being, ever since that visit by Vitelli when she painted the starling. He has been waiting for her to wake. He means it to happen now.

Lucrezia tries to swallow but her throat is arid and parched. When did she last take water? Last night, was it? When they stopped at the base of the mountains? That was hours and hours ago – too many to count.

He is talking now, about how he has come to wish her a good morning, how he has been walking out with his steward and then he had a bout of fencing with his friend Leonello, who accompanied him from court earlier – she will meet him, perhaps at dinner. He is most desirous of being presented to her.

Desirous. The word seems to hit her like hailstones. So close is it to *desire*, which of course describes what men feel for women, for the act of marriage; it is sanctified by the Church, within wedlock, otherwise it is a grave sin; and she has seen it in the faces of men, at court, at feasts, as they watched the swaying figures of women when they passed by. She is familiar with that expression: it is half dreamy, half determined, wholly distracted, yet focused and single-minded at the same time, the eyes at half-mast, the mouth open, as if tasting something delicious. And here it is now on the face of this man. Her husband. Alfonso. Who numbers her among those who love him.

Desirous, she thinks feverishly, must share the same etymological root as the word—

'Your hair,' he murmurs, 'is an incredible colour, one not often seen.' He reaches forward and takes a plait in his fingers, as though to find out if it is real. 'Did you sleep well? Do you feel rested?'

Another question, she thinks. But easy to answer.

'I do,' she says.

'You have slept a long time.'

'I'm sorry, I—'

'No, no, it is nothing to apologise for. I told them to leave you. I wanted you to rest, to recuperate. This villa was built by my great-grandfather, and it was his intention it be used for exactly that: pleasure and relaxation. A place away from the rigours and trials of court, for this family. To which you now belong.'

He pauses, apparently for her response. She has no idea what to say, but manages to nod and say, 'Yes.'

He lifts the braided skein of hair, smoothing it, examining it, holding it close to his face, then stretching it out, as if to measure it. She feels a gentle tugging on its roots, and is forced to sit forward, leaning towards him.

'Was all . . .' she wonders how to phrase the question '. . . well at court?'

'Oh, yes,' he says, without taking his eyes off her hair, 'naturally.'

'I was worried when . . .' She trails off, hoping that he will take up the subject without her having to explain, that he will reassure her, perhaps share with her the problems pertaining to his mother.

Instead, he looks at her, his head on one side. 'Worried? Why?'

'Because you left . . .' she begins, but the expression on his face is one of bland perplexity, and she falters, wondering if perhaps what Emilia said about his mother was not true, that it might have been another matter entirely that called him away from her, and she is making an idiot of herself for asking '. . . you left and I . . . I was . . .'

He smiles at her, as if she hasn't spoken at all. 'You look . . .' he says, still holding the wedding plait taut, so that she cannot draw back if she wanted to '. . . quite different this morning.'

'I do?' She is shaking so much that she is worried he will see it, or feel it, travelling down the shafts of her hair.

He nods, not taking his eyes off her. 'Yes. You were so pale yesterday, white as a little dove. But now, here, you look rosy and beautiful. Like an angel. With all this glorious hair. I had no idea how long it would be. How glad I am, now, that I designated this room as your chamber.'

'Thank you,' she whispers, and her voice sounds hoarse.

'Angels above,' he points upwards with his free hand, to the ceiling frescos, 'and an angel below.' The hand swoops down, landing on her cheek. He cups her face, angling it up towards him. She presses her jaw together, firmly, to stop her teeth chattering. She has never been so close to a man: not the priest, not her cousins, not any male servant. No man has ever been permitted to touch her. The scent of him – the sweat from fencing, the odours of the fields and forest, where he walked this morning – floods her nasal passages, filling her face. The hand against her cheek is hard, unyielding, its heat pressing into her bones.

She waits there, in the bed, clutching the sheet to her chest. From the doorway, Neptune seems to stare down on them, impassive, his trident dripping saltwater.

'We shall have to have you painted, one day soon,' he mutters; she feels the words leave his lips and land on her cheeks as tiny explosions of air. 'How the court artists will fight over the task. They will all want to do it. The very paint shall adore you.' He surveys her brow, her eyes, her chin. 'A portrait . . . or perhaps a classical scene. Hmm.' He seems to be conversing with himself so Lucrezia makes no reply.

'Some time ago,' he continues, 'my people sent to your father to request a likeness of you. And your father,' he says thoughtfully, turning her face gently to one side, then the other, 'sent a portrait, done in oil, finely framed. It was, I believe, a copy of one in your father's possession, perhaps done by an apprentice. The figure in it is depicted in a black dress, with pearls around the neck, one hand raised like so. A somewhat gloomy background. Do you know it?'

Lucrezia gives a single nod. It is an awful copy of a portrait for which she has no affection. Even the original by the master artist Bronzino, for which she sat long hours, her raised arm aching, her back rigid, her neck turned painfully, came out badly. She sees nothing of herself in it and cannot bear to look upon it.

He is examining her at close quarters, eyes narrowed, as if discerning her thoughts, as if reading them like words on a page.

'Do you know what I said when I saw it?' he asks.

She shakes her head.

'I said, "This cannot be the same girl. Either she has been very ill since then or this is a terrible portrait of her."'

Lucrezia is so surprised she lets out a laugh, then covers her mouth with her hand. 'I have always hated it,' she whispers, and it is an immense and novel relief to be able to voice this.

His mouth curls with amusement. 'Really?'

'Even the original. It is better than the copy you were sent, but not much. I look so sallow and sullen when—'

'When you are nothing of the sort. Why did your father not demand that it be repainted?'

She tries to think of the words to choose in reply, but the answer is too great, too visceral. My father doesn't care enough, is what she wants to reply. It doesn't matter to him whether it is a good likeness or not. The original hangs in an unvisited corner of the *palazzo*, unloved, unlooked on. Her brothers and sisters all had two or three portraits done, as children and also as young men and women; she was often told that she was too restless and fidgety to sit for an artist, so she only ever had one, painted in an unseemly and humiliating hurry, just after her betrothal. She feels the sudden pressing ache of this old injury, somewhere below her ribcage.

'If it had been me, I would have sent it straight back to the workshop. Do your father and mother not value the veracity of portraits?'

'Oh, no,' Lucrezia burst out, 'they do. My sisters were painted several times, as children, and then more recently. My brother Giovanni had a portrait made when he was only a year old. You may have seen these on the walls of my father's rooms. My mother sat with my brothers for Bronzino, twice, and my father—'

'But only once for you?'

The question is like a sliver of ice entering her skin, and his eyes, which have unusually wide pupils, take this in. She is sure of that. He sees the answer before he hears it; he grasps its myriad implications.

'Only once,' she mutters.

His response is to catch her face between both of his hands. 'I find that astonishing,' he says, in a confiding murmur, 'and the height of stupidity. We shall rectify this, you shall see, before long. You shall be painted, and by a master, by the best of my court artists. And if it turns out to be anything less than exquisite, I shall insist that it be done all over again until it is perfect.'

She is reeling from this speech, from the idea that he attached the word 'stupidity' to her father, that he would dare

to say this of Grand Duke Cosimo I, that anyone would criticise him and his judgement in this way.

'Very well,' she gets out.

'You are afraid,' Alfonso says, one of his fingers grazing
her cheekbone.

'No, I—'

'Of me.'

'Not at all.'

'You are. But you do not need to be. I will not hurt you. I
promise you this. Do you believe me?'

'I . . .'

He regards her for another long moment, then says: 'I will
not come to your bed now. You understand me? I am not an
animal. I have never forced a woman and I never shall. You
need not be afraid. We will take our time, you and I. For now,
you will get up and I will send for your maid and you will
take a meal. Yes? Then you will explore the villa and see what
there is to see.'

Abruptly, he stands, releasing her, and goes to the window,
where he throws open the shutters.

'Look at this sun,' he exclaims. 'Shining down on the land.
Does it not beg us to be out in it?'

He strides towards the door, his shirt inflating with air, then
quickly doubles back, as if he has forgotten something, pacing
across the floor to her again. He bends at the waist and, sliding
a hand around her neck, stoops and presses his lips to hers – a
brief, emphatic pressure. It reminds her of her father, bringing
his seal down on top of a document, marking it as his.

* * *

She is walking, in soft shoes and a flowing yellow dress. She has a pale blue cap on her head, on which the sun throws down gentle, probing arrows; they land on her crown, her forehead, like the pats of a tame animal.

She holds out a hand on either side of her, each palm brushing against the upper leaves of the box hedges that line the path. The sun finds her hands, too – such a thorough, tireless sun, this – making the skin prickle and seethe.

Her footsteps are slow and measured. She can walk, with every footstep pressing a print into gravel, at her own pace, in any direction she chooses, for as long as she wishes. There is nobody here to bother or pester her or put her in danger. She can go where she pleases: Alfonso told her so, using these exact words. Where she pleases.

This thought effervesces inside her, bubbling up her throat, to exit her mouth as a sound halfway between a laugh and a squeak.

Around her, the garden stretches, impassive and incurious. She is alone. (Apart, that is, from a man with slightly bandy legs and a curved knife in his belt; Alfonso said this man would accompany her on her walks, always at a distance, and that she must not give him a second thought, and that if she wanted for anything, she could summon him and he would be at her side in seconds.)

For now, today, she wanders past a bank of flowers with thick purple blooms, which undulate and vibrate with the preoccupied movements of hundreds of bees, rising and reset-tling. She ducks beneath the bower where the star-like petals of jasmine leak their scent into the air. The hem of her dress trails after her, netting twigs, fallen petals. She passes herb beds, a row of peach trees, some waving grasses, and then she finds she has circled back, without realising it, to the fountain at the centre of the garden – an oval, tiered structure in veined marble, with a sea monster joyfully gargling water into the bright, scented air.

She still cannot believe that such liberty, such motion, is allowed to her. After she had breakfasted on the milk and honey cakes brought to her chambers, and dressed with the help of Emilia, she had been led across the villa's courtyard to a long room where Alfonso had been sitting at a table, attending to some papers and giving orders to a man who held his cap in both hands.

He had leapt up upon seeing her, pushing aside his papers, dismissing the man, and taken her arm, bringing her out here, through the courtyard, to the villa's gardens, and told her she could 'wander at will' whenever she liked. The garden, he said, had been laid out with the leisure and pleasure of ladies in mind.

Impossible to say to him, as her arm lay through his, her fingers aware of the smooth fabric of his shirt sleeve, that she had never been permitted to wander at will, anywhere, that her parents believed girls should be kept under attentive watch, in a limited number of rooms, until marriage, that they should be closely supervised and never left alone.

But here, Lucrezia had thought, was marriage. The arm of a man cradling yours, his tall presence beside you on a path, his voice telling you which architect had laid out this walkway, that arbour, where the marble for the fountain was mined. A walled villa with angels and gods on the ceilings, and all about it rolling fields and dense woods and, in the distance, the meandering line of a river, like a line of gold-brown embroidery thread tacking through the valley.

Alfonso had accompanied her through the first garden and into the second, his head turned towards her, as if everything she did – walk, speak, gesture, shade her eyes from the sun – was interesting to him. He was just about to take her through a third gate, telling her that this was his favourite part of the walk, when he suddenly and without warning broke away, his attention drawn by the unobtrusive cough of a person, who materialised from a line of almond trees, a sheaf of papers dangling from his hand.

Lucrezia had stood for a moment, uncertain, her arm falling back to her side, wondering if she should wait for him, if she should approach him or stay back – what was the best course of action? But he had waved her on, retracing his steps to speak to the man, and she had needed no further encouragement. She continued, secretly delighted to be alone, even for a minute or two. She moved along the path with rapid feet, under the frothing almond blossom, and out into the third garden, with a symmetrical network of narrow paths, lined by low hedges, along which she was now trailing a hand.

The cool prickle of the waxy evergreen leaves against the lines of her palms. The options of left, right or straight on at each junction in the path. The warring wafts of scent from different flowers. The enormous expanse of blue sky that stretches from one distant horizon to the other. Never has Lucrezia seen as much sky as this – above the roofs and windows of Florence, the sky is hazed by smoke or mist, and seen in hemmed-in patches.

She turns to face the villa and sees the low reddish side of the building, the line of trees, and Alfonso, his head bent, in conversation with the man who holds the papers. Alfonso: a tall figure in dark hose and pale shirt, bareheaded; the man shorter than him, in a grey shirt, a cap set back on his lion-coloured hair.

As Lucrezia watches them, the shapes they make against the thick foliage of the trees, she realises that the man with the cap is not a servant. Lucrezia has spent her life observing people at some remove; it is an ability she has, or one that she has developed over her lifetime. She can decode stance, clothing, gesture, the positioning of a head, a facial expression, with a mere glance; the moment she walks through a door, she can tell who in the room possesses the most power, and what type, and who is whose rival, whose ally, who might be withholding some secret.

As she wanders there, among the flowers and fruit trees of the villa's garden, she casts covert glances at the man who is now her husband, and the person next to him, who has drawn Alfonso's attention. His clothes do not speak of servility – the shirt is finely cut, with draped fabric and embellished lappets; the cap glints with spiked *ciondoli* decorations – and his stance, next to the upright height of Alfonso, is casual. He leans towards Alfonso, his weight on one foot. There is, she can tell, an ease or intimacy between them. The elbow of the man glances against Alfonso's, briefly, as they peruse the papers' contents together, and Alfonso does not draw away.

Lucrezia watches, fascinated. Could this be the friend Alfonso mentioned, the one he practises fencing with? Or perhaps a brother or cousin, come from the city? She is sure she has been told that Alfonso's only brother is a religious man, a cardinal, and lives in Rome.

The man is talking now, upturning one palm, then the other, placing them together, as if entreating Alfonso in some way. Alfonso is thinking, she sees, his head lowered. She wonders if it is to do with his mother again, or perhaps some other trouble at court. Her father had told her to expect that Alfonso's first year as duke might be difficult: there will, he had said, be many who wish to test or challenge a young new ruler, both inside and outside his court. Your Alfonso, Cosimo had said, will have to demonstrate that dissent will not be tolerated; he will need to prove to everyone that he is up to the task of ruling Ferrara. He may be required to make a show of strength and mettle: such is the way of these things.

Over by the hedge, Alfonso says something, with a decisive nod, and claps a hand to the other man's shoulder, then turns and starts towards her, coming along one path, then turning right, then left, navigating the maze of pathways.

The other man melts back into the greenery, disappearing, almost as if he was never there in the first place.

When Alfonso reaches her, he says he has to take his leave of her, for now, he must return to his office, but she should remain here in the garden for as long as she wishes.

'I am sorry,' he finishes, with a brief smile. 'I shall see you tonight.'

Lucrezia's mind seems to fold in on itself, the garden and the bees and the flowers vanishing, so that all she sees is the bed beneath the frescos, its sheets turned back.

'Yes,' she falters. Tonight, she thinks, tonight.

'You do not mind?' He is looking at her with his penetrating dark stare.

'Of course not. Please don't worry about me. I am very happy here.'

'Do not stay in the sun too long,' he advises, lifting her hand to his lips. 'It may be stronger than you think.'

'Who was that man?' she asks, quickly.

'Which man?'

He releases her hand and it drops into the gap between their bodies.

'The one who came with the letter.'

'Oh.' Alfonso turns towards the large hedge, as if to look for him. 'He's gone? That was Leonello.'

'Is he . . . your friend?'

'My very good friend. Since childhood. We grew up together. My father educated him alongside us. He is like a brother to me, or a cousin. He has for a long time helped me with matters of state, and taken care of—' Alfonso breaks off, shading his eyes. 'Where has he gone? I told him to wait for me.'

He strides away from her, towards the end of the path. 'Leonello!' he calls, and lets out a piercing whistle, like a hunter calling his dogs. 'Leo?'

Away in the distance, muffled by greenery, comes a reply: 'What?'

'Where the devil have you gone? Come back!'

There is a rustle, a thud from the hedge, then an offhand voice: 'Very well.'

'You need to come and meet my new wife. Where are your manners?'

The man emerges, shoulder first from the branches, the

papers still clutched in his hand. He makes his way through the garden but, unlike Alfonso, he doesn't pick his way along the paths: he walks through the flowerbeds as if they aren't there, striding over the low green hedges, through the blooms, scattering bees and petals in his wake. Here is a man, Lucrezia thinks, as she eyes his progress, who waits on no one, who lets nothing get in his way.

He stops a few paces from her.

'Leonello, may I present to you my wife and consort, the new Duchess of Ferrara? Lucrezia, this is my friend and cousin, Leonello Baldassare.'

Leonello makes a deep bow, almost – it could be said – too deep, as if he is exaggerating the courtesy of the moment, satirising it. Lucrezia does not miss this. She trains her gaze upon him: sharp cheekbones, yellow-brown eyes, a slightly thin mouth, hair perhaps lightened by the summer. He has a well-shaped form, with wide shoulders and narrow hips; she can picture him wielding a fencing foil, swishing its blunted tip through the air.

'My lady,' he says, in a languid drawl, 'I am your humble servant.'

'I am very happy to make your acquaintance. Any friend of my husband I hope will be a friend of mine.'

Leonello regards her, as if considering these words. His name, she thinks, is entirely apt. He has a russet-brown mane framing his face, and his skin is smooth and golden. After a moment, he inclines his head, unsmilingly signalling his agreement. He is, she reflects, nothing like other *consiglieri ducali* she has met – he hasn't a trace of Vitelli's learned poise or reassuring deferential protectiveness. There is something unsettled and febrile about this man: she would not like to be alone in a room with him.

'Is she not a beauty?' Alfonso says to him, pinching Lucrezia's chin. 'Have you ever seen such skin, such clear eyes? Not to mention this hair.'

Again, she feels those tawny eyes on her but this time she does not meet them. She looks instead at her husband.

'Indeed,' the inscrutable Leonello replies. 'Her Ladyship is an exquisite example of womanhood.' He taps the furled papers against his chin. 'We had hoped as much, had we not? And, just as you said, that portrait was not a good likeness at all.'

'Oh, but I am going to commission a new one immediately,' Alfonso exclaims. 'An allegorical scene or a religious one. Or, now I look at her here, I am thinking perhaps just a three-quarter profile, exactly as she is. A marriage portrait. What do you think?'

Both men study her, stepping back to do so, their heads on one side, her husband's face thoughtful, Leonello's unfathomable, assessing.

He doesn't like me, Lucrezia realises, with something akin to confusion, and she wonders why this is. He barely knows her – they have only just met. What about her can he have found to cause such instant hostility? What can she have done or lack in the eyes of this man?

'We should go,' Leonello murmurs to Alfonso. He raises the papers, as if to remind Alfonso of whatever the contents are.

'Indeed.'

Alfonso hastily kisses her hand once more, then turns, and together he and Leonello stride away, their shoe soles spitting gravel. And Lucrezia is left alone in the middle of the garden, the flowers undulating beneath a fleece of bees, the fountain still expressing itself in its indecipherable silver argot.

It begins with her lying on the bed. Such an ordinary thing to do but she is trying, as she holds herself there, not to cling with her fingers to the long cuffs of her shift, as he moves across the room with careful steps, carrying a book in one hand and a candle in the other. He is saying something about the weather feeling uncertain, about how they must fasten all the shutters tonight for it is getting windy.

It is late, very late; dinner has been served, a rabbit stew with griddled radicchio; she has rubbed her skin with mallow tincture; she has taken to the sheets, which smell of rosemary and lavender.

She knows what will happen. She thinks she knows. She has been told. She has grasped the mechanics of it, believes herself possessed of a sufficiently clear idea. She is fortunate, she tells herself, to have been united with a man who is considerate and kind, not to mention pleasing to the eye. Has he not promised that he will never hurt her? Not all girls are as lucky. And she knows herself to be possessed of a toughness, a resilience that will carry her through. She is not easily cowed, can withstand pain and discomfort and fear. She can get through this. She can. There will be a time, and soon, when it will be over. It must happen, it must be borne, and she can do it.

But she had not expected this: for him to walk up to the bed and remove his clothes, layer by terrifying layer, until he stands before her, unclothed and smiling. She tries not to laugh. She tries not to cry. She does not want to look, and yet she does, and yet she cannot. She had not expected him to lie down beside her, and then near her, and then nearer still. And she had not expected him to talk, to make conversation, to ask her questions, some of which are about her journey or foods or how she liked this fresco or that, which is her favourite, what music she prefers, what instrument is most pleasing to her ear, lute or viol, does she like madrigals, he has heard Florence is famous for its madrigals. Such ordinary topics to be discussing, such things that might be said in a salon or at dinner, and all the while his fingers are patient yet restless, touching filaments of her hair, brushing against her face, tracing the outline of her lips, as if they will gather information about her. She had never expected that.

There had been dogs at the *palazzo*, and cats. She had seen them in the act, the male preoccupied and evasive, often looking off to the side, the female beneath, face resigned. And Sofia had told her, as best she could. She had gestured outside Lucrezia's gown, around the area of her navel, and performed a mime with her thumb sliding into her curled fist. She had given her a vial of ointment, stoppered with wax and string, and told her to apply it before he came to her, for the first few weeks. Her mother had pressed her palms together, as if in prayer, and made vague statements about 'God's will' and 'a woman's duty' and 'part of marriage'. So she has a notion of what will occur next.

His calm surprises her, his matter-of-factness, his single-minded approach, and the time he takes.

'Don't worry,' he murmurs, cupping her cheek in his palm, while lower down the bed she can feel his shin slide between her feet. 'Don't be frightened.'

'I'm not,' she whispers.

He smooths her brow with the pad of his thumb. 'I shan't hurt you,' he says, 'I promise.'

'Thank you.'

'Do you believe me?'

'Yes.'

'Do you trust me?'

'I do.'

She has to believe him. What choice does she have? She is miles and miles and days away from her family. There is no one else here.

'You trust me?' he says again, taking her hand and placing it flat on his chest.

She has not yet touched him, not yet made acquaintance with his skin, with his unclothed form. The iron hardness of it startles her, the muscle and heat and bone of it, the animal rhythm of his heart.

'Of course,' she says, and she sees she has answered well because he smiles. He presses her hand to his chest and then, shockingly, he places his other hand on the corresponding part of her, the neckline of her shift, beneath which is the hollow between her breasts. It makes her flinch – she cannot help it – and he sees this but he does not take his hand away. Is it her imagination or does a flicker of sympathy pass over his face? She thinks so – she hopes so. It is his right, she knows, as her husband, to touch her wherever he wishes, and Sofia had warned her of it, but, still, it is a shock. But the fact that he sees her plight, and comprehends it, is reassuring. He will not hurt her, he has said. She has nothing to fear.

He lifts her hand away from his chest and places it on his shoulder, again mirroring the motion so that his palm lands on her shoulder, curving over the rounded bone there. With a smile, he next moves her hand to his throat, then his cheek, then his ribs, then his waist, with his hand following suit. The places where he has touched her feel seared and cold at the same time, as if his hand has printed her shift with some kind of invisible marker or ink. Her hand, meanwhile, as he guides it, is learning the different textures of him: the rough grain of his stubble, the puckered skin of his lips, the satin of his bare shoulder, the whorled hair on his chest. It is interesting to her, and the repetition, the game of it lulling. Chest, shoulder, throat, cheek, waist, then back again to chest. They are still talking at this point, about his three hunting dogs, and their different natures, about the food she likes most of all to eat, and everything between them is strange, yes, but calm. She feels soothed by the repetition of his mirroring game; she can do that, she can cope with that. Perhaps, she thinks, things will go no further tonight; perhaps he means to do this game and nothing else.

She is unprepared, then, unready, when after they are touching each other's waists, he moves her hand not back to his chest but down, further down, much further, to a place she has never seen, never allowed herself to dwell on.

There are statues of naked men and gods and cherubs, all over her father's *palazzo*: no mystery, then, what is down there. She grew up with brothers, of course. She saw them, as young children, standing in tubs of water as the nurses washed them. She has seen what males have, the pouched appearance of it, and the appendage, so vulnerable-looking, so comic, all curled and folded into its own little jacket, like a creature afraid of showing its face to the world. Her sister Isabella had intimated to her that men varied in size in this respect, and Lucrezia had asked how Isabella could say this as, surely, she had known only one man in this way, her husband, Paolo, and, mystifyingly, it had made Isabella let out a peal of laughter as she landed a somewhat painful smack on Lucrezia's leg.

She had not expected this. She had not thought she would be required to touch it with her hand. That someone would take her fingers – those same fingers that have turned pages and tied ribbons and sewn with needles and broken bread and lifted cups and written words and drawn pictures – and wrap them reverently yet firmly about it so that they could learn its ways. She had not known of the transformation this part of the body undergoes, how it alters its form, metamorphoses into something quite other. And she had not known that this change spreads itself throughout the man, that he becomes a different person, enslaved to this part of himself, losing himself, that everything beyond that moment is different and swift and charged.

The talk is mostly silenced now. There are no more questions about favourite frescos. He asks, in a voice hoarser than usual, if he may remove her shift, and when she says yes – because what else can she say? – he does it with the urgency of a creature under a spell, and then his hands, like ravenous animals, begin to rummage about, insistent, purposeful, as if searching for something lost in the crevices of her.

She had not known he would need to lie on top of her, that she would be pinned down, covered by his body. She had not known that she would be required to fold up her legs in such an ungainly way, like a cicada, or that the bones of her spine and pelvis would creak under his weight.

He says again that he will not hurt her, she must not be scared, he will not hurt her, he will not, he promises, the words whispered in his new rasping voice.

And then he hurts her anyway.

The pain is startling, and curious in its specificity. It tunnels a scalded route into a most private space in her, a place of which she had previously only the dimmest sense. She has never felt discomfort like it: burning, invading, unwelcome, overfull. She is aware of her face twisting into a grimace, of a whimper escaping her lips.

He hears this, she is sure. He brings up a hand to cradle her head. In apology, she believes, and now he will stop, surely. Because he promised her that he wouldn't hurt her – he may not have meant to but nevertheless he has. Because he has done what he intended to do. Because he has fulfilled his part of the marriage contract, and so has she. Because he cares about her, loves her perhaps, and would not want her to be in pain. Because now it can finish and be over, he has done what he came to do, she has done what was required, he can let her go.

Strangely, though, he does not stop. He does not withdraw. He remains in the place of pain, inscribing more pain over the original pain. He says to her that she is fine, that she should hold still, that all will be well, she is fine, she is fine. But how can he say this, how can he think this? I am not fine, she wants to hiss, it hurts, you are hurting me, you are breaking your promise.

She had thought she knew what would happen. She had believed herself prepared; but she had not been, not at all.

Isabella told her that it might be sore for a moment and then it would stop, and later she would come to enjoy it. These statements swoop through her mind, backwards and forwards. They are the only thoughts she can allow.

She, herself, her frame, her being, is pressed between mattress and another person, like a sheaf of papers between the covers of a book: it goes beyond astonishment, beyond shock.

The heat, the labour, the noise of it, is appalling – she had had a vague expectation of a mingling of a celestial or spiritual sort, a gentle confluence of beings, in silence – but how close this seems to fury, with its constant and repeated motion, its pounding action, its invasion, the distortion of his features, the panting like one possessed.

She had known. She is sure of this. She had known but, also, she had not. The idea that she had once perceived the male organ as shy or afraid seems so distant, so misplaced, that she believes it must have been some other girl who stood before her father's painting of Jupiter and covertly examined the curious tube of flesh that peeped out of a nest of hair.

Lucrezia counts the thuds of her heart. Up to twenty, then forty. She loses track after sixty. How long does this go on? Impossible to know. Why hadn't she asked Sofia or her mother or even Isabella?

The weight of it – of him – makes it hard to catch enough breath.

Outside, she can hear a wind starting up. It has presence, this wind, and a character. It frisks against the shutters, sliding narrow fingers between the slats, rattling the locks. It purses its lips and blows down the chimney, scattering fragments of soot on the hearthrug. It rubs itself against the tiles of the roof above her head, as if it will prise them off with its insistent fingers.

Difficult to know where to put her hands. She wants to clear the hair from her face, from her mouth, but he is so much larger than her, there is so much of him, and he has two muscled arms that are pressing down into the mattress on either side of her so that she cannot move, and they are pressing down, too, on hanks of her hair. One of her palms, which has been flailing in the air, grazes some part of him, his back, perhaps, his hip, and the damp fleshy burn of it, the flexing motion, is so frightening, she removes it at once. Better then, she decides, to let her arms fall aside, apart, out of the way.

In the dining room, before any of this happened, as the rabbit stew was being cleared away, he had asked her if she would loosen her hair from its bindings for him, so that he could see it. She had done so. She had sat there, at the table, and undone the wedding plaits on one side of her head, while Emilia, who had been summoned for the task, did the others. This was in the before-time, prior to any of this, while they were finishing dinner. He had watched, reaching for a peach from the bowl set on the table, a paring knife in one hand. He had insisted she try the fruit, telling her that they were grown here, on the estate, that he had ordered they be picked for her, that the valley was a beautiful fertile plain, with perfect soil for agriculture. She had looked away at the word 'fertile', as perhaps he had known she would – when she looked back, there was a smile on his face and he was holding out a slice of orange-pink peach flesh to her, not unkindly. Go on, he said, try it. And he reached out and placed it between her lips, as if such an act was entirely natural – she had to open her mouth to accept it, she was left no other option but to take food from his hand. The taste of it instantly flooded her mouth, trickling down her throat so that for a moment she thought she might choke. It was startling, soft as moss, nectar-sweet with an edge of tartness. Well, he had murmured, watching her, leaning forward on his elbows, how do you like it? It tastes, she said, of the sun. It's like eating sunshine. It must have been a good reply because he laughed and repeated the phrase to himself. Her hair, unravelled, still held the impression of the wedding plaits, rippling like wheat down her back.

Bed: once a place for sleep, or for staying awake to listen to the breathing of her siblings, to the nocturnal noises of the *palazzo*. And now another person may pull back the covers and enter it, and do – this.

The wind filters through a gap in the window. She can feel its cool, whispering caress on her cheek, like an invitation or a suggestion.

She discovers that if she turns her head to the side, it is easier to breathe, possible to draw in air that doesn't feel as though it has already been shared in the small gap between them, sucked in and out again, in and out.

And with that breath comes a sensation like the weft and warp of fabric separating in two, and some part of her, the best part perhaps, answers the wind's call. It shakes itself free. It gets up from the bed, leaving the bodies there, to do what they will, and moves away. The relief at putting distance between herself and that bed. The self, the part of her that is leaving, seems amorphous, shapeless. It is at once padding on noiseless feet across the floorboards and also floating somewhere up near the ceiling. This bodiless Lucrezia brushes past the rafters, the painted cherubs; it reaches out a hand to trace the lines of the rainbow. It is enormous, stately; it is minuscule and obscure.

Where the two people are stretched out on the bed, the form of one obscuring the other, is far below. That is a place of shadow and darkness. There is nothing to see of it. What is happening there is of no consequence to her now.

She passes through the walls, disintegrating and dissolving into plasterwork, beams, struts, wattle, brick, and then she coalesces again, in the air on the other side.

She is here now, outside the walls of the villa, where the night has painted its own version of the valley, in bold indigo strokes; where the wind animates this mysterious shaded landscape, setting the trees in motion, flinging night birds up to the blue-black air, driving angry blots across the unreadable face of the firmament. She is on the pantile roof, creeping along gullies and gutters, feeling the ministrations of the spirited wind, the spring of moss beneath her feet, but she is also down there on the ground, where the branches of the trees fan themselves out for the breeze, tugging one way, then the other. Where small, sharp stones push themselves up into her bare feet. Where the forest is a dark shape beyond the manicured hedges, beyond the pollarded fruit trees. It crouches, waiting.

Lucrezia is vigilant. Lucrezia is herself. Lucrezia can choose her own tempo, can increase it, can slow it down. She can gallop, sprint, through the gardens; she can spring over the hedges and paths, her body a streak of colour in the dim light, her ribs a vessel for her leaping heart. And when she reaches the forest, the trees will close about her, all the animals and birds within will send up their questions to the sky in squawks and cries, and she will wait with them, watching, for the first rays of cold morning light, which will feel restorative and forgiving on the complex silk of her skin.

She wakes with a gasp, flinching from a dream in which Maria is pulling her by the hand along a corridor, urging her on, and Lucrezia cannot disentangle herself because, strangely, she and Maria are inside a single dress, a stiff, weighty gown, and Lucrezia is trying to keep up with her sister, who will not slow down, and Lucrezia is worried about tripping over the hem. Just as she falls, her dream-feet tangling with Maria's, her dream-self about to strike her head on the floor, she lurches from sleep to consciousness in the space of a heartbeat.

She finds herself lying on her side, at the very edge of a bed, in an unfamiliar room, the ceiling high, the walls pale and glowing with an inconstant dappled yellow light. Maria is gone, the shared dress is gone. Her hair has been spilt, like liquid, all over the pillows and the bed; it falls in confused gilded streams down to the floor; it tangles in her fingers and covers her mouth. What is going on? Something must have happened. She never goes to bed without weaving it into a long rope that lies obediently beside her all night, like a pet or a familiar.

From behind her comes a noise so unnerving and un-accustomed that her scalp shrinks. The suck and draw of breathing. The rise and fall of another's chest. It is heavy, measured: the sound of someone's slumber.

Lucrezia's mind leaps like a flea from the sight of her hands up close, the alluvial puckers and creases that striate their innards, to the ache she feels in her lower body, which seems to pull down, as if her interior is attached to a rope, to her unfastened hair, to this edge of the bed and the rug beneath it, to the dust motes circling in the golden slabs of light, to the ache, to the breathing behind her, to the ache, to her hands, up close.

She raises her head, slightly, ever so slightly: she does not want to wake the person behind her, so she is careful to move herself an infinitesimal amount at a time, barely rustling the bedclothes.

There he is. The sight of him is a shock. Hair like black feathers on the pillow, face devoid of any expression, as if whatever dreams he is having soothe and transport him, the stubble on his chin and cheeks emerging like a miniature forest on a mountainside.

Lucrezia stares at him, as if she were considering a sketch: *Man, Asleep. Ruler, at Rest.* When he is awake, she is unable to look at him for long – the fact of him, the presence of him, is too overwhelming. The way his gaze seems to miss nothing, to take in every detail, his mind always working and inter-preting and assessing, that knack he has of being able to pluck your every idle, private thought from the air and consume it so that it is part of himself, comprehended, filed away. This, she supposes, is what it means to be a ruler. But like this, his eyes shut, his mind at ease, she can examine him without embarrassment. He is, just for now, not the ruler of Ferrara, not the newly appointed head of a powerful court, but a being asleep, no more and no less.

Here, on the pillow next to hers, is yet another version of the man she has been given to. There are, it seems to her, many Alfonsos, all fitted inside one body. There is the heir she met on the battlements, as a child, then the person behind the marten painting and the loops and dashes of the letters sent from France during the two-year wait for marriage, then the duke who claimed her at the altar, the person in the carriage, and the man in shirt sleeves who gave her a tour of the garden. And now, here is another: a sleeping satyr, with a naked chest, his unnerving lower half concealed by the folds and drapes of sheets.

What a boon it is, what a piece of luck, to be able to take her time like this, to examine every part of him.

She takes in the rings on his fingers – two on his right hand, and one on his left, the signet ring, bearing a tiny inverse impression of his eagle crest – the thin gold chain around his neck, and the way it catches and tangles in the hair. His lips are parted so she may also observe his teeth, how white and sharp they are, how evenly spaced, and that he is missing one on the lower left side of his mouth: evidence of some accident or other loss. The hair on his upper body is darker than that on his arms, she can see. The hair on the chest grows in two waves, which approach each other in opposing directions, meeting in the middle in a sort of cresting line. It is as if he is formed of two halves of a cast, like a sculpture, and has been fused down his central line. His nails: clean, clipped short. His lashes: black. His eyes: shielded by lids, ever-moving from side to side, as if even in sleep he is reading and decoding information – missives from court, letters of state, accounts, political treatises, reports of unrest.

Slowly, so slowly, she eases herself away from him, sliding

between mattress and sheet, until she is out of the bed, away from it and all that has happened there, and moving in her disturbing nakedness across the room, registering the ache and soreness between her legs, her hands finding her slippers and smock, lifting her *zimarra* from the floor and pulling it hastily about her.

She glances for a moment at the painting of *la faina*, propped on the mantelpiece – and how well it looks there, against the pale plaster of the walls, its eyes following her across the room – then lifts the latch on the door, swings it open, and passes through it, closing it behind her.

She moves along the corridor, silent in her lambskin slippers, past the small anteroom where Emilia is sleeping, past a narrow and dark staircase used by the servants, on and on, down some steps, and out on to the loggia.

It is early in the morning, the sun inscribing long shadows from the bases of the columns and trees and the group of servants standing in the courtyard, conferring with each other about something, safe in the knowledge that their masters will not be up for hours.

Lucrezia, however, is awake. She is also adept at making herself unobtrusive: a childhood of mapping out hidden passageways has taught her this, if nothing else. She steps back from the bright lip of the loggia, into the recesses, and glides noiselessly along by the villa's wall.

Through the first courtyard, skirting the kitchens and the gaggle of housemaids who are clattering brooms and dustpans as they throw open windows. She evades them, sliding once more into the shadows. She has no clear idea of where she is going, but when she turns the corner, she knows.

There, before her, is something she has never seen in her life. Something she has really never thought of as possible. Something so thrilling and unexpected, her hands fly to her mouth.

The heavy wooden doors to the villa stand open.

Nobody guards the entrance. There are no soldiers with weapons, no men in livery; no hasty slamming of the doors is about to take place; no weighty bar will be replaced to repel enemies and assassins. Nothing, no one. Just a portal, flung wide, for all to see. It is the act of a household expecting no threat, no attack, no thieves, no interlopers. Here is a building with no need to assert its might, a *delizia* intended only to delight, a place at ease with itself and with its hinterland.

Beyond the shape of the gateway – rectangular with a peaked arch – she can see a gravelled path winding away from it, a row of cypress trees, their pinnacles piercing a sky that is blush-streaked by dawn. Wildflowers cluster along the pathway and they nod their heads at her, blue, red, yellow.

Lucrezia takes a step forward, then another. She darts a look behind her. Will anyone stop her? Will a battalion surge forward the minute she sets foot outside the villa walls, ready to drag her back and slam the doors?

She hesitates on the threshold, casting her eyes over the thick wall of trees. Then she steps out.

The wind from last night is here again, but she doesn't want to think of last night or anything to do with it, she will not, because thoughts such as those cannot be allowed on a morning like this and, anyway, the wind has changed, shrunk itself down, civilised itself; it is behaving; it has remembered its place. It moves low to the ground, like an animal on its belly, it stirs the flowers that line the track, it rustles the lower branches of bushes, it toys with the hem of her wrap, with the tassels of her hair.

She steps away from the villa, her slipper soles scuffing along the path. She moves with an increasing pace, suddenly aware of a lightness or relief within her. She has done it. She has been through it – the thing she dreaded, the act she feared. She had thought it might be terrible, unendurable – and, in truth, it was – yet, look, here she is, on the other side of it, walking in the sun. She has done what she was meant to do; she has not let down her family. What she wishes she had asked either Sofia or her mother or Isabella was how often it would be expected of her. Now she has endured it once, perhaps it will be a good long while before she must do so again.

The sky above her head is vast, stretching from the tops of the cypresses all the way to the distant peaks of the Apennines, which can be seen, far off, in the purple-grey haze. As she walks beneath it, she is aware of its spectrum shifts, from the pink of sunrise, to red, to orange.

This, she thinks. All this. The cypresses like rows of upended paintbrushes, waiting for the giant hand of an artist, the low and subjugated wind, the jagged line of mountains drawn in charcoal on the horizon, the muted calls of servants to each other, somewhere behind her, the open doors of the villa, the clink of bells around the necks of cattle, the lines and lines of fruit trees that open into avenues as she walks by. She wants this. She feels the bliss of it all on her skin, like the graze of drizzle after a parching drought. She can take the other, she can bear it, if it means she can have this. She will exchange that for this. She will, she can.

From somewhere off to her side comes a crack, then a rustle, and she whips round. It is not, as she feared, some wild beast come to devour her. Instead a shape clarifies itself against the trees of the forest. For a moment, her alarmed mind perceives it as a centaur, half man, half horse, a creature sent by mythical forces with some message for her, perhaps. She backs away, clutching her wrap around her.

Then the head of a horse appears, bridled and reined, with a rider mounted above. No centaur, after all, but a hunter, out in the early morning, tracking his quarry, carrying bow and knife and a blunt club through his belt.

It is Leonello, friend and *consigliere* of Alfonso. She recognises the bright hair under the hunter's hat. Slung over his saddle, suspended from their heels, are the slack, loose bodies of three hares, eyes resolutely shut, forepaws defenceless and dangling.

He brings the horse to a standstill and rests his hands on his pommel, looking down at her. She looks back. The eyes under his hat are unsmiling, expressionless. She is filled with an urge to say to him: why do you dislike me so, whatever did I do to displease you? The words are there, ready, in her mouth. It baffles her, this instant and instinctive hostility; she has come across its like before and it is always perplexing, why someone should hate her on sight. She has done nothing to warrant it; it causes her a small but nagging injury, like the sting of a nettle.

She says none of this, of course. She raises her head and looks him in the eye, as she has been taught – she can feel her Spanish mamma's pride as she stands undaunted by this man on a horse – and wishes him a good day.

He nods at her, once, the horse shifting under him. Its flanks, she notices, are damp, its sides heaving.

'Good day to you,' he says, in the curious way that he has, barely moving his lips, his words leaning into each other, 'Duchess.'

The final word is spoken with a drawn-out emphasis. It is an utterance that has been held back by a minuscule but deliberate pause. She knows it; he knows it. It has air and space around it, that word, that title, and in that space swarm many things he is not saying, numerous ideas he is thinking but at the same time withholding.

Lucrezia does what she always does in situations such as this. She did not grow up with four older siblings, who continually put her down, kept her in her place, excluded, teased and belittled her, and learn nothing. The dynamic he is hoping to create is as familiar to her as the shape of her own fingernails. She is expert at dodging such invisible blows.

'How are you, cousin?' she murmurs. She will not raise her voice to him any louder than this; if he wishes to hear her, let him bend down from his saddle. 'I see you have been successful in your hunt.'

How will he take the 'cousin', which lays claim to a familiarity and establishes the irrefutable fact of a marriage that has taken place, possibly against this man's advice and wishes? Lucrezia understands enough about how such things work. Leonello perhaps had a sister or a family member he wished to elevate by marriage to Alfonso. Maybe he favoured a match with a foreign princess or a daughter of another region, and Alfonso went against his advice in choosing her. Or he might bear some grudge against Lucrezia's father's house or influence. Who knows? Lucrezia will not ask; she will never let on to Alfonso or anyone else how this Leonello treats her. To ignore it is to drain it of its power.

Leonello, still high on his horse, waits before he speaks. 'Success indeed.' He adjusts the string harnessing the hares to his saddle, so that the animals, for a moment, appear to stir, to come back to brief life. 'Did you sleep well?'

Despite everything, despite the outer calm she has willed upon herself, she feels her cheeks flush. He knows, of course; he can guess at what took place last night. But she manages to hold his gaze, to look into those gold-brown eyes, unabashed, defiant, and to say, in a steady voice: 'I did, thank you. It is so peaceful here.'

'You weren't disturbed by . . . the wind?'

'Not at all.'

She bestows upon him a gracious yet distant smile, that of her mother.

'I see we are both early risers,' she says, then adds, with the same intonation he used, 'cousin.'

There is a flicker of something across his face – mild surprise, perhaps, at her verbal parrying. Lucrezia realises, in a rush, that she was mistaken: Leonello had no other bride in mind. What he dislikes is that someone else has been allowed, in the finely calibrated hierarchy of court life, to step between him and Alfonso; Leonello enjoys being the new Duke's closest companion. It is his whole purpose and identity, and he doesn't wish to share it with anyone else, including a young wife. This makes her want to laugh – his hostility to her seems suddenly child-like, riven with insecurity.

He eases his feet out of the stirrups and dismounts.

'Allow me,' he says, 'to escort you back to the villa. It is not good for you to be out here alone.'

'There is no reason I should not—'

'Alfonso will not like it.'

'But he—'

'You are, as I'm sure you're aware, a very valuable asset. Perhaps his most valuable, at present, given the situation in Ferrara.'

He speaks these words as if he is in jest, as if the idea of her as a possession, a costly one, is a joke between them. But she is not taken in by his jocular tone; she knows he means every syllable and that his purpose, in saying these things, is to disconcert, to unseat her peace of mind.

'What do you mean? What situation?'

Leonello smirks, slapping the reins across his gloved palms. 'You don't know?'

'I merely—'

'Alfonso hasn't told you?'

'He—'

'I'm referring to the old Duchess, of course, his mother. Her continued refusal to comply with Alfonso's wishes, consorting right under his nose with known Protestants. The edict from the Pope, ordering her exile back to France. And, now, this new desire of hers to take Alfonso's sisters with her.'

Lucrezia listens, aghast. She cannot take in the enormity of this information. 'The Pope?' she repeats. 'He has ordered her exile?'

'Yes.' He slaps his reins across his glove again. 'I assumed you knew.'

'And Alfonso is . . . going against this order?'

'Not against,' he squints up into the morning sun, 'but not necessarily with. He has decreed that the old Duchess must leave only when he chooses. He wants it known that she will act according to his own orders, no one else's.'

'And does he not take a great risk, in provoking the displeasure of the Pope?'

Leonello shrugs. 'That is the least of his worries. If his sisters were to go to the French court with their mother, and find husbands there, their offspring could lay claim to Alfonso's title. And the duchy would pass into the hands of the French. He could lose everything. Everything. Unless—'

'But can he not persuade his sisters to remain with him in Ferrara? Even if the mother must go into exile, then certainly—'

'What he needs to do, as a matter of some urgency,' Leonello says, looking her straight in the eye, 'is produce an heir. And then,' he wafts a gloved hand through the warm air, 'the whole problem disappears. And so here you are. At last. The great hope of Ferrara.' Leonello bares his teeth at her in a smile. 'You must understand the pressing nature of this. There are – how can I put this? – no other possible contenders for his heir.'

Lucrezia takes a small step back, away from the man and his horse. 'I'm not sure what you—'

'No previous, shall we say, indiscretions? No illegitimate issue?'

She shakes her head. 'I—'

'He has never fathered a child.'

Lucrezia looks down, away, anywhere but at this man who spouts words that are so base, that go beyond sense. She wants to cover her ears, to protect them from his vile sentences. But his voice continues, in the same dispassionate tones.

'Most men in his position – as you yourself know only too well – have at least one or two bastards, sometimes more, sown in the folly of youth, children who can be ushered into use, if all else fails. But not our Alfonso. People are beginning to say that perhaps he is incapable in some way, a rumour that must, of course, be disproved.' Leonello draws off one glove then the other. 'So now he has you, daughter of the famous La Fecundissima of Florence, and all those troubles, I am certain, are at an end.'

Leonello tugs at the bridle of his waiting horse and presents her with his arm. 'Shall we?' he says, indicating the villa.

Lucrezia ignores the proffered arm. She will not touch this man; she will not go anywhere with him.

'We all have our part to play,' he says mildly, 'don't we? And mine, at this present moment at least, is to make sure that nothing untoward happens to you.'

Lucrezia is silent. She is considering Leonello's extraordinary revelations. Everything he has said – the sisters who want to leave, their putative children who could strip Alfonso of his dukedom, how he urgently requires an heir, that he might be incapable – threatens to pierce the armour she has constructed against this man and his sardonic tone, his vying for position. But, she reminds herself, she sees him for what he is, a person who always wants to be first, to win in the race for the affections of Alfonso. She will not engage with this particular competition. She will not listen to him, to his nasty whispers and insinuations. She refuses.

'You are not accompanied by your guardsman, are you? You've left the villa without him?' Leonello makes a show of looking up and down the path. 'He is a good man, with a family to provide for – I chose him for the job myself. It would be a pity if he were to be punished for letting you leave alone. Would it not?'

She allows there to be a pause. It grows between them, there on the path. A dignified silence, one that tells him that she is a duchess, above behaviour as petty as his, that she is considering his suggestion and will let him know her answer in good time.

She will not look at him while she maintains this stillness. She considers the path leading away from her, the way it draws the eye along the valley floor, between fields and enclosures, through woodland, narrowing and vanishing. She looks back at the villa, its gables glowing red, the windows reflecting repeating squares of clouds.

'Very well,' she says finally, and she turns back the way she came. Leonello gives the bridle of the horse a sharp tug, and walks along beside her. From their saddle gibbet, the hares swing and sway.

A curving meander of the river

'I must get up,' Lucrezia says, and begins to push back the covers.

'No, no,' Emilia, who is kneeling at the hearth, trying to rekindle the fire, protests. 'You should stay in bed.'

'Really, I must.'

Lucrezia edges towards the side of the bed and pauses there, resting her feet on the floor. The room swings slightly, its corners coming closer, like people in a dance, then receding back to their rightful place. Her limbs feel weak and boneless but she forces herself upright, allowing Emilia to place the furs about her shoulders.

She staggers to a chair, head clasped in her hands. What to do? She poses this question to herself in a tranquil cadence, as if it is of no more significance than what she should wear that day or whom she should invite to a gathering. She needs to do something, to take some course of action. But what? What is a woman supposed to do when she suspects her husband of trying to murder her? To whom should she appeal?

She tells Emilia to bring her ink. Her hand trembles as she presses the penknife to the shaft of the quill, her arm remembering the force of the sickness, still quaking in fear of it.

The knife slices cleanly through. She is in luck. The nib she has cut is a good one – strong, ending in a sharp point that will not fray on first contact. She presses it to the pad of her index finger, watching as the blood flees from it, creating a white depression in her flesh, cringing away from its power.

She lowers the quill into the waiting ink and writes, in a laboured, uneven hand, the words *I need help*. She dips into the ink again: *Please send assistance*.

To whom is she writing? She has no clear idea. To whom should she address this plea? Her mother would dismiss it, saying she is being dramatic, that Lucrezia is, as usual, letting her imagination run away with her. Her father, then. Would he read this letter, if she could get it to him, if it could be brought to his attention in time? Or would it be buried by the heaps of letters arriving at his desk?

And how will she send it? There is no one here to take a letter, no courtier who would be on her side, who would take the risk of dispatching a letter of hers without taking it first to Alfonso. There are only herself and Emilia, her sole ally, whose presence is a secret that no one else must know.

The person she really wants to write to is, of course, Sofia. She wants to say: tell me what to do, how best to face this, how do I escape, I need a plan. She wants to say: help me, please.

Even though she is aware of the letter's futility – she cannot send Emilia with it, for she would be seen by one of the Duke's men – she presses ahead because she must, because there is a modicum of comfort in writing this down, in scratching a small record of what is happening, in forming letters that are bolder now, surer, in the script of the Ancient Greeks she and her siblings studied together as children, in a schoolroom under the eaves of the *palazzo*: *I fear for my life. There is very little time. He means to kill me.* She signs the letter with a single flourishing initial, *L*, and writes *To my sister, Isabella,* at the top.

Emilia takes the letter from her and sets it on the mantelpiece, just as she does with Lucrezia's letters at the *castello*. As if this is a perfectly normal situation, on a perfectly normal day: a mistress writing her correspondence, which her maid will ensure is sent.

With her face averted, Emilia says she will deal with the letter later, and Lucrezia sees that she, too, knows it will never reach Florence.

With effort, Lucrezia raises herself from the chair and goes to the window, where she can watch the course of the river. She needs to think, to weigh options, to come up with a way to get herself out of here.

The river is wide here, complacent and slow, taking a curving meander around the base of the *fortezza*. Its surface is opaque, blistered by deep and unseen currents, its edges lapping at the banks with lassitudinous ochre tongues. It pulls along with it, snared in its current, leaves, twigs, the swollen bellies of small and drowned mammals, particles of mud; the grasses on the bank, it tries to yank out and carry along, but they resist, holding firm to the soil with their long-reaching roots, their green stems supple and playful, bending with and against the currents' wishes.

This Po is unrecognisable from the slender, quick-moving

tributary of the city or the murmuring shallow waters near the *delizia*. Impossible to believe it is the same one, that what she sees here, below this window, will pass through the channels of Ferrara and the villa, and will go on, towards the coast, where it will become erased, swallowed by the mighty, all-powerful sea.

Lucrezia is back on the bed, lying propped on the pillow, her eyes shut, when there comes the sound of horses moving over the drawbridge.

'Who is that now?' Lucrezia says, trying not to listen to the hopeful whispers telling her: *palazzo* soldiers, her father's guardsmen, here to rescue her. Impossible that news of her situation has reached her father's ears, of course, but still her heart beats hard against her bones as she imagines Isabella magically receiving her Greek pleas – which remain on the mantelpiece – raising the alarm, and her father dispatching a whole regiment to come to her defence.

Emilia puts down the stocking she is darning and stands to peer out of the narrow window. 'Oh,' she says, 'it's only . . . them. Finally.'

'Who?'

'You know . . .' She circles her hand in the air. 'What's his name, the artist?'

'What?' Lucrezia lifts her head, wondering if she's heard correctly.

'Yes, him, you know,' Emilia says, uninterested, moving back towards her sewing, 'the one I came with.'

Lucrezia tries to assimilate this information. 'Do you mean Sebastiano Filippi?'

'Who?'

'Il Bastianino?'

'That's him. He—'

'You came here with Il Bastianino? The painter?'

Emilia nods, wetting the end of the thread on her tongue, then poking it through the needle's end. 'I told you that,' she says.

'When?' Lucrezia demands. 'When did you tell me?'

'Earlier, when you were in bed. I said that Baldassare left court, with a small group, but he refused to let me join them. And then that Il Bastianino fellow turned up at the *castello* unannounced, with your portrait, but no one was there to receive him because, naturally, the Duke was here, and Baldassare on his way. And then—'

'Just a moment,' Lucrezia says, holding up her hand, struggling to follow this account. 'How do you know all this?'

Emilia shrugs, as if the answer is obvious. 'Because I was in the courtyard, of course, trying to persuade one of the grooms to let me have a horse, so I could come after you. When I realised he was intending to find the Duke – and you, of course – I intercepted him. Il Bastianino, that is. I told him I knew where the Duke was, and where you were. At some *fortezza* out in the middle of nowhere beyond a village called Bondeno.'

'How on earth did you find that out? I didn't even know where—'

Emilia bites off her thread with sharp teeth. 'I eavesdropped on Baldassare when he was telling the secretaries. I said to Il Bastianino that if he was so desperate to see the Duke, and to give him the finished portrait, he could take me with him. And if he agreed to that, in return I would tell him where to find you all. To tell you the truth,' Emilia adds, 'I think he is after money – his payment for the work of the portrait. I have a feeling that he is—'

'Emilia,' Lucrezia says, her hands over her ears, 'let me understand you. You travelled here with Il Bastianino?'

'Yes,' Emilia says, in tones of impatience. 'What of it? I've told you that three times now, madam. I said I'd take him to you all if he brought me along, and he said to climb up behind one of his men, then, if I was in a fix, so I—'

'But,' Lucrezia tries to think what she needs to clarify in this confusing turn of events, 'why is he just arriving now? You have been here an hour or more so—'

'Well, would you believe it, we got all the way here, and at the end of the driveway, he said he wanted to stop and walk into the woods.' Emilia screws up her face in disapproval. 'Something about how he needed to examine the light falling on the branches, or some such nonsense. So I got down off the horse and said I wasn't waiting around, light or no light. And I just walked up the drive and came in through the back entrance. There was such confusion and noise in the kitchen, with everyone shouting to each other about the Duke's breakfast and the arrival of extra people from court, that no one questioned who I was or what I was doing there. I just asked one of the kitchen boys where you were. And here I am.'

'Here you are,' Lucrezia murmurs. 'You are so much cleverer than me.'

'Nonsense.' Emilia puts aside her darning. 'Now, get back under those blankets, please, madam. You mustn't catch a chill. That would be the very worst thing at this—'

Lucrezia waves her away. 'Ssh,' she says. 'Let me be. I need a moment to think.'

And so Lucrezia thinks. She thinks about Leonello Baldassare, her husband's loyal *consigliere*, riding to the *fortezza*. The dinner last night. The venison, the wine, the sickness in the dark. She thinks about the unexpected appearance of the court artist, Il Bastianino, with her finished portrait, at the *castello*. Emilia insisting that he bring her with him, bargaining with him so that he would agree to take her. And Alfonso. She thinks about Alfonso. Why he left her bed. Why he hasn't yet been in to see her this morning. Where he might be right now – somewhere below, in the dining room, or outside hunting or conferring with Baldassare. And what his next move might be. If he thought she'd eaten as much as he'd intended her to last night, he might suspect she is already dead. Or at least very sick indeed. He might be counting on that, might at that very moment be telling Baldassare that he had put into practice their poisoning plan, that she had had no suspicions, that she fell for it, and hasn't appeared this morning, just as they had planned. And perhaps he means to come into her chamber very soon, in order apparently to discover the dead body of his young wife, raise the alarm, call a doctor, but – alas – it's too late. She thinks about how everything will have been carefully planned, so carefully, down to every last detail. Except, of course, that she was not very hungry last night. Except that the artist will have surprised Alfonso by turning up unannounced at his country *fortezza*, at his secret destination. Which is why, Lucrezia thinks, Alfonso has not yet appeared in her room, to discover that she is very much alive.

Il Bastianino, in his haste, in his desire for money, has given her time. Just a little, but perhaps enough to wrongfoot the Duke. She will not stay here in this damp chamber, like a lamb in an enclosure, waiting for the axe to fall, she will surprise her husband.

Lucrezia draws her hands over her face, and swings her legs off the edge of the bed.

'Emilia,' she says, 'help me get dressed.'

Honey water

Delizia, near Voghiera, 1560

The strangest thing, for Lucrezia, about life at the *delizia*, is that so little is required of her. She is accustomed to days with structure, according to a routine imposed by her mother: a strict rotation of Mass, religious instruction, meals, personal care and manners, tuition, lessons in music, deportment and languages. Here, there is no one to tell her that she must do this, or wear that, go to this room or that room; no tutor appears before her to say that she must make a fair copy of this manuscript or that sketch. Nobody tells her that she is lacking in this regard or that. She can stay in bed, drowsing or day-dreaming until midday. She can wear whatever she wants: there is no stern-faced Mamma bursting into her chamber to say, not that gown, whatever were you thinking, put this on, now, quick, make haste, there are guests waiting, why is your hair not done, where is the maid, why are you wasting your time painting that tiny piece of wood over and over again, what means this strange and repetitive task? She can squander a whole day, should the mood take her, on drawing the distant Apennines, giving each peak a ludic facial expression, or making a tiny painting of a bumblebee with its head buried in a flower (beneath which is a girl growing wings and taking to the sky – but nobody need ever know that). Even meals can be ordered whenever she likes; if she feels hunger uncurl in her stomach, she may ring a bell and a servant from the kitchen will come hurrying along a corridor, bearing a platter of cheeses, fruits, jellies, miniature pies – whatever she feels like eating.

Alfonso comes and goes; sometimes he looks in on her in the mornings, or he might take a turn about the loggia with her when the heat of the day has receded. He goes riding in the forest with Leonello and his men. He spends a great deal of time shut up in his receiving room, where people from court arrive and depart all the time; Lucrezia can see this window lit up, late, across the courtyard. She never disturbs him there but passes quietly, her head down.

There is one day when they have just begun their meal, and Alfonso is talking about seeing a family of deer that morning, saying that perhaps he will take her to the spot so that she, too, can see them, and she is just about to answer him but a secretary appears at the open window, rapping gently on the wood. Alfonso rises, mid-sentence, and leaves. Lucrezia is alone, then, with only the vases of flowers for company, an image in her head of her and Alfonso riding together through the woods. She eats a little food, she adjusts the arrangement of lace around her collar, and watches as the servants come in and out to clear plates and present new ones. Before long, there is so much food on the table, far more than she could ever eat, and the sight of yet more servants and more dishes arriving makes her laugh, behind her hand at first and then more overtly. The servants grin back at her, delighted with the joke of so much food, pleased to see their little duchess so happy. When Alfonso returns, much later, she is surrounded by an opulent, uneaten banquet, and she turns to him gaily, saying: 'I hope you've worked up an appetite in your office because, look, can you believe—'

She stops. His face is strained and oddly haggard. He sits down and picks up his napkin as if it weighs heavily in his hand.

Two servants enter through the door, with a playful cry – 'Look now, Your Highness!' – bearing still more food to entertain the Duchess. On seeing their master's demeanour, however, they fall silent, leave the dishes and flit away.

Alfonso, his head lowered, takes a mouthful of ham and chews it rapidly, shifting himself in his chair.

'That must be quite cold by now,' Lucrezia murmurs, and she is recalling the soothing, lulling way her mother speaks to her father when he is preoccupied by problems in his province – she can bring off these tones, can't she? 'Let me call and ask them to warm it for you, so that—'

'No need,' he answers, removing a piece of gristle from between his teeth and laying it on the rim of his plate.

She casts her gaze around the room, seeking a topic to divert him. That is what good wives do: take their husband's minds off whatever troubles are besieging them. How, though, should she do this? Her mother would sometimes stroke her father's brow or tweak his beard. Lucrezia does not dare try this with him.

'My apologies,' he says suddenly, making her jump, 'for leaving you so long at the table.'

'Oh,' she says, 'it's of no consequence. You have a great deal on your mind. I know that.' She ventures to put out her hand and brush the backs of his fingers. 'It is only to be expected. My father is exactly the same, with so many demands on his time and attention, always being called away exactly like that. I am only sorry you must work so hard.'

He is watching the action of her hand, stroking his, as if observing an animal. Then he looks at her, his eyes travelling all over her face, seeming to check that she means what she is saying.

'Is there . . .' she dares to push her fingers between his '. . . can you say . . . did that man bring bad news? I would like to know about what is happening, if you are willing to tell me. Perhaps I can help you in some way or—'

He lets out a short exhalation that sounds almost like a laugh. 'You wish to help me?'

She draws back. She would like to take her hand from his, but wills herself to let it remain.

'Yes,' she says, with dignity, 'of course.'

He picks up his cup, smiling wryly, and takes a long sip of wine.

'If there is something at court,' she continues, 'or some family matter that is causing you concern, maybe I could . . .'

He puts down his cup with a bang. The look on his face – flaring, suspicious – causes the words to shrivel in her mouth.

'What do you know of my family?' he asks, low and deliberate. 'Or of my court?'

'Nothing.'

'What have you heard? What have you been told?'

'As I said – nothing.'

He leans forward. The hand beneath hers turns upwards and imprisons her fingers in a strong, cool grasp.

'Your father? He has told you something?'

She shakes her head.

'Or someone else in Florence? Your mother?'

'No.'

'Someone here?'

She sees, for a moment, a man on a path, his horse behind him, and three hares strung from a saddle. She could not say how but she knows it would be a bad idea to disclose what Baldassare has told her.

'No,' she says again.

He remains motionless, and silent, for several moments, still gripping her hand, still leaning towards her. She keeps her gaze on his, steady and unwavering, but inside she is striving to empty her mind, to keep it blank as parchment; she is letting all she knows drain away. She will not admit to any knowledge, the conversation with Baldassare about Alfonso's sisters wanting to leave for France, or the instruction she received from her father, from Vitelli, about the Ferrara court and how it has been riven with dissent since the old Duke's death, about the problems Alfonso is facing with his widowed mother, the rumours of her insurrection and disruption to his rule, the struggle he is having in getting the province to obey him. She knows none of this; she has heard nothing; she has forgotten it; she never knew it. She presents to her husband a face that is pleasant and inexperienced. She is his young, guileless wife who is entirely ignorant about the governance of Ferrara.

After an agonisingly long time, he seems to relent. He sits back, he takes another morsel of meat.

'I would never,' he says, as he chews, resting his head on the back of his chair, 'talk to you about such matters. I wouldn't wish to burden you with—'

'Oh, but you can. It would be far from a burden and—'

He allows a steely pause for her interruption. 'It does not,' he continues, 'fall within the role of a wife.'

'But it could. I am—'

'Perhaps I am not making myself clear,' he says, rising from his chair and coming to stand behind her. 'It does not fall within the role of my wife, my duchess.'

'I see,' she says, trying to twist her neck so that she can see him, but he remains just out of sight, his hands resting on her shoulders.

'My wife,' he leans in close, and between each word, he presses a kiss to the skin beneath her ear, 'has quite another role. And one I think she will be fulfilling very soon.'

As snow collects in a hollow, dread begins to fill her, forming great unseen drifts against her edges. She casts her eyes over the food spread across the table: roast meats, almond tarts, a milk pudding, apricots cut in half and filled with cheese, flowers fried in oil.

'Don't you want to eat something?' she says. 'Aren't you hungry?'

'Not for food,' he murmurs. 'Come. Let's go.'

During her days at the *delizia*, nothing is asked of her; at night, however, a great deal is expected. She has to give and surrender herself, to hand over her being to another, to grant him access and ingress, each night, every night. He is like a man possessed, a man on a quest: to conceive an heir, to ensure the continuation of his line. He goes at the task in the same way he approaches everything, with determined concentration and focus.

He becomes, at night, in her chamber, someone quite other. He sheds the skin of the Duke – it drops off him, she believes, along with the clothes he tosses aside as he crosses the floor between doorway and bed. He likes to rip back the sheets and look at her. This she finds hard to bear – the sudden shock of night air meeting her bare skin. She must not squirm with the embarrassment, must not hide herself or shut her eyes: he doesn't like to see her do this. He is no longer Alfonso, anyway, no longer the man who sat with her at the long table over dinner. He has changed, shifted his shape, discarded that guise. He is a creature from myth, all skin and sinew and shocking swathes of hair; he is a river god, a water monster, crawled up from the Po river that meanders along the valley floor, assuming human shape to make his way to her chamber, to her bed, sliding himself between her bedlinen, and seizing her with his webbed fingers, rubbing his scaled skin against hers, subduing her with strength gained in aquatic depths, in struggles with twisting currents, the hidden gills in his neck pulsing and pulsing, drawing in the alien air of the room.

At this point, she is permitted to shut her eyes, while he enters a state that is with her, yet not. He is there, unmistakably, overwhelmingly. And yet he is elsewhere. He is transported, his face unrecognisable, in those moments when she forgets and opens her eyes and sees the grotesque mask above her: a face of fury, of intent, of unslakable need. She is quite forgotten, she thinks. All she has to do now is wait, count down the moments. The river god is enacting his nightly ritual, seeking that mysterious and necessary relief, pursuing his urgent need for human congress, pushing and pushing, as if to make his mark within her, his skin expressing droplets of river water, which drip down on to her, as if he contains the silty depths within him, as if all he seeks is to release them into her, so that she, too, might become, like him, a water creature, a mer-girl.

She has learnt to breathe, to request her muscles not to resist, to press herself further into the mattress to find a small amount of space for herself, not to flinch at the touch of his hand or other parts of his body. She has found that Isabella is right, that it does hurt less as time goes on, that he does not like it if she makes her displeasure evident, that the act takes longer if she absents her body, if she lies there in passive stillness. He is happier, and it will be over sooner, if she mirrors his movements, his expressions, if she smiles when he smiles, if she sighs when he sighs, if she meets his eye.

She might be anyone, at these times.

But she is not anyone. She is his wife, bound unto him by the Church, by her father. She is the girl who took her dead sister's place. She is the link between the House of Tuscany and the House of Ferrara, and will bear children who can lay claim to both provinces, both houses. This is the price to be paid for the freedom of the *delizia*.

She also knows that it will not always be so. They cannot remain at the *delizia* for ever. Soon, Alfonso will have to return to Ferrara, and she will go with him, and she will be expected to reside there, in the *castello*, alongside his mother and sisters. She has no idea how she will be received, how Alfonso's family will treat her, whether they will be kind to her, or hostile, or suspicious, or whether the court itself will be a place of welcome or one of disharmony and distrust. The *delizia* and all its charms are just for now. Before long, their lives will be transported to Ferrara, her marriage will begin in earnest, and she will need to take up her role as duchess consort.

Soon, too, she knows that she will be with child. She may be already.

This thought resides within her, like the engraved brass button she once swallowed as a child, after a dare from Isabella and Maria, never to be seen again. She thinks of her mother, that pale body swelling and shrinking inside its garments, swelling and shrinking, over and over again, her spine weakened from the many pregnancies, the iron corset made for her by the physician, who said it was required to support Eleanora's back. La Fecundissima. She thinks, too, of the women who do not survive the act of birth – the many cousins, aunts and wives of courtiers who drop out of sight, who are spoken of in hushed tones, who are prayed for in the chapel. Will she, Lucrezia, share this fate? Or will she be one of the fortunate, who lives through to the other side, able to watch her children grow into adults?

She wants to ask him this, sometimes, in the middle of these nocturnal couplings, when he is shifting her into one position, then another and another, as if her body is a puzzle he needs to solve, or a tract of land he must conquer, when he is on the verge of emptying himself into her, when he clings to her as if he is drowning or choking in the warm, dry air of the chamber and she is his last hope of returning to his rightful river state. She wants to turn her face towards the shell whorl of his ear and whisper: what if I don't survive? What if this kills me? Do you ever think of that?

If he hears her, silently mouthing such things, he is never moved to make a reply.

It is mid-morning in the villa and Lucrezia is wandering about her chamber, picking things up and putting them down: a brush, a beaded purse, a carved wooden bowl, a horn cup. She drifts to the window overlooking the courtyard, then to the one on the opposite wall, with a view to the mountains. She puts on her *zimarra*. Then, finding it too hot, she lets it slide to the floor.

Alfonso did not stay in her bed last night. Sometimes he falls straight to sleep afterwards, and lies there, insensible until morning, sprawled across the sheets. Other times, the act seems to make him restive, fills him with a peculiar energy; she has learnt that if she feigns sleep at this moment, he will rise from the bed carefully, put on his clothes and leave the room. Always, before he goes, he will lean over, press a light kiss to her temple. The first time he did this, she flinched from the shock, and almost reared up from the mattress; now, however, she has learnt to expect it, even to look forward to it. No one, she believes, has ever kissed her in her sleep before. She likes to place a palm over the place, after he has left the room, as if to keep it there, to stop it floating off into the air, like pollen.

Lucrezia stands at the window, gazing out over the orna-mental gardens, with their mathematically angled hedges and raked paths. Beyond them is the dense forest of Alfonso's hunting grounds; beyond that the flat plain of the valley and, far beyond, the mountains. Beyond them, she knows, is Florence, her family, the *palazzo*, but she will not think about them, refuses to picture them all there, without her.

She allows her eyes to focus instead on the glass of the window where, she sees, a girl is looking back at her. She has a flushed, well-slept appearance: eyes bright, cheeks pink. The shadowy crescents that have always lurked under her eyes, giving her a sleepless and watchful aspect, have vanished. Lucrezia has never considered herself to be pretty, like Isabella or Maria. She has a look of both: the heavy-lidded eyes and pronounced bottom lip. But, somehow, the arrangement of her features has never been as pleasing as theirs. The difference is subtle but there – her eyes are deeper set, her cheeks thinner, her chin narrower. She has an unsettled, pensive air; even in repose, her face harbours a look of preoccupation. This girl in the window, however, might be thought attractive. Beautiful, even.

Lucrezia turns one way, then the other. What is this change that has come over her? She no longer appears so sallow and pasty; her mother could not now pinch her cheek and say, you look as though you live under a stone.

Swift as an arrow, a thought streaks through her head, pulling a disquieting suggestion after it. Surely not. Lucrezia lifts both hands and presses them to her abdomen. Can it be that? But such a state is said to rob a woman of her beauty, not the other way round.

She is assessing her stomach, its muscular spring, wondering if it feels any different, deciding it does, then that it doesn't, when she is startled by a knock at the door.

Immediately, she snatches her hands away from her middle. Is it him? Alfonso? Is he back to—?

She smothers the thought. Not when the sun is high in the sky, when there is work to be done, letters to answer, documents to attend to.

She clears her throat, clasping her hands in front of her, then moving them quickly behind her, then placing them on her hips. How do her hands and arms usually look? Where do they naturally fall? She cannot for the life of her remember.

'Come in,' she calls.

The door is pushed open and Emilia steps into the room. Her appearance is so welcome that Lucrezia lets out an involuntary sound of relief.

'If you please, madam,' Emilia begins, clearly confused by this reception, 'His Highness asked me to come and prepare you for the day. I told him you might be sleeping but he said he has something to show you and—'

'Very well,' Lucrezia says. 'Thank you, Emilia. Let us begin.'

Emilia nods, then takes a square of linen and rubs it over Lucrezia's skin. Then she warms violet oil in her palm, massaging it into the legs, chest and back. Lucrezia submits to these ministrations in silence, lifting an arm, turning a wrist, bending at the knees, twisting her neck one way, then the other. This series of preparations always makes her think of her mother: it was she, after all, who devised them, who decreed the strict order in which they should happen, who insisted that all *palazzo* handmaids be taught them, so that all the daughters be turned out to their best advantage.

Lucrezia sighs. She knows, and Emilia knows, that after the violet oil must come the foot washing, then the nail cleaning, then the bean-flower water on the face, then the hair brushing. How tedious it is, all this upkeep, all this tending, as a gardener must weed a flowerbed or trim a hedge. Why must she and Emilia enact this ritual every day? Does it make that much of a difference? It occurs to her, for the first time, that she need not submit to this, if she doesn't want to. There is no one here to check, no one here to inspect her.

The idea seems to infiltrate her from below, like a plant drawing up water, rising through her legs, into her torso. It feels revelatory, phenomenal. She wouldn't be surprised if she looked down and discovered she was an entirely different person.

'Leave it,' she says, pulling her hand out of Emilia's grasp.

'But . . .' Emilia looks puzzled, holding the stripped hazeltwig, with which she is preparing to push down Lucrezia's cuticles '. . . I was always instructed that—'

'Just attend to my hair, please.'

Emilia's hand puts down the twig, letting it go with reluctance, and hovers over the bottle of bean-flower water.

'Shall I . . .?'

Lucrezia shakes her head. 'Just the hair.'

She sits resolutely on the stool, blood pumping through her veins.

'And don't put it into the *scuffia*. It's too hot today for that. Plait it loosely and let it be free to hang down my back.'

Emilia looks as if she may speak, but then thinks better of it. She takes the brush and combs, and begins to divide the hair into sections.

'It is permissible for a woman to wear her hair uncovered for the first year of marriage,' Lucrezia says, lifting her chin and staring at herself in the mirror, as if daring her reflection to disagree.

'Yes, madam.'

'The Duke told me that. It is the custom in Ferrara.'

'Yes, madam.'

'We are not in Florence now.'

'No, madam.'

She shifts her glance to the serving girl in the mirror; their eyes meet briefly and Lucrezia sees that Emilia is suppressing a smile; a short giggle escapes Lucrezia.

'I don't know what Her Highness, your mother, would say,' Emilia mutters, through a mouthful of pins.

'She's not here.'

'True.'

Lucrezia continues to look at herself and Emilia in the mirror. 'We have similar colouring,' she says, 'you and I, do we not?'

Emilia shrugs. 'Your Grace's hair has more red, and is finer. Much longer, too. My father was a guard from Switzerland and my mother said I got my fair hair from him.'

'Was he a nice man?'

'I never knew him, madam.'

Lucrezia thinks about this, about the Swiss Guards and their barracks in the basement of the *palazzo*: broad, strapping men, they are, with pale blue eyes.

'Why is it,' Lucrezia says, fiddling with a hairpin, 'I never saw you at the *palazzo* before my wedding day?'

Emilia seems to hesitate a moment, then resumes brushing with doubled effort. 'I don't know, madam.'

'Were you perhaps a servant elsewhere?'

Emilia looks up, surprised. 'No, not at all. I was born in the *palazzo*. I lived there all my life.'

'So why did we never see each other before?'

Emilia brings the brush down through the hair, twice, before answering. 'I used to see you, madam, quite often,' the maid speaks with care, as if choosing her words, 'when you were a very little girl, but it's likely you don't remember. And I used to see you again, when you were bigger, from time to time. I worked in the lower floors, alongside my mother, so was not often in your presence.'

'Where does your mother work?'

'In the kitchens.'

The terseness of this reply makes Lucrezia lift her eyes from the brass pin in her fingers to the servant standing behind her in the mirror. Emilia's beautiful, ravaged face is shuttered, deliberately blank.

'Is your mother . . .?' Lucrezia says tentatively.

'She died, madam.'

'Oh, I am so sorry, Emilia. I—'

'Three months past.'

'May God have mercy on her soul.'

'Thank you, madam. I . . . she . . .' Emilia frowns and bites her lip, then speaks in a rush: 'My mother was particularly fond of you. When Sofia asked for me to be trained as your maidservant, she was so pleased. It made her . . . very happy to know I would be with you.'

'Your mother was fond of me?' Lucrezia repeats.

'Yes . . . she . . .' Emilia hesitates again, the brush aloft. 'Did Sofia never say?'

'Say what?'

'My mother was . . . your *balia*. Your milk-mother. You didn't know that?'

'I did not.' Lucrezia stares at Emilia in amazement. 'I knew it was a woman in the kitchens but I was never told . . . I'm sorry, I had no idea. So, you were . . .?'

Emilia smiles at her as she gathers the mass of her hair and, with practised movements, separates it into three.

'I am, I think, two years older than you. I remember you as a young baby. I used to play with you. You were there when I . . .' Emilia gestures towards the scar on her face '. . . when I was injured.'

'How did it happen?'

'You and I were playing a game of hide-and-seek. We'd been told not to play near the fire. A boiling pot fell. It missed you by this much.' Emilia holds up a hand, finger and thumb indicating a tiny space between them. 'You screamed when it happened, as if you had been the one hurt, and you hugged me very tightly. I've never forgotten that.'

'Emilia, how terrible. I—'

Emilia gives a sad smile. 'Better that it was me and not you.'

'Better that it had been neither of us.'

'But if it had to be one of us, it was better that it was me who was disfigured.'

Both girls are silent for a moment. Lucrezia tries to think of something to say, to parry this sentiment, and she is searching her memory for any traces of the incident – the hide-and-seek, the clang of a pot falling to the ground, the scorch and steam of boiling water.

Emilia, however, is moving on.

'Then,' she continues, 'when you were older, when you were walking and talking already, Sofia used to smuggle you down to the kitchens.'

'Smuggle me? Why?'

'This was after you were sent back to the nursery. Sometimes you would cry and cry, and nobody could quiet you, and the only thing that would soothe you was . . .' Emilia looks stricken. 'This is not to disrespect your mother, Her Grace, you understand, I mean no offence, madam—'

'I am not offended. Go on. Tell me about Sofia and the smuggling.'

'Well, she used to bring you down to the kitchens. You would be crying and crying, and then when you saw my mother, you would stop and hold out your arms, with a big smile, your eyes still streaming with tears. Everyone would laugh. I used to take you under the kitchen table – my mother gave us pots and spoons to play with, and we used to make messes with flour, and sometimes—'

This extraordinary speech is interrupted by the door opening once more – it bangs back against the wall, revealing Alfonso, standing there, his face shadowed by a soft cap.

'Is all ready?' he asks.

Emilia starts, drops the brush, bends to retrieve it, with her head bowed.

'Very nearly, Your Highness.'

'I am just coming,' Lucrezia says, moving her eyes towards him, so that Emilia may finish plaiting her hair.

'I have a surprise for you,' he murmurs, and she can hear that he is smiling. 'Come, quick as you can.'

Alfonso turns and strides off down the corridor.

Emilia leans towards her. 'I have heard that there is trouble at court,' she whispers.

'In Florence?'

'No, madam. Ferrara.'

Lucrezia turns in her seat. 'What trouble? What have you heard?'

Emilia glances through the open door, as if to be sure the Duke isn't lurking there. 'A servant who came with the emissary from Ferrara this morning told one of the grooms, who told a housemaid, who told me, that Her Highness, the Duke's mother, is at this very moment secretly preparing to leave the Ferrara court. She means to go before His Grace, the Duke, finds out but, of course, he has people at court who are watching her and one of them—'

'Why would she do that? Alfonso told me she would not be leaving for France until he and I had arrived to pay our respects, and then, in time—'

'No. It turns out she's been planning this for a while, ever since His Grace last went to court. Remember when he left in the middle of our journey? Apparently, he and his mother had a terrible row, and ever since she has been determined to go. Last night, the informant said, she ordered the horses and carriages be made ready for tomorrow so that—'

'Poor Alfonso,' Lucrezia exclaims. 'I must . . .' She starts to stand up, but then sinks back into her chair. What must she do? What can she say, when he has made it clear that he doesn't like her to know of these things? 'I should . . .'

'I heard that the Pope himself,' Emilia whispers, awed, 'ordered her exile, but His Grace, the Duke, wants it to be known that his mother will leave when it pleases him.'

'Yes, I know.'

'But now it seems that her daughters are intending to leave, too, and so—'

'She means to take Alfonso's sisters with her?' Lucrezia interrupts. 'He won't like that. He'll never allow it and—'

'Why not? Why can't the sisters go with their mother, if they—'

Lucrezia shakes her head. 'Doesn't matter. Go on. Tell me what else you know.'

Emilia shrugs. 'I heard the argument between the Duke and his mother is about religion. Which is passing strange but then the old Duchess, being French, may be—'

'She is a Protestant,' Lucrezia says, 'and was meant to have given it up but it seems . . .'

Emilia crosses herself, quickly, efficiently, as if to protect herself from such heresy. 'Whatever she is, the Duke was very unhappy when the emissary told him all this. The servant who was in the next room said that he heard the Duke throw something at the wall and say that he'd have his mother and his sisters captured and whipped if they disobeyed him like this. Can you imagine? A man's mother—'

'He would never have said that,' Lucrezia cuts in. 'The servant must have misheard. Alfonso was perhaps speaking of a courtier, or . . . or a valet. His mother is Renée de France. She is a duchess in her own right. He would never, with a noblewoman . . .'

'Yes, madam.' Emilia lowers her head. 'I'm sure you are right.'

Lucrezia stands up abruptly. Her scalp feels strained where the pins have been inserted at the temples; her *camiciotto* is pinching under the arms. The day, which had begun so well, seems suddenly ominous and pitted with danger.

'Everyone is saying that the Duke will go to Ferrara as soon as he can.' Emilia's words continue to rattle on as she fixes the neckline of Lucrezia's gown. 'I don't know what he'll do there but—'

'Thank you, Emilia,' Lucrezia says, waving her off. 'You may go.'

She crosses the room and steps into the corridor, shutting the door behind her with a forceful snap, leaving the maid to restore the chamber to order.

When she steps outside into the loggia, she is assaulted by glaring white daylight. It has poured into the courtyard, filling it mercilessly to the brim; the sky above the rectangular space seems to seethe and glower, like a furnace, breathing ferocious fumes down on to the villa.

Her eyes, accustomed to the dim cool of the interior, cannot adjust. She takes a step, and another, then has to lean her hand against a pillar, half closing her lids.

Before her, she sees the bleached shapes of people: two standing together opposite another. The heat and the light seem to strip them of all colour and contour, so that they resemble skeletons or branchless trees. She is aware of their voices, an ascending and *tremulo* lilt, weaving through the thick air. She can discern the tones of her husband, deep and rumbling, a voice of a slightly higher pitch, and another, flat in intonation and delivered down the nose – Leonello, she would guess.

Lucrezia adjusts her head; she strains her ears. Like a plant, she leans out towards the light, extending her neck, opening herself out to whatever the air may hold.

Increasingly erratic, she hears her husband murmur. An insult, says Leonello, designed specifically to undermine you, and you cannot be seen to let this pass. You must make an example of her, of all of them. And the third man, the emissary, says: perhaps if Her Highness and her daughters could be—

A figure, tall and lean, breaks away from the arrangement, and comes towards her, limbs and torso filling out as it gets nearer, acquiring dimension and features. A finely embroidered shirt, a head of black hair.

'Lucrezia,' Alfonso says, in that way he has, barely moving his lips to form the word, and he reaches for her hand.

She looks up at him. He does not seem like someone who has received bad news or had a terrible rupture with his mother or whose court is in dangerous uproar. There is not a single glimmer of tension on his face: he looks calm and poised. Can what Emilia said be true? Is it possible she has misunderstood?

'Shall we walk?' he asks, tipping his head in a minuscule motion towards the men he has so recently left, indicating that they are excluded from this pairing, that he finds their presence irksome and wants only to be with her. How adroit he is at communicating so much with so little.

'Of course,' she says.

He draws her arm through his and they proceed along the length of the loggia. Her gown trails after them, making a *suuh-suuh* sound over the tiles. Lucrezia is aware of Leonello and the other man observing them; she focuses her gaze on the end of the walkway, then her husband, who is saying something to her about a hunt he undertook that morning, then the walkway again. She will not turn her head towards the watchers, not let them know she even cares that they are there: she wants Alfonso to believe she knows nothing. This, at least, she can do for him.

As they near the end of the loggia, Alfonso does something unexpected. In one swift movement, he steps behind her, and covers her eyes. She cannot see, suddenly, she cannot move; his palms obliterate most of her face, his arms pinion hers, the length of his body is pressed against her back.

She draws in a quick, shallow breath. How can she tell him that this is a game for which she has a particular dislike? Maria had a habit of seizing her, blindfolding her, either with her hands or lengths of cloth, then leading her carelessly about the nursery for sport, laughing when she bumped into chairs or tripped over fenders.

Her hands rise up of their own accord. Instead of her own familiar features – the protrusion of her nose, the smoothness of her cheeks and brow – she feels instead fingers, the hair on his wrists, the ridged row of his wide knuckles. She tries to prise his hands away in what she hopes is a playful manner, but she feels her panic rising. What is he doing? Why is this happening? Does it have anything to do with his mother or the trouble at court?

'I have a surprise for you,' she hears him murmur.

'For me?' she says, trying to keep her voice even. He would never lead her deliberately into a hard object. He would never want her to bruise her shins or her knees. Would he?

'Yes. I . . .' there is a rare hesitation in his speech '. . . I have to go away, unexpectedly.'

'Where?' she hears herself ask, even though she knows the answer.

'To Ferrara. I shall be gone a day. Perhaps two. No more than that. There is something that requires my presence, unfortunately, otherwise I would leave it to Leonello. So I shall have to go, my little bride, but not for long.'

'I could . . . come with you?' she suggests, from behind his hands. She can feel the heat and sweat gathering where his skin touches hers, her lashes scything against his palms.

'Not this time. Before long, I will take you to Ferrara, to present you at court. I had thought we would spend another month or so here but I think we shall need to return sooner than that now. We will ride through the city gates together – there will be a festival, people will line the streets, and all shall see you for the beauty you are. But for today, I have to travel quickly and without fuss.'

'So you wish me to remain here?'

'You will be quite safe. I am taking Leo but everyone else stays. You will have all the guards, and the servants, the padre, and . . .'

He steers her around a corner, then removes his hands, placing them instead on her waist.

She blinks. The light is brighter than ever, beating down on their heads.

Before her is the shape of something, its outline pulsing against the light, its shadow hinging away from it on the ground. A beast of some sort – an enormous dog. No, a horse. What is it?

She holds up a hand to shade her face. There, tied to a hazel tree, is an animal like a horse, but smaller, with a graceful, sloping head and a long, whisking tail. It is pure white, from the long mane that drapes over its neck, down to the smooth fetlocks. Strapped around its middle is a red leather side-saddle, embossed in gilt, with gold bells on its fringes.

'This is . . . for me?' she whispers.

'For you,' Alfonso says, embracing her from behind, his chin resting on her head. 'She is a rare creature, this. Half horse, half donkey. She was bred by a farmer near here. A white mule. They come along perhaps once every hundred years or so. As soon as I heard about it, I arranged to buy it. And I want you to have it, my gift to you.'

Without further discourse, he lifts her from the ground, his hands encircling her waist, and carries her from the loggia step towards the mule, placing her on the red saddle.

'There,' he says, lifting her leg so that it fits over the support, adjusting the stirrup so that her foot rests comfortably in it. 'And there,' he puts the slender red-and-gold reins into her hand. Then he seizes the bridle and clicks his tongue. The mule moves forward, startling into life.

They make their way around the lower courtyard, around the hazel tree, flickering in and out of the shadows cast by the villa's roof. The mule's rhythm is steady and lulling; she lifts her legs high, with the graceful gait of a dancer. Lucrezia grips the reins, straightens her back, allowing her spine to sway with the beast's steps. She smooths the white velvet of the mule's flank with her palms, leans out to watch the pale hoofs pick their delicate way over the earth.

Alfonso leads her one way, then the other. They pass Leonello and the emissary, who fall silent as they approach. The emissary gives a low bow as Lucrezia rides by, the embossed saddle squeaking, the little bells jingling. Alfonso is talking about the mule and how she will be stabled with the horses, that horses are calmed by the presence of a mule, and Lucrezia may order her to be saddled whenever she likes.

Lucrezia watches the back of her husband's head as he walks beside the beast, the movement of his shoulders beneath his shirt, his loose and assured grip on the bridle, the way he pats the mule's milk-white neck and lowers his face to kiss the soft nose.

They are conversing like any husband and wife. He is talking about how she has a good seat on the animal; she is replying that she was given riding lessons as a child, on a pony, by the groomsmen in the *palazzo*, that her father considered it part of their education. Alfonso is saying, that was very sensible, and he will do the same with his own children, get them riding from a young age. Lucrezia feels a blush fire her cheeks, and Alfonso, glancing back at her, seems to decide to raise his stakes by adding that the mule will be ideal for her when she is with child. He would not have the woman carrying his heir up on a horse – what man in his right mind would? – but a mule would provide appropriate exercise, gentle and not too excitable.

He is running his hand over the mule's mane as he says this. She notices, irrelevantly, that he has an ink stain on his wrist, and another on his index finger. She is trying to keep her thoughts away from heirs and their riding lessons, from the idea of this mule being bought in preparation for her pregnancies. She watches him insert his thumb beneath the bridle straps, as if to check it isn't chafing.

A man who cares about the comfort of a mere beast could not possibly threaten to have his mother and sisters captured and whipped. It is unthinkable.

She wants to ask him about the problem he is facing, whether it is true that his mother is disobeying his orders and returning to France without his permission, what he will do to prevent it, and will his sisters really leave his court and pledge allegiance to another. She wants to suggest that he might try requesting that his mother stay, telling her he would miss her and his sisters if they left. Have you, she wants to ask him, tried kindness instead of commands? It would, she knows, be a scandal for him if they were to leave court when he has ordered them to remain: she has witnessed her father and his advisers talk in derisive tones about men who fail to wield power over their families or their wives. What kind of authority can a man have over a province if he cannot keep his women in check? It gives a fatal impression of weakness to one's enemies, who are always watching. She has heard her father say this. Much can be gleaned from the way a man resolves family problems: this mantra has been repeated to her, by her mother, by Sofia, by various courtiers, with a hint of pride, for Lucrezia's father stood for no disloyalty or rebellion, either within his house or his province. She is sure Alfonso is the same.

What will Alfonso do? How will he stop his mother and sisters leaving? Does he really expect his orders to take precedence over those of the Pope? She feels these words jostling inside her, fighting to get out into the air, in whatever order they can manage.

'Very soon,' he is saying, as he steers the mule away from the loggia, towards the open gates, and it is unthinkable to her how he can appear so composed and unruffled, 'work on your portrait will begin. Preliminary sketches and so forth.'

'Mmm,' she says, only half listening, still thinking about the unruly court, Alfonso's sisters.

'You are not pleased?'

'I am,' she says, hastily. 'Very much so.'

'I had thought it would be diverting for you,' he says, slightly aggrieved.

'It will indeed. Forgive me. I was thinking about . . . something else. A portrait. That will be wonderful to . . . to see.'

'I know you have a great interest in painting so . . .'

'Yes,' she says, struggling to contain a desire to point out that a fondness for painting and sitting for a portrait are two very different things. 'You're right. I do.'

'I have decided,' he continues, 'that it will be a marriage portrait. It is only proper. Further paintings will follow, of course, in time, of you alongside our children. I have chosen the artist – a man well known to me. He has created the decorations in many rooms of the *castello*. Furthermore, he trained under the greatest master of all, Michelangelo himself. What particular form this portrait shall take is still under discussion. But I am anticipating . . .'

Alfonso's voice talks on. Lucrezia's attention slips away from it, fastening instead on the doves that pick their way among the villa's roof tiles, bobbing their heads at each other, beaks emitting low pentatonic trills, wings folded in tight at their sides. Minuscule insects are circling and gathering above the hazel tree, as if they are consulting with each other about some matter, and all are undecided. The mule tosses her head, flicking the soft, furred triangles of her ears back towards Lucrezia, then forward to Alfonso, then back again, as if she is trying to follow their conversation, trying to discern what is happening in this marriage. In the distance, Lucrezia sees that Leonello, unlike Alfonso, is in a state of edginess and haste. He is ordering servants to stow certain objects – clothing, documents, linen packages – in saddlebags; he is ticking something off a list; his foot, encased in its supple leather boot, is tapping against the impacted earth of the courtyard; the tendons in his neck stand out beneath the skin.

Lucrezia watches, from the back of her rare and colourless mule, as a servant – a young boy with an open, tender face, who has been overloaded with luggage – stumbles on a shallow stone step. The boxes and bags slide from his thin arms and fall to the ground. Papers and wax seals spill over the parched earth. The boy kneels, trying to gather them up, brushing dirt off them with his hands. A more senior servant – a secretary from the office – castigates him in a loud voice, cuffing him on the back of his head. As Lucrezia watches, feeling sorry for the boy, and wondering if the papers were important, and whether Alfonso will be displeased, Leonello Baldassare reaches down, without looking, and closes his fist around the boy's collar. He pulls him from the ground and, taking one of the dropped boxes, slams the boy's face, once, twice, three times, into its hard wooden lid.

The bright day goes dark, as if the sun has hidden its face, and the noise of this assault – a soft shape meeting a hard surface, like that of a cabbage falling to the floor – ricochets around the courtyard, bouncing off the tiles, the walls, the shocked faces of the other servants.

Lucrezia stands up in her saddle, her foot pressing into the iron stirrup, her hand held out towards the boy.

'My God!' The words fly out of her lips. 'Stop! Enough!'

With measured slowness, Baldassare turns to look at her. His face is still, eyes expressionless as pebbles. The boy dangles by the collar from his hand, a bloodied puppet making muffled squeaks of distress. Lucrezia is sure that at any moment Alfonso will do something: he will indicate to Leonello to let the boy go. She is certain that this horror will be put to a stop.

But what happens is this: Baldassare, still holding Lucrezia's gaze, strikes the boy one final time with the box, then drops the child to the ground and accepts a handkerchief from the secretary, which he uses to wipe his fingers. Some servants step forward and pick up the boy, removing him, hurrying away his wrecked form.

Alfonso does nothing. Alfonso says nothing. Alfonso makes no sign he has seen anything untoward. Alfonso continues to lead her mule along the terrace, towards the end of the courtyard, and now beyond, so that they are on the narrow path towards the garden, heading away from the villa.

Lucrezia is shaking, all along her arms and fingers; she feels cold; she is having trouble keeping a grip on the bridle. She feels she may slide from the saddle to the ground. She doesn't know what to do or say. She has never in her life witnessed anything like that. Certainly, she has seen servants disciplined, by her parents, by other elevated members of her household, but never to that extent, never more than a shouted word, or perhaps a brief slap. Nothing in her life has prepared her for this.

'Alfonso,' she says, once they are alone, when it becomes clear, from the implacable back of his head, that he will not speak, 'do you not think that was . . . excessive? The poor child – it wasn't his fault. Anyone could see that. Will you now speak to Leonello and say that he was—'

Alfonso turns, pulling on the bridle so that the mule comes to a sharp halt, and regards her, a smile on his face. Lucrezia stares at him, uncomprehending. How can anyone smile after what happened? She has no idea what he will say. Any impression that she has come to know him, that she has reached a sense of intimacy with him, is, in that moment, blown away. A stranger stands before her, a person with whom she has no connection. Instead of agreeing with her, instead of saying that, yes, Baldassare's punishment was too harsh, the boy had done nothing to deserve such brutality, Alfonso reaches out and touches her cheek with loosely curled fingers. 'What a kind and tender heart you have,' he murmurs, tucking a strand of hair behind her ear. 'You will make a wonderful mother.'

His voice and his words are tender but Lucrezia knows that something else runs beneath them, an underground stream with black, corrosive intent. She feels herself shying away from his touch, as if it burns her.

'I have to remind you, however,' he continues, in the same tone, 'that I do not tolerate challenges to my rule, to any of my decisions or actions. If anyone does so, I punish them. Swiftly and severely. Am I making myself clear?'

Lucrezia cannot grasp what he is saying. Who is to be punished? Is he talking about the boy? All he did was drop a box.

'Leonello,' Alfonso says smoothly, 'is my representative. He is my instrument. My father selected him and trained him for one purpose: to be my *consigliere*. He is, if you like, the quill in my hand, the sword at my side. He speaks my words, he carries out my actions. If you question his authority, you question mine. Do you understand me now?'

'Yes,' Lucrezia gets out.

'You are young, I know, and new to this court, so naturally I forgive you this transgression. But it must be the last. You must never, ever again undermine Baldassare. Particularly in front of others. Do you hear me?'

She doesn't trust herself to speak the words he desires – she fears that other words, ones he won't like, will come out – so she confines herself to a single nod.

'Good.' He leans forward and kisses her on the mouth. 'I am glad we are in agreement. Let us return, then, to the courtyard.'

Alfonso jerks the bridle, turning the mule back the way they came.

The boughs of the hazel tree, stirred by gentle gusts of air, make tortured, evanescent shapes against the lapis sky.

Alfonso and Leonello leave as soon as the heat of the day has passed. Lucrezia steps out into the courtyard to bid them a safe journey. Alfonso is mounted on a black stallion with high haunches and a rolling, liquid eye. Lucrezia stands well back, one hand curled around a column of the loggia.

Leonello rides the same horse he was on that morning when Lucrezia met him coming out of the forest. No hares are strung from the saddle now, but bulging leather sacks and a wineskin. She keeps her eyes averted from him.

It will take an hour or two to reach the *castello*, Alfonso has told her.

'Goodbye,' he calls, 'goodbye, and God bless you.'

His stallion prances sideways on its shining hoofs, shifting the metal bit inside its mouth, turning towards Lucrezia, as if it needs to get a look at her, as if it has some message for her;

Alfonso gives the reins an answering peremptory yank and the horse snorts, twisting its head against its tight restraint, trying to wrest control from its master. Lucrezia wishes she could tell the horse that it's no use, that Alfonso never will let him do as he pleases. And, just as she expected, Alfonso lets out a warning *tsk*, shortens the reins even more so that the stallion's head is tucked almost completely under its neck.

'Goodbye,' he calls again.

Lucrezia holds a handkerchief in her fingers, waving it back and forth in the still, humid air. The hoofs of the horses clatter and skid as they canter away from the villa gates.

He is gone for a whole day, and another, longer than she had expected. She does not know if this is a bad sign or a good one. At night, she pushes the bolt across her chamber door and sinks into an undisturbed, dreamless sleep, lying with arms extended either side of her, in a restful cruciform.

She makes enquiries about the injured serving boy, and is told that the child has a broken nose and several cracked teeth, but is making a good recovery. She asks that he be given poppy syrup and nourishing broth, to aid his healing. She sends Emilia with some coins to cover the expense.

She walks about the ornamental gardens, the flower bowers, the walkways. With her guardsman shadowing her, always, she treads between the light-shot trunks of the forest. She gathers bright petalled blooms, springy handfuls of moss, thick and veined leaves, the frilled yellow caps of mushrooms, the shed spines of porcupines. She searches the branches above her head, endlessly, for a stone marten, for she does so desperately want to see a real one, but her guardsman tells her they are rarely here any more – too many of them were taken by hunters, he says. She soaks her wrists in the cool waters of the fountains. She visits her mule every day, taking an apple, a pear, to feed her. She asks for her to be saddled, then rides her around the loggia and into the gardens. Her guardsman steps forward to lead if the terrain becomes rough, even though Lucrezia is more than capable of managing. But she does not wish to hurt his feelings so accepts his aid with a nod. She lets the mule nibble at the bushes of sage and thyme, so that when she returns it to the stables, the animal smells of a meadow, of summer.

She wears loose gowns, much like the *sottane* she had as a child; she discards her shoes; she leaves her hair unbound down her back for most of the day.

Instead of heavy food, like the meat and fish Alfonso favours, she orders milk puddings from the cook, fresh bread with a salted crust, figs cut open and served with soft cheese, the juice of apricots in a dainty cup.

On the third morning of Alfonso's absence, Lucrezia is in the salon, a hempen smock over her clothing. She is shuffling along the perimeter, looking again and again at the fresco depicting the twelve labours of Hercules: the toil and sweat of the man, the way his muscles strain beneath the skin. She leans close to the wall and sees tiny brushstrokes in the grainy surface of the tempera, signs of the long-ago artist trying to wield authority over his pigments, his egg-yolk paste, his fast-drying mixtures. The indigo and the azurite he must have mixed, here, in this very room, under commission by one of Alfonso's ancestors, have faded and softened with time; it is almost as if the colours have retreated into the wall, to hide themselves, to wait out the centuries. Lucrezia imagines them springing back, all at once, in collusion, to their original vibrancy, with some magic signal, with the utterance of some secret shibboleth. Hercules' eyes will once again be sky-blue, his loincloth startling red, instead of faded pink, the mountains beneath his feet the green of new growth. Lucrezia leans close to the fresco and inhales its smell of dust and rust and faint decay.

She turns and regards the arrangement she has placed on a table by the window: a bowl of peaches, a pitcher of water, and a honeycomb on a green dish, sitting in a pool of its golden ooze. She tilts her head one way, then the other. The dark purple cloth is good – the way the colour sings with and against the orange of the peach skin and the gold of the honey and the way it drapes and folds. The sun is placing fingers of light over the curved rumps of the fruit. She should make haste, she realises, as the light may go, the colours change. Alfonso may return at any moment and she will need to set this aside to attend him. She will need to grind saffron, cochineal, the heart of an iris flower, and – what else? Lucrezia steps back to the easel, where she has set up her usual planed square of *tavola*, her brushes, a mortar with its pestle resting on the lip, oyster shells filled with linseed oils, ready to absorb the powdered pigment.

She is about to paint over a scene she did last night, of an aquatic creature, half man, half fish, crawling up out of the shores of a river, silvered tail glistening in moonlight. She feels, not for the first time, a pulse of sadness that this image will disappear, will become just an underpainting, never to be seen by anyone other than her.

But it must be so. No one should see this. An underpainting

it must be. So she will conceal it with this most innocent and appropriate still life of fruit and honey. What could be a healthier pastime for a young duchess than that?

She is about to take a length of chalk and make her first mark on the *tavola* – the ovoid shape of the bowl, with the echoing curves of the peaches above, will bisect the gleaming scaled tail of the mer-man – when a peculiar noise reaches her ears.

A sudden thwack, as if something heavy has hit the floor, several rooms away: a sack, perhaps, or bale of cloth, thrown down. Lucrezia listens for footsteps, walking away from whatever it was.

But there's nothing. No sound. No footsteps. No movement at all.

Lucrezia looks at the chalk in her hand, at the undulating ripples of the river she painted late into the night, at the faded but frank eyes of Hercules on the fresco, as he raises his sword to the many-faced Hydra.

She lets the chalk stick fall from her hand; she wipes her fingers on a cloth; she walks across the salon, through the atrium, her footfalls leaping from the floor to the ceiling and back again, through a chamber with an alabaster relief of Athena emerging from a grimacing Zeus' head, through an antechamber where a table is spread with what appears to be drying rushes, and into a corridor that leads from the central courtyard to an arched window looking out over the valley.

And, here, lying on the floor, is the body of a man.

Lucrezia blinks, then ventures forwards. A man, lying there on the tiles, as if dropped from the sky, his shirt very white against the terracotta.

'Signore?' she says hesitantly. 'Can you hear me?'

She taps him with the very tip of her foot. Nothing. She crouches beside him and places a tentative hand on his shoulder. 'Signore,' she says again, and shakes him gently.

He doesn't respond but the motion turns him on to his back, and Lucrezia can see right into his face.

It is not someone she recognises. He has a crown of light brown curls; there is a capacious leather bag strung about his shoulder. His clothes and shoes are not those of a nobleman – no embroidery adorns his cuffs; no jewels encircle his fingers; the cloak spread out behind him is of a coarse weave. But, equally, he doesn't have the aspect of a servant either: his shoes are stout but also have intriguing webs of stitching; his hands aren't roughened by labour but have long, expressive fingers.

Where did he come from? Lucrezia looks up and down the corridor. She calls, but nobody comes. It is clear that this man has just arrived here – his clothes are dusty from the roads, his bag is laden with whatever he is carrying or delivering – but where has he come from, and why?

What is also clear to Lucrezia is that the man is gravely unwell. He is completely unconscious, sunk into an unresponsive state, his eyes rolled back in his head, the lids heavy, his jaw slack. When she touches his hand, she finds the skin is marble-cool and clammy, slippery with icy sweat. This is no fainting fit, from hot weather or lack of water: this is something quite other.

'Signore!' she says again, more sharply. She slaps his cheek, trying to rouse him, but his head lolls alarmingly to one side. His breathing, she sees, is shallow and fast.

She isn't sure how but she somehow knows that this man, this stranger, is close to death. That he is dying, right in front of her, here, on the tiled red floor of the villa. She can feel it via the contact of her palms: his life is ebbing away; he is drifting off to a place of no return.

Panic seizes her. She shakes him, hard, by both shoulders. She inflates her lungs and shouts: 'Help! Somebody, please! We need help!'

The skin on his face is turning a greyish colour, his eyes seeming to sink back into their sockets, his lips bloodless. Frantically, she loosens the ties at the neck of his shirt, hoping that this will allow more air to pass into him. Some part of her mind registers how strange it is to be handling this man's body, her fingers on his throat, his clavicle, the stuttering pulse in his neck; his body is so different from Alfonso's, which is hardened by fencing and riding and hunting and lifting weights. Alfonso is all muscle and bone under burnished brown skin. This man, or boy perhaps, is softer, the flesh more yielding, pale like distemper.

'Please,' Lucrezia whispers, into the stranger's unconscious face, 'please. Wake up.'

It comes back to her, then, as she stares down at this dying man, the time when a visitor to her father's court – a foreign dignitary – had collapsed at Mass. Down he had gone, face first, on to the floor of the chapel, like a felled tree. Lucrezia had been a small child but she still remembers the man's grey pallor, the looseness of his limbs. Sofia had told her – what was it? – that there was a kind of sickness to do with the blood, an imbalance of some kind, if a person had too much red blood or not enough, Lucrezia can't recall now, but she does remember that they brought the dying dignitary back to life by dripping honey water into his mouth. There was a man with him, an older man, perhaps his father, who knew exactly what to do; Lucrezia remembers him calling for honey, a cup of water; she remembers him rushing to snatch these things from the hands of a servant.

Within seconds, Lucrezia is running back through the ante-chamber, the alabaster chamber, the atrium; she is seizing the dish with the honeycomb, the pitcher and a spoon from the table. Then she runs back, as fast as she can, water slopping out to soak her wrists and front.

When she crouches again beside the young man, she can see that he is worse, further away from the shore than he was, his breathing hoarse and rasping, his face a mask of clay.

It seems important that she talk, that a voice might reach him, wherever he is, that he might know he is not alone, that there are people trying to keep him on the side of the living, that there is something for him to come back for, to struggle towards. So she keeps up a torrent of words as she tips water into the dish and mixes the honey into it with hands that are urgent and shaking.

'I don't know who you are or where you have come from but I want you to stay, do you hear me? You are to stay. We are in the *delizia* at Voghiera and I wonder what brought you here, with this very heavy bag of yours. Now here, try this, just a little.'

She tips a spoonful of the honey water between his parted lips but his head is lolling at the wrong angle, and the precious fluid seeps out of his mouth, on to the floor.

'Please,' she whispers to him, adjusting his head, which

is so slack that she must remove one of her shoes, then the other, to keep it propped straight, 'you must try. Do you hear? Please.'

She tilts a second spoonful into his mouth and this time it doesn't trickle out. She waits a moment, but nothing happens, so she gives him a third. As it enters him, his breathing turns to an alarming gargle at the back of his throat. He is choking, he is inhaling the honey water. Tears start into her eyes. She puts down the dish and turns the man on to his side. He is heavy and cumbersome. His body flops from her grasp, but she manages to yank him towards her, and watches as the liquid streams from his mouth into a puddle on the floor.

She has killed him. She is sure of it. She has hastened his death, brought it about. What was she thinking, pouring water into the mouth of an unconscious man? Why didn't she run to fetch help or—?

Without warning, there is a splutter, then a cough. The man expels more liquid, then takes a huge, shuddering breath. His eyes are still closed but a faint tinge of pink rises to his lips.

Lucrezia clutches his arm. 'Signore?' she says. 'Can you hear me?'

She flattens herself on the floor next to him, peering right into his face. The man's eyes are rolling like marbles beneath the lids. She reaches for the dish and holds the spoon to his lips. This time, he swallows.

'Yes,' Lucrezia murmurs, relief surging through her, 'that's it. A little more.'

He opens his mouth to admit the spoon, and swallows again. The colour is spreading throughout his face like a tide, creeping up from his mouth, to his cheeks, his brow, his forehead.

'Very good,' Lucrezia says. 'You're doing so well.'

His eyelids open a crack, then fall shut, then open again, wider this time, revealing eyes that are neither green nor blue, but somewhere in between. Or is the right eye bluer than the left? Lucrezia stares into them; he stares back at her.

She straightens. He blinks and brings a trembling hand to his head, then turns over on to his back. She lifts his head, propping it once more on her shoes.

'Don't worry,' she says to him, 'you're going to be all right. All is well. Just try to swallow this.'

He gazes up at her, puzzled, shifting his eyes to the walls behind her, the ceiling above his head. His hand wanders to the strap of his bag, to his loosened collar. When she proffers the spoon, he strains forward to take the honey water.

'I was so worried,' she tells him, in a shaking voice. 'I didn't know what to do. Can you talk yet, signore? Can you tell me your name? Your business here? Are you alone or with an . . . associate?'

He closes his lips over the spoon, then releases it, all the while keeping his aquamarine gaze on her.

'Well, never mind,' she says, after a moment, 'we can wait for that, but I would like—'

Behind her, there is a clatter of footsteps, and a heated exclamation: 'God in Heaven!'

Lucrezia turns to see a second young man, ganglier and thinner than this one, with a similar leather bag about his shoulders, rushing along the corridor towards them.

'Oh, damnation and hellfire,' he says, swooping down on

them, 'did he have a fit?' He comes to a squat, next to his friend, and lays a hand on his shoulder.

'Are you all right? Are you coming round?' His eye falls on the dish with the honeycomb. 'You gave him that?' he asks Lucrezia. 'How did you know what to do?'

'I . . .' she hesitates, suddenly feeling the strangeness of her situation – alone with two young men of indeterminate station she has never met before, she might be in trouble if someone reports this to Alfonso '. . . I once saw a similar type of . . . fit.'

'And they cured it like this?' He gestures at the dish.

Lucrezia nods. 'I wasn't sure if it was the right thing. I just came upon him here, lying on the floor, and I was so frightened. He looked so terrible that I really thought he—'

'How incredible! You did exactly the right thing,' the second young man says, interrupting her. 'You saved his life.'

'No,' she protests, 'I merely—'

'You did,' he insists. Then he nudges his companion with the toe of his boot. 'She saved your life, Jacopo. This beautiful young woman. Aren't you lucky?'

Lucrezia stands. The man takes the dish and spoon from her, with an easy grace, and continues to give Jacopo small amounts, waiting to see when he has swallowed.

'What brings you to Voghiera?' she asks.

'We are here for the portrait,' he says, keeping his eyes on Jacopo.

'The portrait?'

'The marriage portrait. Of the new Duchess.'

Lucrezia leans against the wall. She isn't sure if it is the shock of coming across a dying man, or the fear in the

256

moments when she'd thought she couldn't save him, or the relief that he is now back from the brink, but her limbs feel suddenly weak, her vision clouded. 'Are you . . . the artists?'

This question makes the crouching man let out a cheerful laugh. 'No,' he says. 'Well, in a way. We are his apprentices. Two of them, anyway. I am Maurizio, and this,' he taps the prostrate form with the back of his hand, 'is Jacopo. Who gives us endless trouble. But we love him anyway.'

'How many apprentices are there?'

'It varies. Between five and ten, at any one time, depending on how many commissions we have. Jacopo here is the painter of cloth and I—'

'Cloth?'

'Yes.' He grins up at her. 'The way it drapes over an arm or a leg, the way silk catches the light, the way the colour of fabric alters if near candlelight. It is not so simple. No one does it like Jacopo.'

'But does your master not—?'

'Him?' Maurizio scoffs. 'Il Bastianino wouldn't dirty his fingers for the cloth. Too much like hard work. No, he'll do the face and perhaps the hands, if he hasn't drunk too much – and Jacopo will do them, if he has. Don't tell the Duke, though, eh?' He winks at her, grinning wickedly. 'Jacopo's speciality is cloth. Mine is the landscape behind.'

'Behind the person?'

'Yes.' Maurizio unceremoniously heaves Jacopo towards the corridor wall and props him in a sitting position. 'The hills, the lakes, the trees. That's what I do.'

'I had no idea that the work was shared like that.'

'Oh, always,' Maurizio says. 'Everyone in the studio will

have a hand in it.' He sits down, next to Jacopo. 'So, what can you tell us about the Duchess Consort?'

Lucrezia is silent. She realises that, shoeless as she is, and with an overall covering her dress, she must look to them like a servant.

'We hear she is very young,' Maurizio is saying, 'and very beautiful. Is that right? With hair like Venus herself.'

'I . . . I couldn't say.'

'Have you not seen her, then?'

'Well . . .'

'Her husband keeping her under lock and key, is he? Wouldn't surprise me, from what I've heard.'

Lucrezia presses her palms against the wall, and the back of her head. The solidity of the plasterwork feels suddenly necessary to her. 'What have you heard?'

'Only that he is like Janus, with two faces, two personalities. And he can switch between them,' he snaps his fingers in the air, 'like that.'

Lucrezia gives her head a shake, trying to marshal her thoughts. Lock and key? A Janus? She sees, for a moment, a depiction of the double-headed god, shown to her by her tutor, years ago: a young, smooth face looking one way, and a careworn, brooding face looking the other. Is this what her husband is really like?

'Anyway,' Maurizio is saying cheerfully, 'we can't wait to see this little duchess, especially if she is all that people say she is. Eh, Jacopo?' He nudges his friend, who manages to raise a bleary smile.

'What's your position here, then?' Maurizio asks, looking her up and down, his eyes bright with appreciation. 'I can't say this job will be arduous if there are girls like you around.'

Lucrezia ignores him and addresses Jacopo: 'How are you feeling? I must be on my way but I want to be sure you are fully recovered.'

Maurizio seizes Jacopo around the head with his arm, ruffling his halo of oaken curls. 'He's all better, I'd say.'

'Jacopo,' Lucrezia says, 'are you quite well?'

'Oh,' Maurizio says, releasing Jacopo's head, 'he doesn't speak.'

'Really?'

'Yes.'

'Never?'

'Never. He's a mute.'

'I had no idea, he—'

'Or he speaks some strange tongue that none of the rest of us can understand. We're not quite sure where he came from – Il Bastianino says he found him in an orphanage somewhere in the south. He somehow heard of this child who could draw anything, even after looking at it for only a moment, so he bought him from the monks. You get used to it. It's quite restful, actually. Most people talk too much, myself included. Now, what's your name and will we see you again while we're here?'

Lucrezia looks at them both, sitting there, with their backs against the wall, their apprentice bags by their sides, Maurizio's face so affable and open, Jacopo's wan and watchful.

'I think you will,' she says.

She has ground her pigments and mixed them with the oil; she has applied paint for the curves of the peaches – ochre and cochineal mixed with lead white – and is beginning to mix a green for the bowl. The water-creature is half gone when Emilia comes to tell her that Alfonso has returned from Ferrara.

Lucrezia stares at the maid, brush raised. The way the light from the window is falling upon Emilia at this particular moment means that the scar on her face is hidden in shadow: she appears perfect, exquisite, her fair hair held back under a cap, her capable hands folded in front of her.

'Did he . . .?' Lucrezia tries to speak but she is still in the world of the painting, her mind running on its interplay of light and shade, the arrangement of shapes, and the ever-intriguing conundrum of how to render something three-dimensional on the flat surface of paper.

'Has he . . .' she tries again '. . . sent for me?'

'Not yet, madam. I thought you'd like to know that he's arrived.'

'Yes,' says Lucrezia, abstractedly, wiping a brush on a rag. 'Certainly. Let me know, please, if he . . . when he . . . asks for me.'

Emilia nods, then shuts the door behind her, and Lucrezia returns to her painting, relieved, delighted at this reprieve.

She paints for a long time, standing back from the *tavola*, leaning in close. She progresses from bowl to honey to the pleats and wrinkles in the cloth. She navigates her course through the arrangement of objects, how they interact with each other, the spaces and conversations between them, shrinking herself to the size of a beetle so that she may wander through the crannies between peaches, along the interlocking hexagons of the honeycomb. She feels her way around the corresponding painting, using her brushes like feet or antennae, seeking a route through the unfamiliar terrain of the items, hacking her way through the undergrowth of the work.

She paints while the sun is high in the sky, as it slips down over the pitch of the roofs, while servants rush up and down the loggia. She does not even notice the fading light, or the bustle and flap of the villa around her, or that she hasn't eaten since midday. She is absorbed in her work; she is her work; it gives her more satisfaction than anything else she has ever known; it intuits the need, the vacancy, within her, and fills it.

It is late afternoon when Emilia knocks again on the door. She doesn't meet Lucrezia's eye as she says: 'His Grace is asking for you, madam.'

Lucrezia puts down her brush. She feels light-headed, almost dizzy, to be confronted like this with the real world. 'Thank you, Emilia. I will go to him directly and—'

She stops, catching sight of Emilia's face, which is horrified. Lucrezia looks down at herself – the overall, the paint smears, the bare feet – and lets out a laugh. 'Perhaps I should change.'

'Yes, madam,' Emilia says, with some relief. 'I will come with you.'

Not long after, attired in a *sopraveste* of primrose satin, the ruby collar around her neck, Lucrezia is rather hot. The windows of the salon are open on both sides of the room, but there is very little passage of air: nothing moves. The trees outside in the courtyard hold out their motionless leaves at the end of their branches. A few darkening clouds, stained pink and orange, hang above the villa, as if too exhausted to move on.

Lucrezia waits, seated in a chair she dislikes – it has an unyielding pad, and horsehairs poke through the fabric to prick her legs. She attempts to fold her hands meekly in her lap, but that doesn't feel right, so she leans an elbow on the table next to her, but that feels unnatural. With a suppressed sigh, she picks up some embroidery she has half-heartedly been doing in the evenings spent with her husband. She cannot remember how to be a wife, a duchess consort. It has not been long since Alfonso went away, but somehow during those few days the habit of it has slipped away from her.

The truth is, though, that she is still caught in the microcosm of her painting: that is the only place she wishes to be. All other sights, all other worlds, will be dissatisfying to her until she finishes it, until the painting is complete and will release her back to where she belongs. Here, this salon, waiting for her husband to appear, an embroidery hoop in her hands.

Lucrezia sighs again and stabs the needle through the cloth, pulling the thread taut. The embroidery is one Isabella embarked on months ago, a rose surrounded by a border of gold: Lucrezia has no idea why it is now in her possession. Most likely, Isabella abandoned it, tossing it aside when something else caught her attention, and somehow it ended up among Lucrezia's luggage. It is useful to her, as a theatrical prop, to make those around her believe she is the type of person who fills time with such pointless pursuits.

She is trying to add a butterfly on one of the outer petals, but it is not turning out well: one of its wings is larger than the other, giving it an unbalanced look. Perhaps she, too, will not finish this; perhaps this rose will never be completed.

She cannot work with needle and thread – her fingers become stiff and strange to her. Paint is what she loves best, and chalk, and ink. She turns the hoop over and inspects the underside. She has always had a secret liking for this part of the embroidery, the 'wrong' side, congested with knots, striations of silk and twists of thread. How much more interesting it is, with its frank display of the labour needed to attain the perfection of the finished piece. She runs her hands over its cartography: she can tell which stitches are hers and which Isabella's. Her own are clumsier, hastier, with an air of impatience and displeasure.

She turns the hoop over once more and pushes the needle through the cloth. Instantly, she receives a sharp pain, just below her fingernail: she has misjudged it and pricked herself. She watches, with a ghoulish fascination, as a perfect bead of crimson rises out of her cuticle.

Without warning, the door is flung open. Lucrezia starts and, putting her finger in her mouth, jumps to her feet.

Alfonso is moving swiftly through the room. He has taken extra pains, she sees, with his toilette, his hair smoothed back and oiled, his face freshly shaved, and he is wearing cuffs with gold trims.

'My dearest,' he says, and, bowing over her hand, he kisses it. 'How I have missed you. Are you well? Did the time hang heavily upon you?'

'No, not at all,' Lucrezia says. 'I—'

'What?' he exclaims, throwing himself into the chair she has just vacated. 'You didn't miss me at all?'

'Oh,' Lucrezia says, a furious blush heating her face, 'no, I did, really, I—'

'Not even a little bit?' he teases, drawing her on to his lap and, seeing her finger, he catches her hand in his. 'But you are hurt. How did this happen?'

'It's nothing. I was doing my embroidery and the needle slipped and—'

'Here.' He pulls a kerchief out of his sleeve and wraps it tenderly around her finger.

'Thank you,' she says, then carefully, without looking at him: 'How was everything in Ferrara?'

'Good.' The word is clipped and efficient. 'All good.'

Lucrezia, perched self-consciously on Alfonso's knee, watches as a red stain appears on the snowy whiteness of the kerchief around her finger, blood making itself known, refusing to be concealed.

'Did you manage to . . . attend to the matter you were concerned about?'

Alfonso clasps his arms around her and, once again, she experiences the sensation of being pinioned, imprisoned. The embroidery of his cuffs catches and chafes against her dress, whispering to her, telling her something she cannot understand. 'I did.'

'Was it . . .' she knows she should not pursue the matter as he doesn't seem to wish to discuss it, but she cannot contain her fascination over what might have occurred at the Ferrarese court in the last few days '. . . did you . . . was it resolved . . . to your satisfaction?'

He draws back and gives her a level look. 'Of course,' he says, and he toys with a curl at the side of her head, winding it around and around his finger. 'Do you know why?'

Wordlessly, she shakes her head.

'Because everything,' with each word, he gives the curl a gentle tug, 'is always resolved to my satisfaction.'

'Oh, I am glad,' she cries, relieved. 'You managed to persuade your mother to stay in Ferrara? Will she wait at least until I arrive at court? I do so long to meet her. And your sisters. Did they agreed to remain with you? Have they—'

She stops. Alfonso is leaning back in the chair, scrutinising her. She has gone too far, she sees, and wishes she could pluck her hasty words from the air and stuff them back inside her.

'You seem,' he says, at last, 'remarkably well informed.'

'Forgive me,' she says, and realises that she is filled with inexplicable terror, her heart pounding, the skin of her neck prickling. Will he become angry? Will he castigate her as he did after she asked Baldassare to stop beating the young boy? 'I spoke out of turn and—'

'No, no. It is interesting for me that this news has reached you. Useful to know.'

'I'm sorry, I should not have—'

He cuts her off with a slow blink, making it clear with this minuscule gesture that he does not want or need her apologies. 'I wonder, however, how you came by this knowledge.'

She sits on his lap, an ornately plumed bird in a hand. Emilia, she thinks, Emilia. But she will not give him this name, will not surrender her maid to him. Never.

'It was . . . that is, I overheard . . . something about it. You know how it is, when people talk—'

'What people?'

'I'm not sure.'

'Servants or officials?'

She has to think. Which would be best? Which would be worse? Which would cause the least damage or punishment?

'Well . . . I don't recall . . . perhaps both?'

He looks at her for several moments, mouth hidden by the hand propping up his chin. Then he nods. He asks what she has been doing, did she find some occupation for herself, and she realises that the subject has been dropped, but she still doesn't know whether or not his mother has left for France, and if his sisters have remained in Ferrara. She cannot ask now. He is easing her off his lap and walking towards the easel, where her unfinished painting is resting, covered with a shawl. He pulls this off and, dropping it to the floor, bends to examine her work.

'This is charming,' he says, inspecting the still life, the peaches and the honey, which, she is relieved to remember, completely cover the moonlit river beast with the scaled tail. 'Quite charming. Such a pleasant pastime for you, my love, although—' There is another knock at the door, and Alfonso, without looking round, calls, 'Enter.'

And Lucrezia turns to see the two apprentices appear in the room, Maurizio ahead, bounding in, beaming, with the expectation of pleasure on his face, Jacopo behind him, eyes lowered. They have changed out of their travelling clothes; both are in clean collars, their boots polished to a shine.

'Ah,' Alfonso says, pausing briefly for their murmured greetings. 'Allow me to present to you two apprentice painters, assistants to Sebastiano Filippi, otherwise known as Il Bastianino, who will be painting your portrait when we return to court.' He extends a hand towards her. 'This is my wife, the Duchess.'

Lucrezia steps out of the margins of the chamber, into the flickering, intersecting circles of light around the candelabra. The filigreed lace on her sleeves, her ruby pendant, her head-dress instantly flare and spark in reply, and the two young men turn towards her.

Maurizio blanches, recognising her, his mouth falling open, but recovers himself quickly, courteously inclining his head, murmuring that he is honoured, he is humbled, he is her devoted servant. Jacopo stands immobile, like an animal afraid of attack, eyes locked on hers. Lucrezia recalls, fleetingly, the clammy give of his skin under her fingers, the terrifying loll of his neck, the slender jut of his collarbone.

For a moment, in the salon, nobody moves.

Then Maurizio jabs Jacopo with an elbow; he startles into life, like a marionette whose strings have been jerked. He snatches the cap from his head, he makes a low, sweeping bow.

'Forgive my friend,' Maurizio says. 'He has been a little unwell today and—'

'Unwell?' Alfonso interrupts. 'What manner of unwell?'

'Nothing in the way of contagion, Your Highness,' Maurizio says hastily, 'I assure you. He was perhaps . . . a little overcome by heat and – and the journey. Nothing more.'

'I see.' Alfonso steps towards Lucrezia and takes her hand. 'This, gentlemen, is to be your subject, your muse.' He makes a gesture indicating the length of her, from her feet to her head. 'I expect your master has told you but I have commissioned a marriage portrait of her, as is fitting. You, I gather, are expected to make preliminary sketches so your master and I can decide the best way to approach the work. Is that understood?'

'Yes,' Maurizio says, nodding, 'and may I say what a muse she will be, Your Highness, what a delight and a—'

'Your friend,' Alfonso points at Jacopo, 'why does he not address us?'

'He never speaks, Your Grace,' Maurizio says, clapping a hand to Jacopo's shoulder. 'We believe him to be a mute.'

'Is he deaf?'

'No, Your Grace. He hears perfectly well, he just doesn't—'

'But he is . . .' Alfonso frowns '. . . a capable draughtsman?'

'More than capable,' Maurizio replies, with a grin. 'He is highly skilled, the best apprentice in the workshop. Our master would only send his very best assistants to you, Your Grace. Please be assured. Jacopo's figures and fabrics are exquisite, second only to those of the master himself. You shall see when we are given the opportunity to pose Her Highness and—'

'Yes, yes,' Alfonso cuts him off, with a curt gesture. 'I see that you are more than able to speak for both of you. Well,' he claps his hands together, 'I see no reason to prevent us from beginning right away.'

Lucrezia turns to him. She has had no dinner; her stomach feels hollow with hunger; she is tired; her head aches. The very last thing she wishes to do this evening is to pose for sketches by two apprentice artists. But Alfonso is all action. He is pacing the room, saying that he shall direct the pose himself, that he has studied painting in depth, both its practice and its theory, that he will observe how the pair of them fare. He is pausing to say that he should warn them he will not tolerate anything less than perfection. If he is not pleased, they will know it immediately. He is leading Lucrezia by the arm, to a chair at the fireplace, moving back her easel, placing two candelabra next to her on a table, where sit a marble sphere and a goblet.

When she raises her gaze, she finds that, just as she expected, Jacopo is looking straight at her, and his face is curiously dear to her. He is thinking, she knows, that he might have died today, that without her intervention he might not be here, standing in this room, paper in hand, that there would be a vacancy in the air right there, by the credenza. If she hadn't come to see what the noise was, if she hadn't found him, if she hadn't known what to do, if it wasn't for her. She isn't sure how she knows this, but she does. She then sees that he is looking at the painting of the peaches on the easel, then back at her, a quizzical expression passing over his features. How peculiar it seems to her, in that moment, to have saved the life of another. It has, she is dimly aware, created an invisible yet indissoluble tether between her and this man, this silent person, who is now weighting down the corners of his paper on the table and taking up his stick. She feels it; he feels it. They know it and they know each other's thoughts and they sense each other's actions and fears.

She does not know why this is or where it might lead, but she knows it must remain hidden, and silent as the tongue in his head.

The apprentices make their sketches during the course of two days. They take over the alabaster room with their rolls of paper, their graphite, charcoal and chalk, their travelling bags and discarded cloaks and tunics. When Lucrezia passes the open door, she catches a glimpse of Jacopo, sleeves pushed up, leaning over a desk; she hears Maurizio's one-sided chatter, and Jacopo answering him with a laugh.

The laugh surprises her. It is the first noise she has heard him make. And it sounds at once unique to him, and also similar to any other laugh a young man might make, like the ones she heard from her brothers when they wrestled each other.

It makes her peer again through the crack in the door, and see them both standing in the golden glow of the alabaster relief walls, like lithe fish in a clear pond. Maurizio is looking down at Jacopo's work; Jacopo is pointing at something on the paper and Maurizio is considering whatever it is, then shaking his head. This display of wordless comprehension that passes between the two of them intrigues her. How can Maurizio understand what Jacopo was asking him about the work?

She moves off, reluctantly, along the corridor, and goes to the stables to visit her mule, taking a cup of oats, saved from her breakfast.

Over the next day or two, she is frequently summoned to the salon, where her husband will be examining the sketches, holding one in his hands, then discarding it, and reaching for another. Maurizio and Jacopo stand to the side, waiting and watching as Alfonso peruses their work.

'Not like this,' Alfonso says, dropping the curled paper to the floor, 'or this. Or this.' He extracts one from the heaps of papers and unrolls it on the table. 'This, however, has potential. It has captured her sweetness but also her spiritedness, her—' Alfonso breaks off, turning to look at the apprentices. 'Which of you made this sketch? You?' He points at Maurizio.

Maurizio shakes his head. 'No, Your Highness. That one was done by Jacopo.'

'The . . . tongueless boy?'

'Yes, my lord.'

'Well, ask him to do more like this. You, too. I want her whole face to be visible, looking at the viewer, with space in the frame for her shoulders and arms and most – if not all – of her dress. Do you understand?'

Maurizio and Jacopo scramble into position behind their paper. All Lucrezia has to do is stand in exactly the pose her husband has decreed. Simple. Yet not so easy. After a minute or two, the muscles in her raised arm begin to ache, then burn. She finds she needs to blink more than usual – it is something to do with being looked at so intently. Her feet, beneath her gown, feel thin-skinned, as if their bones are pressing, unshielded by flesh, into the floor. Her gown weighs on her shoulders, constricts her lungs. She would like to stride off. She would like to go to the stables and order her mule to be saddled, then ride it out of the villa gates, up the path, and away.

She allows her eyes to wander about the room; it is the only part of her permitted motion. Alfonso has folded his long frame into a chair; he sits, one arm draped over his knee, his head swivelling between her and the apprentices. Maurizio stands near the wall, his habitually cheerful face grave with concentration, his brow contracted; he looks like a man undergoing a trial, suffering some agony of the soul. He makes a hesitant mark on the page, then looks up anxiously at her. Jacopo, by contrast, Lucrezia sees, is composed, still as a tree trunk. His hand passes over his page, making sure strokes;

his gaze flickers up, just for a brief moment, then down; up, then down. When he glances up, she thinks, he doesn't see a person. He sees an arrangement of shapes, an intersection of planes and angles, a meshing of light and shade.

'Are you perhaps finding this irksome, my love?' Alfonso has come to stand in front of her, addressing her in a low tone.

'Not at all.' She suppresses a yawn. 'Why?'

'You seem . . .' he circles his hand in the air '. . . distracted. Weary. As if we are holding you against your will.'

'No, all is well.'

'You aren't enjoying this?'

'Really, I am.'

'Well, could you then make an effort,' he whispers, 'to comport yourself with a little more dignity?'

'Dignity?'

'Hold it in your mind that you are my duchess. We need to see this in your bearing, in your features, in everything about you.'

Lucrezia presses her lips together, then nods. 'I will try.'

When Alfonso steps away, she sees that Jacopo's eyes are resting upon her. Lucrezia looks at Jacopo and Jacopo looks back. His drawing hand has ceased, hovering over the page. She has, she can see, become visible, no longer the subject of his sketch, but as a person. He slides his eyes towards Alfonso, who has returned to his chair and is intent on picking stray dog hairs off his hose, then back to Lucrezia. His mouth twitches, not in amusement, but something else. Disapproval? Concern? It is hard to say. Lucrezia stares at him and something seems to solidify in the air, in the beams of their eyes, flowing from her to him and back again, creating an almost tangible channel between them. Lucrezia wouldn't be surprised if others in the room were able to see it: it would be coloured red, or blue, or fluctuating between the two, towards purple, and it would crackle audibly. It would be impossible to cross the room at this moment without getting caught by it: the channel or connection between them would repel others from it. It occupies a space of its own.

Jacopo is the one to break it. Alfonso shifts in his chair, crossing one leg over the other; the apprentice seems to snap to attention, as if remembering why he is there, and he bends his head once more over his paper, bringing his pencil towards it to make an uncertain mark somewhere near the top. His hand, Lucrezia observes, is trembling, ever so slightly, as if someone stands behind him with their fingers on his elbow, lightly shaking it back and forth.

Lucrezia swivels away, towards the window, where she can see, in the slice of sky above the villa's roofs, a gathering of dark anvil-shaped clouds.

The weather breaks that night, cracking open, the heavens unleashing a storm. Lucrezia watches at her chamber window as the mountains appear through the darkness, illuminated by a flash of lightning, then vanish, appear, then vanish – a series of rocky peaks made visible by a flickering celestial torch flame. The thunder comes a few seconds later, rumbling, like a large stone rolling towards her.

Outside the chamber, the villa dogs are howling from wherever they have been shut; servants are running to and fro, seizing whatever furniture has been left outside; the trees are thrashing back and forth.

The apprentices, she knows, were due to leave this evening; they were meant to pack up their materials and ride back to the city. They will not go now. She and Alfonso were to leave not long after them, but the sky and the wind have decided otherwise; they have different plans for them all.

As if sensing her thoughts, the storm responds, tightening its grip on the valley, asserting its dominance, unleashing its next round of weaponry. She hears the rain begin before she sees it, a percussive tapping on the roof tiles, a wet sloughing in the courtyard, a rushing and a gurgling in the gutters. The *delizia* is engulfed by it, all its walls and roof drenched and streaming; within seconds, the leaves of the trees are sluiced clean of their summer dust.

The sky splits open again over the mountains, two forks of lightning branding themselves into the scene – bright river deltas – the valley flashing in and out of visibility. The stupefying heat of the past few weeks has retreated somewhere to hide, to lick its wounds. Raindrops fall, large as coins, through the open window and on to Lucrezia's face and neck. She holds out her hands, palms upwards, wanting them to land there, so that she may feel this wildness, capture something of the storm's spirit.

Behind her, Emilia is packing Lucrezia's possessions into trunks and bags. Lucrezia can hear her footsteps, pattering over the floor, and the shushing sound of silk gowns being laid inside boxes.

She knows Alfonso has arrived when she hears Emilia murmur a greeting. She turns towards him, to say something about the incredible storm, hoping that he will stand at the window with her, looking out.

'Whatever are you doing,' he says, 'at the open window like that? Shut it, please.'

For a moment, she believes he is being playful, that his tone is only mock-angry. Her father often addresses her mother thus, when Eleanora is teasing him or behaving in a skittish fashion, Cosimo's words severe but his eyes resting on Eleanora with affection and indulgence. So Lucrezia smiles at Alfonso.

'Look at this storm!' she says, delighted, opening the window even wider so that he may see. 'It's so dramatic. Do you see how the sky has gone dark and—'

He bears down upon her, reaches out and seizes her wrists. 'I told you,' he murmurs, 'to shut the window, and when I ask something of you, I expect you to do it. Without delay. Without hesitation. Do you understand me?'

His grip is tight, unyielding, and only then does she realise, with a sickening drop in her stomach, that he is in earnest, that she has angered him. Without slackening his hold on her, he reaches behind her to close the window with a bang.

'People die of less,' he is saying. 'Are you mad? You're frozen. And soaked through.' He snaps his fingers towards Emilia. 'Bring something to dry your mistress. Quickly, please.'

He pulls her away from the window and his touch is far from gentle, his hand closed about her upper arm like a manacle, talking about cold and storms and chills, all the while untying the ribbons on her shift. He snatches the cloth Emilia brings and rubs it roughly over her brow, her cheeks, her now-bare shoulders. When he strips off her shift, she goes to cover herself with her arms, but he will not permit this.

'Stand still,' he commands, 'until you are dry.'

Emilia steps towards her, so close that Lucrezia can feel the maid's breath on her exposed neck. It is all she can do to stop herself reaching out and grasping the girl's hand for comfort. Emilia carefully places Lucrezia's *zimarra* across her shoulders, then steps away again.

'I'm sorry,' Lucrezia gabbles, sliding her arms into the sleeves and fastening the cord. His behaviour is not something she has witnessed before – it is alien and frightening. She is sure her father has never seized her mother by the arm and dragged her across a room, castigating her all the way. Lucrezia has never seen Cosimo touch Eleanora with anything other than tenderness and reverence. It is suddenly apparent to Lucrezia, as if the words are being written on the air before her, that Alfonso's feelings for her resemble in no way her father's for her mother. Lucrezia had thought her wedding might mean love and affection, an unbreakable bond, a parity, a partnership; she had hoped it would bring her joy and respect. But she suddenly fears, in the fury and contempt of Alfonso's grip on her arm, that her marriage will be something very different.

'I did not mean to provoke your displeasure,' she says. 'I was just—'

'This kind of recklessness is something I might have expected from an infant, not a duchess such as yourself. What kind of example is this to others? What if somebody outside had seen you, displaying yourself like that at the window?'

'I don't think anyone—'

'Did your mother not teach you to conduct yourself with decency? And to safeguard your health?'

'She—'

'Did it cross your mind that you might already be with child? Did it? Anyone would think you do not wish to bear my heirs.'

Lucrezia is seized with a terrible and urgent desire to laugh, and has to lower her head so that he will not see the sudden grin on her face. Can he really believe that watching a storm will have an effect on pregnancy?

'I was merely—'

'You find this to be a source of amusement, I see.' His voice has reached an even lower pitch. He is not touching her now. 'However can I trust that in future you will—'

Lucrezia can bear this no longer. What madness has possessed him? She does not deserve this: all she did was open a window to see the lightning. She lifts her head to tell him so. 'Alfonso—'

'Do not,' he holds a finger aloft, closing his eyes, as if summoning all reserves of patience, 'be foolish enough to interrupt me when I am speaking. Now or ever. Do you under-stand me?'

She bows her head again. 'Yes, Your Grace.'

Her smile and the suppressed hilarity have vanished, as if they never existed; there is no danger now that she might laugh. She stands before her furious husband in the posture of a penitent. She pictures herself from the outside: a girl with her shoulders slumped, her head lowered, hands upturned. No one would think she was anything other than apologetic and remorseful, filled with regret for her misdemeanour. Only she knows that within, just under her chilled skin, something quite other is taking place: flames, vibrant and consoling, lick at her insides, a fire kindles, cracks and smoulders, throwing out smoke that infiltrates every corner of her, every fingernail, every inch of her limbs. Her hair surrounds her – all he can see of her is the top of her head. He must believe she is listening to his lecture, to his chiding, but no. She is stoking this conflagration, letting it blaze, encouraging it to sear every inside space. He will never know, will never reach this part of her, no matter how violently he grips her arm or seizes her wrists.

She wonders, however, over the roar of the flames, what will ensue. Will she be sent back to Florence, in disgrace, just as her father once predicted? Will she have to face her parents again, so soon after her departure? Better, perhaps, for her to contract a fever and die here than risk her father's fury and her mother's scathing disappointment.

Within the tent of her hair, she can see her feet, bare and wet, facing his, booted and polished. She can see the front panels of her *zimarra*, decorated with delicate threadwork, and her arms hanging by her sides.

She knows what she has to do but part of her baulks at it, wants to run from the room, down the stairs, across the courtyard, out of the villa, and into the forest, where she might conceal herself inside the undergrowth, shelter there with the porcupines and stone martens, with pine needles in her hair and moss matting her hem. She need never come out.

With a small sigh, she reaches out a cold hand and ventures to take one of his. This is what is required: this is the only exit from this scene. She cannot run to the forest, however much she would wish it. When he doesn't resist, she raises his hand to her mouth, and kisses its hard bones, again and again.

'I'm so sorry.' She says these words like an actor reading

lines. 'Please forgive me. I'll never do it again. I was so intrigued by the storm and the lightning. I wasn't thinking. I cannot bear that you are angry with me.'

There is a pause. She cannot look at him, in case his face is still distorted by fury and incomprehension. She waits, still holding his hand to her face, sensible of the fire within retreating from her edges, dying down, the flames shrinking, and this gives her a feeling of such profound sorrow that actual tears – not conjured or affected ones – gather behind her eyes and spill down her cheeks.

At the touch of saltwater on the skin of his hand, his anger vanishes, like clouds cleaving apart to let in shafts of sun. His face of fury disappears, to be replaced by one of indulgence. His other hand rises up to cup her cheek. He wipes at her tears with the sides of his thumbs. It seems to her that he is, all of sudden, himself once again, that for a moment he had been inexplicably replaced by a vengeful, irascible monster in human form, a devil in collar and cuffs. But now the beast is banished: Alfonso is back.

'Very well,' comes his voice, and it is once more his even, affectionate tone. He leans forward to kiss her brow, then her temple. 'We shall speak no more of it. Do not distress yourself, dearest.'

He pulls her towards him and embraces her. Her face is crushed against his *giubbone*, his arms about her head. To disguise the strange shaking of her hands, she passes them around his waist and fastens them behind him. She breathes in and out, inhaling his scent; she finds she has to keep swallowing, as if she has eaten something she cannot digest; she wonders what will happen now.

But she doesn't have to wonder for long. One of his hands is toying with her hair, letting its rippling length run through the palm. Then it removes itself. It drops lower, towards her waist. It pulls open the knot there and loosens the sash. It pushes aside the *zimarra*. It gestures towards Emilia.

'Leave us,' its owner says.

When he eventually departs, walking away from her and through the chamber door, she stays for a while on the bed, looking up at the frescos, allowing them to come into focus and recede from it, as gradually she lets herself comprehend his absence, permits herself to believe that, yes, he has gone.

Then she rises and moves about the room, stepping through the neat piles Emilia has made, the packing boxes, the trunks; she gathers up her shift, her slippers, her shawl, and puts them on.

Emilia knocks gently on the door, asking if she may do anything to help prepare for the journey tomorrow, if Her Ladyship needs her. Lucrezia says that she is fine, there is nothing she wants, Emilia should go back to bed.

Emilia waits for a moment, on the other side of the door; Lucrezia can hear her breathing, and she hesitates, thinking she might pull the maid into the room, pushing the door shut behind them, and ask her if she saw, if she understood, if she, too, thought that Alfonso morphed from one person to another, before their very eyes, and what does it mean, and will it happen again? Emilia might say, yes, she saw it, too; she might soothe her and tell her that all men are thus sometimes, it signifies nothing. Lucrezia is reaching for the door handle but then she hears the maid tiptoeing down the corridor.

She fastens her attention instead on practical matters. She opens the box of her art materials; she counts the brushes, the bottles of oil; she rubs her fingers around the pearly insides of the painting shells; she touches the wrapped parcels of minerals and pigments. She checks that the marble pestle and mortar are safely padded in straw.

She doesn't bother to open the trunks to check the gowns, the tunics, the shoes, the veils, the scarves, the jewels, the mantles, the *giorneas*, the collars, the belts. Emilia will see to those, folding them carefully along their seams, interleaving them with paper and cedarwood chips.

Catching sight of the mirror, she freezes, her heart leaping like a fish in her chest: for a fleeting second, she sees her sister Maria staring back at her. The high forehead, the anxiously drawn eyebrows, the slightly pouting bottom lip. Then, of course, she realises that it's not Maria at all, she is not experiencing a visitation from the world beyond: it's just her, Lucrezia, but seeming suddenly so much older.

He will always need to triumph, to be seen to win: she admits these words to her mind as she turns her head this way and that in the mirror, to be completely sure the reflection is her. There will never be a time or a situation in which he can readily accept defeat.

She thinks of Maria, how she lay in the bed for days, fever raging through her, her lungs filling with deadly phlegm. She thinks of how, had this not happened, had Maria not contracted the disease, it would have been Maria in this room, in this bed, in this marriage, in this mirror, not her. She, Lucrezia, might still be in the *palazzo*, taking the air on the battlements, visiting Sofia in the nursery, taking riding lessons with her brothers in the courtyard, learning songs on her lute, watching from the salon gallery as her parents host a pageant.

But she knows that had it not been Alfonso it would have been someone else – a prince, another duke, a nobleman from Germany or France, a second cousin from Spain. Her father would have found her an advantageous match because that is, after all, what she has been brought up for: to be married, to be used as a link in his chains of power, to produce heirs for men like Alfonso.

Her brothers, by contrast, were trained as rulers: they have been taught to fight, to argue, to debate, to negotiate, to outwit, to outmanoeuvre, to wait, to spot an advantage, to scheme and manipulate and consolidate their influence. They have been schooled in rhetoric, in narrative, in persuasion, both written and verbal. Every morning they are drilled in running, jumping, boxing, weight-lifting, fencing. They have learnt to handle a sword, a dagger, a bow, a lance, a spear; they are taught how to fight on a battlefield; they have studied military tactics. They have been instructed in hand-to-hand combat, with their fists and their feet, in the event of their needing to defend themselves on a street or in a room or on a staircase. They have been taught the fastest and most efficient ways to end the life of another person – an enemy or an assailant or an undesirable.

Lucrezia is conscious that such knowledge will also occupy space in her husband's head, that he will have undergone similar training. Like her brothers, like all rulers, Alfonso will know where resides the weakness in a human form, where to press his fingers or apply a tight grip, between which ribs a knife should be inserted, which part of the neck or spine is most frangible, which veins, if pricked, will bleed most copiously.

She looks at the reflection, which seems, in the thick, syrupy glow of the lantern, half her and half Maria, and wonders what her dead sister would have done, how she might have coped in this marriage. She cannot, no matter how hard she tries, imagine her haughty, pithy sister submitting to this life, to this man. But, then, Maria would never have stood like that, watching a thunderstorm: she would have been sitting composedly in a chair, wrapped in shawls and woven blankets, perhaps turning the pages of a religious text or creating a canvaswork hunting scene with coloured silks. She would, in this way, have made a better wife for Alfonso, would not have angered him as Lucrezia did.

Lucrezia suddenly sees that some vital part of her will not bend, will never yield. She cannot help it – it is just the way she is built. And Alfonso, possessed of such a swift and perceptive way of reading people, must have sensed this. Why else would he have become so furious with her, if not to try to break down the walls of that citadel, capture it and declare himself victor?

If she is to survive this marriage, or perhaps even to thrive within it, she must preserve this part of herself and keep it away from him, separate, sacred. She will surround it with a thorn-thicket or a high fence, like a castle in a folktale; she will station bare-toothed, long-clawed beasts at its doors. He will never know it, never see it, never reach it. He shall not penetrate it.

* * *

The next day, when Emilia wakes her, she learns that the apprentices left early, saddling their ponies just after dawn.

Lucrezia and Alfonso, and the household retinue, ride out after midday. The air is washed clean by the storm, with a hint, Lucrezia thinks, of autumn's chill. She wears a fine wool shawl about her shoulders as they ride, Alfonso on his stallion, she on the cream mare; her mule, Alfonso has said, will be brought later, by a servant. It would be inappropriate for the court or the citizens of Ferrara to see her mounted upon it.

High on the back of her long-maned mare, Lucrezia turns in her saddle as they depart from the villa. She wants to etch its square red roofs and the symmetry of its fountained gardens on to her memory. She grips the reins, overcome with a peculiar certainty that she might never see it again, might never be as happy or as free as she was here. Life at court awaits her, and her role as duchess consort is about to begin.

With her head held high

Fortezza, near Bondeno, 1561

Emilia is laying out a velvet dress and the jewelled *cintura* but Lucrezia shakes her head. 'Not that one.'

'But, madam, there will be people for you to receive – courtiers and the artist and—'

'Doesn't matter. Give me the woollen one. I'm so cold.'

With a truculent flounce, Emilia turns her back on the velvet dress and starts to fiddle with the woollen one Lucrezia discarded last night. Can it have been only a few hours ago? It feels as though she has been in this place for weeks, perhaps months. She is a different person from yesterday, from the girl who rode from Ferrara, from the duchess who sat down to eat dinner last night. She has changed her shape, shed her skin, been painted over, or remade in a new form.

'We need to hurry,' Lucrezia says, seizing the bodice from Emilia and wrestling it on to her body.

'I still don't see why you need to go down. You ought to be in bed, you ought to . . .'

Lucrezia lets Emilia's words run over her. She bundles her

hair into a *scuffia* and, without pausing to let the maid fasten the *cintura* around her waist or thread earrings through her lobes, she snatches up her furs and makes for the door.

She will walk into that room with her head held high. She will do it. The fever still clings to her as mist lingers on the surface of a lake: a film of sweat chills her brow, and there is a dull, pervasive ache in her lower spine and in the places where her bones fit into their sockets. Her ankles, as she descends the winding stairs, feel tender and spongy. But she will do this. She grips the rough grain of the stone walls with certainty, with a crystalline, righteous anger.

Sisters of Alfonso II, seen from a distance

Castello, Ferrara, 1560

As they depart from the *delizia*, her husband rides next to her. He has fitted leather gloves over his hands; his cap is set back on his head, so that she can see his face when he turns to address her. The air, after the thunderstorm, is cool and clean, the ground still damp. There is a sense, as they pass through the fields, that it is possible to hear the roots of the fruit trees thirstily drawing up this sudden gift of rainwater. Leonello is behind them somewhere, the guards out in front.

When they reach the city, there are lines and lines of Alfonso's men waiting outside the walls for them, bearing swords and flags; there are musicians, who herald their arrival by raising instruments into the air and sounding loud notes. The noise is harsh and atonal, and it is all Lucrezia can do not to wince. Then crowds of people surge out of the city gates, spilling into the street around the horses, calling, cheering, waving handkerchiefs and hats. Lucrezia's horse skitters anxiously sideways, whisking its tail, and Alfonso reaches out to seize the bridle, yanking it back into line. Leonello shouts an order to the soldiers who push back the crowds, clearing the way for them. As they pass through the arches of the gates, the porters bow, pulling off their hats, while covertly casting their eyes up to look at their new duchess. There are yet more people lining the streets, faces turned towards Lucrezia and Alfonso as they make their way along a straight road with trees and high, symmetrical buildings along its edges. The Ferrarese put down their bundles, abandon their stalls or pull their children by the hand, so that they might rush to stare at her, or cheer, or throw into her path flowers and handfuls of grain. Windows of houses open and figures lean out, calling greetings and felicitations, making the sign of the cross in the air. She isn't sure if she should smile or wave; Alfonso, when she casts a look at him, keeps his eyes ahead. She tries to arrange her face into a pleasant yet dignified expression, neither too prim nor too joyful. How should a duchess look? She cannot help but glance into the faces of these people, who celebrate her appearance here with such glee. She sees: a man with a small child on his shoulder, the child waving its hand vacantly, as if it has been instructed to greet the new Duchess but has no idea why. A young boy holds the collar of a brown dog, which is crazedly barking at the horses and the soldiers; the boy's face joyous, delighted by the spectacle. An elderly couple, arm in arm, stand by a vendor selling woven baskets, the man leaning towards his wife, speaking into her ear, as if explaining what is before them. As Lucrezia rides by, she sees that the woman's eyes are occluded, sightless, her face turned up towards the sky, as if appealing to its power, as if its brightness is the only thing she can see. At a street corner, there is a girl with a sack balanced on her head, her feet bare and filthy, and here is a mother with a baby tied to her back, and by a small fountain, a group of children are tossing beads of water into the air, calling to each other. When they see the procession, they run from the well, clapping and shouting, jumping up and down, their thin limbs contorted with excitement. Lucrezia raises her hand and waves to them – she cannot resist – and the children burst into laughter, throwing their arms into the air to wave back, crying *La Duchessa, La Duchessa!*

Her smile falters when they turn a corner by a cathedral into a large piazza, overshadowed on one side by an imposing structure rearing up from an expanse of green moat, with tall towers at each corner. The *castello* is waiting for them, its drawbridge lowered in readiness.

It is vast, fortified, the walls thick, the battlements high – it is easily three or four times the size of her father's *palazzo*. Its foundations stand in water and the tops of its towers pierce the clouds. Rectangular windows interrupt the red brickwork on the upper floors, and a walkway runs from one tower to the next. Nobody could get in here, if uninvited, and nobody could get out, without permission. It is less of a *castello* than an edifice of power, a building that has its defence prepared in advance.

The hoofs of the horses clatter on the bridge; she sees a swallow veer along the surface of the moat, a blue-black arrow, then disappear under an arch. Lucrezia passes under the portcullis, pulled up, its metal spikes pointing down towards her, and then she is inside, the doors pushed shut behind her, the *castello* secured, and they are entering an open courtyard surrounded on four sides by vertiginous walls; Alfonso and Leonello are dismounting, tossing their reins to waiting groomsmen; Alfonso is pulling off his riding gloves, stretching his neck from side to side, and coming towards her horse to help her down.

Taking her arm through his, he turns her and together they face the mass of bowing servants and soldiers assembled before them. Alfonso passes his eyes over them, acknowledging their respect, accepting their deference, then gives them a nod and moves, with Lucrezia, towards the loggia's cool shade.

Then they are ascending a wide marble staircase, Alfonso saying something about a Dutch viceroy and a treaty over his shoulder to Leonello, who is following them, and something else about Urbino and a letter of intent. Leonello is saying, hmm, hmm, as if neither agreeing nor disagreeing with what Alfonso is saying, but committing it to memory. Lucrezia tries to stay several paces ahead, pulling the orbit of her skirts away from him: she hates to think of him coming up behind her, where she cannot see him. She tries, too, not to recall the noise of the serving boy's face as it struck the travelling box, that yielding thud.

The three of them arrive, Leonello and Alfonso still conversing about state matters, on a landing with tapestries hung on the walls. Lucrezia is turning her head to examine them – scenes of a mythic nature, with unicorns curled at the base of trees – when some servants dart forward to open heavy wooden doors, and they are passing through them, into a large state room with a lofty, vaulted ceiling; the walls are elaborately painted with, Lucrezia sees out of the corner of her eye, unclothed males, in a row, their arms held up in what might be joy or anger – it is hard to tell.

'Allow me,' Alfonso says, with a brief inclination of his head, 'to present my sisters.'

Lucrezia is taken aback. She had assumed she was being guided towards her chamber, where she might change out of her travelling clothes and prepare herself to be received by Alfonso's family, for the formal *menara a casa*. She had thought she would have several hours for this task. But here she is, still in her dusty *giornea* and cloak, her hair blown about, her gloves grimy. And here are they: distant figures at the far end of the room, on a dais, moving from sitting to standing, turning their faces towards her. Trying to hide her discomposure, Lucrezia slides her arm out of Alfonso's and curtseys deeply in the direction of the figures – were there two of them, or three, and was Alfonso's mother there? – bending her neck, just as she has been taught, so that her gaze rests on the rug.

There is an exclamation, then the sound of feet on the patterned marble, and a soft, musical voice saying, 'We are so glad you have come. What a joy it is to finally meet you, Lucrezia.'

A hand lands on her arm and Lucrezia raises her head to see a woman in an inky-blue sleeveless gown looking down at her. She is considerably taller than Lucrezia, with the same dark eyes as her brother, but with a fragile face, high cheekbones and a curving red mouth.

'Thank you,' Lucrezia falters, unnerved by the woman's warmth, her poised beauty, 'Your Highness. It is an honour and a—'

The woman takes Lucrezia's fingers in her own. 'Please, call me Elisabetta – we are sisters now, are we not?' She gestures at a second woman, coming haltingly forwards. 'And here is Nunciata.'

Lucrezia curtseys once more, conscious that Nunciata is looking her up and down. The sisters could not be more different. Elisabetta's shining dark hair is divided and piled up behind a lace band. She wears a stiffened ruff around her lovely column of a neck and a pearl choker. The slashed fabric of her gown reveals pale rose silk beneath and her slim feet are encased in gold leather shoes. Lucrezia wants to stare at her face, her dress, her jewels, so that she may memorise it all. She would guess her age to be around twenty-six or twenty-seven. Nunciata, however, is not so well favoured: her small eyes peer out of pasty skin, her neck is thick, with a soft chin disappearing into it. She is stout and short in stature, the crease between her brows suggesting that she is given to frowning, and her dress is dun-coloured, rigid with brocade. Tucked beneath her arm is a small spaniel with silky ears and a hostile, imperious face.

'Welcome,' Nunciata says, in a tone that pulls away from the meaning of the word, and gives a stiff nod.

Lucrezia smiles, hoping to communicate to her that she brings no judgement on her appearance, that she knows what it is to be the overlooked, less-admired sister. But Nunciata is looking away, across the room, towards the windows, where Alfonso stands conferring with Leonello.

'I see that marriage has yet to improve his manners.' Nunciata sighs and calls across to him querulously. 'Aren't you going to come and greet us? Or are you now expecting your little bride to do it for you?'

Alfonso gives no sign of having heard her, continuing his conversation.

'She is a *very* little bride,' Nunciata remarks, peering short-sightedly at Lucrezia's feet, then her arms, her hair, anywhere but at her face. 'Somewhat delicate-looking, is she not?'

Elisabetta flicks her gaze between sister and brother, then back to Lucrezia, giving her hand, which she still holds, a small and reassuring squeeze.

'She is lovely,' Elisabetta says, 'perfectly lovely. What a fortunate choice for—'

'Perhaps what I mean is young,' Nunciata interrupts. 'You seem very young,' she adds, more loudly, in an accusatory tone, as if Lucrezia is somehow at fault in this. 'I thought you were near twenty or so—'

'No.' Elisabetta cuts across her swiftly and smoothly, and they know, all of them, that Nunciata is mixing up Lucrezia with Maria, the bride who never was, and Lucrezia feels sure that if she were to turn her head, she might see Maria standing beside her, arms folded, peeved, much in the stance that Nunciata has adopted. 'Lucrezia is . . . fourteen, I believe, or fifteen?' She turns to Lucrezia for confirmation.

Lucrezia nods. 'I will be sixteen in—'

'A charming age!' Elisabetta exclaims. 'To be almost sixteen is—'

'Very young,' Nunciata mutters again, in the direction of her sister's ear, her face twisted with anxious displeasure, like someone who suspects she has been cheated in a purchase. 'Not too young,' she adds, in a whisper she apparently, and mistakenly, seems to think Lucrezia cannot hear, 'we hope?'

Colour rises to the delicate cheekbones of Elisabetta and she appears to struggle to know what to say. For a split second,

Lucrezia believes that Elisabetta is embarrassed by her sister's lack of tact, by her blundering indiscretion, but then Elisabetta looks quickly at the floor, bowing her head, and Lucrezia, aghast, sees that Nunciata has, instead, pinpointed and voiced Elisabetta's own concern, that they are, all of them, perhaps everyone in this building, just biding their time, desperately waiting for her to become pregnant.

Lucrezia stands there, in her travelling dress, in her fifteen-year-old skin. She feels as though these people desire to see right through her; they are like anatomists who peel back the hides of animals to peer inside, who unclothe muscle from skin and vein from bone, assessing and concluding and noting. They, all of them, pulse with the craving, the need, to see a child growing within her, to know that an heir is secured for them. They see her as the portal, the means to their family's survival. Lucrezia wants to fasten her cloak about herself, to hide her hands up her sleeves, to tie her cap to her head, to pull a veil over her face. You shall not look at me, she wants to say, you shall not see into me. I will not be yours. How dare you assess me and find me lacking? I am not La Fecundissima and never will be.

There is a movement to the side of her and Maria once again flits across her mind but the hand that closes over hers is familiar and warm: a tall presence is stepping in next to her. Alfonso.

He surveys his sisters, then looks at Lucrezia, scanning her face. If he manages to divine what has passed between the them, he doesn't let on. Instead, he lifts her hand and, in front of his sisters, clasps it to his chest.

'What do you think?' he says to them. 'Is she not a beauty? Did I not tell you I had chosen well?'

'Oh, yes,' Elisabetta says, with visible relief, 'oh, you did. It is wonderful to meet her. I am so happy, she is lovely.' Nunciata nods, her mouth pursed into a line, then mutters something about how they had feared he would never settle down but would continue in his youthful ways for ever, so it is a greatly fortunate event for this family that he has entered into matrimony, finally.

Alfonso allows a short silence after Nunciata subsides. He is unmoving, his eye trained upon her. Then he transfers Lucrezia's hand to his sleeve and holds it there, tight, in the crook of his arm. She can feel the iron-like contraction of muscle against her palm.

Lucrezia clears her throat. She feels that if anyone is to speak, it should be her. 'Is there . . .' She hesitates, looking about the room, as if she might find a different topic of conversation among its furnishings and chairs. 'Will I have the pleasure of meeting your honoured mother today? And your elder sister?'

Elisabetta flinches, her brows lifting, and she glances at Alfonso.

Nunciata snorts. 'Are you,' she gestures with the arm not holding the little dog, her gown rustling indignantly, 'intending to travel on to France?'

Lucrezia is thrown by this reply. 'I . . . no . . . Are they—?'

Elisabetta sighs. 'What do you wish us to say, Fonso?' she murmurs.

Alfonso doesn't reply. He disengages himself from Lucrezia, walks towards a table and pours himself a draught of wine. 'What do I wish you to say?' he repeats. 'Whatever do you mean, Elisabetta?'

'You know exactly what she means,' Nunciata snaps, and the spaniel, as if sensing its mistress's irritation, lets out a sharp, high bark.

Alfonso takes a sip from his glass, eyeing Nunciata and her dog over the rim. Lucrezia takes a step back. It is as if the room is filled with flickering flames, visible only to these three siblings, hidden conflagrations that would burn if she came too near them.

'My mother,' Alfonso enunciates these words clearly, and Lucrezia realises with a jolt that he is addressing her, 'is now in France, with our sister Anna. As I told you. So I struggle to comprehend why, my darling,' he says, swirling the wine around in its vessel, 'you would ask about them.'

Lucrezia opens her mouth to say, you never told me, you never told me anything. I assumed they would be here in Ferrara. You said that everything had been resolved to your satisfaction. But she closes it again. Elisabetta has seen this: she is looking at Lucrezia closely, sympathetically.

'Let us not talk of sad matters,' Elisabetta declares, clapping her hands. 'We must plan a celebration of your arrival, Lucrezia. I shall arrange a *festa*, with music and plays, to welcome you – we shall have the singers Alfonso likes so much, the ones he ordered from Rome. Not tonight, however,' she adds hastily. 'You must be tired from your journey. May we steal her away, Alfonso? Nunciata and I will take her to her chambers. I'm sure you would like to rest and unpack. We will have lots of time for conversation in the weeks to come. First, come with us and see your rooms. They are all prepared. I saw to it myself.'

'Thank you,' Lucrezia says. And when she sees the rooms, she says thank you again. Thank you, thank you. There is a private salon, which is perfectly square, occupying the highest floor of one of the *castello* towers; it has thick wall hangings, a writing desk, plush chairs, a huge fireplace, and two windows with cushioned seats. And through a door there is a smaller chamber, with a curtained bed, a mirror, cupboards and chests for her clothes. Already she can see servants placing her trunks and boxes in orderly piles. Emilia is moving among the luggage, counting off items on her fingers.

Nunciata struggles into the tower room, puffing, and lowers herself on to a chair, complaining about how fast they went, how she had forgotten the distance. The spaniel she puts on the floor, whereupon it disappears under the wide spread of her skirts.

'I hope you will be comfortable here,' Elisabetta says, while her sister, who is fanning herself, is still complaining about the stairs. 'I arranged these rooms myself, but you must say if there is anything not to your liking or—'

'Oh, no,' Lucrezia bursts out. 'It is all perfect. I wouldn't change a thing. They are beautiful rooms. You have both been so kind.'

'Not at all.' Elisabetta seats herself on one of the velvet settles. 'It was my pleasure. We were so happy when Alfonso got married. Weren't we, Nuncià?'

Nunciata grunts, fumbling in her pocket for a handkerchief.

'It was everything my sisters and I hoped for. And . . .' Elisabetta pauses to adjust her cuff '. . . also my mother. I only wish she . . . could have been in attendance.'

Lucrezia sits down next to her; she wants so badly to ask about the mother, why she left, what Alfonso said, do Elisabetta and Nunciata miss her, do they think she will come back, and what of Anna, their eldest sister, will she marry and produce an heir, and will that heir want Alfonso's title, *castello* and lands, and does this now mean that all hope for Alfonso's line is pinned on her, has the pressure for her to produce a child increased tenfold, that she blurts out instead: 'You are not married?'

Elisabetta turns her dark eyes on her.

'Forgive me,' Lucrezia says, 'I speak out of—'

'Nothing to forgive,' Elisabetta says, in a light tone. 'No, I am not. And neither is Nuncià. I cannot speak for her but I have yet to receive an offer that tempts me.'

'Into matrimony,' Nunciata murmurs mockingly, 'that is. For you are tempted by other types of offer, are you not, Elisa?'

'Nuncià, please.' Elisabetta's colour is high, her cheeks burning. For the first time, she has lost her poise, her veneer of calm.

'One in particular,' her sister continues, in a malicious whisper.

Elisabetta turns towards Lucrezia and says, through a set mouth, 'My sister likes to tease.'

'I have sisters, too,' Lucrezia says, 'so I know how it is.' Then she corrects herself confusedly. 'A sister, I mean. I had two but. . .'

Elisabetta reaches out and covers Lucrezia's hand with her own. For a moment, the three of them – the bride, the two sisters-in-law – sit in silence, a triangular shape inside the square of the room.

Then Elisabetta, with refined skill, removes her hand to gesture at the window, where the blue Ferrara sky is already darkening. 'It is getting late. We will leave you. Nuncià, shall we?'

Nunciata, putting away her handkerchief, nods, but neither gets to her feet. Lucrezia shifts inside her dress. The spaniel pokes its face – snub nose and bulging eyes – out of Nunciata's skirt to stare fixedly at Lucrezia.

'Will you take supper here in your rooms tonight?' Elisabetta enquires. 'We can order it to be brought.'

'I'm sure she is capable of ordering her own meals,' Nunciata snaps. 'Such things were possible in Florence, were they not?'

Lucrezia looks from one sister to the other. What would be the correct reply? She does not understand what has passed between the two of them, but she is aware that Nunciata has scored some acrimonious triumph or other over the beautiful Elisabetta, who is discomposed and flushed. Lucrezia knows enough about siblings to be aware that when Elisabetta and Nunciata leave this room, bitter words and accusations and justifications, perhaps reaching back over their shared lifetime, will be exchanged and aired.

'Yes,' she says. 'Of course. Please don't trouble yourselves any further on my account.'

'Very well,' Elisabetta says, in her musical voice. She gathers her skirts around herself, preparing to leave. But she does not look at Lucrezia or Nunciata when she says, 'You will not repeat my sister's silly remark, will you? To Alfonso, that is?'

Lucrezia blinks.

'It would only . . .' Elisabetta chooses her words '. . . worry him. He has so much on his mind. I wouldn't want to add to his cares. And Nunciata was only teasing. Weren't you?' she appeals to her sister.

Nunciata is fussing over her dog, letting its ears slide through her hands, ignoring Elisabetta. Again, Lucrezia has that sensation of flames flickering in the air between them.

'Was I?' Nunciata says eventually.

'Yes, you were.'

'If you say so.'

'Do you promise, Lucrè?' Elisabetta says, with an attempt at playfulness, but Lucrezia can hear the knife-edge of anxiety in her voice. 'I may call you Lucrè, may I not?'

'Of course,' Lucrezia says. 'My sister calls me that.'

'Then it is entirely fitting. We are sisters now, also.'

'And I promise,' Lucrezia says, 'that I won't mention this to Alfonso.' She thinks she would promise anything to the lovely creature who has furnished these rooms for her, who is so anxious to conceal something about herself that she has to pretend it doesn't matter at all.

'Thank you,' Elisabetta says. 'It is of no consequence, you understand. Just a trifling matter. But thank you.'

Elisabetta's heart-shaped face relaxes with relief. She reaches out and gives Lucrezia's cheek a light pinch. 'Such a sweet and pretty thing you are,' she murmurs. 'Alfonso made a wise choice. Don't you think, Nuncià?'

Nunciata makes a non-committal noise. The spaniel, sighting a pigeon on a balustrade, emits a tiny growl, lurching forward on its slender lead.

Elisabetta touches her fingers thoughtfully to Lucrezia's hair, bound as usual inside its band and *scuffia*. 'This is a Florentine fashion?'

'I . . .' Lucrezia raises her hand to the net, feeling the seed pearls pushing back into her palm '. . . it . . . My mother wears it like this. I believe it was a custom of her own mother. And we, her daughters, always—'

'Your mother is Spanish, is she not?' Nunciata asks.

'She was born there but spent her girlhood in Naples, where her father was—'

'And you speak Spanish?'

'I do.'

'What else?' Nunciata demands.

'French, a little German. And I can write Latin and Greek.'

'I see. Quite the little scholar, aren't you?'

Lucrezia makes a lightning decision to sidestep the aggressive tone; sometimes this worked when Isabella and Maria were taunting her. 'My father,' she says evenly, 'believed in educating his daughters, alongside—'

'You have ladies-in-waiting with you, I assume?'

Lucrezia shakes her head. 'I thought perhaps I would—'

'No lady-in-waiting?' Nunciata regards her with a shrewd gaze. 'Not even one?'

'I brought a maid,' Lucrezia says, 'and I'm very fond of her. She is in there.' Lucrezia points to the chamber.

Nunciata leans sideways, peering through the open door to the chamber, where Emilia is bending over the boxes, lifting out garments and shaking them in the air. She is evidently unimpressed by what she sees because she says: 'I will send a woman to you directly. A companion. Someone befitting your status. She can wait on you, introduce you to the fashions of this court, and perhaps attire you appropriately.'

Lucrezia, unnerved, can make no reply. The thought of admitting into her rooms a lady-in-waiting she has never met, and one selected by the unpleasant Nunciata, is not a welcome one. A spy in her midst. What is so wrong with her attire now, and her hair? She would like to lean forward and say to this woman that her mother is considered a great beauty, and highly stylish, that people come from all over the province, and beyond, to look upon her, to copy her dress and her manners.

Elisabetta must have divined her unease because she says, without warning, as if to change the subject: 'Tell us about Alfonso.'

'What of him?'

'He seems well. So restored by his time in the country, by his time with you. It is a delight to see. Is it not, Nuncià?'

Nunciata doesn't reply, but keeps her head bent over her lapdog, still murmuring into its ear.

'He is . . .' Elisabetta seems to hesitate '. . . attentive to you?'

Lucrezia nods. 'Yes.'

'And . . . kind? He treats you well?'

'Yes.'

Elisabetta looks at her for a moment longer, then says: 'Good. I am glad to hear it.'

She helps Nunciata to her feet. 'We will leave you now. Please send me word if you need anything. My rooms are adjacent to the state room where we first met. Nunciata's are next to mine.' She crosses to the door, her arm through Nunciata's, where she turns to say: 'Alfonso's apartment is directly below yours. There is a staircase linking your rooms with his. I'm sure he will be up to see you soon.'

He doesn't come that night. Lucrezia listens out for the purposeful tread of his boots up the private staircase, for the sound of the door latch lifting without so much as a knock. But neither comes.

She makes preparations for retiring, Emilia turning back the covers, then drawing the curtains around the bed, with Lucrezia inside: a songbird in a fabric cage. Still no sign of him.

Lucrezia waits. The room fills with darkness, the stars pushing their distant cold light through pierced holes in the sky. She pictures herself, in her tower room, at the corner of the *castello*, where two of its sides meet. This room seems to hover in space, above the city, high above the green moat. If she were to lean too far out of the window, she would lose her footing and drop like a stone into the water.

She asks Emilia to sleep not in the small closet off the chamber's anteroom but on a pallet beside her bed. The maid obliges, carrying her bedding through and settling herself quickly, without fuss.

But sleep will not come for Lucrezia, refuses to hear her call. Her mind, made restless by the journey, by the new rooms, has too much to do, too many impressions to review and polish and store away, too many questions to pose and ponder. Elisabetta and her high gold shoes, her delicate cheek-bones, the secret Lucrezia barely comprehends but must keep from Alfonso, Nunciata and her ill temper, her stubby fingers, the sleek, peeved face of the spaniel, with teeth like white needles, the vanished French mother, the elder sister whose putative marriage would pose a terrible threat, the court over which Alfonso must exert his authority, like a falconer bringing a bird to glove, the feast to come.

The *castello*, under its mantle of night, respires with strange noises: the creak of joists, faint ripples of footsteps, a shuffle and clink outside in the passageways, which Lucrezia tells herself will be the guards doing their rounds, but which the fevered part of her brain tells her is some spectre or dead spirit, dragging chains and instruments of torture around the *castello*'s quiet spaces.

She tries to harness her hearing, to bring it under control, like a wayward bloodhound, orders it not to listen out for all that is distant, but to focus instead on what is in the room: the brush of the bed curtains as they move in the draught, to the deep and regular sound of Emilia's breathing.

Lucrezia is the guide for this night, its companion, its confessor. She hears doors swing open and slam closed; she hears a cart clatter along the street below; she hears the rumble of a voice – male – perhaps on the floor below, and a woman answer it, in tones that, to Lucrezia, seek to reassure; she hears, far in the distance, beyond the city walls, the plaintive cry of a wolf. She sees the darkness weaken, grapple by degrees with the dawn, then cede its sovereignty to a vitreous grey mist. And, just as this night, her first, is very nearly over, as it is ushered into obliteration, she falls asleep, an exhausted guide, her task complete.

Alfonso's singers at the banquet stand at either side of the dais, their heads tilted upwards, their voices seeming to rise not from their mouths but from a place somewhere behind them. The sound is like nothing Lucrezia has ever heard: their voices carry more strength, more power, than any other singers'. They begin a note and, without pausing to draw in more breath, sustain and stretch it for so long that Lucrezia feels a sympathetic dizziness. How can they sing for the count of eight, nine, ten and beyond? Their voices intertwine, rising to the vaulted ceiling, twisting and growing; they sing with each other, against each other, the melody veering back and forth between them, like a shimmering kite on a string.

She glances around, wanting to know if others share her astonishment. Nunciata, on the other side of the table from her, seems oblivious, deep in conversation with someone introduced to Lucrezia as a poet. Her spaniel stands on the table, lapping from a dish, its little haunches convulsed by shivers. Elisabetta is facing the performers but her gaze has slid sideways, fixed on the far side of the room. Others listen for a moment, then turn to their neighbour to murmur a remark or an aside; two women, one in an emerald-green dress and a frothy half-ruff, the other's hair adorned with small, stuffed birds, are whispering together, their faces close, their shoulders trembling with silent laughter. A man at the end of the table has one hand inserted into an arrangement of fruit, his fingers straying over grapes, peaches, apricots; he settles on a fig, drawing it out of the heap and dropping it, whole, into his waiting mouth. Catching Lucrezia's eye, he gives her a wink, his lips mobile and moist. She looks away. Only Alfonso, Lucrezia sees, is intent on the music. He leans forward, one elbow on the table, chin resting in his hand, his index finger beating out the tempo of the song on his temple. He is rapt, transported; he is caught up in the music, a willing butterfly in its beautiful frail net. She pictures the notes and phrases rippling through his head, like many-coloured pennants.

She is wearing her wedding gown as she sits at the banqueting table. He had come to her rooms earlier in the day, looking tired and unslept, to request this of her. He was sorry, he said, that he was not able to visit her yesterday evening. State matters had required his attention – many people had needed to speak with him, it is often so when he has been absent from the *castello* – but would she please wear the gown to the *festa* arranged in her honour? Courtiers would be happy to see her in her wedding clothes, and he would be proud to escort her into the room and present her to the court. She had looked like a goddess and he wants the whole of Ferrara to see her thus, at his side. Emilia clapped her hands when he had gone and ran to fetch it. She was so happy, she said, as she straightened its skirts and teased out the gold panels, that Her Highness would wear it again, and so soon.

So Lucrezia has put it on, once more: the blue skirt, the huge sleeves, the gold *cintura* Alfonso gave her. This time, however, she was able to instruct Emilia to fasten the bodice as she wishes, to ignore the marks made by her mother, indicating where the lacings should be tied, to make it her own. Tonight, it doesn't feel like Maria's but hers and hers alone. She is no longer an imposter, an interloper assuming the life of her sister, but herself: Lucrezia, Duchess of Ferrara.

There had been music when she and Alfonso entered the banqueting hall – trumpets sounding out trilling arpeggios – and outbursts of exclamation and applause. People were lining the long sides of the room, and Alfonso had led her on a circuit, pausing every now and again to present a particular person to her: a cousin, a friend, a courtier, a poet, a sculptor, a companion, some of Nunciata and Elisabetta's ladies-in-waiting, a lute player, the head of the guardsmen. Lucrezia had inclined her head to these people, accepting their curtseys and bows, trying to imprint their names on her mind so that she would remember them. The dresses of the ladies were narrower than in Florence, with higher collars, more lace, and bodices longer at the front. She examined these gowns from the corner of her eye, as an adviser of Alfonso informed her of the number of exits and entrances in Ferrara's city walls, while Alfonso stood at her side, his hands clasped behind him. She could feel him vibrating with amusement at the man's determination to reel off the names of all of the gates, enumerating them on his stubby fingers. She nodded, as if fascinated by this information, all the while wondering if she could draw these Ferrarese dresses in a letter to Isabella, who had told her to write with detailed descriptions of the fashions here.

It is through this lens that she views the entire *festa*. How would she relate this to Isabella, she is wondering throughout a long and somewhat meandering theatrical performance of a historical dramatic verse about a king who accidentally poisons his wife, and is then for evermore haunted by her ghastly and reproachful apparition. Which of the dishes, she considers as she eats, will she describe in her letter? The stuffed head of the *cinghiale* – its mouth forced open with a yellow quince, its eyes closed to the indignity – the fish broth, the twists of almond pastries, the *frittata*, the white slabs of *lardo crudo*, the slices of cheese so fine you can see the light through them.

She composes sentences in her head, as she sits at the table: *It is a very refined court,* she will write to her sister, who has remained in Florence, at their parents' side, who has not been sent to live with her husband. *They value not acrobats or* nano *antics but theatre, poetry and music.* Or: *The ladies wear their hair piled high above the radius of their ruffs.* And: *There was a recitation of an epic poem, followed by two singers with extraordinary voices – I only wish you could have heard them.*

The thought of writing this letter brings a sharp and novel pleasure. She will be able to tell Isabella about things she does not know. She allows herself to imagine Isabella reading closely, avidly, then feeling pangs of jealousy, of wishing that she, too, could go to Ferrara. She might visit, perhaps. Lucrezia could invite her, if Alfonso permits it, and Isabella could ride over the Apennines and reside for a time here with her, in the *castello*.

Lucrezia sighs. The music and the voices of the singers have taken a melancholic turn, sliding into a minor key. It is unlikely that Isabella will come. She is so caught up in her life in Florence, so absorbed by it. If Lucrezia wrote to her, describing this *festa*, in all likelihood Isabella would lose interest halfway through the letter, toss it aside, and go off to find one of her friends or whichever courtier is her current pet.

The sentences fade in Lucrezia's mind; they fall silent. She smooths the folds in her skirt and concentrates instead on the room, which flares with murmured conversation and song, the swaying light from the candles, which finds its echo in the jewels about the ladies' necks, in their rings, on the hilts of the men's weapons.

The song builds to a climax, both singers hitting the same high note, its sound swelling and amplifying in the air between them. Then, glancing at each other, they close their mouths in perfect unison, snipping the silken rope of the note in half.

Applause descends like a rainstorm. People stand up from their seats, raising their hands to clap; women wave their handkerchiefs; men call, bravo, bravo, more, again. The people who applaud the loudest, Lucrezia notes, are the ones who talked through the performance.

She claps and claps until her palms sting. The singers blow kisses into the crowd, moving towards each other, with a curious sideways gait, clasping each other's hands and bowing low. Lucrezia is used to tumblers, acrobats, jesters, but there is something elevated and indefinable about these singers. They are tall, with long, tapering limbs, and pointed feline faces; the flex and motion of their wrists, their arms, is mesmerisingly agile, as if their joints are oiled to move more smoothly than others'. While they were singing, that is what they were – singers, geniuses, angels – but standing, as they are now, bowing and calling words to people in the room, they are once more human.

Alfonso bends towards her through the noise, shrinking his height so that he might look into her face. 'You are enjoying the music?'

'Oh, yes,' she says. 'It is like nothing I have ever heard. It is sublime – they are extraordinary. Their singing, the way they can switch from a low note to a high one – I don't know how they do it, how they flex their voices in that way.'

He is regarding her, intrigued, still clapping. 'You are right,' he says, surprised. 'I had not thought of that. They do have an extraordinary ability to go from a low register to a high one. It is a skill unique to their kind.'

'Their kind?'

'They are *evirati*. I ordered them especially from Rome. They are trained, most rigorously, from a very young age, even before they undergo . . . ' He makes an indecipherable gesture with his outstretched fingers. 'It produces a voice extraordinarily pure, with unprecedented range. Their vocal cords are those of a young boy, in a body the size of a man.'

In a rush, she understands. She has read about such customs in the ancient world but had no idea it happened in her own. She feels colour invade her face, while a peculiar suffocating sensation grips her throat. She glances quickly at the figures by the candelabra – their long, slender wrists, their smooth and ageless faces. She cannot help but picture them as small children, about to be operated on, without knowing what was ahead. What pain and shock they must have suffered, all for the whim of a wealthy man, what helplessness and confusion. Did they have any choice? Who would perform such a procedure?

The room is falling silent; people are resuming their seats, their whispered conversations. The singers are preparing for another song.

As the first phrases of the music float out over their heads, Alfonso reaches out and covers her hand, resting on the tabletop, with his own. Her disquiet at the enforced gelding of the *evirati*, treated no better than performing animals, battles for a moment with the simplicity of this gesture, its heartfelt nature.

Alfonso's hand dropping on to hers like this, its fingers curling around hers, carries enormous, significant weight. For her it means he must love her, must feel for her – but also for the entire room, the gathered assembly. To do this, here, in front of his whole court, with all his friends and associates and courtiers and guardsmen and servants and artists and musicians and poets looking on, is a statement, a message, of commitment and love, and also perhaps renewal. Maybe she, the new Duchess, can heal the rift in this court caused by the old Duchess, its evident instability and unhappiness, the religious schism, the attempted annexation of her daughters, the absent sister?

Resplendent in her bridal dress, Lucrezia sits with her hand in that of her husband. She is so pierced by happiness that she believes she must be glowing, like a lantern in the darkness. Someone loves her – a man, a powerful and erudite man. She has invoked and inspired love in the heart of a duke: she, Lucrezia. More than anything, she wishes she could write this down, for Isabella, for anyone to read: *He took my hand at dinner, in front of the whole court.* She sees Nunciata noticing, and looking away. She sees the woman with the birds in her hair cast a brief, stabbing glance at their joined hands, then whisper something in her companion's ear, her pretty vixen face distorted by ire and envy. She sees that the man who ate the fig is now picking at his teeth with a small chicken bone. She sees Nunciata plucking at the sleeve of the poet, who, with a weary courtesy, leans towards her to hear what she is saying. She sees Elisabetta moving along the far edge of the room, weaving through the chairs and seated guests, making her way past a figure standing beside a pillar. It is a uniformed soldier: Ercole Contrari, the head of the guardsmen, to whom Lucrezia was introduced an hour or so ago. She recognises his moustache, his handsome, even-featured face. He is leaning with one arm on the pillar, and as Elisabetta passes, his body inclines towards hers. He murmurs something but Elisabetta affects not to have heard him, turning her face resolutely towards the room, the tables, the rows and rows of guests. Lucrezia sees, however, that Contrari's hand extends, and it holds, between its fingers, a folded piece of paper, which Elisabetta, twisting her arm up and behind her back, plucks from him, quickly, deftly, and conceals up her wide, tapering sleeve, and then she moves on, as if nothing at all has taken place. It is an act so smooth, so practised, yet so charged with danger, for him and for her, that Lucrezia's breath leaves her chest. Lucrezia swivels her eyes towards Alfonso, but he is still focusing on the singers; she swivels them back to Elisabetta, who is taking a seat across the room, next to some cousins, and her face has an air of calm but her eyes – her eyes! – are alight with a treacherous, beguiling happiness.

The *evirati* tilt back their heads, open their throats, and pour forth notes that soar to the ceiling like the arrow-winged swallows who flit along the surface of the moat.

Later that night, long after the feast has been eaten, after the revellers have left the state room, have taken to their beds, after the servants have cleared the tables, washed the dishes, pans and spits, swept the tiles, after everyone in the walls of the *castello* has gone to their chambers, Alfonso falls asleep in Lucrezia's bed, his arm clamped around her.

She lies beneath its weight until she is sure he is deeply asleep, then eases out from under it, sliding a cushion into her place, so as not to wake him. She is just about to push her way through the curtains when she is jerked backwards by the hair and, for a horrifying moment, she thinks he has seized it and is dragging her back to bed.

But when she turns, she sees that he still sleeps, his all-seeing eyes closed, his hands uncurled. The ends of her hair are trapped between his torso and the mattress.

Lucrezia eases them out, freeing herself, strand by strand.

In the other room, a silver crepuscular glimmer lies low on the floor. She tiptoes through it, fancying that her feet will become stained by its luminous glow, that by morning she will discover she has left tell-tale bright footprints behind.

She sits down at the desk and takes out a roll of vellum and a sheet of paper. She cuts herself a new nib, brushing the shavings into a neat pile. She draws the feathered tip of the quill against her lips one way, then the other, feeling the hooks of the filaments unlatch then reconnect, unlatch, reconnect.

She has no sense of what she wants to do: write a letter, draw, read, commit a verse to memory. She just knows that sitting here, in front of her desk box, with its cargo of ink and charcoal and penknife and paper and brushes, brings her a peace that she can find nowhere else.

Sleep will not come for her; it is a steed she cannot catch or harness; it throws her off, it takes flight if she comes near, it refuses her entreaties. She doesn't know if it is the rich food she has eaten or the tall man sprawled across the middle of her bed or the distracting blue-white light spilling into her rooms.

She dips the quill in ink and lets it dry as she stares, unmoving, at the coin-like face of the moon, which has pasted itself to the outside of her window. She dips it again. She resolves to write not to her sister but to her mother.

Dearest Mamma,

It is late at night and I am thinking of you all. I hope this letter finds you in good health and even better spirits. I send my love to you, and Papa, Francesco, Isabella, Giovanni, Garzia, Ferdinando and Pietro.

Please ask them all to write to me, as often as they can. I wish to hear everything that goes on. How are Papa's hounds, the cats in the nursery, and also the little chestnut pony? Who is riding her now, I wonder? Please don't let it be Pietro – he will kick her too hard and she is too sweet-natured for that.

We arrived in Ferrara yesterday, where hundreds and hundreds of citizens were waiting for us. Alfonso's people are very loyal to him: he looked very handsome and grand, sitting up on his horse as we rode through the streets. I wish you could have seen it. I have met his sisters, two of them (his mother and the eldest sister have gone to France – I do not know why – maybe Papa has heard something of this?).

Tonight was the festa. *There was music (evirati – have you ever heard their singing?) and a recitation. I have written on the back of this page a list of the food that was served, and also sketched for you the dress of a Ferrarese lady. Isabella might find this interesting. Their fashions, as you can see, are quite different from ours.*

The castello *is so large and is certainly a change from the* delizia. *I am worried I will get lost in all the corridors and staircases! My rooms are in the south-east tower, on the floor above Alfonso. His sisters fitted them out for me, and they are very nice. If you like, I will do a drawing of them for you next time I write.*

Tell me news of Sofia. I hope her knees aren't troubling her too much in damp weather?

I pray for you all and I wish I could see you. I send a thousand salutations, and even more kisses,

Your affectionate daughter,
Lucrè

She reads over her page. How bloodless it all seems, how craven: the questions about pets and siblings, the lists of food, the quince-dumb *cinghiale* and dishes of figs. She hates the self she is in these words. It could have been written by anyone.

What she really wants to know is: is it raining in Florence tonight? Has the thunder of autumn begun? Is Papa swimming in the Arno? Are the starlings swarming above the piazza at the day's end? Does the light still slant into my chamber in the evening, just before it disappears below the city's roofs? Do you miss me? Even a little? Does anyone ever go and stand before my portrait?

She melts the sealing wax over a candle flame, then presses her insignia into the molten drips: her father's crest of a shield with six *palle*.

She puts the finished letter to one side and, glancing over her shoulder, she reaches into the desk box once more, this time taking out a small square of *tavola*, one she planed and sanded herself, only last week. It is untouched; she runs her fingers over its smooth surface, weighs it in her hand. She takes up a piece of red chalk and moves across it, from top to bottom, sketching an upright object, narrow, double-sided. A pillar. Next to it emerges first a triangular shape, which, with a few more strokes of the chalk, acquires a head and arms, resolves into a figure.

Lucrezia grinds pigments, mixes them with drops of oil. She takes a slender-tipped brush and paints a fine, heart-shaped face, a narrow neck, a diminutive chin, lowered eyes, a dreamy expression. Behind this woman, she puts a man, barely seen, merging into blue shadow; this second figure is leaning towards the first and its face is tender and gentle.

When it is finished, the palm-sized painting fills Lucrezia with satisfaction and also fear. She looks at it for a long time; she watches as the paint dries and solidifies, the couple's features resolving into permanence, the man for evermore leaning towards his lover, her face suffused with pleasure.

Lucrezia touches her fingertip to the oil paint, to ascertain that it is indeed dry, irrevocable, and the moon suddenly clothes itself in mist, as if it, too, is alarmed by what her hand has created.

She glances behind her, as if to check that the door to her chamber is shut, that Alfonso is not looking over her shoulder. Then she takes a stiff-bristled brush and loads it with a dark greenish-brown, the colour of forest shade, and with sweeping movements, she covers the image with darkness, obliterating the lovers, sealing them inside a tomb of paint. The woman's dress disappears, the man's hand, their faces, the column. In moments, it is all gone, hidden for ever, the only sign the scene was ever there the slight undulations in the paint's surface, like rocks on the bed of a lake.

She cleans the brushes with a rag; she tidies the desk; she props the now-blank *tavola* against a vase to dry; she extinguishes the candle and, after ensuring that all traces have been eliminated, returns to bed.

Alfonso's routine at the *castello* is obscure to her; she knows only that he is much busier here than he was at the *delizia*. He rises early, for exercise, usually accompanied by Leonello and two or three other young men. They ride in the hunting ground outside the city walls or fence together in the courtyard. He then goes to his offices, to read his correspondence, to write letters and directives, to hear pleas and commissions, to give orders to his guards and secretaries and officials and advisers and politicians and architects and cardinals and councillors, to work tirelessly and determinedly at bringing the region under his control. Emissaries, courtiers, military personnel and ambassadors arrive and depart all day long. He often takes his midday meal there, if he is particularly busy. Emilia reports on what she has heard, via his under-secretaries, who talk to the grooms, who in turn talk to the guards, who talk to the kitchen servants, who then talk to the maids: that Alfonso has stationed spies in all parts of his region, and also in neighbouring ones, that the province is reasonably peaceful but the court itself is another matter.

Lucrezia can pass a whole day without seeing him, beyond a brief glimpse as he crosses the courtyard, with a stern and preoccupied air, flanked by officials, or a wave from him to her, as she takes the air on the loggia and he rides in through the gates on an exhausted horse, or a hasty farewell in the morning as he leaves her bedchamber.

He visits the chapel on the lower floors once a day, he has told her, not so much for Mass or confession, but to sit at the back to hear the choral master put the *evirati* through their practice. This master, he said to Lucrezia, is one of the best in the world: an Austrian sent from Vienna, who insists on a strict two hours every morning devoted to vocal exercises and harmonic improvisations. In the afternoon, they rehearse musical performances, to be presented at court gatherings, according to Alfonso's wishes. Alfonso tells Lucrezia that he likes to sit there and listen; it clears his head, he says, lulls his mind. If ever he has to make a difficult decision, regarding policy or finance or family, he finds that being in the chapel during their practice helps him reach a solution.

After four or five days at the *castello*, Lucrezia realises that what she will have here is long periods of liberty. She cannot believe it. The days offer so many hours in which she might do as she wishes. She can sit at her desk and sketch what she sees from her window or inside her head or whatever items she has arranged beside her – a globe, a leather glove, a telescope, a dead pigeon from the kitchens, the skeleton of a squirrel that she found near the *delizia* – and consider how best to transpose them to paint and canvas. She can dispatch Emilia to the apothecary to purchase a certain weight of cochineal or verdigris; the maid returns with waxed paper twists filled with pigments, tightly wrapped conical parcels from which spill the ingredients for a rainbow, for bears and beasts and rain and leaves and hair and flesh, for anything in the world, if only she is able to find the exact mix, the perfect brushstroke. She can take the private stairs down to the ducal apartment and make use of the orange-tree terrace, where she can gaze out at the city streets through the diamond-shaped openings in the walls. Everything feels, during the first week in Ferrara, attainable and possible. There is some-thing about these days spent within the *castello* that fills her with a molten sense of potential: she might do anything, paint anything. All she needs to do is put out her hand and grasp what she wants.

Alfonso's sisters, however, have other plans for her. After several days in which Lucrezia shuts herself into her rooms, intent on experimenting with miniature bird's-eye perspectives of different buildings – the *delizia*, the *palazzo* – Elisabetta begins to send for her, most mornings. Her rooms are draped in deepest pink, like the interior of a soft fruit, and Lucrezia is obliged to sit and watch while her sister-in-law finishes her hair or covers her face and hands in a beautifying paste, as she consults with her ladies-in-waiting about this gown or that letter or this recital or an upcoming *festa*.

She will then link her arm through Lucrezia's and they will walk together along one side of the *castello*, one room opening into another, down a staircase or up to the private loggia. Elisabetta might beg Lucrezia to pick some of the orange blossoms that grow on the terrace in the ducal apartments.

'These blooms,' she will say, when Lucrezia brings her a basket of them, 'are so good for brightening the skin. Not,' she will add with a smile, 'that you need it, dearest.'

She asks Lucrezia about her childhood, about her brothers and sisters, about the city of Florence, where Elisabetta has never been but has heard much of its charms and its exquisite buildings. She listens carefully to Lucrezia's answers, and remembers the details of her family, their names, ages and predilections.

'Perhaps,' Lucrezia ventures, because it becomes rude not to, 'you will go there one day.'

Elisabetta's mouth turns up into a smile. 'I should like that very much.'

Lucrezia tries to picture Elisabetta in her parents' *palazzo*: her narrow dresses sweeping the tiled floors, her observant eyes gazing upon the gilt ceilings, the crackle of her ruff-lace as she turns her head this way and that, her modulated tones conversing with Isabella, with Eleanora. She cannot picture it and she wonders, with a stab of unease, if Nunciata would insist on coming, too, and how she would cast her eyes critically over her parents' opulent frescos and statues, how she would wince at the noise of the musicians as they played rousing tunes to accompany the acrobats. She hates the idea of Nunciata telling her ladies what a garish place the Florentine court is. The thought of Nunciata and her snappish spaniel there makes her, for the first time, feel protective of her parents, of the world they have built around themselves.

She will never take Elisabetta or Nunciata there.

Elisabetta ensures that Lucrezia doesn't spend too long in her rooms, drawing her into life at court. You are not to shut yourself up in here all day, she says, walking in unannounced, pulling back the window coverings, ruining the light that Lucrezia has carefully filtered for whatever painting she is working on. Elisabetta glances at Lucrezia's easel but doesn't say anything beyond an encouraging, how pretty. She will take Lucrezia's hand, ordering Emilia to remove the painting smock, and will then lead her down to one of the salons, where writers are discussing poetry, or philosophers are debating ethics, or a player is giving a recitation, or noblewomen are whispering to each other about this husband or that lover or which dressmaker is the laziest. Lucrezia will sit, mostly silent, at these events. She will endure the stares and glances of the men and women of court, the way they assess her posture, her jewellery, her worth, her standing, her appeal or otherwise. She will switch off the surface part of her that notices these arrows and lances, and instead tune herself, like a lute string, to pick up only what is being said across the room, by the philosophers, by the player and his lines about Ithaca. If she hears the people around her murmur the name 'Alfonso', she will refuse entry to her head the words around it; she will not slip into the pool where these people swim; she will not, even, turn her eyes towards the door, where stands the broad and straight figure of chief guardsman, Ercole Contrari; she will not blink when Elisabetta slips out, shortly followed by him. She sees all this but does not admit it, to herself, or anyone else.

If there is a cloud on her horizon at this point it is only Nunciata, who becomes suddenly alert to the amount of time Lucrezia is spending with Elisabetta when she sees them pass the open door of the chapel one morning, where Nunciata sits alone with her dog. Lucrezia is relating to Elisabetta her mother's habit of keeping only Spanish ladies-in-waiting and how this often gives rise to linguistic misunderstandings between them and the *palazzo* servants; Elisabetta is laughing, she has her arm through Lucrezia's, she is saying how funny Lucrezia is, please tell her more. When Nunciata calls to her sister, asking where they are going, Elisabetta doesn't break stride, just says over her shoulder that she and Lucrè are going out for some fresh air. It isn't long before Nunciata comes after them, tracking them down to the courtyard, where Elisabetta has requested that Lucrezia's white mule be brought to them so that they may feed it orange peel and pastry crusts. Elisabetta is weaving coloured ribbons into the patient animal's mane while Lucrezia holds it still, and telling her women to brush out its tail, when Nunciata appears, spaniel under her arm, her face shiny with exertion. She watches with narrowed eyes as they decorate the mule, then lead her around the courtyard, asking each other if they should fetch more ribbons, in a brighter colour perhaps, or even lace, Elisabetta is suggesting that they call Alfonso, so that he may see, it might divert him. Lucrezia, carried along by these high spirits, is starting to nod, but Nunciata cuts across them.

'Our brother,' she says, apparently addressing only Elisabetta, 'would not appreciate being disturbed. Especially for this frivolity. Have some sense.'

Her voice is like water tossed on to a fire: the joy, the spark goes out of them all. They unwind the ribbons, they hand the reins of the mule back to the groom, they disperse from the courtyard.

After this, Nunciata is sure to attach herself to them every day. She ensures that she arrives early at Elisabetta's chamber so that she, too, may fetch Lucrezia from her rooms. She attends every salon gathering Elisabetta gives, even though she yawns and fidgets through each recitation or recital, often inserting herself in the seat between them, speaking over Lucrezia if she addresses a remark to Elisabetta, answering for Lucrezia if Elisabetta asks a question. It is an awkward grouping; Lucrezia longs for the days when it was just her and the lovely, light-hearted Elisabetta. This triangular dynamic, with the two of them warring over her attention, is confusing and uncomfortable, a far cry from Isabella and Maria's aloof and excluding pairing.

Elisabetta seems amused and delighted by Nunciata's behaviour, thinking up more and more remote places in the *castello* for them to hide, murmuring to Lucrezia that Nunciata will never find them here. She is so jealous, Elisabetta whispers, delighted, pressing Lucrezia's hand as they conceal themselves behind the window drapes in her salon. But when Lucrezia writes of it to her mother, thinking that she, too, will find it entertaining, she is taken aback when her mother replies in a very serious tone, warning her to be on her guard:

Dearest Lucrè,

Do not be deceived that Alfonso's sisters are engaged in this rivalry because they are fond of you. Never mistake such behaviour for affection. Remember that any alliance at court is always about power and influence. To be the confidante of their brother's wife, his duchess consort, is their aim. They want to be close to you so that they may be close to him, to secure their position. They see you as a way to him. Take care, always, not to show favour to one above the other. Conduct yourself with fairness, as well as a seemly distance. You are the Duchess, not them. Ask yourself why they are urgently seeking your favour. Is there any reason to suspect that either of them is acting against their brother in some way? Or perhaps you?

You are in my prayers, daily,
Your devoted mother

Lucrezia conceals this letter hastily, in a locked drawer. She takes it out, every now and again, to reread it. Can her mother be right? Perhaps it is just that Elisabetta enjoys her company and that Nunciata feels excluded by this. But doubts begin to pluck at the edges of her mind whenever she is with Alfonso's sisters. What do they want from her? Are their motives clouded, as her mother claims? Could their invitations and offers of company be moves in a sophisticated and invisible game of power?

After Elisabetta starts to take Lucrezia on daily rides with her, outside the city gates, and Nunciata cannot join them as she is not fond of horses, Nunciata sends to Lucrezia's door a lady-in-waiting. Clelia appears without any warning one afternoon, just as Lucrezia is returning from a ride, saying, with a deep curtsey, that she has been asked to wait upon the Duchess Lucrezia. She comes into the room, her deferential tone belied by the way she looks about her with naked curiosity, taking in the painting table, the easel, Lucrezia's collection of bird feathers, the delicate ivory of the fox skull on the windowsill. Her eyes have a slight bulge and tend to open so wide that the white sclera is visible all the way around the iris; she has, Lucrezia feels, a curious way of moving her feet, slapping the soles of her shoes down on the ground, and sighing deeply at intervals. Emilia is put out by her presence; Lucrezia catches her hovering, watching, as Clelia is performing some task – laying out clothes or polishing shoes. The two begin to compete, in what they believe are imperceptible ways, to be the one to take Lucrezia her morning drink, to slice her bread, to plait her hair, to fasten her bodice. Clelia is, Nunciata tells her, when she visits to find out how Lucrezia likes her new woman, the cousin of a noble family that has fallen on hard times. 'She has breeding,' Nunciata raps out, casting a disparaging glance at Emilia, 'and is a perfectly suitable companion for you.' Lucrezia is obliged to send Clelia on invented errands if she wants to paint or sketch or read, otherwise Clelia will move about the room with her slapping steps or gaze out of the window, sighing, as if she would rather be anywhere else but here.

'Give her a little longer,' is Elisabetta's advice, delivered with a gentle pat on the arm, when Lucrezia tells her how burdensome she finds Clelia's presence. 'She may settle. You may yet get used to her. She has,' Elisabetta says, 'done wonders with your dress and your hair. Do you not think?'

Lucrezia's hair, that day, has been done in the Ferrara style, similar to Elisabetta's, with curving wings at either side of her temples, and a great many sharp-ended pins holding it on the crown of her head. She is not sure if she likes it, and the sensation of that great weight of hair balanced on top of her head makes her neck feel stiff. But she does not say this: she nods, she smiles, she says she will indeed give Clelia more time.

Elisabetta nods, pleased, then says she has to go: she has an appointment. Her eyes meet Lucrezia's, as if to say, you know, don't you, you have worked it out? And Lucrezia rises to walk with her to the door, matching her step to Elisabetta's, silently telling her that, yes, she knows and will never tell.

Alfonso appears in her rooms earlier than usual that evening. Lucrezia is still preparing for bed: Emilia is removing her collar, pin by pin, and Clelia is unwinding the *cintura* Lucrezia wore at dinner, when he comes through the door.

'Please,' he says to the maids, who have paused, uncertain, in their tasks, 'continue.'

He seats himself in a chair, on top of several items of clothing, but neither Lucrezia nor Emilia nor Clelia dare to point out to him that he is crushing the fabrics. When Clelia places the *cintura* inside its box, which is on a table next to him, he lifts it out and holds it in his hands, letting its gold links and studded rubies pass through his fingers.

'Your hair,' he says suddenly, 'is different.'

Lucrezia is by now in her shift and skirts, standing in the middle of the room.

'Yes,' she says, turning to look at him. 'It is a new style for me.'

She waits for him to say that he likes it or perhaps doesn't like it or that it is the same arrangement as Elisabetta's, but he is silent.

He gets to his feet, still with the *cintura* in his hands, walks to the window, then back, as if to regard her from all angles.

'I have some exciting news for you,' he says, with a smile. 'Il Bastianino will arrive here tomorrow morning, for the portrait.'

'Yes, I've heard,' Lucrezia replies, 'and—'

'You have?' He pauses in his pacing. 'I wonder who told you.'

'Nunciata. She said—'

'And how did she come by this information?'

'I think she said . . .' Lucrezia wishes she had never spoken '. . . a friend of hers has commissioned something from Il Bastianino but the work will be late because he will be here, with us, instead of—'

'I see.'

He circles the room, from fireplace to window to doorway to chair. The maids have their heads down, their movements quick: they want to be out of here, Lucrezia knows, away from him. She is just about to dismiss them – the sooner Alfonso does what he came here to do, the sooner she can be alone – when Alfonso speaks again.

'You are spending a great deal of time with my sisters, I am told.'

Lucrezia looks at him. Is this a question or a statement? What would be the best reply here?

'I . . . yes . . . I suppose I am.'

'With Nunciata?'

'Yes.'

'Just Nunciata or Elisabetta as well?' His eyes travel up to her hairstyle as he asks this, then back to her face.

'Both of them. Initially, it was just Elisabetta who . . .' She trails away, suddenly feeling herself on unstable ground.

'Go on.'

'Who . . . Elisabetta . . . it was she who first . . . sought my company. She was very welcoming to me when I arrived, and then . . . Nunciata . . .' Lucrezia falters. She doesn't know how to articulate it all to him; she cannot understand what he wishes to hear or whether she might unwittingly say the wrong thing. 'She . . . Nunciata . . . seemed to desire to join us. So now . . .'

'Now?' he prompts.

'They . . . she . . . they are both . . . kind enough to . . . spend time with me and . . .'

'It's always the three of you together?'

'Sometimes.'

'And other times – what? It is just you and Nunciata? Or you and Elisabetta?'

Lucrezia nods.

'Does anyone else ever join you?'

'No,' she says quickly. 'Yes. Sometimes Elisabetta's ladies. Or . . . or some courtiers. That poet Nunciata likes.'

'Do you spend more time, would you say, with Nunciata or Elisabetta? Or is it about the same?'

'Perhaps . . . a little more with . . .'

'Elisabetta?' Again, his gaze flicks up to her hair.

'Probably, yes.'

'What do you do together?'

'We . . . take walks . . . around the loggia. I am invited to . . . gatherings in her salon.'

'And you leave the *castello* with her, every few days, do you not?'

'I do.'

'On horseback?'

'Yes.'

'To go riding?'

'Yes.'

He nods, thinking over this information, letting the *cintura* drop, link by link, into his palm. Then he places it back in its box and takes her hand, guiding her towards the chamber.

'Come,' he says, 'it's late, and you are probably tired.'

'Could I trouble Her Highness to please lift her chin a little? More. A touch more. Good, good, beautiful. Now turn your face towards the window, slowly, please, slowly. Yes, there! Hold that, please, Your Highness.'

The artist stands in the middle of the Salone dei Giochi, drenched in sunlight that falls from the windows. He is motionless, Lucrezia sees from the corner of her eye, for her gaze is directed towards the wall, feet together, arms aloft, like a swimmer about to dive or an acrobat finding poise before a trick.

'Yes,' he murmurs to himself, his fingers circling gently, as if he is holding invisible brushes, as if he has already begun, in his imagination. Then, without turning his head, he addresses someone behind him. 'Do you see, Your Grace? I feel this may be better than the previous pose: we get the curve of her jaw, the elegance of her neck, although how I will ever find the paint to reproduce that flush along her throat. It is exquisite, too exquisite. And that brow!'

Alfonso, clothed in dark colours today, moves about in the shadowy recesses of the room. He is examining sketches arranged on a long table, bending over one, then another, moving along the row, then back again. He told Lucrezia last night that Il Bastianino was the artist responsible for the frescos in this very room. There had been a wingbeat of silence before Lucrezia managed to get out a noise of approval. In fact, she does not like these frescos – babies riding dolphins, mer-folk astride serpents, men with impassive faces engaged in combat. They are, to her eye, oddly static and unappealingly fleshy. Alfonso, however, told her that Il Bastianino was the right artist for her portrait; how apt, he said, that he should have decorated the very walls of her home, and now he will paint her.

For several hours now, Lucrezia has been asked to pose in one way – seated, standing, feet crossed, hands laced, hands apart, head forward, head aside, arm up, arm down, wrist turned – while the artist makes a sketch. He then repositions her and does another.

He arrived at the *castello* this morning with a great deal of equipment, carried on the backs of several apprentices. Lucrezia's eyes swept through them: several young boys, a sullen youth, and Maurizio, who was telling the younger apprentices where to set up the materials, where to stack the shells, where to place the paper and the canvases. He was wearing the same blue jerkin as when she first met him, in the corridor of the *delizia*. No sign of Jacopo. Lucrezia felt a bright flare of anxiety in her chest: was he ill, had something happened to him? She checked the doorway, but it was empty, then looked back at Maurizio, questioningly. He must have been following her with his eyes because he gave the slightest downwards nod, as if to say, do not fear, he is well, nothing amiss has befallen him.

The artist, Il Bastianino, approaches her, lifts an arm or a fold of her skirt, moves the arrangement of the *cintura* about her waist, straightens the lace at her throat. And Alfonso stands by, observing, his hands clasped behind his back. Lucrezia finds the situation ludicrous: the idea that Alfonso is permitting another man to touch her dress or her hand or her jewels is so peculiar. If this man weren't painting her, it would not be out of the realm of possibility for Alfonso to unsheathe the dagger he keeps in his belt and run him through – she has heard of men killed for less.

Every now and again, Il Bastianino murmurs, 'With His Highness's permission,' as he comes near, and without waiting for Alfonso's response, his fingers will insert themselves into Lucrezia's cuff, to pull down the lace there, or he will touch her cheek or her temple.

What Alfonso does not know is that Il Bastianino gives her hand or her chin, or whatever part of her he is touching, a secret, surreptitious squeeze – just a minimal hidden pressure. The first time this happened, Lucrezia raised her eyes to the artist, startled, only to find him looking back at her, his face mischievous, provoking. He has a drooping moustache, longish hair that is starting to grey at the sides, pink jowls and animated green eyes. Lucrezia knows exactly his type, a man who cannot resist flirting with a woman, even if she is the duchess consort of his patron, even if she is thirty years younger than him, even if it means risking his life. Eleanora would stare him down – Lucrezia has seen her do this many times, to similar men – with a chill gaze, then tell Cosimo that he was 'a man not to be trusted'.

Lucrezia does not look at him again, will not meet his eye. She sits within her pose, as the artist and her husband and the apprentices and various courtiers look at her and discuss her and contemplate what would be desirous in this portrait – more gold, more jewels, a globe, a locket, an animal, a table, a book? What would give the correct impression? How to show the House of Ferrara to its best advantage? The artist sketches, Maurizio advises, Alfonso paces one way, then the other. Nunciata, her dog under her arm and accompanied by the poet Tasso, comes to stand next to Alfonso, peering over Il Bastianino's shoulder. She gives a small shrug of disdain, as if she doesn't like what she sees, and whispers something to Tasso, who smiles and shakes his head indulgently. Towards the end of the day, Leonello steps in through one of the doors, positioning himself next to Alfonso, glancing from the sketches to Lucrezia and back again, saying nothing.

She keeps still as best she can, unhitching herself from what is happening in the room, allowing her mind to roam. She becomes other and elsewhere, as she does at night, with Alfonso, leaving just her skin and bone behind, in her stead; only her outer layers remain. The rest of her withdraws, escapes, slips away. She thinks of her white mule, the jangle of its bridle as she rides through the forest; she thinks of Sofia and how she must be setting the nursery table with plates and spoons, perhaps asking one of the other nurses to rub her feet; she thinks of her mother's beloved insectarium, the oozing digestion of the worms, their adhesive strands of silk; she observes the way the mobile surface of the moat casts a silvery simulacrum of itself on to the walls and ceilings of this room. Then something out of the window catches her eye, pulling her back into the present, into the room.

There, on the narrow battlement of the opposite tower, she sees two figures, walking towards each other: black cut-out puppets against a blue sky. The woman moves towards the man, who is moving towards her; halfway along, they meet. Their bodies merge, the light between them is eclipsed.

It is, of course, Elisabetta and Contrari. Lucrezia recognises the quick step, the profile of the former; the latter has the guardsman's broad frame and plumed hat. For a moment, she is there with them, feeling the sensation of wind up on the tower, the urgency of their stolen embrace; she is Elisabetta, she is Contrari; the intensity of their love courses through her.

She regards them for a fleeting moment only, before bringing her gaze back into the room.

Alfonso is staring right at her, his eyes narrow.

Lucrezia attempts a smile but her heart is suddenly thudding against her dress. Is it possible that Alfonso could divine something? From her face or the way she was looking out of the window? How could he?

He has noticed something, however. Lucrezia sees that he is now looking out of the window, at the battlements, at the tower, at the sky, and Leonello, also, who has come to stand beside him.

Lucrezia risks a glance: Elisabetta appears to be alone. Contrari has gone. She lets out the breath she has been holding. Perhaps it will all be well.

Alfonso watches his sister move from one end of the tower to the other. His expression is thoughtful, his head tilted to one side, his arms crossed. When Elisabetta disappears from sight, into the doorway at the tower's centre, he turns back to the room. Lucrezia watches as he unfolds his arms, then walks over to where Il Bastianino is standing. He takes a long, measured look at the sketch the artist is working on, before reaching out and removing the paper from the easel.

'I thought I had made myself clear,' he murmurs, barely opening his lips. 'I want something that conveys her . . . how to put this? . . . her majesty, her bloodline. Do you understand? She is no ordinary mortal: treat her thus. Ensure, please, the portrait reflects that, above anything else. I want everyone who looks upon this to know instantly what she is: regal, refined, untouchable.'

Il Bastianino gapes at him, for a moment, stunned, then recovers himself.

'Of course, Your Highness,' he says, with a bow. 'I shall do my very best to fulfil your wishes.'

Alfonso nods. He casts the sketch to one side, then exits the room, without looking at anyone else.

A note sent early to her door, in her husband's handwriting: she is to be painted in an outfit designed to his specification, which was delivered late last night. Would she please put it on, along with the betrothal gift, and come down to the salon? He signs this missive, *your Alfonso.*

In the square room, from a hook in the wall, hangs the skirt of the gown. The bodice and sleeves are separate entities, draped over the credenza and the table. To Lucrezia, as she steps over the threshold, it looks as if a woman has been cut into four pieces and calmly arranged around the furniture.

Emilia is excited, clapping her hands, going up to the skirt and stroking her palm over its whispering silk, picking up a sleeve, then putting it down, chattering about the fine cloth, the embroidery, the bold pattern. Even Clelia has managed to raise what might pass as a smile. She, too, cannot keep from touching the dress.

Lucrezia stands to let them clothe her. She raises her arms, she drops them, she turns, she bows her head, keeping her face averted, so that her gaze is trained on the sky, which is grey and bilious, hoarding rain.

When Emilia and Clelia lead her to the mirror, she sees a person looking back at her with a faintly perturbed expression. The dress is slender, with a skirt that spills and swirls around her. A high collar rises up around her neck, making it hard to turn her head: the lace claws at her throat. Her arms are swathed, invisible, inside huge ballooning sleeves that rear over her shoulders, and end just below her wrists: her hands appear like the pale and ineffectual paws of a mouse, peeping out of frilled and ornate cuffs. It is like nothing she has ever worn in her life: the waist clamps her middle, the enormous sleeves and gathered skirt making her seem as inconsequential and slight as a reed. She cannot recognise the person she is in this gown. It doesn't look like the dresses she brought from Florence but it doesn't look like what Elisabetta, Nunciata and the other women at court wear. What, she wonders, as she lifts an arm, as she pushes a toe against the hem, does it signify that her husband had this made for her, that this was how he wanted her to appear in the marriage portrait? Most disturbing is the fabric itself: dark red with a raised black damask pattern, which, if stared at, can seem to recede behind the red at certain moments, then leap out and impose itself on top the next. Is the black over the red or the red over the black? Lucrezia stares and stares but cannot make it out, cannot see if the intricately wrought black lattice imprisons the red or sets it free. It makes her feel dizzy, uncertain, as if the relations and boundaries between things might all begin to collapse and merge.

In the Salone dei Giochi, among his frescos of men wrestling and fighting, stands Il Bastianino. When he sees her, he gives a wide grin, revealing his mouthful of snaggled, wolfish teeth. 'Yes, yes,' he says, folding his arms and shaking his hair out of his eyes, 'it is perfect, Your Grace, quite perfect. What a portrait this will be.'

Alfonso stands with one foot resting on a stool; in his hand, he holds a book or pamphlet, which he doesn't close. He regards Lucrezia over the top of whatever he is reading. Il Bastianino is ushering her towards a chair, where he arranges the dress around her, all the while letting out a litany of compliments and hyperbole, smoothing the skirts, twitching the hem one way, then the other, inching it back so that the tips of her shoes are revealed. He places a cushion behind her back which forces her to sit up straight, moves her arm to the table.

He then takes three rapid paces backwards, then another, more slowly, and another. 'Now,' he says, holding out his arms, as if he means to rush forward and embrace her. 'Do you see?'

Two figures move towards him: Lucrezia sees them advance from opposite sides of the large salon; one is Alfonso, walking from where he had been reading near the fireplace; the other comes from the furthest reaches of the room, where Il Bastianino has set up his materials. One is tall, with long legs and boots that echo on the tiled floor, the other is stockier, with a thick mass of curls and shoes that slide noiselessly over the floor.

One is her husband; the other, she sees, as the quivering light reflecting up off the moat falls on him, is the apprentice Jacopo.

Lucrezia is immediately conscious of the ridiculous figure she must cut, sitting as she is, enclosed in a lake of finery. She feels the tightness of her bodice, the prickle of starch in her collar, the shuddering motion of the ruby that hangs from her neck. Jacopo doesn't look at her. He comes to stand behind Il Bastianino and looks perhaps at the floor in front of her, the hem of her dress. He holds, between his fingers, sticking out like weapons, a brush, a charcoal stick, a palette knife, a small phial, perhaps some type of fluid to cleanse the brushes and canvases. The skin over his knuckles is raw, reddened, and stained with flecks of colour: madder red, orpiment yellow. She wonders for a moment what he had been painting to have accrued those colours. The wings of a cherub? The petals of a flower? The favourite pet of a patron's family?

A movement to the side of Jacopo distracts her from this train of thought. Alfonso is nodding, one hand tucked into his *giubbone*. Then he smiles and, among all his many yet rarely appearing smiles, it is her favourite: unguarded, spontaneous, wide, involving his whole face, transforming it from forbidding to lively and handsome.

'There she is,' he murmurs, the words reaching her where she sits, across the room, and she smiles back at him. Then he adds: 'My first duchess.'

She is still smiling when she sees Il Bastianino direct a fleeting, puzzled frown towards the floor. Jacopo turns his head slowly towards Alfonso, which in itself seems shocking – a commoner in rough clothing daring to behold a duke at close quarters.

But Alfonso amends his utterance to 'My beautiful duchess,' and Il Bastianino composes his face once more into an obsequious smirk, and Jacopo turns away, and Lucrezia feels the strange buzz of tension and fear move further away from her, like a craft on a river.

That is what he meant, she is certain. 'Beautiful', not 'first'. Why would he say 'first', when she is his wife, his only wife? A slip of the tongue, a momentary lapse. She herself has them all the time, words inserting themselves without warning, forcing entry without permission or consciousness. Utterances inappropriate and unintended. He would have meant to say, 'beautiful duchess', not 'first duchess', because 'first duchess' makes no sense, none at all: it sounds as if he believes there will be others, in the years to come. And that in itself is so wild, so strange a notion, as to be impossible.

He meant 'beautiful' all along. She is certain of it.

By the time her attention returns to the room, Alfonso has left. Clelia and Emilia sit on a window seat, the latter stitching at something white with a blue trim, the former making apathetic stabs of a needle into what looks to Lucrezia like the embroidered rose, once Isabella's, once hers, now Clelia's. Il Bastianino has lapsed into silence, concentrating on his canvas, on his paints and perspectives. And Jacopo is sometimes drawing and sometimes writing on a large board that he holds balanced between his waist and his arm. He works, Lucrezia sees, with his left hand, glancing up at her, then down.

At one point, he comes right up to where she is sitting and looks, she thinks, at the fall of the gown over the knee, the way it peaks, then cascades towards the hem. She wants to say this to him, to ask: is it the folds of cloth you are studying, the variation of colour, the way the pattern is interrupted by a pleat and then resumes in a different place? Do you hate this pattern? Because I do. It makes me feel confined, as if its symmetry and curlicues imprison me. Do you see that, do you? I am sure you do, though I cannot exactly say how I know this. I just do.

She watches him as he stands there, right by her, the paint ingrained in the skin of his right hand, the hemispheres of colour under his nails, like separated bands of a rainbow, the ever-moving left hand, curled backwards around the stylus, the way he presses the tip of his tongue to the corner of his mouth when he is thinking. That tongue intrigues her, the human instrument, which, with him, lies dormant, unused. How like any other tongue it looks. You would never know, from its pink and speckled appearance, that it was in any way different from—

Jacopo goes to rub at something on his page, fumbles, and the stylus drops to the floor. A tink-tink-thud as it bounces off the hexagonal tiles, first one end, then the other, and comes to rest by her foot.

And her ears, always sharp, always alert, pick up something else. Jacopo murmurs, quite distinctly, in self-castigation, in a language she knows, a dialect she grew up hearing, in the *palazzo* nursery, from the mouths of her Neapolitan nurses: 'Clumsy idiot.'

He kneels, still holding his board, without looking at her, and searches on the floor for his stylus.

Lucrezia glances around her. Her maids are right at the other end of the room, Clelia yawning, Emilia bent over her darning. Il Bastianino is behind his easel. The guards are by the door, propped against the wall, faces glazed with boredom.

Lucrezia takes a light inhalation. 'You are from Naples?' she whispers, barely enunciating, her lips almost static, in the same dialect.

Jacopo's head jerks up. She had forgotten the shifting maritime blue-green of his eyes, the sharp angles of his face, features cut from marble.

'I am,' he says, in a tone so quiet it is as if he breathes the words, rather than speaks them. 'I was. How do you—?' He breaks off, sending a swift look over his shoulder.

Lucrezia shifts her foot sideways, an incremental movement, and presses her toe down on the stylus, which she then pulls in beneath her skirts. Jacopo sees this and, after a moment's hesitation, he continues the pretence of looking.

'My nurse,' she whispers, by way of explanation. 'So you speak only this dialect?'

Jacopo casts about on the floor, his hands sweeping semicircles on the tiles. 'I can speak like them, more or less,' he tips his head towards Il Bastianino, 'should I choose to. But,' he looks up at her and, for a moment, she recalls the feel of his weakening pulse under her fingers, the struggling rasp of his breath, 'I do not choose to.'

'How is it possible,' Lucrezia begins, 'that—'

She is interrupted by Il Bastianino, calling, 'Jacopo? Whatever is the matter? Why are you grovelling on the floor like that?'

Lucrezia lifts her toe off the stylus; Jacopo's hand disappears in a flash under her hem, then emerges, holding it between two fingers. The moment is over, their chance to speak gone; their final words have been said.

Jacopo, however, as he moves from crouching to standing, breathes into the air near her, in Sofia's language: 'I shall never forget that you saved my life.'

Then he leaves, walking away, down the long room. She watches, observing the spring of his gait, the way one foot seems to turn in slightly. Tucked under his arm is a board filled with images of her wrists, her neck, the plane of her cheek, the socket of her eye. He has them, has taken possession of them: he will keep them safe, will ensure no harm comes to them. This thought makes a small, spreading warmth percolate through her.

Lucrezia rides out with Elisabetta and their guards, along the straight road leading from the *castello* to the city walls, and out to the hunting grounds. The first frost of the year has encased each branch, each blade of grass, the bolts and handles of the *castello* door as they depart. The air carries an iron-like chill that hints at winter's arrival. The forest seems unusually still, as if silenced by the cold. Lucrezia urges her horse to a canter: she wants to feel the world reel by, wants the bright gaps between the trees to meld into one entity.

Elisabetta, in a fur-lined riding cloak and feathered cap, allows her horse to fall back; Contrari rides beside her, his reins held in one sure hand. They will converse like that, heads inclined towards each other, for hours.

There is something in the way they are that brings Cosimo and Eleanora to Lucrezia's mind. The way Contrari hooks his finger into Elisabetta's sleeve. The tenderness in his eyes when he looks at her, the way a love like this can render a man of great physical strength to gentleness. The way Elisabetta seems to know before Contrari speaks that he is about to say something; she is able to intuit what he will utter. Lucrezia sees all this, and it is familiar to her; it fills her with a longing to have such a connection with someone; she would like someone to look at her as if she were a rare and valued thing, to wear absurdly in their hat band a sprig of holly she gave them, to ask what is her opinion of this or that.

When Lucrezia glances back at them from her saddle, they look like ancient sylvan spirits, faces tinged green by the ever-moving leaves of the forest.

Unable to sleep one night, Lucrezia parts the curtains, rises from her bed, walks about her chamber, and into her salon. She passes the closet where Emilia is sleeping, closed in. She draws back the bolt on the door and leans out into the stairwell.

It is not quite midnight, she estimates. The *castello* feels active still, albeit in a minor way. There is a distant sound of footsteps receding from her; perhaps a servant, summoned late to a chamber. There are hushed voices out in the courtyard.

She feels the sensation she has had all her life, for as long as she can remember: a draw towards exploration, towards movement. She thinks for a moment, then pulls her head back inside the door. She walks backwards, several paces, then eases open the door to Emilia's bed. The maid is lying on her front, face pressed to the rush matting, an arm curved about herself.

Lucrezia lifts from the floor next to her bed a brown dress, a linen apron, a cap.

She pulls the dress over her head – not too small, not too big, just a little loose around the shoulders – then the apron. She settles the cap on her hair; it is a capacious coif, shaped like a fleur-de-lis; it can be pulled right over the face, obscuring the wearer's features.

Silently, carefully, she steps out into the stairs, the clothes of the maid chafing her ankles. She is careful to walk quickly, her head bowed, her hands clasped in front of her. She is a maid; she wears coarse cloth next to her skin; she has an explanation ready, should anyone ask. Her mistress, unable to sleep, asked her to fetch some milk and honey from the kitchen.

Milk and honey, milk and honey. Lucrezia incants these words to herself as she walks down the stairs, along a corridor, past a row of windows that look out over the moat, its surface glazed with ice. She passes two guards, one of whom says something ribald, which makes the other laugh. She passes another maid, an older woman, who is staggering under the weight of a bowl of water, above which shivers a veil of steam. She grunts at Lucrezia in acknowledgement but doesn't stop.

Lucrezia walks all the way from one tower to the next. She walks in the opposite direction, then goes down a floor, and then another. She hears the spaniel yapping behind a door, and Nunciata crooning to it, giving it morsels from her plate. She walks past three courtiers jealously discussing a posting, and why that man was favoured over them. She sees the woman who wears birds in her hair leaving the chamber of an equerry in the early hours, her gown awry, her feet bare.

None of them looks at her beyond a brief glance. It is the perfect disguise. What liberty she gains by casting off her identity, by donning Emilia's clothes, what fortuities are hers! She can go anywhere, be party to anything. These people do not see servants, do not recognise them as vessels of judgement or emotion. A maid in a brown dress might as well be a table or a sconce on the wall. She has access suddenly to the private, hidden life of the *castello*, the wrong side of its embroidery, with all the knots and weave and secrets on display.

She returns to her room, after an hour or so, breathless, invigorated, her skin tingling, her mind fed and soothed, all at the same time. She will replace Emilia's clothes and return to bed, withdrawing into that private space, to think about all she has seen.

She is sleeping, however, on the night she hears the terrible noise – she is not conscious of having fallen asleep but she must have because suddenly she is lurching out of a dream, like a drowning person from water. She finds herself not circling the walkway in Florence, as she had thought she was, but crouched in a dark, cold place. For a moment, she cannot tell where she is, so profound is the blackness. She gropes around. Is Alfonso in the bed? Is he in the room? But she encounters space, a blanket edge, then the brush of the bed curtains.

What was it that woke her? Lucrezia twists her head, one way then the other, trying to ascertain what she had heard and if it was real.

The answer arrives in the form of a noise: a scream, high-pitched, desperate, torn from the depths of a person's very soul. It stabs through the *castello*'s night-time silence, again and again, razoring the air, dragging sharp, serrated teeth against Lucrezia's ears.

Whatever can have happened? She lurches from the bed, through the curtains, through the chamber door. In the darkness of the salon, she encounters Emilia, blundering towards her, hair tangled, face contorted with fear.

'Did you hear that?' Emilia says.

'I did.'

'What was it?'

The two girls grip each other by the arms. The maid is trembling, a hand held to her chest, as if to still her heart.

The scream comes again, louder this time, and with words attached: 'No, no, no!'

It is a woman, frantic with distress. Lucrezia moves towards the door, Emilia clutching her hand.

'Please,' the woman is sobbing, 'please, no!'

Lucrezia presses her ear to the wooden panels of the door.

'Who is it?' Emilia whispers.

'I don't know.'

'What should we do? Should we call the guards? Should we—?'

'Ssh,' Lucrezia urges, still listening.

The woman, whoever she is, is asking for mercy, saying stop, please stop.

Lucrezia's fingers find the bolt and slide it back.

Emilia, realising that she intends to go out, tries to stop her. 'Your Highness, no, you mustn't, you—'

344

'Let go.'

'Don't go out there.'

'She may need help.'

'But something bad is happening and—'

'Let go, I tell you,' Lucrezia commands.

Emilia releases her grip. Lucrezia pulls back the bolt, opens the door, and steps out.

For a moment, all she can hear is the rush of her own blood. Then she is conscious of a scuffling, perhaps coming from the floor below, the clink of weapons, the scrap-tap of many feet, moving rapidly about, in and out of a doorway, up and down a corridor. There is a rumble of male voices, talking in urgent tones to each other.

Then a female voice, cracked, pleading, choked with tears: 'I implore you.'

Lucrezia is about to go down the stairs, to see who this woman is, to try to help her, in whatever way she can – there must be something that can be done for the poor creature. But then she hears, quite distinctly, the woman say, 'Alfonso, please.'

The name raps against Lucrezia's head, each vowel striking a blow against her temple. Alfonso is down there? He is present? Is he trying to stop whatever is happening or is he witnessing it, perhaps even partaking in it? Lucrezia cannot believe it. She must have misheard.

The woman's voice comes again: 'Alfonso, I am begging you. Please don't do this.'

On the floor below, a door slams, there are footsteps going down a flight of stairs. Then silence.

Lucrezia stands for a moment in the corridor, the icy breath of the *castello* moving about her. Then she stumbles towards her door and, ignoring the questions of her maid, pushes the bolts into their locks, one after the other.

The next day, the *castello* has a suspended stillness, its corridors and salons filled with a silence that presses at the walls, a pressure from within. Lucrezia doesn't take her morning walk around the terrace; Elisabetta doesn't send for her, requesting she come to her rooms; she doesn't see Nunciata putting out her spaniel on the loggia for its morning air. Even the city, or the slices of it visible from Lucrezia's high windows, seems subdued, with swirls of grey fog lingering at street corners and the edges of the piazza.

Breakfast is left outside Lucrezia's door. The usual bowl of warmish milk, with its yellowing puckered skin on the surface and its silky, opaque texture, turns her stomach. She replaces it, undrunk, on the tray.

Emilia tiptoes around, straightening the wall hangings, wiping dust off Lucrezia's paintings, the packets of pigment, the bottles of linseed oil. Clelia sits in an armchair by the window, sighing heavily at intervals, stitching inept petals along the edge of one of Lucrezia's smocks.

Lucrezia sends her down to Elisabetta's rooms with a message: would Elisabetta care to take a turn around the terrace?

Clelia comes back saying that there was no answer at the door.

Towards the middle of this long morning, a servant from the lower floors knocks on the door to ask that the dress for the portrait be boxed up so it can be taken away, and also to deliver a message that the Duchess is to remain in her rooms today until further notice.

Lucrezia rises from her chair and goes to the door, where Clelia stands, talking to the man.

'Why am I to remain here?' Lucrezia asks. 'Who sent this order?'

The servant bows low and says, 'It was the request of His Grace, the Duke. He sends his regrets that he was not able to deliver this message himself but—'

'The Duke said this?' she asks. 'Why?'

The servant looks panicked, unable to find a place to rest his eyes. 'I . . . I cannot say, my lady, I was just told to . . .' His speech peters out, and he bows again, his face scarlet with embarrassment.

She wants to reach out and grip this man by his sleeve, to demand what he knows, what this signifies. But she tugs at the front of her bodice, mustering an appearance of calm.

'Why is the dress to be taken?' she asks him. 'Where is it going?'

'To the. . .' the servant stammers, 'Sala . . . the Sala dell'- Aurora, where His Grace will be waiting. I believe . . . it is for the purpose of . . . Her Highness's portrait.'

'The portrait?' She presses her lips together, mind whirring. 'You are dismissed,' she tells him. 'I shall bring the dress myself.'

The servant blanches. 'But His Grace said that—'

'I know what he said. But, nevertheless, I am coming down.'

Inside, she tells Emilia and Clelia to prepare the gown. She watches the lid go down, sees the final flash of the plum-coloured silk, the black lattice design, which this morning seems to occupy the foreground, standing dominant over the delicate red. Then she tells Emilia and Clelia to bring the box; she walks ahead of them, head high, down to the Sala dell'Aurora.

The square room is empty, the painted faces of the deities and skies looking down on nothing. Lucrezia walks to the vacant space at the middle, estimating where the very centre might be. Just as she believes she has reached it, the door opens.

She turns and sees her husband, accompanied by three of his advisers and Leonello. There is something stern and forbidding about the five men, the way they walk in formation, as if they are carrying something heavy between them.

He is silent as he crosses the room, as he takes in the scene before him: his wife, her maids, the servant he dispatched, the box containing the dress. His appearance is immaculate: black hose, black *giubbone*, black boots.

'My dearest,' he murmurs, as he reaches her, his eyes flickering from her to the box to the maids, gathering information, calculating what the situation holds.

He takes her hand, standing very close to her, and bows over it for a moment, then says: 'I did not expect to see you.'

How very like him this utterance is, Lucrezia thinks. A mere seven words, a seemingly bland construction, but it carries so much. He appears to say simply that he is surprised to see her, but what he is actually conveying is his displeasure that she has taken it upon herself to come down to his apartment like this. Why, she wonders, does he not want her here? For what reason does he require her to stay in her rooms?

'I thought,' she says, 'I would come down myself, to ensure the dress was delivered safely, and in case I was needed for work on the portrait.'

His face doesn't move; her hand, still in his, grows hot beneath his touch.

'I would have sent for you,' he replies, 'if that were the case.'

She shrugs. 'The change of air does me good.'

He nods, drops her hand, turns towards the table where the box has been laid. He places his palm upon it. 'This is it?'

He seems to be asking the maids but since he is not looking at them, Emilia doesn't realise and doesn't answer. He waits, the picture of patience and forbearance, one hand still on the box, until Clelia leaps to her feet, curtseys, and says, 'Yes, Your Grace.'

'Why . . .' Lucrezia addresses his back: she is going to ask him the reason for her to be kept to her rooms, she is, she is about to, but somehow she feels that to keep him talking, not confront him, might be her best course of action, the way to get as much information as possible out of him, so she swerves instead into '. . . is the dress to be taken away?'

'It is the usual practice,' he says. 'To spare your time, to avoid trespassing on your patience. Il Bastianino will take it for a short while to his studio, where he will pose and paint it. Then,' he turns towards her, 'it will be returned, when the portrait is complete.'

Lucrezia sees, for the first time, that he has an injury to the left side of his face. Under his cheekbone, just in front of his ear, are three scratches, fresh and vivid, cut deeply into the skin.

'Your face,' she exclaims, moving towards him. 'Did you—?'

'It is nothing.' He touches a fingertip to the livid stripes. 'I had quite forgotten.'

'But you need a salve or a—'

'It's nothing,' he says again. 'Do not concern yourself.'

'Alfonso,' she says, in a low voice, unable to hold it in any longer, 'I am . . . I need to ask you something.'

He doesn't reply, just keeps his eyes on her.

'There were dreadful noises in the night. And this morning I sent word to Elisabetta but heard nothing back. What is happening?'

'Leave, please,' he says, without moving, and for a shocking moment, she thinks he is addressing her, that he is ordering her from the room, in that imperative voice. But, without hesitation, Leonello, the advisers, the servant and her maids all get to their feet and file out of the door.

And then, she and Alfonso are alone, in the beautiful room where, above their heads, Aurora in her golden carriage pushes back the gloomy presence of Night.

'There are things,' he begins, in a voice barely above a murmur, 'that will happen in our lives, from time to time, that may seem inexplicable to you. You do not need to involve yourself. It is my duty to deal with anything that threatens our status and our reputation. Not yours. I sent word requesting that you remain in your room, and yet here you are. What occurred last night was—'

This astounding speech, which causes Lucrezia's limbs to tremble beneath her skirts, is interrupted by the door opening at the far end of the salon.

Jacopo the apprentice is walking towards them, his cap held in his hand. Alfonso gives him a sideways glance, then holds out a hand and points at the box. 'There,' he says.

Jacopo directs his steps around them, circumnavigating the centre of the room, where Lucrezia stands with Alfonso. He takes out a leather strap from his bag and begins to fasten it around the box.

'There will be many things,' Alfonso resumes, as if Jacopo isn't in the room, and Lucrezia recalls that Alfonso perhaps still labours under the impression that Jacopo is deaf as well as mute, 'that it is better for you not to know. But I ask you to ensure at all times that the compass of your loyalties is pointing in the correct direction: you are my wife and I scarcely need to remind you that your first and foremost duty must always be to me. No one else. Not your women, not my sisters, no one. I am your husband and also, yes, your protector. So allow me, please, to protect you.'

She sees, behind him, Jacopo cast a sideways look at him, at her. He is hefting the box to his shoulder. He does this slowly, with great caution, taking as much time as possible. His steps, as he moves towards the door, are slow, and it seems for one unsettling moment that he might change course and walk towards them. But then he seems to think better of this. He adjusts his hold on the strap, on the box, and it comes to her that he is carrying her gown, that he will, very soon, be opening the lid at the studio, inhaling the air trapped there, air from her chamber; he will be touching the cloth with his hand, lifting it out, shaking it, examining it, deciding on the right combinations of pigments to replicate it on Il Bastianino's portrait. He will be picturing her inside it, considering how it held her body, draped over her limbs; he will linger over it, examine it; it will haunt his days and flit through his dreams at night.

'I'm sure,' Alfonso is saying, 'that your father operates in the same way, shielding your mother from elements of his rule that he deems—'

'On the contrary,' Lucrezia cuts across him hotly, forgetting who she is and to whom she is speaking, 'my father shares everything with my mother. He consults her on many issues, he cedes his rule to her whenever he is away, he seeks and values her opinion and her—'

'That is all very touching.' Alfonso utters these words through rigid lips. 'But your father is one man and I am another. And you, my love, are no more than a child.'

Over the shoulder of her husband, which looms above her, blocking out most of her surroundings, she sees that Jacopo has reached the door of the salon. He seems to hesitate on the threshold for a second or two, placing a hand on the door latch.

'So, please, do me the courtesy of returning to your rooms, as instructed, and remain there until I tell you that you may leave,' Alfonso says, grazing the line of her jaw with his thumbnail. 'Do you understand?'

She nods, with a rapid dip of her chin. Jacopo pushes open the door, steps through and, casting one final look at her, closes it behind him. Lucrezia has to quell a strong urge to break away from her husband and run after him. She wishes, for a wild moment, that she had concealed herself within that box, that she had folded herself down within the dress so that Jacopo could spirit her out of the *castello*, through the gate, over the drawbridge, and away.

'Yes,' she says, instead, tilting her face to look at Alfonso, at his hair, which still carries the tracks of his comb, at the still-raw gouges on his cheek, as if someone has clawed at his face with their fingernails. 'I understand.'

* * *

Back in her room, Lucrezia dismisses her maids. She draws her shawl more tightly about herself and stands at the window, where she has a view of a section of the moat, the main draw-bridge, and a number of streets, which lead off the piazza at opposing angles.

Winter seems to have arrived with a peculiar abruptness. She doesn't know if it is the northern climate or the dank humours of the Po valley but the seasons in Ferrara turn like the handle of a crank; one day it is summer, the next, the trees are dropping their leaves, then frost descends and icy winds are seeking out gaps in the walls and windows. She is used to the Tuscan climate, where there is a slow tapering-off of warmth and light, a gradual tip into autumn, winter arriving in an apologetic creep.

She waits at the window, fingertips pressed to the pane, forehead leaning on the cool glass. A modest patch of mist appears before her every time she breathes out, and disappears when she breathes in.

A group of guards marches out across the bridge, in a controlled formation, three sets of two, their swords held over their shoulders. They move across the piazza, and vanish down a side-street. A man in a black cloak comes striding over the bridge and is admitted by the gatehouse. Two ser-vants carrying baskets scurry out, parting in the middle of the piazza, the taller one calling something to the shorter, who waves a hand.

And then the drawbridge rattles with the sound of wheels. A cart is speeding out of the gate, pulled by a piebald horse, a servant standing up to wield a whip over the beast's back; three other servants run along beside it; they are calling to each other, words of admonishment. Several guards run after the cart, their hats in their hands, their heads bare and their faces wild and anguished.

In the back of the cart – Lucrezia cranes her neck to see, straining up on to her toes – a long, rectangular shape is covered with blankets.

This, Lucrezia realises, is what she had been waiting for. She doesn't quite know what it means, what it signifies – any of it. The haste of the servants, their alarm, the vicious crack of the whip, the ragged running of the guards who are following the cart, even now, as it careers through the piazza, then turns a corner and is swallowed by a narrow gap between dwellings.

Lucrezia fixes her eye on this gap, long after the guards have given up the chase and returned slowly to the *castello*, one with his arm about his comrade's shoulders, long after the cart has gone. She doesn't move her gaze from it, as if the cart might reappear to explain everything, as if the servant on it will be calm, his cargo entirely innocent and normal.

She argues with herself, with her eyes, with what they thought they saw, what they might have seen, how mistaken they could be. But she knows; her heart knows. The shape in the back of the cart had been long and thin, with squared edges. Like a box or a bed. Or a coffin.

She stays at the window for a long time. She watches the people of Ferrara come and go, walking one way across the piazza, then the other. She watches children hold the hands of their parents. She watches a woman lug a large bale of cloth on her back, a man roll a barrel using his bare and filthy feet, a young girl tugging a dog after her on a length of rope, two brothers carrying armfuls of firewood. She watches as the sky empties of light and the stone of the buildings acquires shadow.

She is still at the window when the cart reappears. The servant is now sitting on its edge and he lets the horse idle its way across the bridge; the whip is folded and furled, under his arm. The back of the cart is empty.

Emilia and Clelia find her there, stiff with cold, when they return. They help her to a chair, they chafe her frozen hands and feet, and Emilia spoons hot broth into her mouth. Clelia chides her for letting herself get so cold.

Something has happened, she says to them, over and over again. I know it has.

Emilia avoids her eye, focusing instead on the broth, the fetching of blankets, the building-up of the fire.

I know, is all Lucrezia can say to them.

How can she know? Clelia mutters to Emilia.

Don't think about it now, Emilia tells her, patting Lucrezia's arm. Don't think about anything.

But when Clelia leaves to order water from the kitchens, so that they may bathe her, Lucrezia turns to Emilia, she grips her by the shoulder, she makes her sit down next to her, and she says: tell me what has happened. I know you know.

Emilia begs, no, do not ask. It is better you don't dwell on it.

Lucrezia says, tell me.

Emilia suggests they play a game of cards or that Lucrezia does some drawing. Would her mistress like her to bring some paper?

Lucrezia says: Emilia, your mother nursed me, we are milk-sisters, you and I. You have known me longer than I have known myself. We have come a long way together. Please tell me.

Emilia touches the scar on her face, with first one finger, then another; she lowers her eyes; she speaks falteringly. She heard, she tells Lucrezia, from a kitchen maid who heard it from a man who serves in the Duke's office that His Grace, the Duke, discovered that Ercole Contrari had – and here Emilia hesitates, choosing her words – had compromised the honour of the Duke's sister the Lady Elisabetta. The Duke had condemned Contrari, head of the guardsmen, to death.

Here Emilia's story stops, with what Lucrezia immediately sees as an inconclusive suddenness.

Go on, she says.

No, Emilia whispers, shaking her head.

Yes, Lucrezia says. Tell me.

So, Emilia says, her voice wavering, because the Lady Elisabetta showed no remorse, and refused to condemn Contrari, saying that she loved him and that he loved her, the Duke ordered – Emilia pauses, swallows – he ordered that Contrari be strangled to death and the Lady Elisabetta be forced to watch.

Lucrezia listens to every word, to the separate sound of each, their syllables, the gaps between them. She runs them through her head, sentence by sentence. She picks over them, with care, with her full attention, so that she is sure of their meaning, their significance, so that she completely comprehends what Emilia is saying.

And, Lucrezia begins, while unsure of what she means to ask, but she hears her voice continue without her knowledge or consent, this has . . . been done?

Emilia nods. The Duke ordered two of Contrari's men to do it. This afternoon, in the Salone dei Giochi. But they . . . could not. So Baldassare did it.

Baldassare? Lucrezia repeats. Leonello Baldassare?

Yes.

And Lady Elisabetta . . .?

She was there.

My husband?

He was watching. He commanded the guards to hold her fast, so that she could not get away.

Lucrezia makes herself speak. She bids her mouth and tongue to make sounds. She tells Emilia and Clelia, who has arrived back, that she has changed her mind about bathing; she wishes to be alone, please.

They leave, Emilia backing out of the door, then closing it behind her.

Lucrezia stands in her salon, watching the curlicues of steam write themselves on the air above the basins of hot water, brought up from the kitchens by Clelia. They twist and writhe, like serpents responding to pipe music, finding their way to the windows, their shed skins adhering to the cold panes. In the space of a moment, the views down on to the piazza are obscured, and Lucrezia is no longer standing in a tower room but in a box, shuttered off from the world.

Then she walks quickly through the steam, to the chamber, where she dons her mantle and shoes. She fastens a cloak around her neck, pulling the hood up over her head. Then she goes through the door and out into the corridor.

She moves quickly over the brick floor, gripping the edge of the hood to keep it from falling back, stepping from one circle of brazier-light to the next, a dusky-winged moth. When she hears voices in a corridor perpendicular to the one she is in, she takes a sidestep into an alcove, flattening herself to the wall.

Tasso the poet is coming along, with a woman beside him; Lucrezia recognises her as one of Nunciata's ladies-in-waiting. She hangs off his arm, her shawl sweeping the floor; he looks lugubrious, downcast, almost indifferent to the presence of his companion.

'. . . he has summoned the physician,' the woman is saying, peering up into Tasso's face, 'but she will not see him.'

'It is a terrible situation,' Tasso says, in his rumbling voice. 'Tragic, grim.'

'Let us make haste,' the woman says, shivering, looking over her shoulder. 'Come. It feels wrong to be walking about on a night like this.'

They disappear around a corner and Lucrezia steps out. She has an instinctive dislike of that woman but, at the same time, knows what she means. The *castello* has a strange feel tonight: the air that fills its rooms and passageways seems malodorous and heavy, as if weighted down with all that has taken place within it. There is an unnatural quiet, which is broken at odd intervals with strange noises, some muffled and mysterious, others amplified by distance. Lucrezia's footfalls, as she descends a staircase, seem to ricochet off the walls, their tap-tap-a-tap splintered and distorted into a monstrous beat, which sends needles of alarm into her chest.

She hurries, almost runs, along the lower floor. If Alfonso were to see her, if Baldassare or any of his men were to cross her path, if Alfonso goes to her chamber and finds it empty – then what? She has no idea.

She doesn't care, she doesn't care. Let him see, let him know. She doesn't care.

She is saying these words to herself as she runs, the hood falling back off her head, as she bangs on the door of Elisabetta's chamber, as she pushes past the lady-in-waiting who answers, who is saying that she is sorry but Elisabetta is not receiving anyone.

Lucrezia, panting, bursts into Elisabetta's rooms. Tonight, the berry-pink wall hangings seem to have harvested the darkness around them, taking on a lowering, purplish hue.

The lady-in-waiting is trying to get Lucrezia to leave, her voice twittering entreaties and apologies. She won't touch her, Lucrezia knows, but she holds her arms wide, as if to shield the room from Lucrezia's burglarising gaze.

Lucrezia knows how to deal with this situation – she is, despite everything, her mother's daughter. She raises her chin, she looks down her nose at this woman. I am duchess of this castle, the stance says, and you are in my way: Lucrezia knows this; the woman knows this.

'Stand aside,' Lucrezia says, 'please.'

The woman, with a sigh, steps towards the wall, still murmuring apologies.

There is a slight rustle in the room, and the sound of something like a cough or a grunt. What Lucrezia had, in the dim light, assumed was a heap of clothing on the settle makes a sudden movement.

'It's you,' says a voice, flat and displeased.

Lucrezia flies to the side of the settle and kneels on the floor. In the gloom, she sees a face, puffy and sallow, round as a moon. For a moment, she thinks there has been a mistake, and this is Nunciata lying here, but she recognises the rings on the hand she has seized as Elisabetta's, the high brow, the black eyes, which are the same as—

'How dare you come here?' Elisabetta says, in her new hoarse voice. 'What do you want?'

Lucrezia presses Elisabetta's hand. 'I had to see you. I heard . . . I am so sorry – so very sorry. . . I cannot believe it, I cannot—'

'Then you are even more of a fool than I took you for,' Elisabetta snaps, pulling her hand out of Lucrezia's, and turns away, pressing her face into the cushions.

Lucrezia draws back, stung. She waits for a moment, still kneeling. She is aware of the lady-in-waiting, hovering somewhere behind her, ready to escort her away.

'You are grieving,' Lucrezia says. 'I understand, and—'

Elisabetta lets out a short, bitter laugh. 'Do you? Do you really? They made me watch. They held me down as they murdered him with their bare hands.'

'I cannot begin to—'

'Tell me, do you love my brother?'

'Of – of course I do,' Lucrezia falters.

'Really?'

'I—'

Elisabetta pushes herself to a sitting position. Lucrezia is shocked, all over again, at the change in her appearance. Her hair is matted and hangs in a clump on one side of her face; it seems much shorter than Lucrezia would have expected, and she realises that the high crown of hair that Elisabetta wears must be a false extension, taken from the head of another woman. The skin around her eyes is red and angry-looking, as if scrubbed with rough cloth.

'You don't have the faintest idea of what love is,' Elisabetta is saying. 'You are just a child.' She reaches out and cups Lucrezia's cheek, her fingers pincering her earlobe. 'A pretty, silly child dressed up in jewels and silks. Like a pet monkey.'

Lucrezia feels like a flag on a windy parapet, pulled one way then another. She has no sense of where this conversation is going, of what might happen within it.

'I am so sorry,' she says, 'for what happened, for—'

Elisabetta puts her face close to hers, breathing sour metallic exhalations on her. She is, Lucrezia thinks, like a shattered windowpane, her whole being splintered into crazed fractures.

'You told him, didn't you?' she whispers, at their new proximity, her eyes boring into her. 'Why would you do that? I thought we were friends, you and I.'

'We . . . we are friends,' Lucrezia stutters, appalled. 'I didn't tell him! I promise you.'

'Is that true? Somebody told him. And I believe that it was you.'

'It wasn't me. I would never have done that. Never.'

'Do you swear?'

'I swear it, Elisabetta. He . . .' Lucrezia tries to think of how to put it '. . . he has a way of seeing the truth, the crux of a situation. I don't know how he does it but he can gaze on someone and see whatever it is they most want to keep hidden. He can peel away the layers people use to clothe their secrets, he—'

Elisabetta makes an involuntary noise of revulsion and jerks back, away from her. 'You are right. This is exactly how he is.' She puts her hands to her face, closing her fingers over it, and stays like that for a moment or two. When she removes them, her beautiful face is still ravaged and ruined, but it is no longer bitter.

'I believe you,' she mutters, and takes Lucrezia's hand, with an abstracted air. A tear collects in her eye and slides quickly down her cheek, followed by another, and another. She makes no move to wipe them away but lets them drip off her face into dark circles on her shift.

Lucrezia kneels before her, gripping her hand. And then Elisabetta says something unexpected. 'Poor Lucrezia,' she murmurs, still looking away from her.

'Me?' Lucrezia replies. 'It's you who—'

'No, no.' Elisabetta sighs, straightening a fold in her shift. 'I am leaving. As soon as day breaks. I will go to Rome, to Luigi, my other brother. I may never come back here. Alfonso is not my husband. I can leave. You cannot.'

Lucrezia has again that sense of an erratic, unpredictable wind, pulling her in opposing directions. 'I am quite content with—'

'Listen to me, little Lucrè,' Elisabetta croons, crooking a finger towards her, drawing her so close that their foreheads touch. 'You have no idea what he is capable of,' she breathes, pressing her forehead so hard into Lucrezia's that it hurts, 'and that to rule as he does, so well, so decisively, you need to be entirely heartless. He has brought this court under his control in so short a space of time, but at what cost? The things I have seen him do!' She curls her hand into a fist and bangs it against her chest, making Lucrezia wince. 'He has nothing here. Nothing at all. And you know what else?'

'What?'

Elisabetta's face cracks into a pained, ugly smile. 'He has

never,' she hisses, 'got a woman with child. Not a single one, not—'

'Perhaps you—'

'—not any of his women here, or any woman anywhere. Never! Not once! Do you understand me? It is rumoured that he will never produce an heir, that the duchy cannot remain in our lineage, which of course makes him angry beyond reason, because he always knows what is being said about him, I don't know how, but what I do know is that one person will be blamed for this, and you know who it is?'

Lucrezia feels overcome, by the pressure of Elisabetta's forehead on hers, by the unwashed and unkempt scent of her.

'You,' Elisabetta breathes, maliciously, almost delightedly. 'You will be blamed. So be careful, Lucrezia. Be very, very careful.'

Then she pushes Lucrezia away from her and signals to the woman standing in the corner. 'I am tired,' she says. 'Show her out.'

Lucrezia goes into her chamber; she locks the door; she lights a candle and brings it into bed with her, drawing the curtains; she does not answer when Emilia or Clelia knocks. She does not open it when they bring her breakfast, when she hears the rattle of what must be Elisabetta's carriage leaving, when they cajole her through the keyhole, or even when Nunciata raps with her knuckles, demanding that Lucrezia let them in.

Only when Emilia whispers through the keyhole that His Grace, the Duke, and his *consigliere* Baldassare have left for Modena, and will be gone for several weeks, does Lucrezia pull back the bolts.

She asks Emilia to bring her furs: she has a notion that what she needs most is to be outside, in the air. She cannot bear to be in this chamber, enclosed by walls, and Alfonso is not here to tell her to remain in her rooms. She must have sky above her head; she must have wind tugging at her hair. She knows she will not be permitted to leave the *castello* – the guards at the gates will never let her through, not without Alfonso's express permission – and so she seeks out every outdoor space available to her. She takes to the orangery, walking from one of its walls to the other, weaving in and out of the trees, bare and leafless and blossomless now. She climbs the stone stairs to each tower, in turn, and strides round and round each battlement. She paces from terrace to terrace, looking out over the city, its roofs and gutters, and beyond, to the flat valley on one side and the peaks of the Apennines on the other.

She is assailed, from nowhere and for the first time, by a longing for home. She is swamped by it, drowned by it, as if a wave has crashed over her head. There is, suddenly, nothing she wants more than to be in the corridors of the *palazzo* in Florence, to be passing through its rooms and terraces. She misses, with a pain sharp and distracting as toothache, the view from the top of the walkway, down into the piazza, the tops of the statues, the hidden scent of the Arno. She cannot fathom that the onset of a winter in Florence is happening in her absence. Can the trees be shedding their leaves? Can the citizens be putting on their woollen caps? Can the Swiss Guards be donning their warm cloaks? In her mind, as she moves compulsively from one *castello* terrace to the next, she marks the passage of her family's days, thinking, Now they will be clearing the nursery table for their midday meal. Now my father will be taking his exercise. Now my mother will walk out with her ladies. Now she will be calling for Isabella to come and join her in the salon. Now Sofia will be easing off her shoes and putting her feet up on a stool by the fire.

How can all this be taking place without her? It makes no sense, as she paces round and round the orange trees, that they are there and she is here. She is one of them; she has the same-shaped eyes as her father and brothers, the same brow and nose as her mother and her sister; they all grew up at the same table; her portrait hangs among theirs. She is one of them. She is not one of these people, who maim and fight, banish and imprison each other, who kill and scheme, depart and plot.

Towards the end of the first day of Alfonso's absence, Emilia and Clelia become wearied by Lucrezia's constant movement. Clelia, who doesn't like heights, will not come out on to the battlements; she remains inside the tower, whimpering, imploring Lucrezia to come down, come inside, to take some food and rest, His Grace wouldn't like her to be out in the cold for so long, he will not be pleased if he hears about it on his return. Emilia, although not keen on the narrow stone battlements, will not leave Lucrezia's side. She shivers in her thin shawl; Lucrezia tries to get her to wear one of her furs but Emilia will not. It wouldn't be right, madam, she says. She clings to the wall, edging along as best she can in Lucrezia's wake, eyes averted from the drop, patting Lucrezia's clenched fists, pushing her wind-tangled hair from her eyes, trying to persuade her to go back to her rooms, where she might eat some broth and drink a little wine.

But the longing to be back in Florence, to be away from here, is so potent that it creates a sickness in Lucrezia. She cannot bear the thought of food; she cannot remain still. She cannot sit at a table or lie down; if she does, she is hit by images of Contrari, his handsome face distorted by the agony of his death, his neck ringed with bruises, or Baldassare's hands with their broad knuckles and short fingers, or the beautiful Elisabetta, dishevelled and haggard with grief. Lucrezia will not remain indoors, despite the pleading of her women. Sadness keeps attempting to tie weights to her wrists and ankles therefore she has to keep moving, she has to outpace it.

And so she walks, along one terrace then another, from one battlement to the next, and as she goes, she concentrates on recreating a part of the *palazzo* for herself. The route from one window of the nursery to the other – the uneven board that squeals in damp weather, the fringe of the tablecloth, the smooth wood of the chairs, the sounds of her brothers' footsteps – or the painted ceiling in the salon, each face, each ripple of cloth, each scudding cloud.

She asks Clelia to bring her desk box out to the loggia, and a small table. When these things arrive, she stops her pacing, takes a sheet of paper, and writes a letter to her parents. *Please*, she inscribes in dark ink, the breeze coming up from the moat tugging at her quill, as if it desires to snatch it from her, *let me come home*. She thinks carefully about what to say, how to put it. *I miss you all*, is what unscrolls from her nib. *Can you send for me?* She tries to think of how to describe what has happened here. She cannot form the letters for his name – Contrari, her mind hisses at her, Contrari, over and over again, until she feels quite mad with it – but she refers to him as the Head of the Guardsmen. She writes the phrase, *put to death*; she writes, *forced to watch*; she writes, *Elisabetta has gone* and *she was my only friend here*. Just before she signs her name, she writes down what is in her heart: *I no longer feel safe in this place*.

She seals the letter and gives it to Emilia to dispatch, not Clelia. She does not trust Clelia, and never has. The sly, sideways gaze of her, the way she watches Lucrezia all the time, her pale hands, always damp in the palms. Clelia, Lucrezia suddenly sees, with the clarity of misery, has always been a spy for Nunciata, feeding back information on and impressions of Lucrezia. Never mind – she will not take her when she goes home; she and Emilia will go together, alone. Alfonso cannot object, if her father requests her return. Perhaps in a day or two her father will send horses, and men to accompany them, to lead them back over the Apennines. And then, perhaps by early morning, they will see Florence, laid out before them, the Arno river cutting through the houses and buildings, the cupola shining in the sun, and the battlements of the *palazzo*, like the strong teeth of a bear. Her parents will greet her with joy and relief, glad to have her back among them, telling her they have missed her, admiring how much she has grown, how accomplished and gracious she looks.

On the third day of Alfonso's absence, a lady-in-waiting of Nunciata comes to find her. Lucrezia is on the ducal terrace on the north-eastern side of the *castello*; she has ordered all the windows behind her to be thrown open, for she wants to be sure that the rooms will be swept through and refreshed by clean air. The lady-in-waiting puts her head out of one, frowning. She takes in Lucrezia, swathed in her furs, pacing from one end of the terrace to the other. She tells Emilia and Clelia to bring Her Ladyship within, this very minute, or she will catch her death of cold. Lucrezia ignores her, will not answer even Emilia's entreaties to come inside, to rest awhile.

Nunciata herself appears, the next day, panting from the climb up the stairs, and stands in the doorway out to the orangery, where Lucrezia has spent the day, moving among the branches of the trees. She holds a cloth over her face, so as not to catch whatever it is that ails Lucrezia. As Alfonso has had to go away, she says to them, through the fabric, she herself is responsible for the Duchess. What is all this she has been hearing about Lucrezia refusing to come indoors? What kind of notion is this? Is this all about the dead Contrari? Lucrezia must know that to demonstrate such excessive grief for that man is tantamount to treason. Her loyalties must always lie with Alfonso. Doesn't she realise that?

Lucrezia, with her face turned outwards, towards the city, says she has no wish to discuss it. It is, she says, of no significance to Nunciata.

'No significance?' Nunciata repeats, her words muffled by the cloth. 'Whatever do you mean?'

'You have never liked me,' Lucrezia says, the words clear and carrying. 'And, anyway, I shall be leaving here soon enough.'

'Where are you going?' Nunciata enquires crossly, from her position by the door, shivering in the wintry breeze.

'Back to Florence, of course,' Lucrezia says, believing that the conversation is at an end and that Nunciata will now withdraw.

But Nunciata does not leave. She conducts a hissed conversation with Clelia instead. Has Lucrezia a fever? Whatever can be making her behave so oddly? What nonsense is this about Florence? Is she suffering from a skin disorder, a cough, a pain of the throat? Clelia shakes her head each time. What, then? Nunciata asks. Clelia shrugs and says something about Lucrezia feeling nauseous and refusing food, that it is all she can do to persuade her to take a little milk, every now and again. Nunciata lets the cloth fall from her face, and looks thoughtfully at Lucrezia, all the way from her pale face to her feet, before bustling off with new purpose, apparently thrilled about something.

It is unclear to Lucrezia how much time passes here. She walks every loggia, every terrace, every battlement of the *castello*, over and over again, coming inside only at dusk. She is aware of fitful nights, drifting in and out of sleep, of the fire dying down to embers, then being fed with logs. Ice appears on the windows in the early mornings, in patterns of long, frayed fronds, as if cold feathers are pressing themselves up against the glass. Warm broths and preserves are brought to her bedside, and she waves them away. As soon as day breaks, she puts on her warmest clothing and goes out to the terrace or the orangery, Emilia trailing behind.

She is climbing the narrow stairs up to the south-west tower when a servant brings a letter. Lucrezia catches a glimpse of her mother's precise, sloping handwriting and snatches it from the man's hand. She sits on a cold step and pulls it open.

It is brief, hastily written, and contains no invitation or offers of horses. Lucrezia can picture her mother, about to leave her rooms, to join Cosimo in the offices, pausing at the desk in her *scrittoio*, pulling a sheet of paper towards her, and dashing it off. She would then have thrust it into the hands of a servant, with an impatient, there.

Lucrezia holds it in trembling hands as she scans it.

My dear Lucrè,

What a wild and worried letter was your last! You must be careful not to let your imagination run away with you – you are aware, I'm sure, how that tendency has been in you from a very young age. Remember that your Alfonso is an honourable man, so let him be your guide, always. I am sorry to hear that Lady Elisabetta's departure has upset you – the loss of a friend is indeed a sad thing. Perhaps, however, this will give you opportunity to spend time with Lady Nunciata, free of the rivalry you mentioned before. Most of all, I would advise you most strongly, my darling, to pay attention to your own position at court, which will only be truly assured by the birth of an heir. I have no doubt that motherhood will bring you the peace and security you so desire. Your father is in agreement with me on this.

All is well here. Isabella has taught everyone a new card game, and we spend more time than we should engaged upon it. I am having a fitting for a new gown this afternoon – cream silk with embroidered panels. The boys are doing well in their lessons. We send our love and prayers.

Your loving mother

Lucrezia reads it twice, first quickly, then more slowly. She places it on her lap and looks down, letting her eyes rest upon it, unfocused, so that the words and sentences fade into black lines, like columns of ants.

She then leans over and thrusts the edge of the letter into the sconce burning on the wall of the stairwell. For a second or two, it seems the flame cannot believe its luck, refusing to consume the page. Then it comes to its senses, asserting its grasp, turning the edges of the paper black, shrivelling and devouring them.

It burns quickly, merrily, casting a leaping orange glow on to the damp steps, making Emilia start forward with an exclamation and shake Lucrezia's wrist. When the burning letter falls to the floor, Emilia stamps on it, again and again, extinguishing the fire.

The marriage portrait of Lucrezia, Duchess of Ferrara

Fortezza, near Bondeno, 1561

She descends the staircase, haltingly, from the *fortezza*'s damp chamber, leaving Emilia behind. When she reaches the dining hall, she stands in the doorway, catching her breath, holding on to the door frame. There is Il Bastianino, at the side of the great hall, his back to her, talking about the brilliance of the commission. It has been one of his favourites, he is saying, and he hopes His Grace is only half as delighted with the result as he himself is, what an honour, what an accolade, for a humble painter such as himself to paint a woman of such virtue and beauty, he will never, never surpass such a—

One by one, the men in the room notice her, standing on the threshold: first Baldassare, who is nearest, leaning against a table, his arms crossed, then the four servants who wait at the far side of the room, then the two apprentices, Maurizio and Jacopo, who are propping up in their hands a large, flat object swathed in linen, then Alfonso, who is seated by the fire, his legs crossed, his hunting dogs asleep at his feet. The artist himself is the last to realise she is there, so deep is he in relating the story of her portrait.

His words flow on, eddying around them all, transfixing them. At last, he turns his head and sees her and his voice stops.

She finds, reflected in their startled faces, a testament to how changed she is. In the raising of Maurizio's brows, she knows that her face is pale and gaunt; in the dying stutter of Il Bastianino's words, she feels the ragged tresses of her severed hair, tied at the nape of her neck. Baldassare looks quickly at her, then away, unfolding and refolding his arms, and Lucrezia wants to go to him, to beat her fists against him and say, yes, yes, do you see how sick I look, but do you know what else? I'm still alive, I will not be so easily dispensed with.

For a moment or two, no one speaks, no one moves. The room hangs suspended, as if these men are all people in a painting, satyrs in a forest, perhaps, or penitents in a saint's procession. Then the spell, if that is what it is, is broken. Alfonso, who knows better than any of them what rituals should be observed, what must be said and left unsaid, comes to life. He uncrosses his long legs, rises from his chair and walks towards her, his hand outstretched.

'My love,' he exclaims, 'you look most unwell. Let me fetch the physician.'

'No need.' Lucrezia raises her chin to look him in the eye. 'I am quite recovered.' She permits her hand to lie in his for a moment, then removes it and advances into the room, away from Baldassare, only a little unsteadily.

'I would prefer the physician to make that judgement. I was this moment about to visit you in your rooms as I was wondering why you had not come down this morning, but then Il Bastianino arrived unexpectedly and, look . . .' he points towards what the apprentices are holding '. . . he has brought your portrait.'

Lucrezia regards first Maurizio – his amiable smile, his broken front tooth – then allows her eyes to rest on Jacopo. She is aware, to an almost unbearable degree, of the different gazes in this room, and the way they stream towards her, like the sticky, silken threads of a spider's web. That of her husband, somewhere to the left of her, standing just behind her; that of the artist, no doubt comparing her appearance today, haggard and ill, with the woman he rendered into paint only a few weeks ago; that of Baldassare, boring into her back, where the criss-crossing ties of her bodice cover her spine; that of Maurizio, which is filled with kind sympathy; and that of Jacopo. His is unlike any of the others. It is a beam of comprehension, from his eyes to hers. It draws up awareness and knowledge as a thirsty plant will water. Does he see that she will die? Can he understand that her time on this earth is now so limited, so short? Can he glean all that from her face, from the way her husband looks at her, from Baldassare's posture, there, as he balances, poised like a hawk awaiting the right wind, on the edge of the table, watching, watching, always watching.

'Let us see the portrait,' Alfonso says, 'now that the muse herself is here.'

Il Bastianino claps his hands together, as if nothing at all is amiss or peculiar in this dank and lonely fortress, and gestures impatiently at his apprentices.

Maurizio and Jacopo hoist the painting, still covered, to a table, where they balance it between them, turning their heads to their master, waiting for his signal.

Il Bastianino, never one to miss a dramatic moment, steps forward and, with one final glance over his shoulder at Alfonso, rips away the covering.

'There,' he announces breathily, arm aloft, the cloth billowing to the floor around his feet. 'Behold the Duchess.'

Before her, held up on each side by Jacopo and Maurizio, is an image so arresting she almost gasps. In the painting is a woman who looks like her, or a version of her, or an ideal – she cannot tell which. This is her, yet not her; it is so disturbingly like her, while being completely unlike her. It is Lucrezia, but it is also someone else. This girl is a duchess it is clear to see from the jewels that adorn her ears and neck, wrists and head, from the gold-and-pearl *cintura* around her waist, from the ornaments on her bodice, from the pleating and embroidery of her gown. Here before you, the portrait shouts, is no commoner, but someone high-born and exalted. She stands, looking out at the viewer, with the green fields and valleys of her province behind her. But there is something else lurking here, in this picture, almost as if another person hovers there. Lucrezia, standing in the *fortezza*'s hall, can sense it, like the scent of a fire. The girl stands next to a table, where a pile of books is stacked, a quill resting on the top. Her hand is next to them – she can tell it is hers because there is the ring Alfonso gave her, and her fingernails, and there is the thumb that slants to the left, the very digit that she is, at this moment, clutching in the opposite hand – but it is not like hands in other portraits, languid and still. This hand is flexed, tendons visible, something gripped between thumb and finger: a paintbrush. A slender one, with a narrow tip, designed for detailed work, for fine rendering. It is held in a sure, definite grasp. A hand with a purpose, a hand filled with intent. And, she now sees, the look in the girl's eye is lucid and charged. She stares out at the viewer with frankness close to defiance, her head high, her lips showing the hint of a smile. The dress, with its voluminous dark red folds, and its pattern that either imprisons or cringes behind the colour, seems tame and insignificant, utterly overshadowed by the boldness of the girl's expression, the way she seems to pose questions to the viewer: what do you want from me, why have you interrupted me, whatever do you mean by gazing at me like that?

Lucrezia regards the portrait; she stares; she cannot look away. It is at once scaldingly public and deeply private. It displays her body, her face, her hands, the mass of her once-long hair, which ripples down either side of the dress, with a brand of insolent indifference to its geometric pattern, but it also excavates that which she keeps hidden inside her. She loves it, she loathes it; she is dumbstruck with admiration; she is shocked by its acuity. She wants the world to see it; she wishes to run and cover it again with the cloth at the artist's feet.

She turns to Il Bastianino, as if to say, how did you know, how did you see all that, but she finds that his attention, and that of everyone else in the room, is fixed on one person only: the Duke of Ferrara.

Alfonso is considering the portrait, tapping a finger against his teeth. He walks one way, his head tilted, he walks the other. He advances towards it, he retreats.

Lucrezia watches him, out of the corner of her eye; she sees the anxiety rising in Il Bastianino, with every passing moment of the Duke's silence, a muscle in his cheek beginning to spasm; she sees that he has come here, to the *fortezza*, pursuing them out of the city, because he needs money. He must be in debt or need to buy materials for a new work – something like that. She sees Baldassare push himself away from the table and come to stand near Alfonso, less for the purpose of seeing the painting – he gives it a cursory glance – but more because he scents possible displeasure from Alfonso, and knows that he must be present if words are to be said, that he must be the one to speak them. She feels, she realises, as if she is suddenly absent from this room, or disappearing from it, evaporating into the air. The Duchess is present, in the painting. There she stands. Lucrezia is unnecessary; she can go now. Her place is filled; the portrait will take up her role in life.

Perhaps it is this feeling of incorporeality, of displacement, but it is as if her perception is suddenly heightened, or perhaps as if she is already dead, has already passed over into another realm, as if her soul has brimmed up and over, flooding everything in the vicinity. She can hear the squeak of Alfonso's boots as he paces the floor; she can sense the air taken in and expelled by Baldassare's chest. She can feel the boredom of the servants, at the far end of the room, the spiralling monotony of their thoughts. And she can look at Jacopo and know that it was he who painted this portrait.

It was him. She knows it. He mixed the pigments, prepared the canvas, stretching and smoothing its surface, he applied the coats of the *imprimitura*, deciding where the shade would fall, and also the light, then arranged the composition so that the perspectives and the colours all agreed with each other, like nouns and verbs and participles in a sentence of translation. He painted her hair like that, shining and unbound, he placed the painted quill upon the painted books, he put a paintbrush into her painted hand and that gleam and spirit into her eye. It was him. Il Bastianino might have added a stroke here and there, might have said, Like this, no, and this; Maurizio might have painted those orchards and hillocks, seen far behind her. But it was Jacopo who did this, who made this work.

As if he read her thoughts, as if he and Lucrezia are, after all this time, still connected by the strange event they went through together, in the corridor of the *delizia* last summer, he looks at her.

So much is taking place in the room around them, albeit in silence, for no one would dare to venture an opinion before the Duke has spoken. Il Bastianino is wondering if he will be paid, if he will be asked to do the work again, if he will continue to have the Duke's patronage. Baldassare is trying to ascertain Alfonso's mood, which has been erratic of late, what Alfonso might expect of him, and whether he will be required to dismiss this artist and his boys, and what form this dismissal will take. Maurizio is thinking that he would like to leave, to ride back to Ferrara, to get away from this gloomy place.

Lucrezia and Jacopo regard each other. She turns her eyes towards the portrait, then back to him, as if asking the question. He gazes back, utterly still, his hands gripping the edge of the painting, as if he will never let it go.

'It is,' the Duke's voice cuts into the thin silence, 'a wonder.'

Il Bastianino almost collapses with relief, his shoulders dropping, his knees buckling as he makes a deep bow, saying that he is so pleased the Duke is happy, he is overjoyed, Her Ladyship was such a gift of a subject, every moment of the work was pleasure, pure pleasure.

The Duke is nodding, saying that it is, he thinks, the artist's finest work to date, the effect so lifelike, the interplay of colour and light, the expression on the Duchess's face – the depth and earnestness are so like her – that it is evident, clearly evident, that Il Bastianino was influenced by Michelangelo. The comparison is one that will be noticed by others, the Duke is sure.

Il Bastianino bows, again and again, beaming. It has been an honour, he is assuring the Duke, perhaps the greatest of his life; he is most grateful, always, for His Grace's patronage, and if there is anything else, anything at all, His Grace should not hesitate to ask.

One by one, the men begin to leave the room. First, Alfonso, still talking about Michelangelo and brushwork, then the artist, who snaps his fingers behind his back, which makes the apprentices place the portrait on the floor, leaning against the wall, then Baldassare, then the servants. They file out through the door, Il Bastianino dropping back to ask Baldassare if it would be possible, if it wouldn't inconvenience His Grace at all, for him to receive payment, an advance on payment, a partial payment, anything at all would be most gratefully met, and he, Il Bastianino, is only ever too happy to put himself at His Grace's disposal in the future.

Lucrezia, alone in the hall, feels suddenly weak; she staggers to a chair and sits down, just before her legs give way. She grips the chair arms, feeling the sawdust spring of its stuffing, aware of the poison from last night still slinking through her blood, like a pack of wolves with muzzles close to the ground. Above her head rows and rows of stone bricks are arranged in arches that curve over her solitary figure. Or, rather, she is not alone. Across the room, propped against the wall, is herself – another self, a former self. A self who, when she is dead and buried in her tomb, will endure, will outlive her, who will always be smiling from the wall, one hand poised to begin a painting.

The sound of footsteps makes her turn her head. And here, coming through the open doorway, accompanied by a snatch of Maurizio's voice saying, 'We must have left it in the hall, we'll fetch it,' are the two apprentices. Maurizio hurries towards the portrait and begins to lift the linen covering off the floor, shaking it in the air, then folding it, corner to corner. Lucrezia is watching this, mesmerised, still gripping the chair arms, when she realises that Jacopo is standing next to her.

'You are in danger,' he says to her.

The sound of the dialect, Sofia's dialect, makes her want to weep. She looks up at him wonderingly – the aquatic eyes, the heavy brow, the frayed edges of his jerkin – but it is her, this time, who has no words, who cannot bring herself to speak.

'I . . .' she begins, but what she needs to say dies in her throat. She attempts a gesture in the direction of the door, and Alfonso, but a terrible lethargy has seized her arm, and her hand falters, falling into her lap.

'Yes,' she manages to say, her mouth finding the familiar shapes required for the dialect, 'but there is nothing to be done.'

Jacopo looks at her. He requires no further information, just as she knew he wouldn't, but glances quickly around the hall, then back at her.

'There is very little time,' he murmurs, 'they will be back in a moment. So listen well. There is an entrance for servants, at the back of the kitchens. Maurizio and I will stuff the lock with rags on our way out.'

'What?' she says, in her own tongue, distracted and stupe-fied by the sight of herself, in splendid attire, across the room, visible over the back of a person who is trying to fold a billowing sheet into submission, by the headache that has descended on her with the claws of a raptor, by the way the air feels so cold when she breathes in, packing her lungs with frost, by these words spoken to her in such a rough and rude voice.

'So that you may open it,' he says quickly. 'I will be there waiting for you, in the trees, as soon as it is dark. I will stay until dawn. After that, it will be too dangerous.'

'You'll wait for me?' she repeats, her tongue thick and unwieldy in her mouth. 'Whatever do you mean?'

He looks at her, his face attentive, full of concern. Then he reaches out and touches her, at the place where the neckline of her bodice ends and her shoulder begins. She flinches with the shock of it. Part of her wishes to lash him with her voice, to say, how dare you, do not touch me, people like you are not permitted to approach me, have you any idea what my husband would do to you if he saw, what my father would—

But the feel of his fingertips – stained today, she has noticed, with patches of green, irregular in size and shape, as if his hand is the open ocean, studded by an archipelago of unmapped islands – against her skin produces a sensation the like of which she has never felt before. It is the opposite of the convulsions that shook her in the night: it is light, fluttering, and causes concentric circles of heat to expand down her arm and up her neck. It is gentleness, it is care. It is far from anything she has felt in the bed at the *delizia* or in the *castello* or here in the *fortezza*. It is a touch that topples a wall built somewhere within her, that crashes through a thorned thicket that has grown and spread about her heart, through necessity and neglect. It is contact that removes obstacles, sweeps them away, hurls them into the air.

She opens her mouth to speak, to say she doesn't know what he means, that he must be out of his mind, but also to say, if only I could, if only that were even slightly possible.

Maurizio, across the room, is muttering, Enough, Jacopo, enough, someone might come, let's go, now.

Jacopo removes his hand, steps away from her and she only just manages not to reach out for him and grasp his arm. The circle of flesh at her neckline feels singed and bare.

'You cannot stay here,' he whispers, in the language of the faraway south. 'You know that. You must leave, as soon as you can. Make sure you come.'

Then they walk away, without looking back, and she is alone again.

A presence malign and predatory

Castello, Ferrara, 1561

After her mother's letter, the need for motion leaves Lucrezia. She still spends her time outside but instead of pacing, she stands staring up at the sky. She eats little, has no desire for the company of any courtiers. Nunciata orders the *evirati* to sing for them after dinner one evening, but Lucrezia leaves before they finish, saying she is tired. By all means, Nunciata cries after her, rest! You should rest!

That night, enclosed in her *castello* bed, Lucrezia dreams that she is moving through a damp, misted place with narrow streets and unmoving channels of water. Behind and in front are children, walking along with her. They don't assume a clear corporeal form but she knows, with the clarity of a dream, that they are her children, those yet to be born. The ones waiting, like actors poised to enter a stage, ears cocked for the cue that will summon them forth. Despite her diurnal fears about conception and motherhood, she longs to touch these creatures, to feel their small bodies against hers, to stroke the silk of their hair, to kiss the creases of their palms: she can feel these impulses beat through her, and the sensation is like a river breaching its banks to form small tributaries that course off in unexpected directions. The dream-children, who are visiting from an unknowable future, elude her grasp, though. When she reaches for them, they slink sideways, they duck into the doorways of the buildings or they skip towards curious little stone footbridges, and her hand closes on nothing but moist air. Their faces are indistinct, turned away, but their little hands brush hers, every now and again, their pliable fingers working their way between hers. Where are you? she tries to ask them. What is this place? How can I find you, and when will you come? But they don't answer or don't hear her. They are busy, calling to each other as they bound along, down alleyways and on to jetties, their voices passing back and forth like shuttles, the foggy air the loom cloth, their words a phantasmagorical thread.

In the room, before she goes to her own bed, Emilia is burning amber resin in a bowl. She wants Lucrezia to sleep well, and for a long time. Only through sleep, her mother always told her, will recovery come.

Grey feathers of smoke waft over the bed where Lucrezia is lying, eyes shut tight, hands gripping the bedclothes.

Lucrezia dreams she is in one of the paintings that hang on her father's walls, walking shoeless over dark, leaf-strewn soil, which is studded with spring blooms – white, red, delicate yellow. She worries, in the dream, that her feet will crush the flowers, so she steps carefully, choosing her path, dreading the sensation of a stem snapping beneath her or the cold crush of petals against her sole. Through the thick foliage, she can hear the voices of women singing; she catches glimpses of their thin, pale robes as they circle each other in a loose, improvised dance. But they themselves remain elusive, always ahead or to the side of her. Somewhere in the branches is a presence malign and predatory: she either knows this or recalls this, she cannot say which. But an icy breeze threads from him, through the tree trunks, to lick insistently at the bare skin of her arms. The awareness that she must keep watch, must avoid this being at all costs, swirls about her mind like smoke. He is a demi-god, perhaps, or the personification of an element or some tree-spirit intent on revenge or capture. He seeks the women in the pale robes, or perhaps it is her he has come for. It is impossible to know. Can the women save her? Lucrezia cannot tell. She clears the ivy and branches from her path with her cold, cold hands, and keeps walking, hoping for the best. It is important to step around the flowers, not to touch the low-hanging fruit above her head: this is all she knows.

Around her, the *castello* is quiet, Lucrezia in her bed, curled into herself, Emilia on her pallet, mouth open, emitting soft snores. On the floor below, Nunciata sleeps, turned on to her side, her spaniel cradled in her arms. Far, far below them, in the moated gatehouse, a guard is woken by a single rap to the vast wooden door, then another. Barely conscious, he shakes his companion awake and they raise themselves, yawning, stumbling from their rush mats.

The chains of the drawbridge do not rattle as the guards lower it: the mechanism is oiled several times a week. It is part of their duties. Important, the *consigliere* has always told them, for the drawbridge to be opened and closed without waking anyone, for the Duke, if it pleases him, to be able to come and go without alerting others.

The guards, still half asleep, remove their caps and bow low as two horses enter the *castello*.

Lucrezia is dreaming again. This time, she is standing in a round structure, a mill perhaps. There is a sound of grinding, of stone rasping on stone. To her left, she sees Sofia bending over, turning and turning a wheel with her hands. It is a strenuous task and Sofia's face is slicked with sweat; her hands grip the wheel and she pants with the effort. Lucrezia walks towards her, wanting to assist, but Sofia shakes her head. Without looking at her, she says, 'You know what you have to do.'

The grinding around them intensifies and Lucrezia, in the dream, wants to put her hands over her ears. 'I don't know,' she shouts, over the noise. 'What do I have to do?'

Sofia turns to give her a stern look. 'You know,' she says.

Lucrezia jerks awake, yanked into consciousness, her mouth forming the words: Tell me, tell me.

The room is empty. A clean, white light is softening the outlines of the furniture, leaching the colour from the fabrics. A charred scent like resin hangs in the air and the walls look oddly bare.

She turns her head and there is Alfonso, sitting on the edge of the bed, close to her, his hand resting on her hip. He is back, apparently, from Modena, but why, when she has been told he would be away for another fortnight? What is he doing here? She has not seen him since she handed over her dress for the portrait, and he ordered her to stay in her chamber. How long ago was that? A week, or perhaps more?

'I didn't mean to wake you,' he murmurs. 'Did you sleep well?'

She watches, dumbfounded, as he leans towards her, closer and closer. What does he mean to do to her? His face and torso are getting nearer and she shrinks back into the pillows but there is no escape, no possible way she can put distance between them.

He places a brief, dry kiss on her temple, then leans back, apparently unaware of her reluctance.

'You were dreaming,' he is saying, 'and muttering something – I couldn't tell what. It sounded very serious.'

He talks on, about the way his dog twitches in sleep, apparently convinced that it is hunting rabbits, the way Nunciata was prone to nightmares as a child, and how this drove their nurses to distraction, because she would wake them all up every night with her shouting. How strange it was, how Nunciata struggled and screamed.

Lucrezia is stunned, by his presence in her room, after a long absence, by this flow of chatter. Has he forgotten what happened with Contrari, what passed between them? Has he no memory of ordering her to remain in her rooms? His appearance is no less startling for he is, once again, the Duke she first met, on the arm of her sister, on the battlements that day. The man who pulled the face of the mouse. He is the man who married her at the altar of Santa Maria Novella, not quite a year ago. He has many incarnations and she is not sure she has yet met them all. There is this man – amusing and amused, his head on one side, able to chat, to take her hand, to conduct himself with kindness and concern, to roll up the sleeves of his *giubbone*, revealing the brown skin of his wrists.

She thinks of all the things she wishes to say to him: that she would leave and go back to Florence, that what he did to Elisabetta, to Contrari, was barbaric and inhuman, she can never love him, ever again, that she hates what he does to her at night, that she is filled with horror at the thought of giving him a child, that she wants to be far, far away from him. These utterances stream through her head, like the cold wind through the forest of her dream. But she cannot catch hold of them, cannot voice them, not now, when he sits here so amiably, so affectionately, holding her hand, and asking her how she is feeling, saying he is so sorry she has been unwell, that he has summoned the physician to see her because he, Alfonso, does not want her to ail in any way at all.

This is a different man, surely, from the one who ordered Contrari's death. It cannot have been him. This is her husband, who loves her, or seems to; that was the ruler of Ferrara. They are the same man; they are different men, the same yet different.

'You are nauseous and cannot keep down food, I hear. Is that right?'

He is leaning close to her, fingers curled around her arm, a lopsided smile on his face.

'I . . . No, it is more . . .' Lucrezia tries to order her thoughts. 'Who told you this?'

'Nunciata wrote to me. It's true?'

'I have felt . . . I have no appetite.'

His face breaks into a wide grin. 'The physician is outside,' he says, springing up from the bed. 'May I ask him to come in?'

Lucrezia is mystified. Why would Nunciata write to him about her appetite? And why is he suddenly being so charming and attentive to her?

'A physician is not necessary,' she protests. 'I don't need—'

'You have nothing to fear. He is the best in the whole of the region. He will take excellent care of you. I have sent away your women but I shall remain in the room with you the whole time.'

Lucrezia raises herself to a sitting position. 'Alfonso, why—?'

The physician steps over the threshold, performing a deep bow first to Alfonso, then to Lucrezia. He has a bald pate that gives off a glaring sheen and carries a bag of rigid leather.

'Your Highness,' he says, coming to the side of the bed. 'His Grace, the Duke, has requested that I examine you. Might I be permitted to take your pulse?'

He bows again at the end of this speech and, when she nods, lifts her wrist in icy fingers.

He waits, eyes raised to the ceiling. He then asks her to open her mouth, so that he can examine her tongue. He looks into both ears, he kneels and looks into the contents of the chamber pot beneath the bed. He lays a hand to her forehead, her arm; he asks to view her breasts and abdomen. He palpates her stomach, with care at first, and then with more pressure.

'Well?' Alfonso says, when the doctor has indicated that Lucrezia may once again lower her shift. He is, Lucrezia suddenly realises, simmering with unaccustomed tension, a tendon standing out in his neck, eyes gleaming with an avid light.

'I believe it is unlikely that Her Grace is with child. The stomach is soft, the veins are not enlarged, and I would venture to suggest that there is an excess of choler in Her Ladyship. She seems low in spirits and perhaps might benefit from—'

Alfonso slams a hand against the wall, startling both Lucrezia and the doctor.

'You think her *spirits*,' he spits out, 'are my concern here?'

He turns away and stands with his back to them, head bowed. The doctor glances helplessly at Lucrezia and she gives a silent shrug, as if to say, do not look to me for help.

The doctor straightens, as if summoning courage, and changes tack.

'I understand this must come as a disappointment to His Grace, but we must not give way to despair. I see no reason at all why Her Ladyship will not be in a happy state very soon. She is young, she is healthy. Her colour is excellent and her body is neither too fleshy nor too thin. She has a pretty, rosy sort of face, and good circulation, all of which indicate that she will conceive a son.'

Alfonso turns around. He has tucked the hand that struck the wall into the fastenings of his *giubbone*, as if to tame its impulses, as if to ensure it doesn't give him away again. He shoots Lucrezia a level, evaluating glance, then leaves the room, indicating with his head that the doctor should follow. The door between chamber and salon closes.

Lucrezia listens for a moment and, when she discerns voices beyond the door, she gets out of bed and presses her ear to the wooden slats.

'. . . has been almost a year,' Alfonso is saying, in a low tone, and he must be pacing about because she hears his voice get louder and then softer, louder again, and the tap of his boot soles, 'which ought to be sufficient time, would you not agree?'

'The body,' the doctor says, 'of a woman is like a fine instrument and it takes care and practice to produce the desired music—'

'How much longer, in your opinion, will it be before she will produce a child?' Alfonso demands.

There is a pause, as if the doctor is assessing the situation in which he finds himself, its pros and cons, and its possible implications for himself.

'Forgive me, Your Highness,' the doctor says, 'for such a question but how often do you lie with her?'

'It depends. Frequently. Every night.'

'Might I suggest a regular system of every fifth day, with a gap of abstinence in between? Such a practice ensures that the seed be enriched and matured, and falling on the replenished soil of the female. Any more than that and too much strain is placed on the male body and brain.'

'Every fifth day?'

'Yes, Your Grace. And let her see her confessor in the gap, so she may be appropriately shriven. This has proved a most efficacious method, in accordance with Greco-Roman science. Also, with the utmost respect, and the forgiveness of Your Grace, at such a time, it is considered best that a man should confine himself solely to the embraces of his wife, not to expend himself elsewhere, in—'

It interests Lucrezia that Alfonso interrupts the doctor at this point, speaking over him, cutting off what he was about to say.

'There is something about her, though,' Alfonso mutters, and Lucrezia can picture him, his frown, his restless striding. 'Do you not see it?'

'See what, Your Grace?'

'Something amiss.'

The doctor hesitates. 'Amiss? I am not certain that I—'

'It is hard to define. There is something at the core of her, a type of defiance. There are times when I look at her and I can feel it – it's like an animal that lives behind her eyes. I had no knowledge of it prior to our marriage, no sense of it. I was assured of her balanced disposition, her good health. She seemed so biddable, charmingly so, young and innocent. But now I see it I do not know how I missed it. It makes me fear that there will always be a part of her that will not submit or be ruled.'

The doctor makes a neutral noise. 'Her Ladyship appears to me to be a most—'

'I have a suspicion,' Alfonso speaks in so quiet a tone that Lucrezia has to strain to hear him, 'that she keeps pregnancy from her body by force of will, by some malady of character. Is it possible for a woman to be so unsettled in spirit that a child will have no hope of taking root within her?'

Beyond the door, Lucrezia hears the doctor hesitating before making his reply.

'I have never,' he says tentatively, 'heard of such a thing. Her Ladyship comes from a very good family. Could it be that what you are referring to in the Duchess is a tendency to emotional excess?'

'Perhaps. That is one way to put it.'

'It is, I can assure you, a common state in young women. Your wife, I would venture to say, has too much heat about her. Her blood is hot and this can overexert the female mind. I can, of course, treat this. It should be simple to redress. I recommend a course of bleeding and cupping, some preparations of herbs and minerals. I will see to the precise concoctions myself. She must eat cool foods, a little poultry, green vegetables, red meat, cheese and milk every day. No spices, no broths, no peppers or tomatoes. Let her also be surrounded by gentle and fruitful things. None of these images of wild beasts that I see on the wall here. These bones and feathers and savage artefacts should be removed from her. She may engage only in careful exercise, once a day, and should rest after meals, in bed, and after waking. No excitement, no dancing, no music, no creative endeavours, no reading, except for religious texts.'

'Very well.'

'I am certain that the event you so desire will come to pass.'

There is a shuffling, a rustling, as if the doctor is taking his leave, bowing, backing away. Lucrezia is about to move back towards the bed, in case Alfonso comes into the room again, when she hears the doctor say: 'Oh, and I recommend that her hair be cut.'

'Her hair?'

'It is the colour of fire, Your Grace,' he says, as if the idea is distasteful to him, 'and there is so much of it. Very heating, very inflaming. We need to cool her, remember, to contain her. Cutting off her hair will help, I assure you.'

A group of servants is sent up. They arrive with boxes and sheeting. Clelia supervises as they remove the paintings from the walls – the betrothal stone marten, Lucrezia's sketches of the white mule, a small oil painting of a fox, a scene depicting a doe chased by dogs, a portrait of a woman with a pet leopard she found in a salon at the *delizia* and relocated to her private rooms. When they begin to dismantle her collections of feathers and pebbles and fragments of bark, Lucrezia springs forward and inserts herself between the servants and her treasures. They will not listen to her protestations and so she tries to gather up as many items as she can, filling her arms and hands, but before she realises what is happening, two guards have stepped in from the corridor, and they are taking the feathers and stones away from her, they are putting their hands on her, holding her back. Emilia is shrieking, don't you touch her, don't you dare, get away from her, and Clelia is scolding, telling her to hush, and the guards' faces are grey and miserable, like those of stone gargoyles, so Lucrezia takes to the window seat, and huddles there, with her head buried in her knees.

Her sheaf of streaked porcupine spines is taken, the dried mosses and lichens, the dish of apricot pits, cleaned and polished to a gleam, are all packed into boxes and carried away.

In their place, Clelia hangs a picture of a bowl of lemons and figs, a classical scene of men standing in a circle, solemnly holding spears, and a depiction of a blank-faced Madonna with an overlarge halo, holding a passive Christchild swathed in a loincloth.

Her books are taken away, 'to prevent excitement', Clelia explains, and her paints and vellum and chalks. She is allowed a small amount of paper and ink, for letters.

* * *

A packet of herbs is brought, with instructions to drink it before her evening meal. Clelia pours hot water on to the dried concoction, and an evil-smelling steam is released into the air.

Lucrezia looks down into the cup. The liquid is dark green, with particles of black afloat on a foamy surface. She raises it to her mouth but the smell rising off it is so noxious, so powerful, that she gags before the drink even touches her lips.

'That's good,' Clelia says, observing her from across the room. 'It is purging you of the heat. It's working already.'

Lucrezia holds her breath, tips the cup, tries to swallow. The mixture is thick, viscous in texture; the warring tastes of mulch, bitter mint, a pepperish aniseed flood her mouth, coating her tongue and airways. She gags again, coughs, splutters, feeling a portion of it slide down her gullet; the rest diverts into her throat, the back of her mouth.

'Quick,' says Emilia, who is standing at her elbow, 'eat this.' She hands her a morsel of cheese. 'It will take away the taste.'

Lucrezia pushes the cheese into her mouth, its dairy blandness smoothing away the bite of the doctor's herbs. She shudders, once, then hands the cup back to Clelia.

A secretary is sent up after the midday meal, with a reminder from His Grace that the Duchess must rest.

Lucrezia is put to bed by Emilia and Clelia; they pull the bedclothes tight and tuck them under the feather mattress. She lies there, feeling fury smoulder and build within her. To lie like this in the middle of the day, staring up at the bed canopy. It is insupportable. She cannot do it.

* * *

Clelia brings scissors with handles in the shape of long-billed cranes, and instructions from the Duke that her hair be cut, in accordance with the doctor's advice.

Lucrezia takes the scissors and weighs them in her hand, slips her fingers into the vacancy created by the crane's legs and dipped beak.

She will not let anyone perform this task: not Clelia, not Emilia, not Nunciata, who arrives intent on using the scissors, almost as if she relishes the idea of severing those locks from Lucrezia's head. It is all for the best, Nunciata says, trying to snatch the scissors out of her hand, you will see. Soon you will be with child and you won't miss all this hair one little bit.

She will do it herself, Lucrezia says, or not at all.

She stands before the glass, her hair loose. She can feel the luxurious length of it, covering her back, brushing against her legs, stretching from scalp to ankle. Her mother once referred to it as 'her only asset', gathering a hank of it in one of her hands, as if unable to believe that such hair had been bestowed on her least promising daughter. It was, Lucrezia knows, the envy of her sisters, who could never get theirs as long. Maria and Isabella would rub preparations of *malvavisco* and willow sprigs into each other's locks but their hair wouldn't grow past their waists before it began to split and dry. Lucrezia, on the other hand, who never did anything other than to brush it once in a while, was possessed of a mane that grew lushly, thickly, with waves and meanders like the braided course of a reddish-gold stream. Maria used to grab it in her fist and pull it towards her own head, saying, 'I'll cut it off and use it for myself,' and this threat always made Lucrezia scream – the idea of Maria walking about with her hair clipped on to her head seemed violating and treacherous – and Sofia would have to come and separate them.

Maria never carried out her threat. And now Lucrezia must sever it herself, from her own head, and Maria will never be able to thieve it from her.

She regards her reflection. Her face is pale and bloodless, her eyes huge in their sockets. She looks fearsome, she looks determined. She sees the waterfall flood of her hair, the sunlight invading the kinks and curls, inhabiting its warm spaces. It heats her, the doctor had said, her cape of hair; it creates rebellious feeling, disturbs the natural order of her, causes her humours to become unbalanced.

She lifts the blades in one hand and a fistful of hair in the other. Behind her, in the mirror, she can see Emilia wince and cover her mouth. Nunciata is still twittering about pregnancies and continuing the family line, and how in life everyone must make sacrifices, and she sits forward, keeping Lucrezia keenly in her sights.

Lucrezia's fingers tremble a little, not from reluctance, perhaps, but a kind of raw thrill. She is doing this; she is about to do it. She does not want to but she sees no other path open to her. If she doesn't do it, someone else will, and she will not let anyone cut the hair from her head. If it must happen, she will take charge of it herself. It is her hair. It is her head. They can take away her pictures and her paints; they can fill her body with medicines and cold foods and other things besides; they can poke and palpate her stomach and peer down her throat; they can lock her up in her rooms, but she will cut the hair from her own head before she lets anyone else near her with shears.

She stretches open the scissors and slides their blades in beside her ear, readying herself to snap them closed.

No, cries Emilia, not there.

Not so close to the head, Nunciata calls out, there's no need for it to be as short as that.

Emilia steps forward and indicates with her fingers a place on Lucrezia's upper arm, glancing at Nunciata in the mirror for her assent. Nunciata shakes her head. Emilia raises her finger to just below Lucrezia's shoulder, which is, Lucrezia reflects, about the length of Emilia's own hair when released from her cap.

After a short, considering pause, Nunciata nods.

Lucrezia slides the blades of the scissors to the agreed place on her hair, and, without closing her eyes, she presses them together.

The noise is louder than she might have thought. A clean, metallic *shuurassh*.

The severed hair shies away from the forked blades. There it is, in her palm: a life's worth of growth, the nearest and darkest part belonging perhaps to her early womanhood, the very furthest and fairest part her infancy. Extraordinary to think that these strands have been attached to her all that time, from when she was a small child in the nursery, to now, here, in this room, this moment, where her life has ended up.

She lays the strand carefully on the coffer beside her, and returns to the glass.

Snip, snap, snip, go the blades, working with and also against each other, and soon all her hair is gone, cut off so that the ends brush her shoulders, and her reflection shows not Lucrezia but someone other, a marionette or a woodland creature with large eyes and a white, shocked face. An invalid, a penitent.

She places the final bright tress on the coffer and runs a hand down the length of her shortened hair. The ends are sharp and bristly against her fingertips. Surprising how light her head feels, how easily it turns, how her neck feels cold and exposed.

Behind her, Emilia is crying as she lifts the severed strands. She is saying that they will keep them, that they can use them to dress her hair, pinning them into the remaining tresses, and it will look just as it used to, if done properly, should Lucrezia wish it.

'I do not wish it,' Lucrezia says.

'But, madam—'

'Burn them.'

'I cannot. I—'

Nunciata is putting her dog on the floor, shuffling forward. 'Alfonso said he wanted the hair.'

Lucrezia turns. 'Alfonso?'

'Yes. He asked me to—'

'Why?'

'How should I know?' Nunciata says testily. 'It is not for us to question his whims.'

Lucrezia watches as Clelia takes the hair from Emilia, binds it, combs it, coils it around itself, and wraps it in linen. Nunciata takes this bundle and holds it at arm's length as she leaves the room, her spaniel yapping at the end of its leash.

Lucrezia is filled with the urge to pull the packet of hair from her grasp, to keep it, to destroy it. She does not like to think of part of herself being taken away and put into Alfonso's possession. What will he do with it? Keep it in a chest, lock it in a cupboard?

The door closes after Nunciata, and the hair is gone. Lucrezia turns away. The maids sweep the floor, they tidy the coffers, they clear away the dishes, they prepare her daily herbal draught; the day turns, continues and closes, like any other, as if nothing at all has changed.

The beautiful rooms are bare. Lucrezia paces from one wall to the other, from the bedchamber to the window overlooking the piazza. She does not look at the painting of the Madonna or at the bowl of fruit – swollen lemons, figs on the point of bursting. She keeps her head averted from them. If they will not let her have her own paintings, she will not let her eyes fall on these.

From this small rebellion she draws solace.

She is permitted to leave her rooms for a quarter of an hour, to take the air on the loggia, as long as she is wrapped in furs to protect her from the damp winter winds.

She walks as fast as she is able, feeling the blood tick along her veins, her heart work away in her chest. She keeps one eye on the sundial, watching the progression of the shadow. Her guard will tell her when her time is up, when she must return to her rooms.

Emilia devises a way to dress Lucrezia's hair so that the loss of so much length is concealed. It involves twisting strands at the front to give an impression of mass, looping these strands over the ears, and pinning up the remainder in a pearl diadem from the wedding chest.

Clelia says it is not to her taste. She does Lucrezia's hair the next day, wetting her fingers and teasing it back into curls.

Emilia says she thinks this does not suit their mistress's long neck.

On the third day, Lucrezia says she will do her hair herself.

The maids watch, each from the corner of their eyes, sullenly, not looking at the other.

Lucrezia invents some message for them to take to distant places in the *castello* or asks them to fetch things for her, from the kitchens, or to take treats to her mule in the stables. Anything to be rid of their glowering presences for a while, to be alone in her thoughts.

Every five days, Alfonso comes to her. He, too, dismisses the maids but for different reasons.

No longer does he remove his clothes as he crosses the room or pull back the bedclothes to look down upon her. He kneels at the bedside instead, insisting she does the same, and, with his rosary beads in hand, leads her in prayer. The act itself is swift, his movements deliberate and careful.

He does not once mention her hair.

He is always courteous afterwards. He tells her what has been happening at court – what songs were sung over dinner, who recited which poem, who is having love affairs with whom. He mentions matters of state, both in Ferrara and abroad. He says he has visited the studio of Il Bastianino, to see the progress of her marriage portrait, and he was much pleased by how it is coming along. He asks her how she is feeling:

calm, calmer, warm, cooler? Not too hot, hungry, thirsty, at peace, at rest? Does she feel any change in herself, in her body? Is there anything she craves to eat or drink? Can he do anything for her?

She is, he reminds her, obliged to visit her confessor. For this, too, she may leave her rooms.

Lucrezia becomes very frequent in her visits to confession. She insists for the first time on attending Mass at least once a day.

As she goes to and from the chapel, everyone remarks on how apt and right this is, that she should appeal to the Lord for a child. The whole *castello* is praying for the bestowing of an heir on the couple. The guards, maids, servants, stewards watch with reverent eyes as the little Duchess crosses herself before the altar.

She must walk down a flight of stairs, along one loggia, then another, and across the orangery to reach the chapel. She passes the entrance to the Sala dell'Aurora and also the smaller hall. She does this very slowly, as instructed by her physician. She must not rush, must preserve her strength. Often, she catches glimpses of courtiers, the servants who are employed to run between kitchen and hall, between salon and gatehouse. She can very easily see between fifteen and twenty other faces.

When she gets back to her room, she sketches these faces, quickly, with the ink and paper intended for letters, then burns the evidence.

* * *

The physician comes regularly to check on her. At first, Lucrezia hates these visits, the way his fingers probe her body, grip her pulse point, place heated glass cups on her back, draw information from her skin and neck and tongue.

After a week or two, however, it begins to be a welcome change, a distraction from the monotony. Lucrezia asks him about his family, the names and ages of his children, has his whelping dog given birth to her puppies yet, and how does his wife? Are her leg pains improved? Does his eldest son still show signs of melancholy? Is his daughter still refusing to practise her music?

Her monthly bleeding arrives, on the expected day. Alfonso does not visit for over a week.

If the tedium becomes too much, Emilia will play a game with her. The cards are ones Lucrezia brought from Florence; they are painted with images of towers, bridges and trees. Their edges are softened from the many times they were used in the *palazzo* nursery: Lucrezia brushes these against her cheek, then sniffs them, just in case a hint of Sofia, Isabella or her brothers remains on the surface.

After the game ends – and Emilia does well, picking up rules and strategies with alacrity – Lucrezia will sit at the window and lay bets on which way the people in the streets below will turn: left or right? Emilia will bring her paper and ink, and turn away, pretending not to see if Lucrezia starts to sketch instead of writing a letter.

And if Lucrezia cries in the night, Emilia will come and hold her, tight, just as Sofia used to. She will smooth the hair on

Lucrezia's brow, she will dab her face with a handkerchief, and say, there now. She will relate stories her mother told her – tales of fairies who grant wishes and goblins who possess a magic iron sword. She will tell her that, in the *palazzo* in Florence, the servants were in awe of Lucrezia, that some feared her.

This makes Lucrezia stop weeping. Why? she will want to know.

Because, says Emilia, there was a rumour about you. Someone swore that, when you were a little girl, he once saw you touch a tiger. And the tiger didn't harm you, it let you stroke it. It was always said that you had charmed the beast, like an enchantress. Impossible, of course, but—

Not impossible, says Lucrezia, not at all.

Then she closes her eyes and falls asleep. In and out of her dreams shifts the barred orange flank of a distantly remembered beast, with large paws and a simmering amber gaze.

She cannot settle on how she feels about becoming pregnant. She wants this confinement to her rooms and swallowing of herbs and visits from the doctor to end and, it seems, conceiving is the only way to achieve that.

But if she thinks about her body swelling with the growth of a baby, about the concept of birthing that child, about overseeing its education, health and life, then being expected to produce another, she feels overwhelmed and unready. A male child would be greeted with rapture and relief, she knows, but then it would be moulded for one single destiny: a duke. And a female child would be required to do as she has done, to be uprooted from her family and her place of birth and bedded down in another, where she must learn to thrive and reproduce and speak little and do less and stay in her rooms and cut off her hair and avoid excitement and eschew stimulation and submit to whatever nightly caresses come her way.

What would she feel if she were pregnant? How would she greet the news? She would be permitted to leave her chamber, to take part again in life at court. But her body would bud a person, an entirely separate being, on whose head would be heaped all manner of expectations. Alfonso's son, Alfonso's heir, a future Duke of Ferrara.

Her monthly bleeding arrives again, several days early, with an air of insolent disregard.

At this calamity, the doctor is summoned. He requests to examine the cloths. Lucrezia waits on the edge of her chair, head averted, hands tucked beneath her, while the doctor informs a displeased Nunciata, who sits on the settle, and Alfonso, who stands by the window, his back turned, that her menstrual blood is 'thin' and, yes, 'too hot'.

She is given a new herbal preparation, this one with an acidic aftertaste and a yeasty smell.

The doctor instructs that she be allowed to sketch babies, no more than once or twice a day. Strong, healthy babies, he says, and male.

She covers page after page with children. Their supple, unguarded faces, their pearly limbs. Children seen from the windows of the *castello*, or those from her dream, walking along a canal or over a small arching bridge. Babies on the backs of their parents, babies in cradles, babies on horseback, babies taking flight on outstretched feathery wings, to mingle in the blue and skim over treetops.

Nunciata, who seems delighted with her role as Alfonso's sole remaining sister, only too happy to bustle into Lucrezia's rooms several times a day in order to report back to him how his wife is passing her time, comes up behind Lucrezia to see what she is drawing.

When she sees the airborne babies, she frowns.

Lucrezia arranges a row of wineglasses on her windowsill, fills them with varying levels of water, and creates an entire musical scale by tapping their edges with a fingernail. She does this for hours, over and over, until she can pick out several tunes.

Clelia watches silently from the other side of the room, winding yarn off the back of a chair.

Lucrezia takes a handful of polished mineral pebbles, which had been left, forgotten, inside her credenza, and, finding their colours dulled, drops them into a dish of water.

The next day, the level of the water has sunk.

Have the pebbles been drinking it?

She kneels down, fascinated. She lifts one of the pebbles and shakes it, listening out for a tell-tale slosh.

Emilia tells her it is impossible, that pebbles don't drink. It is the warmth of the air that draws off the water. Clelia says it is a fanciful notion. Nunciata sniffs and says she has never heard such nonsense in her entire life.

But Lucrezia is sure of it. The pebbles are drinking. She pours more water into the dish, and covers it with a cloth.

Sure enough, the next day, half the water has vanished.

She tells this to Alfonso, as he is dressing. She offers to show him the pebbles. He turns his neck and looks at her for a long time, standing between bed and window, stalled in the act of fastening the ties of his shirt. His face is inscrutable, fixed, his hair hanging down over one eye, his fingers remaining in position, still grasping his shirt edges. He seems almost sad, and she wishes to say to him, what is the matter? Why do you look like that?

Then he seems to shake off whatever it was that had passed through his mind. He fastens his shirt with haste, pushes back his hair and sits in a chair opposite the bed, arms folded, one leg crossed over the other.

'It seems to me,' Alfonso says, clearing his throat, 'that you are not perhaps thriving under the regimen of this doctor. Would you agree?'

Lucrezia sits up straight; she has to clench her hands under the bedclothes to contain her eagerness, not let it show. Go carefully, she tells herself, appear calm.

'I hate it,' she hears herself say, despite all her intentions. 'I cannot bear being shut up like this. It is intolerable. You have to let me out, you have to give me back my liberty.' She presses her fingernails into her palms – do not appear heated, keep a cool demeanour. 'What I mean is, I am not certain that the medicines are helping me. I feel that—'

'I have been in consultation with another doctor, from . . .'

Alfonso makes a minute hesitation, as if trying to remember, and any such pause in the flow of his speech is unusual – later she will recall this '. . . Milan,' he opts for. 'His advice is quite contrary. He recommends a change of air, plain food, and exercise. It is for this reason that I think we should go to the countryside, you and I, for a short period. So that you may regain your health. And we can rest . . . together. Away from the court. And all its pressures.'

Lucrezia stares at Alfonso. 'The countryside?' she repeats. 'You mean . . .' She cannot finish the sentence because her throat closes over with a surge of unaccustomed happiness. Her mind is filled with images of the *delizia*, the bright pathways of the garden, her rooms with angels on the ceiling, the kind villa servants bringing platefuls of pastries, riding her mule with the red bridle, the corridor where she dropped honey water into the inert mouth of a young man on the brink of death.

'Oh,' she says, unable to prevent the tears pricking at her eyelids, 'I would love that. Yes, the countryside. Please. Let's go there.'

We were happy there, she wants to say to him. Contrari had not happened, Elisabetta had not left, there were no doctors or medicines or prescriptions of rest, there was no Clelia sent to spy on her, no Nunciata to order her around, and Alfonso was an altogether different person – he had liked her then and she had yet to disappoint him. Perhaps it will be possible to return to a time when she and he were in harmony. Perhaps he means to recapture all that. Perhaps there her body will do what he wants, what everyone expects. Perhaps she can still make a success of this marriage.

'Very well.' He stands, pulling on his boots. 'We shall leave tomorrow.'

If Lucrezia is surprised by his haste, she does not dwell on it. Emilia and Clelia pack boxes and bags with gowns, shifts and shawls. Lucrezia orders her paints and brushes to be returned to her; she packs these herself. For a moment, she looks about her, sure that she needs to wrap in cloth the golden fantail of a tiny glass fish, and perhaps an aquamarine fox, but she remembers this cannot be: the *animaletti* were lost to her, broken, a long time ago.

She is going to the *delizia*, she tells herself, over and over again, the *delizia*. There, she is able to wander at will, and perhaps she and Alfonso will gain some sense of unity. At any rate, she is getting out of these rooms; she will look upon something other than the glowering walls of the *castello*.

In the courtyard, she is surprised to see that there is no carriage ready for them, just a pair of guards, some donkeys with luggage strapped to their backs, and two horses – one for her, one for Alfonso.

He is there, giving orders for that groom to hold the bridle, for this saddle girth to be tightened. The drawbridge has been lowered in readiness – not the one he usually uses, which is large and leads out of the front of the *castello*, but a side one so narrow only one rider may pass through at a time.

'We are not going by carriage?' she says.

'No,' he says, taking her arm, 'I thought this would be easier. And quicker.' He leads her to the horse and helps her mount. As she settles the reins in her hands and adjusts her gloves, he is indicating her maids. 'We will take only one of these women,' he says, and points at Clelia. 'This one will stay behind.'

Lucrezia turns in her saddle to watch as Clelia drops a curtsey, then walks away, in the direction of Nunciata's rooms. Emilia looks after her, trying not to seem too delighted.

'Let us go,' Alfonso says to her, turning the reins of his horse. 'The servants can follow behind.'

They clatter over the narrow side bridge, across the moat, between the buildings, past the white-pink façade of the cathedral. It fills Lucrezia with a strange, febrile joy. The vastness of the sky above her, the sight of all the people, out in the early-morning air, the stalls lining the streets, the clothes and hands and noses and shoes of people she has never met and never will.

How the citizens of the town stop and stare, to see their duke, mounted high on a horse, to gaze upon their young duchess, swathed in furs. The two of them, together, riding through town, flanked by their guards.

They pass through the city gates, and out on to the open road. Alfonso urges his horse into a trot, and Lucrezia's mare follows. The countryside slides by, empty orchards, their bare branches blackened by rain, stony meanders of farm boundaries, sodden fields, blank-eyed houses. She is conscious of the jolting of the mare beneath her, the squeal of the saddle, the wind that tries to prise the hat from her head, to insert its fingers between her clothes and her skin, the sharp needles of rain on her face.

They are following the path of the river and Lucrezia thinks that the way looks familiar: she recognises a particular crossroads at the summit of a gentle incline, a rock formation that resembles a loaf. And then they take a turning, on one side of which is farmland in tiers, where a tethered goat turns its doleful eyes on them for a moment, then turns away, as if to pretend they aren't there, and on the other run the grey-brown waters of the Po river.

'Is this the same way we went before?' Lucrezia enquires.

They have slowed the horses at this point in the journey, for the terrain here is rockier; she heard one guardsman say to another that he didn't want to turn the animals' hoofs.

'Before?' Alfonso asks.

'On the way back from the *delizia*.'

'No,' he says, 'of course not.'

'Why of course not?'

'Well, we are not going to the *delizia*, so naturally—'

'We aren't?' She wants to pull her horse to a standstill but a guardsman holds her on a leading rein. 'Where are we going?'

'To Stellata,' he says, his expression one of puzzlement, as if she is being perversely forgetful, when in fact she is sure he never told her this.

'Where is Stellata?'

'Just beyond Bondeno. Very close by.'

'Is it a villa? Like the *delizia*?'

'It is a country lodge, a beautiful place, right by the river, and in the shape of a star. Hence the name. I spent much time there when I was a young child. My father took me riding and hunting. I thought it would be nice for you to see it. A change of scene, some healthy country air.'

'But . . .' Lucrezia tries to articulate her objection, coming up with '. . . how will Emilia know where to come? I told her we were going to the *delizia*, not—'

'Emilia?'

'My maid.'

'The one I instructed to remain behind?'

'No, the other one. I brought her from Florence. She was to come after us, so that—'

'Do not concern yourself. She will be escorted to the right place, and—' He breaks off and gestures with a gloved hand. 'Here it is now. Do you see? There is one of the star points.'

Lucrezia can see, through the complexity of bare branches, a dark, high slice of wall, like an arrowhead. It is strangely geometric, for such a rural place. More than anything, it bears a resemblance to Alfonso's *castello*, with the same repeating arched battlements, as if part of that structure has been broken off, transported and set down among the trees.

'It looks . . .' she casts about for the appropriate words – she doesn't want to criticise a place that has been dear to him since childhood '. . . imposing. Like a fortress or—'

'You are a very clever girl,' he says, with a smile, 'It was a fortress, a long time ago, to control navigation of the river.'

He urges his horse with a click of his tongue. They ride towards the *fortezza* and, one by one, pass over the bridge.

The underpainting and the overpainting

Fortezza, near Bondeno, 1561

L ucrezia makes her way through the *fortezza*, leaving behind her finished portrait in the empty hall. She can hear Alfonso and Leonello out in the courtyard, bidding Il Bastianino goodbye, wishing him a safe journey back to Ferrara. She climbs the stairs, one by one, and stumbles into her chamber. Emilia holds her by the wrist, admonishing her, saying she should never have gone downstairs, never; she should have stayed in bed.

Lucrezia ignores her and sits at the desk, slumping sideways, resting her head on her arm. In this position, she has a new view of the sketches she did last night. She is down at their level, regarding them from an angle. Had it really been she who drew this mule, this unicorn? What was it that had excited her so much about them? She cannot for the life of her remember. They seem devoid of existence now, just lines on a flat page.

She closes her eyes. Emilia is fussing around her, placing

blankets on her shoulders, telling her she should get into bed, she needs to rest.

Lucrezia opens her eyes and sees: the strokes of chalk, the hind hoof of the mule, the wooden surface of the table, with its knots and rings and alluvial grain, the fading light filling the narrow window, a hand with curled fingers lying limp beside a stylus, a ring with a tiny moonstone, a lace cuff.

'Come to bed,' Emilia is saying. 'I will help you.'

Lucrezia shakes her head, interested in the percussive noise her hairpins make against the table. She watches as the hand with the ring and the cuff moves towards the stylus. The fingers grip it. The stylus rises up and settles against the notch in the hand's muscle. Its point is guided towards a piece of paper, where it makes a horizonal mark that tapers off in a curve. Lower down, it makes a second mark, which meets the end of the first. Then it moves again, in confident downstrokes, again and again: legs, in motion, ending in strong feet, four of them, running, sprinting at full tilt. Lucrezia watches as her hand brings forth a vibrant face, a complex pattern on a flank. These markings might, to the untrained eye, appear as stripes or cage-like bars, but to Lucrezia they are camouflage. The animal in the picture is soon surrounded by vegetation lush and dense, by lianas and heavy blooms, and even its startling appearance is soon lost, melded with the jungle.

'Very nice,' Emilia says, looking over her shoulder. 'A leopard?'

Lucrezia, still slumped sideways, shakes her head.

'How well you draw. But I think you should—'

'It was to be the centre of the triptych,' Lucrezia mutters into the surface of the table.

'Hmm?' Emilia says, her fingers moving to untie Lucrezia's neckline, to remove the furs and shawls from her shoulders.

'I shall never finish it now,' Lucrezia says, and she watches as the hand slackens, as the stylus falls to the desk, as the paper rolls up into itself of its own volition, the tiger disappearing. 'It will never be done.'

But Emilia is not listening. She supports Lucrezia to a standing position and suddenly the headache worsens, tightening its hold, delving its fingers into the nerves of her eyes, the muscles that stretch from shoulder to neck. She feels the blood drain from her head, from her shoulders and lungs, pooling uselessly in her legs. She has to cling to the bedpost in order to remain upright.

Behind her, Emilia is removing her gown, the bodice, the sleeves, still chiding her; she has aired and warmed the bed, she says; she gets Lucrezia to lie down, and pulls the covers over her.

Lucrezia is cold, cold; she has never felt so cold in her life. Her legs and feet are insensible, her fingers ice. Her breath rattles and rasps in her chest, her teeth juddering against each other. At all her joints, the places in her body that articulate and bend, there is a deep, dragging ache; she may never move again.

Emilia piles blankets and cloaks on top of her but the chill will not leave Lucrezia. The maid closes the bed curtains, she builds up the fire. Eventually, she gets in beside her mistress in an attempt to warm her, rubbing her feet with her own, huffing hot breath into Lucrezia's curled hands.

'There now,' Emilia whispers to her, 'all will be well.'

Lucrezia turns over to face the wall, away from Emilia, her

jaw clamped tight. Desolation is flooding through her, to her every edge.

'No,' she gets out from between her clenched teeth, 'it will not. I shall die here and—'

'Do not say such things,' Emilia protests.

'—I shall never see Florence again.'

'Why would you think that? Come, you are feeling ill but soon you shall recover. It is just an ague, brought on by the journey and—'

'Poisoned,' Lucrezia mutters.

Emilia shushes her, strokes her forehead until Lucrezia feels the approach of a numbing unconsciousness.

'Sleep,' Emilia tells her. 'Rest.'

'Don't answer the door,' Lucrezia mumbles. 'Don't draw back the bolt. Whatever you do, don't let him in.'

When she wakes, it is much later. Darkness fills the room and the faces of the windows. Lucrezia sits up, her mouth parched, her head as clear as a goblet, ringing with a single, resonant note. She rubs a hand against her face. The pain of the headache has gone but it has left behind an expansive feeling in her skull, a peculiar kind of clarity, as if the agony of it has washed clean her mind.

Her thoughts are diamond-sharp, cut with precision, polished and perspicuous. They follow, one after the other, as if strung together on a thread.

She is hungry, her stomach flat and gnawingly empty.

She is at the *fortezza*.

Death will come for her, if not tonight, if not tomorrow, then one day very soon.

There is no one to save her.

Alfonso will send one of his men. Baldassare, most likely. It would need to be someone he trusts absolutely.

Or perhaps he will do the task himself.

She will die: he means to make this happen. It is unavoidable. It is her fate.

Lucrezia, as if driven by this notion, rises from the bed, where Emilia sleeps on her side, face obscured by the spread of her hair.

Lucrezia stands for a moment in the frost-cold room. What has woken her?

She turns her head slowly, towards the window, then the door, holding her breath, listening out for footsteps, voices, noises on the stair. Are they coming for her? Is the time now?

There is nothing. The star-shaped building stretches out and away from her, silent and undisturbed. She cannot hear a single sound, human or otherwise. She might be suspended in Heaven already.

Except that her stomach growls, gnawing on itself, begging for food. Her body must be empty. She is living entirely on air.

She waits a moment longer, just to be sure that no one is approaching the chamber door. Then she bends over and, with a decisive snatching movement, picks up Emilia's discarded dress. She pulls it over her head.

She must eat something, if she is to work out what to do. She must find food, and quickly, before anyone else wakes up. She must procure something herself, if she is to be completely sure it is safe to eat.

It seems to her that there is another Lucrezia in the room, one who cowers still in the bed, plaintively asking her what on earth she is doing, imploring her to stay here, where she is safe and warm. She tells this girl that she is putting on the maid's dress in order to find food, that she needs to keep up her strength. Perhaps it also seems that there is a third Lucrezia, the one who appears in the painting, and she is questioning her as to where she might be going, an imperious look on her face, one eyebrow raised. This Lucrezia, the Duchess Consort, is horrified by the putting-on of this coarse dress. She is advancing towards her, her *chioppa* rustling indignantly, lily-white hands outstretched, as if to stop her.

But she is too quick for her. The girl in the drab dress skips sideways, past the bed. She unbolts the door, and steps out.

The *fortezza* is suffused with black, dank air; tendrils of mouldering, spore-heavy draughts move through it, curling round her ankles, rubbing themselves against her. The building creaks and rustles with the frigid chill of night. She fastens the strings of Emilia's cap and, putting out a hand to find the wall, moves down the stairs.

The whole place seems empty, deserted, corridors filled only with darkness, but Lucrezia knows better. There are guards and servants and assistants and officials tucked away behind these doors, around corners, in every nook and cranny of the place.

This, she hears someone say brightly, inside her head, is the most dangerous thing you have ever done.

If she were found – what then? If Alfonso or one of his men were to discover her. If they were to stop and question a woman dressed as a maid, only to see that it is, in fact, their duchess.

She tiptoes down one flight of stairs, across a square landing, then another. The kitchen is somewhere behind the hall, she knows, down a slope and around a corner. Just as she is about to exit the second staircase, she hears something that makes the blood halt in her veins.

Footsteps, quick and purposeful, coming from the direction of the hall.

Lucrezia flattens herself against the wall. Don't come this way, don't, please don't. She sees, passing the mouth of the staircase, a lantern encasing a single short candle, then an arm, holding it up, then a shoulder, clad in leather, then a chest and face, in profile, and a head of tawny hair.

Baldassare.

Lucrezia clings to the wall with her palms, with her front, as if she would scale it, like a lizard, and disappear into a crack, if only she could. Baldassare is coming along the corridor, with stealth and speed, using only the balls of his feet. He carries a pouch or small bag of some kind in one hand and the lantern in the other.

Impossible to believe, and horrible to see, but Baldassare comes to a stop. His boots pause, and he waits, motionless, the lantern held out. Then he takes a step back, and another, until there he is, once more, at the foot of the stairs. He is right next to her, so close that she could reach out and touch him, close enough for him to hear her breathing.

She watches, from the shadows, cheek pressed to the *fortezza* wall, which perspires a frigid, slick moisture. Panic swarms over her, like insects. This is her end, right here, right now. She will die on this staircase; he will seize her and put his hands around her throat, and there is no one here to bear witness, to tell her story afterwards, to remember and relate her end. How narrow and slight her neck is. How easy the task will be for a man like Baldassare. He will crush the life out of her in seconds and fling aside her body, like a rag.

Will he turn into the stairs? If he decides to come this way, all will be lost. He will discover her there, within two steps of him; he will want to know what she is doing, where she is going; he will recognise her because he is the kind of person who sees through disguises. She has no doubt of this.

Baldassare seems to be listening. He turns his head one way, then the other. He looks behind him, down the corridor, he turns to look up the staircase.

Lucrezia keeps herself very still. She takes only the smallest sips of air. She doesn't move: not her eyes, not her fingers, not her face. She is sensible of a glacial thread of air running along the ground, and wonders if it will act against her, disturbing the fabric of her skirts, betraying her presence. Her heart, however, thuds away inside her ribcage, stridently, noisily, as if trying to attract her attention, as if trying to warn her of the proximity of the man who, in all likelihood, has been given the task of murdering her.

She finds herself, from the corner of her eye, examining his hands: their blunt nails, the pad of muscle behind the thumb, the articulated bones joining digit to palm, the ring on his smallest finger, engraved with Alfonso's eagle crest. They seem to her, at that moment, extraordinarily powerful, with a sickening, large span.

Baldassare uses one of these hands to raise the lantern above his head. He peers along the corridor. He turns to check behind him, once more.

Then, raking his fingers through his hair, he moves off, away from her, walking fast, as if in a hurry to get to where he is going.

She waits until the darkness has swallowed him, until the stone walls of the *fortezza* have stopped echoing with his footsteps, then slips down the final few stairs, and is out into the corridor, moving in the opposite direction to Baldassare.

She doesn't have long, she doesn't have long. If Baldassare is up and awake, intent on some action, there is a chance that others are, too. Perhaps some officials, perhaps servants. Even Alfonso himself.

To reach the kitchens, she must first pass the door to the hall. As she gets nearer, she thinks of the portrait, how it will be in there, propped up, ready to be hung. She wonders what will happen to it, how it will fare, after she is dead. Will Alfonso send it back to the *castello*? Will it be hung somewhere? Will he look at it sometimes? Will the eyes stare back at him, interrogatively, and will he be able to bear this?

Keeping close to the edges of the corridor, she goes past the hall door, around the corner, down a slope, and through a low doorway.

The kitchen is in stasis. Hams are suspended from the ceiling. Pots lie upturned on the table, next to a partially eaten loaf. An ashy cone of embers smoulders in the large grate. A basket of onions, encased in their dry and aetiolated jackets, lies abandoned on a stool. On the floor by the fire, two servants sleep on woven mats, wrapped in cloaks, hats pulled down over their faces.

She stands by the table, her hand on the humped back of the loaf. She should go back upstairs now. There is the door, behind her, leading back into the *fortezza*. Perhaps all may still be well. Perhaps she is mistaken as to Alfonso's intentions. She might conceive a child, she might bear an heir, she might continue as a duchess. She might.

It comes back to her, then, as a fully formed thought, what Jacopo had said to her as he stood beside her in the hall, his hand on her shoulder. He would stuff the lock of the servants' exit with rags and wait for her in the forest.

She winces at the recollection, giving her head a shake. So ludicrous. How could such a thing be possible? The idea that the perimeter of a *fortezza* like this could be so easily punctured, that Alfonso would permit any such breach to his security, verges on ridiculous. An artist's apprentice could never conceive of the lengths men like Alfonso go to in ensuring their safety. There are guardsmen with him all the time, she could have said, there are people whose very job it is to patrol and secure his buildings, every day and every night. They would never, ever miss a thing as simple as an unlocked door.

Lucrezia takes up the bread and stows it in her apron pocket. She skims several slices of cured ham from a plate and places them next to the bread.

Then she hesitates. Behind her waits the silent *fortezza*, her chamber, her sketches, her husband, his guards, the wandering Baldassare. In front of her is the kitchen, the sleeping servants, the low-burning fire, and a hatch-like exit recessed into the thick defensive wall. This must be the door that Jacopo talked about, the one that admitted him and Maurizio, and the route by which they left.

It is squarish, made of thick planks bolted together, and it draws the eye, like the vanishing point in a sketch.

There is no way, she tells herself, that Jacopo's plan would have worked, even if he had spoken in earnest, even if he had tried. The idea that rags could triumph over all that Alfonso has at his disposal, the thought that an apprentice could outwit the efforts of a duke, his men, his trained guards, a stone *fortezza* built to withstand attack, is nothing less than madness.

Despite all this, here she is, stepping past the slumbering servants, and grappling in the dim light with a thick iron bolt, then another, then a third, her fingers reading their length and breadth, then easing them back. Then she grasps the iron ring of the handle. Will it turn? Was Jacopo serious when he said he would disable the lock?

She tries to twist it. It will not yield, and she is not surprised, not at all, not disappointed or let down, not even a little, because she was not expecting it to. Still, she decides to try the other way, just in case, one final time, before she goes back upstairs, with her improvised meal, to face whatever will come, for she has no choice. She has never had any choice. So she gives the handle one final testing turn, and she feels – she can hardly believe it, she must be imagining it – a sliding, a shifting, deep within the mechanism. There is a quiet clunk, and then the handle yields.

She stands there. She takes a breath, then another. She inserts her fingers into the lock and extracts the rags she finds, one by one, holding up their crumpled, oily lengths in disbelief. How incredible, how unlikely, that such frail things could jam the mechanism of a heavy iron lock. She pulls the door towards her, experimentally, for it cannot be unlocked, it cannot. Alfonso would never permit such a lapse, such a risk. The idea of an entrance or exit to his domain being left unsecured like this is preposterous.

The door swings towards her, just a little, just enough to admit a breeze from the outside, active and sprightly, eddying in through the gap and swirling its way into the kitchen behind her.

Ducking down, Lucrezia steps through the door and stands on the stone ledge of the threshold. She is at the outer skin of the *fortezza*, several feet above ground, at the furthest point of one of its star arms. It is the side wall of the building, facing away from the river and the drawbridge and the main entrance. A secret hatch for servants, for tradespeople, for the apprentices of a court artist.

She grips the edges of the door frame, the loaf of bread making her apron sway. The night is cool and frosty, with a gusting wind that stampedes through the trees, tipping them towards each other, then apart. Above her, blue-fringed clouds are pushed along, like boats on a black sea, revealing and concealing needlepoints of starlight, unreadable maps in the sky.

At her back is death, her death. She is certain of this, as she is certain of the colour of her eyes and that her hair grows in a peak slightly off-centre to her face. To her fore is the unknowable. Death again, she is sure, but a different one. If she goes, if she leaps off this ledge, to the ground and runs towards the trees, Alfonso will come after her. He will dispatch soldiers and guardsmen and she will be hunted down, like an animal.

Her choice, as she sees it, standing there clinging to the

outer wall of the *fortezza*, is death by poisoning, by stealth, death in her chamber, perhaps with a fever, with spasms of pain, unbearable and unsupportable, vomiting into a basin. Or a death out here, somewhere in the woods or out on the road, in the open countryside, with Alfonso bearing down on her on horseback, perhaps wielding his sword. She will turn and face him, she will look him in the eye, daring him to do it, defying his mastery of her. This is what she will do, if it comes to it. She will.

What Lucrezia does not know, as she stands on the ledge, is that Alfonso will never come after her. He is, at that very moment, with Baldassare, climbing the spiral staircase to her chamber, extinguishing their lantern when they reach the top. He is pushing open the door and crossing the room, which is so dark he has to pause for a moment until his eyes adjust. Baldassare, next to him, indicates the form in the bed, barely visible in the gloom. There is her hair, fanned out, her hand uncurled in sleep, the covers pulled up high. Alfonso kneels. He kisses the ends of the hair, he crosses himself, he pulls back the blankets, he takes a pillow and together, he and Baldassare suffocate the young Duchess.

It will not be an easy passing. She will scream and struggle. She will fight. She will flail at them with fist and nails and feet. She will claw at the pillow; she will thrash and buckle beneath their hands. She will, at one point, get her mouth out from under the pillow and they will, through the thick darkness, hear her yell, hoarsely; she will nearly struggle away from them. Baldassare will curse and swear; he will throw his body across hers, to subdue her, to get her to lie still. Who would have thought the little Duchess had such strength and fight in her?

She is, however, no match for the two of them. They are men in the prime of their life, their bodies trained and lethal. They are used to working together; they trust and know each other so well that they can each anticipate the other's next move. The Duchess cannot win but still she fights. Alfonso has always said that she had within her an untameable element to her spirit. It takes them longer than they had anticipated, but of course they triumph in the end.

When she is finally still, after Baldassare has crushed her face and torso beneath his weight for many minutes, until he is certain the breath has left her, they stand up, they brush themselves off, they straighten their clothes in the dark. Baldassare mops his face with a handkerchief by the fireplace; Alfonso smooths back his disarrayed hair, adjusts his sleeves. Then they leave, closing the door behind them. It is only outside the chamber that Baldassare relights the lantern. They do not look at each other as they descend the stairs. Neither of them speaks.

A kitchen servant discovers the Duchess, dead in her bed, the next morning, and raises the alarm. Great consternation fills the *fortezza*. None of the country servants, bar the two who served at dinner, have ever seen the Duchess, but still, they weep and lament over her young body, which is so battered and abused by the seizure that killed her, her face quite ravaged. They put the bed to rights, they tidy her hair and shift, before sending word to the Duke.

The Duke shuts himself up inside his room, immobilised by grief, the poor man, the servants whisper to each other;

the only person allowed in or out is his *consigliere* and cousin, Baldassare. Letters are sent, to Ferrara, to the Pope, and to Florence. The Duke Alfonso himself writes, broken-hearted, to her parents, with the terrible news of their daughter's death. A short illness, an ague, a seizure, a fever of the brain, the damp air. He is devastated and commends her soul to Heaven.

A coffin is brought by carriage to the *fortezza*. Nobody wishes to lay out the body, for it has been so brutalised by illness – unrecognisable, the servants say to each other. No one would ever know it was the same woman as in the portrait still propped up in the dining hall. Someone suggests that the task should be given to one of the Duchess's ladies-in-waiting but unfortunately, Baldassare tells them, they remained behind in Ferrara. In the end, three women come from the village and lay out the Duchess in the dining hall, under the gaze of the portrait, which, the women say to each other, is too tragic to look upon.

The Duchess's body is then conveyed to Ferrara, accompanied by the Duke and his men, who ride behind it, heads lowered.

Meanwhile, an emissary is dispatched from Florence, accompanied by the court physician. They have been sent by the Grand Duke, and commanded to make haste. Cosimo tells the physician to find out exactly why and how his daughter died, so suddenly, so unexpectedly: Cosimo wants information, he wants to know who is to blame for the death of a healthy young woman. The physician carries a letter, addressed to Alfonso II, Duke of Ferrara, stamped with the crest of the Grand Duke of Tuscany, requesting that they be permitted to examine the corpse. They ride the route Lucrezia herself took, not quite a year ago, over the Apennine mountains, and along the valley floor.

The Duke Alfonso does not receive them himself but sends his trusted adviser, Leonello Baldassare, to the courtyard to greet them, when they reach Ferrara. Baldassare communicates the Duke's regret that grief at his wife's passing compels him to remain in his apartment.

The Florentine physician and emissary are shown to the *castello* state room, where a coffin stands on a table. Even from the doorway, the scent is overwhelming – the sweetish, cloying odour of decay. It has, the servant stationed at the door says, apologetically, been five days since the Duchess's passing. What the men see within the coffin is discoloured, bloated, blackened and bruised. It looks barely human: decaying matter swathed in a rose silk dress with a dark damask pattern. The physician takes in the Duchess's rosary, which has been twisted into the hands, the purplish tint to the fingernails, the plait of pale hair which coils into the neck – strange how the hair can fade in death; there is little sign of the red in the Duchess's tresses but he has seen this phenomenon before. Behind him, the emissary retches meekly into a handkerchief.

They will depart, with no small shudder, from the gates of the Ferrara *castello*. They will ride back, and report what they found to the Grand Duke, omitting the parts about the putrefaction, the smell and the retching. The Duchess looked peaceful, they will say instead, and at rest. She was laid out beautifully and fittingly: a duchess to the last.

A Mass will be said in Florence, in Santa Maria Novella, where Lucrezia was married. Her mother will weep throughout; her father will grip his wife's hand, his face white, his teeth set.

The coffin of Lucrezia, Duchess of Ferrara, is taken with great ceremony, from the *castello*, through the streets, to a monastery in the south of the city. Citizens line the streets; they throw flowers; they cry; they look with pity on the set face of their Duke, so stoic, so brave. The Duchess is interred in the family tomb, beneath a slab of marble, which is engraved with a crest that is half her father's and half her husband's and the words: Wife of Alfonso II, Duke of Ferrara.

The marriage portrait is hung in the Duke's private chamber, covered at all times in heavy velvet drapes. No one is permitted to pull back the curtain, and look upon the Duchess's face without the Duke's express permission. He keeps her there, hidden from view. Alfonso retreats from court, and from the world, for several months, as is perhaps only to be expected after such a loss. He is not seen either in the *castello* or in the city. Some say that he has taken himself off to one of his country villas; others report with certainty that the Duke has shut himself inside his rooms in the *castello*, where he sits, brooding over the portrait of his deceased wife.

Then a citizen sees his familiar silhouette up on the walkway surrounding the tower – tall, hawkish, hands behind back – looking out over the province. The rear of the *castello* chapel is once again occupied during the daily rehearsals of the *evirati*. By late spring, in the early mornings, it is possible to hear the clatter of hoofs as the Duke and his men go out riding.

As the summer approaches its end, it is said on the streets of Ferrara that the Duke has entered into negotiations with an Austrian family, for the hand of their daughter.

* * *

Lucrezia, Duchess of Ferrara, pulls shut the small, hidden door of the *fortezza* behind her. She takes a leap from the ledge, brown gown billowing out around her. She lands on the frost-hard grass below, and almost before her feet make contact, she is running.

The ground is unstable, pitted with holes, tussocks and marshy patches, but she keeps going, stumbling, her muscles weak and aching from her illness, almost falling but pulling herself up.

Jacopo is waiting in the trees – she hopes. He will be there – he must be there. He promised he would be, just as he promised to fix the lock on the door.

They will make their way north-east, Jacopo and Lucrezia, via back roads, to a city of uncertainty, where land and sea meet and mingle with each other, where the streets are water, where houses seem to float on bolts of turquoise silks, where she will learn to propel a boat, standing up in the stern, her skirts hitched up around her knees, the wet pole gripped in both hands, dwelling after dwelling sliding by, the windows framing endless portraits of people lighting candles, turning towards each other, lifting infants to their shoulders, putting down pots, shaking clothes in the air, living, eating, loving, talking.

Later – much later – there will be a craze in the city for the work of one particular artist. The paintings are small enough to be held in the palm of a hand, and some collectors decide not to hang them on the wall but to keep them on a table, so that they may be handled and passed around, as a novelty or conversation piece. They are almost all of animals: minks and cats and monkeys, imperious peacocks, spotted cheetahs, mules, lambs, oxen and doves. The paint, while applied thinly, has an intriguing layered quality, standing up from the *tavola* on which it has been applied, by the artist's meticulous and loving hand. The people who collect them – the rich, the dissolute, the aristocrats, the rulers, the noblemen and -women, the courtiers, the bankers, the princes, the courtesans – whisper among themselves that beneath the uppermost painting are said to be other, hidden, secret underpaintings, sometimes many of them, sometimes none at all. Only the bravest, or perhaps the most rash, are ever tempted to take a cloth soaked in a solution of vinegar and alcohol, and rub away at the work, to dissolve the colours, to erase and wash away the iridescent wings and ochre beaks, the resplendent sprays of feathers or the gleaming umber of hides, the sentient and watchful gloss of bestial eyes. Those who have done so, it is said, have discovered quite a different scene underneath: classical compositions of warring deities or landscapes never seen by a human eye, or triptychs of portraits, gazing back at the viewer. Always, in these miniature underpaintings, there is the face of one particular woman, in a crowd, perhaps, or as a dryad in the background. There she will be, often looking out sideways, addressing the viewer with an enigmatic, unfathomable gaze, always with the air of someone who cannot quite believe her good fortune, to be a nymph, swimming in a warm sea, or a peasant with a basket of peaches. But others who worked away at dissolving these paintings have found nothing at all, just a plain piece of *tavola*, carefully sanded to a silken grain.

* * *

Look. Here is Lucrezia, a small figure in the corner of a land-scape with a river, a forest, an imposing stone building. She is moving across open ground, through the dark winter night, running, running, with all her strength, towards the merciful canopy of trees.

Author's note

Alfonso II d'Este, Duke of Ferrara, is widely considered to have been the inspiration for Robert Browning's poem 'My Last Duchess'; Lucrezia di Cosimo de' Medici d'Este, Duchess of Ferrara, is the inspiration for this novel.

I have tried to use what little is known about her short life but I have made a few alterations, in the name of fiction.

Lucrezia was born in the Palazzo Vecchio in Florence. In 1550, when she was five years old, the family of Cosimo I de' Medici moved across the river to the Palazzo Pitti. I kept them in the first location, for the sake of narrative cohesion.

The real Lucrezia was married to Alfonso II, at the age of thirteen, in May 1558 (the dowry paid by her father was an astonishing two hundred thousand gold *scudi*, which is around £50 million in today's currency). She remained in Florence with her family for the following two years, while Alfonso went to France to lead military campaigns for Henri II. On his father's death in 1559, Alfonso became duke, and he returned to Ferrara, arriving in Florence in the summer of 1560 to fetch Lucrezia and accompany her to his court. I have conflated both the marriage and the departure, so that Lucrezia in this novel is married and leaves for Ferrara in one single event at the age of fifteen.

Cosimo I de' Medici became ruler of the Duchy of Tuscany in 1537, at the age of seventeen; he was elevated to Grand Duke of Tuscany in 1569. I refer to him by his latter title for the duration of this novel for the purpose of differentiating him from Alfonso. There was indeed a collection of exotic animals in the basement of the Palazzo Vecchio; the street behind it is still named via dei Leoni. It's been suggested by several biographers that the animals' odour was one of the reasons Eleanora insisted on moving to the Palazzo Pitti. The story of the tigress and the lions was inspired by an incident at the royal menagerie in the Tower of London, when a keeper mistakenly opened the interconnecting door between cages.

The two sisters of Alfonso II who remained at the Ferrarese court after their mother's departure were named not Elisabetta and Nunciata, as here, but Lucrezia and Eleonora. I took the liberty of renaming them here to avoid confusion with other characters in the book.

The grim conclusion to the love affair between Ercole Contrari, head of the guards, and Elisabetta/Lucrezia d'Este took place in 1575, not 1561.

The only portrait of Lucrezia on display in Europe, at the time of writing, can be seen at the Palatine Gallery, two streets away from Casa Guidi, Robert Browning's Florence residence. It is a small oil painting, about the size of a hardback book, commissioned by her parents shortly before Lucrezia left for

Ferrara, and attributed to the studio of Agnolo Bronzino. In it, she is depicted against a dark background, wearing both Medici and Este jewellery; her face bears a slightly uncertain, apprehensive expression. The Uffizi Gallery has other iterations of the same portrait in its archives; a larger (and, to my eye at least, less flattering) version of it, by Alessandro Allori, is in the North Carolina Museum of Art.

The Ferrarese marriage portrait of Lucrezia, which forms the basis of Browning's poem, is, to the best of my knowledge, entirely fictional. If one ever does come to light, I would be very keen to know about it.

A final note about uxoricide among Lucrezia's family: her sole surviving sister, Isabella de' Medici Orsini, met a very sudden and highly suspicious death at the age of thirty-four, in 1575, while on a hunting holiday with her husband at a country villa in Cerruto. According to the official account, written by her brother Francesco, who was by then Grand Duke of Tuscany, it occurred 'while she was washing her hair in the morning . . . She was found by [her husband] on her knees, having immediately fallen dead.' There are, unsurprisingly, differing opinions on the cause of her death. The scene at the close of this novel, with Alfonso and Leonello enacting their violent ritual in the *fortezza* chamber, and the resulting unrecognisable corpse, is taken from another account of Isabella's demise – that of Ercole Cortile, who was operating as a spy in the Florentine court for none other than Alfonso II, Duke of Ferrara. After conducting his own enquiries from eye-witnesses to the deed, he wrote to the Duke: 'Lady Isabella was strangled at midday. The poor woman was in bed when she was called by Signor Paolo . . . Hidden under the bed was the Roman Cavalier Massimo, who helped him to kill the lady.'

Only a few days before Isabella's death, her cousin Dianora – now married to the youngest Medici brother, Pietro – also died a mysterious death at a country villa in Cafaggiolo. Pietro wrote to his brother Francesco with sinister composure: 'Last night, at seven o'clock, an accident and death came to my wife, so Your Highness can take peace, and write to me about what I should do, if I should come back or not.' The reason given was that she suffocated accidentally while in bed. Ercole Cortile, once again writing to Alfonso II, was more forthcoming: 'she was strangled by a dog leash by Don Pietro . . . and finally died after a great deal of struggle. Don Pietro bears the sign, having two fingers on his hand injured from the bite of the lady.'

The deaths of Isabella and Dianora appear to have had the tacit approval of their families. Neither Paolo Orsini, Isabella's husband, nor Pietro de' Medici, Dianora's husband, was ever held to account for the sudden and unexplained deaths of their wives.

Alfonso II, Duke of Ferrara, went on to have two further wives.

Neither union produced any children.

Acknowledgements

Thank you, Mary-Anne Harrington, Victoria Hobbs, Jordan Pavlin, Georgina Moore, Amanda Betts, Christy Fletcher, Reagan Arthur, Josie Kals, Amy Perkins, Yeti Lambregts, Emma Ewbank, Fergus Edmondson, Cally Conway, Hazel Orme, Louise Rothwell, Tina Paul, Jessie Goetzinger-Hall, Rebecca Bader, Elaine Egan, Chris Keith-Wright, Jennifer Doyle, Mari Evans, Alexandra McNicoll, Prema Raj, Tabatha Leggett, and Jessica Lee.

Thank you, Beatrice Monti della Corte and the Santa Maddalena Foundation. Thank you, Emma Paoli, Anna Castelli and Caterina Toschi, for helping me track down Lucrezia's portrait in Florence. Thank you to the staff at the Palazzo Vecchio, the Castello Estense, and the Museo Civico di Belriguardo, and to the custodians of the Corpus Domini Monastery, Ferrara, who kindly allowed me in to visit Lucrezia's tomb, despite Covid restrictions.

Thank you to Dr Jill Burke, of Edinburgh University, for her time, generosity and expertise, and also to Carlotta Moro, of St Andrews University, for her enthusiasm and advice. Thank you, Penny Reid, for discussions about art and portraiture. Needless to say, any mistakes about Renaissance life and art are undoubtedly mine.

I am grateful to the authors of the following books: *How To Do It: Guides to Good Living for Renaissance Italians*, by Rudolph M. Bell (University of Chicago Press, 1999); *How to*

437

be a Renaissance Woman, by Jill Burke (Profile Books, 2023); *Art of the Italian Renaissance Courts,* by Alison Cole (Everyman Art Library, 1995); *The Rise and Fall of the House of Medici,* by Christopher Hibbert (Penguin, 1974); *Medici Women: Portraits of Power, Love, and Betrayal,* by Gabrielle Langdon (University of Toronto Press, 2006); *Gli Ornamenti delle Donne* by Dr Giovanni Marinello (published in Venice in 1562, translated by Jill Burke); *Isabella de' Medici,* by Caroline P. Murphy (Faber & Faber, 2008); *Art in Renaissance Italy,* by John T. Paoletti and Gary M. Radke (Laurence King, 2011); *The Medici: Godfathers of the Renaissance,* by Paul Strathern (Vintage, 2007); *Women in Italian Renaissance Art,* by Paola Tinagli (Manchester University Press, 1997). Any errors or inventions will be mine.

Very special thanks are due to JA, IZ and SS.

And, last but certainly not least, thank you, Will Sutcliffe, for everything.

If you enjoyed *The Marriage Portrait*, read on to learn more about Maggie O'Farrell's inspiration for the novel, in an exclusive essay.

The Stone Lion

The writing of this book very nearly got me arrested.

Last autumn I was in Florence airport, at the end of a research trip, about to catch a flight home. The place was quiet, with barely any queues – most people were still wary of travelling. Everyone around me was masked and subdued. We followed instructions, we shuffled along, we stood the requisite two metres apart as we inched our way through the labyrinth of scanners and searches and checks, the Italian security guards gesturing at bottles of sanitiser at every stage.

I was through the metal detector and waiting, shoeless, to be reunited with my carry-on luggage, checking my watch and wondering why it was taking so long, when two men appeared behind me.

They were in immaculate suits, with lanyards swinging from their necks, their faces expressionless yet alert.

'Is that your bag?' one of them asked me.

I turned and saw my rucksack – grey and innocuous – on a table. All its contents were disgorged and spread out, and an armed guard holding a machine gun stood between it and me.

'Come this way,' the men said, and I had to step out of the queue, still barefoot, away from security and all the other passengers.

In a windowless office lined with mirrors that I assumed were two-way, my boarding pass and passport were taken off me. The problem, it quickly became apparent, was the lion figurine they had found on the scanner. I'd bought it in a flea market at the very beginning of my trip, and had wrapped it in a jumper, stowing it at the bottom of my hand-luggage, thinking that this was the safest way to transport it.

About the size of a small loaf, carved from stone and covered in greyish-green lichen, it depicted the beast at rest, its muzzle resting on its paws, tail curled about its flank. There had been something about the profundity of its repose, the animal's power and strength thrown into relief by slumber, that had appealed to me. I'd haggled enjoyably with the stallholder; we'd settled on the princely sum of twenty euros; I'd paid, he'd wrapped it up, and off I went, pleased. It would, I'd thought, as I walked away, my bag heavy with its weight, sit on the windowsill of my kitchen and would always remind me of this trip I took, alone, to Italy at the end of a pandemic.

We were now, my lion and I, a long way from my kitchen. The lion lay on the table between me and the customs men, deep in a nest of the newspaper in which the stallholder had wrapped it, looking wholly incongruous in this room where, in the corner, a woman was photocopying my documents and telephoning a specialist in the smuggling of ancient artefacts.

The customs men asked me the same questions, over and

over again: where had I got the stone lion? How much had I paid for it? What was the name of the stallholder? Did I have a receipt? Was I travelling alone? What was the purpose of my visit to Italy? Were there other items similar to the lion in my hold baggage?

I kept telling them the same answers: a flea market, no, I didn't know his name, it cost twenty euros, no receipt, I was in Italy for work, to research a book. Twenty euros, they kept repeating, in disbelief, twenty?

The tone in the room changed when the woman running my details through a computer discovered that I had made numerous visits to the Palazzo Vecchio. My Covid "Green Pass" records revealed that I had gone to the museum no fewer than three times in twenty-four hours. Why, they wanted to know, why so many visits?

I took a ragged breath. Did they know, as I did, that an insignia of the Palazzo Vecchio, one of Florence's finest buildings, erstwhile seat of the Medici, filled with priceless artefacts, is a lion? The beasts are everywhere you look – on the walls, adorning the furniture, displayed on ceilings and columns. The Grand Duke kept real lions in the menagerie of the palazzo basement, to be brought out to impress visitors. Did these customs officers suspect I'd stolen it on one of my visits? I began to wonder, at this point, if I would make it home that day, if I would see my children any time soon, if the little stone lion was what it seemed – a charming, mildewed tchotchke – or might I have unwittingly paid twenty euros for a stolen antique?

'*Sono una scrittice*,' I told them, nervously. I am a writer. '*Sto scrivendo . . .*' my extremely limited Italian began to fail me, 'I'm writing a novel . . . *un romanzo ambientato* . . . it's set . . . in the Palazzo Vecchio. It's about Lucrezia de' Medici.'

I pulled some notebooks out of my bag. I wanted to be cooperative; I wanted to help them understand; most of all, I wanted to be permitted to get on my plane which, I could see from the monitor, was now boarding. Look, I said to them, displaying the relevant pages in my notebooks. A novel, I said, *un romanzo*. About Lucrezia de' Medici, who lived in the Palazzo Vecchio. See?

They took the notebook from me. They flicked through the pages. They perused the maps I had drawn of each floor of the museum, of the way one room gave on to another, of the location of various artefacts and furniture and treasures, of the staircases and doors and exits. Too late I realised my mistake: never had anything looked more like the schemes of a thief.

With steely authority, deaf to my protestations about writing and research, they collected up my passport, boarding card, the Green Pass that had betrayed my movements, my notebooks and annotated maps of the palazzo, and left the room, saying something to the armed guard who was stationed at the door.

The lion was still on the desk in front of me. I looked at his curled mane and his crossed paws, and wondered what would happen next, how my husband might react if I phoned him to say: I'm still in Italy and I've been arrested for international art theft.

It's often hard to pinpoint the moment a novel begins; ideas tend to approach, insubstantial and silent, under cover of night; they hang about the house in awkward groups, like shy guests, not speaking or making eye contact with each other, until you – their host, in every sense of the word – take them by the hand and say, let's see what can be done.

I know, however, precisely and exactly when my novel about Lucrezia de' Medici, *The Marriage Portrait*, began. I can identify where I was and what I was doing when I first decided to write it; I can even, oddly, narrow it down to the date and time of day.

It was an afternoon in February 2020 and I had arrived uncharacteristically early to pick up my daughter from her friend's house. To pass the time until my child emerged, I must have rummaged in my bag and found, by luck and chance, not only my diary but also a pen, and written a very long entry in my diary.

I have the relevant notebook open on the desk beside me as I type this, and it's a strange snapshot of a person contemplating a world she has no idea is about to change in ways unfathomable and unimaginable. It begins in faint, scratchy green ballpoint, which I must have abandoned two paragraphs later, in favour of a more reliable black rollerball. There is an account of a recent trip to London, concern about my sister's aged dog, the purchase of a vintage leopard-print coat, my son's recovery from shingles, the whereabouts of some ribbon bunting, some general anxiety about the imminent publication of my novel, *Hamnet*. I describe my troubles over what my next book should be about; I am trying, it seems, to decide between two ideas. Near the end, there are a few lines about 'this virus which is spreading and spreading'. I don't seem unduly concerned but say that there is 'a sense of a dark cloud rolling towards us', and that perhaps I ought to buy some paracetamol. I then go on to make a list of fiction sequels that I liked, and those that I didn't; a few largely illegible words about Hong Kong, and something else about a walk along a river.

Then there is a gap, an empty quarter of a page or so.

I like this gap very much; it makes me happy. I am running my fingertip over it, as I sit here, recalling what it represents, what was happening, what caused me to lift my pen from the page.

This was the moment the idea for this book arrived, blown in like the blast of a gale, to envelop me there, sitting in my car, waiting for my daughter to come out from what would prove to be her last playdate for a long time.

'The life of Browning's Last Duchess', I have written, in a hand rendered shaky by excitement or perhaps uncertainty, followed by an unsightly row of question marks.

I had, at the time, been rereading Robert Browning's dramatic monologues – there is an entry in the diary about it a few pages earlier. I wish I could say that it was something insightful about the poetry itself but, unfortunately, it's only an account of my youngest child's persistence in running off with the book. (It is a particularly lovely edition, bound in green leather with gold embossing, that I bought for almost nothing in a junk shop when I was an undergraduate – my youngest was very much Hogwarts-struck at the time and she kept swiping it from my bedside table to stand in for a spellbook. I soon learnt that if I couldn't find my Browning, I should look for it under her bed, beside a heap of improvised wands.)

In the car, my diary resting on the steering wheel as I wrote, unaware that the world was about to be engulfed in chaos, I was thinking about Browning's poem, 'My Last Duchess', and its brilliance in capturing the sinister narcissism of the Duke. In the space of a few lines, Browning conveys a man so assured of his position and authority that he thinks nothing of telling the family of his new betrothed that he had his previous wife murdered for the grave sin of smiling too much. I recall wondering, for the first time, if the poem was based on real events. Had these people, this Duke and this hapless wife with her white mule and her dangerous fondness for blossom-decked branches ever lived, or did Browning conjure them up out of his imagination?

I must have searched online on my phone because I have the strong memory of, within a few clicks, finding a name: Lucrezia di Cosimo de' Medici. And then an image with a dark background began to load, agonisingly slowly, on to the screen of my aged phone. First there was a glimpse of a black dress, with silver-white lines of embroidery, some pale fingers of a hand resting on a small globe, a table, a jewelled hairband, a stiff lace collar, and then, suddenly, there she was, in her entirety, gazing out at me.

I don't think I will never forget the moment I first saw her face, when I looked into those dark eyes. Here she was: the wife from the poem, the one kept behind a curtain which only the Duke himself was allowed to draw back, so he and he alone could control her smiles. The person in the background of one of literature's most mesmerising poems. But here, thrillingly, was the real, actual woman – or girl, more accurately, as she couldn't have been more than fourteen or fifteen when she sat for the artist – in an image painted just before she departed her home in one of Florence's finest palazzos to begin her married life with her husband, Alfonso, Duke of

Ferrara. She had an oval face with severely pinned-back auburn hair, a hand over her heart, clasping or perhaps plucking at a jewel, and a gold cintura belt circling her narrow frame.

What struck me most was that, despite the impassive, photo-realistic style of Bronzino, to whom the portrait is attributed, there is a deep sense of unease about it. The fathomless black of the background, the frank and beseeching gaze, the tremulous set of her lips. Lucrezia di Cosimo de' Medici does not seem happy; she gazes at us from across time with a charged, heartbreakingly apprehensive expression. She looks as if she has a great deal to communicate, a story she is burning to tell. She is, I thought as I sat in the car, like someone appealing for help, or mutely communicating that all is not well in her world.

As well she might: a year or so later, she was dead.

The official cause of death at the time was given as 'putrid fever' – a catch-all diagnosis that could imply any number of diseases or conditions. Rumour spread that she had in fact been poisoned by her husband, Alfonso, Duke of Ferrara.

Either way, I knew as soon as I saw her that this idea was one with potential and momentum. And my diary attests to this: after the uncertainty of the question marks, everything speeds up. There follows, in frantic, disjointed phrases, connected by dashes and arrows as if I'm trying to write as fast as my racing thoughts, a series of facts. 'Lucrezia di Cosimo de' Medici,' I have scrawled, with an arrow to 'the 5th of eleven children' and then 'sister of Isabella, who was also murdered by her husband', and: 'doesn't move to Ferrara for two years because Alfonso is in France.'

I had, whether I knew it or not at that moment, found my

next novel, the one that would sustain, distract and fortify me throughout the following two peculiar years.

The Marriage Portrait isn't my first encounter with Robert Browning's work. When I was a student in the early 1990s, I attempted to adapt some of his dramatic monologues, including 'My Last Duchess', into a play. This is something I had completely forgotten about until I was searching through a box of old letters in my attic (did anyone else find time hanging heavily during lockdown?). I found a reference to the playscript in a letter from a friend. She was asking about my struggles to find a way to link the different Browning characters. The Duke and his murdered Duchess with Fra Lippo Lippi and Porphyria's psychotic murderer, and Andrea del Sarto with the Bishop giving strict and hopeless orders to his inattentive 'nephews'.

The letter is dated 1992. I was twenty, then, in my second year of university, and going out with an aspiring actor, a somewhat Heathcliffian type with a craggy brow and a six-foot frame. He would be perfect as the duke, I had decided, as I feverishly transposed Browning's lines into something resembling a script, adding possibly more stage directions than ever seen by any cast anywhere (a clue, I now see, to my nascent predilection for prose). I would weave together these disparate monologues. The Duke would open the play, of course, and he would be joined onstage by the hapless representative of the new fiancée. And some sculptures. And his dead wife, who would stand immobile in a frame, a Ferrarese Hermione. And maybe the rest of the characters, who would be waiting for their turn to deliver their soliloquies. I could visualise the whole thing: Renaissance Italy made flesh in an underfunded, ill-attended student theatre.

Unfortunately, or perhaps fortunately, it was never to be. The script was never finished; an essay or exam took precedence; my green-and-gold Browning was replaced on my shelf; the actor boyfriend and I split up, several times, got back together, and eventually separated for good. When the relationship dissolved, so did the theatrical production, and the world was spared my haphazard and optimistic attempt to put the monologues on stage.

Love for the poems themselves, however, has never left me. I read and re-read them at regular intervals: they are masterclasses in narrative and characterisation, in the unreliable narrator, in adherence to strict technique (those iambic pentameters, the rhyme schemes, that enjambment!), in the potency of economy in writing. Again and again, Browning displays the quiet power of the white spaces of the page, all that is left unsaid.

I sometimes wonder if Browning had an intimation, when he finished 'My Last Duchess', that he had written a work that attained perfection. Did he realise its skill and impact? Could he recognise, in its lines, that it would endure for centuries to come? It would have been unthinkable to him, then, that here was a poem that would be studied and analysed and loved and discussed by literature students the world over. He first published it in 1842, with the title 'Italy'; in a later edition, in 1845, he amended it to the title we know today, with the telling subtitle 'Ferrara'. This, of course, identifies it as inspired by the real-life Duke of Ferrara, Alfonso II, and, by extension, his first wife, Lucrezia de' Medici, who died aged sixteen. The

hree-year gap and change of heart intrigues me. What
1appened in that time to make him want to root the poem in
1istory, to identify the protagonist and his silenced wife? Had
1e even a shade of awareness of its brilliance?

When I went to Italy, on Lucrezia's trail, at the end of 2021,
I'd been working on the novel for almost two years. As soon
.he idea for it came to me, in the car waiting for my daughter,
I abandoned the other novels I'd been planning to write and
;witched my attention to sixteenth-century Florence and
Ferrara.

In the usual course of events research comes first and the
writing second. If the world had been running normally I
would have gone to Italy quite soon after I had the idea, to
walk about the locations, draw my maps, take my notes. But
:he universe, as we all know, had other plans. Two or three
weeks after I sat in the car waiting for my daughter, everything
changed: the dark cloud descended and lockdown began.

Most of this novel was written in an atmosphere only too
familiar to everyone: between bouts of homeschooling, daily
constitutionals around the local cemetery, Zoom calls, discus-
;ions about pandemics and why this had happened and when
t might be over, the cooking of food, to comfort and feed my
anxious and bewildered children. It came to life in whatever
:iny breathing spaces I could create; I was lucky, I knew, that
I could make an escape, mentally, to Renaissance Italy, as often
as possible. I worked whenever I could and wherever I could.
One memorable day, when the house felt overstuffed and
noisy, and people kept bursting into my study to ask where
was their pencilcase and could they have a jam jar, now, right

now, and what was for lunch, I was driven to take refuge in the playhouse in the garden. I crouch-crawled inside, balanced my laptop on my knee, pulled the door shut, and there I sat blissfully undiscovered for at least two hours, able to concentrate, to lose myself, for the first time in what felt like weeks. Only the cats were able to locate me: they gathered uneasily at the window, perplexed by this unprecedented behaviour, miaowing for admittance.

As soon as travel bans were lifted I booked a flight to Italy, an act which incidentally required more admin than the purchase of my house (the forms, the test certificates, the passes, the documents). I was worried, of course, and not only that I might catch Covid. I was already on a third draft: what if I'd got everything about the locations in the novel completely wrong? I had lived near Florence for a while and so had a general sense of the city, but had never set foot in Ferrara. How would I cope if everything I'd written about the Palazzo Vecchio or the Castello Estense was inexact nonsense?

What I was unprepared for was the emotional impact of visiting the place Lucrezia had lived. The pandemic had made it necessary for me to create the novel in a counterintuitive direction – backwards, with the writing occurring before the research – but what I hadn't bargained for was the effect of walking along a corridor where a person you have been thinking and dreaming about for two years had lived. By the time I was finally able to move through the rooms of the palazzo where Lucrezia was born and spent her infancy, I'd been living alongside her for so long that she felt like a blood relative, like one of my own children. To map out the castello where she lived the final year of her life, to visit her tomb in the monastery in the south of Ferrara, to lay flowers on her grave, felt devastating. When the custodian of the monastery told me that in all the time he had worked there, not a single person had ever before asked to see the grave of Lucrezia de' Medici d'Este, I'm not ashamed to say that I cried. Because she had been only sixteen. Because she had died a long way from her home and family, surrounded by people she barely knew. Because she seemed largely forgotten by history, with barely any mention of her in the Ferrara museum, and only one tiny portrait of her on display in Florence, low down on a wall in a distant room of the Palatine Gallery, next to a fire extinguisher.

Goodness knows what the custodian of the monastery thought. A strange woman with wild hair and a zealous gleam in her eye, clutching some lilies, pleading in halting Italian to be allowed in to see the grave of a long-dead teenaged duchess. And then, when Covid restrictions have been negotiated and debated, she stands there, looking down at the gravestone, weeping, wiping her eyes with her mask.

The trip to Italy taught me many things but I'd never before fully appreciated the crucial and immutable connection that is built, day by day, line by line, word by painstaking word, between writer and character. And how, if the latter happens to be based on a real person, the connection – albeit one-way – is even more profound.

Is it a spoiler to say that I'm not writing this from a Italian prison cell, that I didn't end up convicted of smuggling? In the airport, I sat in the customs interview room alone, watched over by the guard with the gun, for what felt like an interminable time. My flight, on the monitor, boarded. Final calls were made, then final, final calls. I clutched my perspiring palms together, gazing at my lion, who slept on, blissfully unaware of the crisis he was causing.

Then the men came hustling back into the room. One of them was on the phone.

'It's OK,' he said. 'The expert says it's not stolen.'

'I can go?' I said, leaping to my feet.

'Yes, go, quick!' they exhorted me, as if I had been carelessly loitering in duty-free instead of being interrogated about theft and smuggling.

I snatched up my documents and was just about to sprint away, towards the departure gates, when they stopped me.

'Don't forget this,' one of them said and, stepping forward, he placed the stone lion into my arms with surprising tenderness.

'I can take it?' I said, incredulously. I had assumed that it was no longer mine, this little Florentine lion, that it would be used as evidence in an investigation of the flea market, or to serve as a cautionary tale to other visitors from overseas.

'*Certo*,' the terrifying customs man said, with a nod. 'He's yours. Now go, *signora*, run!'

The lion sits on the windowsill in my kitchen, his back to the garden, his mane warming in the sun. I like to tell people that he almost got me arrested but I'm not sure they believe me. He looks so peaceful, after all.

Maggie O'Farrell,
Edinburgh, May 2022